AUTHOR

Born in Harrow; living

Since leaving school, Chr
of Australia, completed a nu
residency at Darwin Hospital; then as a journalist and war correspondent, visited the four corners of the earth. He has achieved an MD, an MA in the English Language, and another complete MA in Woodworking – three of his main vocations.

A horrendous accident in 2009 ended his career in the construction industry, limiting his time to reading and writing.

He now resides in Norfolk where he loves natural history and the countryside.

Christopher E Howard, MA. MD. .a.

Text Copyright ©Christopher E. Howard – 2021
All Rights Reserved

Cover artwork copyright
Christopher E. Howard & CC Readers,
Norwich, Norfolk.

All rights reserved.

This novel is entirely a work of fiction. The names, characters and incidents portrayed in it are the work of the author's imagination. Any resemblance to actual persons, living or dead, events or localities is entirely coincidental.

CC Readers – Publishing
61 Bridge Street, Kington, Herefordshire, HR5 3DJ
enquiries@ccreaders.co.uk

ISBN: 9798447130381

All rights reserved. No part of this publication may be reproduced or stored in a retrieval system, or transmitted in any form or by any means, electronic, mechanical, photocopying, scanning, recording or otherwise, without the prior permission of the publishers.

This book is sold subject to the condition that it shall not, by way of trade or otherwise be lent, resold, hired out, or otherwise circulated without the publisher's prior consent, in any form of binding or cover other than that in which it is published and without a similar condition including this condition being imposed on the subsequent purchaser.

This book is dedicated to

All peoples around the world who wish
to live and uphold the values of true democracy.
Everyone should have freedom to live without
fear.

Poverty is not necessary
in a world where
compassion for those less able
should be the normal.

Excalibur – *Found!*

Christopher E. Howard

*For Susi
Best Wishes
Always.

Chris
x
x*

EXCALIBUR – *FOUND!*

Prelude:

It's six thirty, British Summer Time.

In a small mystical glade amongst a wooded and scrub area near Tintagel, amid a sparkling pocket of lost time, by the shores of Dozmary pool on Bodmin moor, half-buried in a magical glistening worn chunk of pink and grey granite, lies EXCALIBUR.

Chapter 1

"If that dog bites me, Tom, I'll bloody-well report it," declared Greg Hewden-Wright acrimoniously; squaring his shoulders against the cold of the early morning.

Across from him, his long-time friend and confidante Harry Dean sniggered good humouredly, staring down at Tom Everly's old – and extremely gnarled – bulldog, the thick-set animal standing by his side, patiently eyeing Greg suspiciously, despite knowing him for the past fifteen years; Greg's threadbare cheese-cutter hat; equally tired oilskin overcoat and patched trousers giving the impression of a scarecrow that had come to life.

"He ain't about to bite anyone," Tom huffed, searching the voluminous pockets of his overcoat for a light. "He's lost most of his teeth."

He dropped the lead he'd been holding loosely, almost laying it over his dog's broad back, making a further search of his inner clothing, as Greg straightened with concern, worried Bruiser might suddenly realise he was free and make a dash for him and his sweet little Yorkshire Terrier.

It had to be said however, that the small Yorkie was about as worried as the tired-looking Labrador beside it, both sniffing the air nonchalantly.

"Oh, for God's sake," blurted Harry pulling out a silver Zippo. "Here!" He reached over with the American-style lighter.

"Oh, ta," voiced Tom, befuddled over having misplaced yet another set of matches.

He lit his soggy roll up whilst Greg stamped his feet, agitation gnawing at his senses. "Where is he," he worried – not for the first time?

"He'll be here," Harry averred confidently, replacing his Zippo carefully, glancing around wistfully at the county he'd known practically all his life – not a full Cornishman but accepted as one, having worked as a rep for the small engineering firm alongside Greg and Tom virtually all their lives. He could still recall vividly the squadrons of Hurricanes and Spitfires that had scrambled from the small airfields around about to take battle into the skies around the southern and east coasts of Britain, fighting for freedom from world oppression. But now as around them Southern England began to rouse itself, the sun already high in the sky, the soft whine of the electric milk cart carrying through the empty suburban streets – car doors banging softly as commuters began their short car journey from the villages and shires surrounding Bodmin moor, heading for the more vibrant coastal towns – there was a new threat – one a lot closer to town!

They were on the very edge of Bodmin moor, about as far as the housing and industrial estates had been allowed to encroach, ready to take their early-morning constitutional through the walkways of Bolventor, following some well-worn paths through the scrub and wooded areas.

Such was life today that secluded walks such as these could be considered fairly dangerous for the old or unwary – at any time – hence the grouping; today's society breeding a new kind of foe for the pensioners that oozed from conurbation and slithered throughout the length and breadth of the British Isles like a virus, ready to pounce, rob and maim for a pittance, waylay the unsuspecting – no regard for age or infirmity anymore.

A new dawn of uncertainty and remorseless voracity was upon them, and it was all they could do to outwit the evil – safety in numbers – and (at times) another string to their bow; a six-foot three, square shouldered and heavy set young man known to all as Dan, revered for his size and strength.

"We should go," voiced Greg tiredly. He needed to get the walk over with and get back to his house promptly to settle into his comfortable armchair and doze for a while, an annoying habit of waking at three thirty in the morning becoming an irritable hang up, unable to return to sleep until much later, ruining his waking hours lately.

Danny King was late, his father gripped with emphysema, coughing up his guts just as he was opening the back door, Lucy the family retriever, hovering expectantly – Dan returning to search for his father's inhalers, eventually locating them in the kitchen, sitting him down in the lounge as he set them up for him, mother fussing about upstairs getting dressed.

By the time she'd clomped down to see if he was alright, Dan had administered the steroids and his Dad was breathing better, the virtues of working as a stone mason taking their toll as dust filled with flecks of silicon and mica were breathed in on a daily basis.

Dan checked the time, finding he was already late, having had to wait for the bathroom earlier while father ran the gauntlet, the young man's hours at the fitness centre in Launceston flexible, although he liked to be in early most days to catch the first batch of school kids that habitually used the swimming pool.

"You ok, Dad," he asked once more, eager to get Lady walked and settled down for the morning?

His father waved an arm, indicating he would live another day, and after convincing himself he would indeed be alive on his return from work, Dan made to leave, stopping quickly to peck Mum on the cheek before stepping through to the back door.

The three musketeers were waiting for him as he walked up the driveway of the semidetached property, pulling out the collar to his jacket, squeezing past an extremely old and now rusting Chevrolet convertible – a once dream machine that his father had spent a small fortune on trying to renovate some years ago; the huge car so beautiful but so expensive to run and maintain.

Even the thick heavy lorry tarpaulins that protected the paintwork were beginning to fray, the material constantly harassed by the weather.

"Here he is," he heard Harry Dean exclaim, Lady ambling up to greet everyone!

Dan watched the wagging tails with a smile, always enjoying this early morning routine as the dogs sniffed and welcomed each other, so happy Harry and Tom had suggested it – only Greg having to make changes to his morning schedule in order to meet up. Since they all ventured past his house at some time in the day anyway, it was no trouble to join with them morning and evening – the moor never too unsafe, but with the influx of several thousand holiday makers every year, migrants and deviants alike it was safer early morning and evening to team up – no skin off his nose either way.

"Morning Dan," Greg called softly.

"Morn' all."

"Morning," Harry spluttered, chugging on his roll-up. Beside him Tom smirked, having given up the cigs decades ago, nodding to Danny with unparalleled respect.

Conversely Greg had never started smoking although he seemed to attract almost every ailment going.

Tom adversely appearing the fittest of the three!

"Those things will kill you, you know," Greg warned sternly, watching as Tom returned Harry's lighter once more.

"They probably would – if he could keep one of them alight long enough! Shall we…" Dan urged, feeling he was already half an hour late?

Together they began to saunter resolutely along the roadway until it surrendered abruptly at some brightly painted bollards only two hundred yards further, a demarcation that signified the end of the line for the road and row of semidetached houses; Bodmin Moor, with all its woodland and bogs and pretty glades and grasses stretching out before them –

all four dogs shuffling and trotting ahead, eager to be the first to sniff the scents of the countryside.

Eager to step the route out today, Dan hung back however allowing Greg and his small Yorkshire Terrier to catch up, keeping the group together, feeling it his duty to care for all three of his wards despite Greg being something of a hypochondriac.

Dan stood for a moment, breathing in deeply of the rarefied air, enjoying the sudden peaceful atmosphere the leafy avenue produced, the transformation from one element of the county to the other a real calming resolve, as if moving from a noisy or noisome environment to one of peace and tranquillity. It often caught him off guard, especially at night; the huge beech, birch, oak and ash making an overhanging tapestry fit for a king or opening of a blockbuster film.

Late spring/early summer and bluebells were still evident in the interstices of the enormous boughs, cyclamens, primroses and willowherb giving colour amidst the trees, somewhere a lilac and wild jasmine were pumping out heady mixtures of aromas, filling the spaces with a melody of rich scent.

Replete with fresh air in his lungs, Dan moved off as Greg caught up, the little Yorkie almost as old, it seemed, the arthritic and balding dog padding happily amongst the lanes' grass verges.

"Alright, Greg," Dan called knowing there was bound to be something wrong? Greg had nodded, although he had to confide an old injury to his leg was irritating him today.

"Always something," he grumbled, then puffed out a cough as he joined the body-building giant, eminently happy he had him as a chaperone, even more glad the young man was a considered friend, one who'd make a point of coming over and sitting for a moment in the working men's club, or local watering hole, just to let everyone know Greg was a valued friend – even perchance a relative; his very persona implying anyone foolish enough to upset the old gaffer might have to deal with the man-made goliath as well. Greg liked that, revelled in it a lot in fact, so much happier the young man had sort of come of age.

Danny put a warm hand out to Greg's shoulder as he passed him, Lady looking back from where the three other dogs had scampered ahead, making sure he was intending to follow. Tom and Harry had stopped for a moment too, (another attempt to light a roll-up), a tried and trusted arrangement that allowed for the four to travel in unison.

It was promising to be an extremely good summer this year, Dan ruminated, keeping pace with the ailing Greg, with March and April being increasingly warm and sunny, the paths a little further in where the trees crowded round drying out considerably this year already; the walkers able to pick their way easily along the route today, not step carefully as usual as water encroached to the paths and avenues during the autumn and winter months.

It was the dog's sudden alertness and pensiveness that first attracted the four walkers that something was amiss. Danny and Greg noticed it first, the four dogs that usually ran together stopping suddenly to about turn as one, as if a deer might have been nearby, The Yorkshire terrier, *'Bruiser,'* and the two Labradors abruptly backing up some way to the small avenue of verdant lime green grass that was wending its way off to their left, sniffing with apparent excitement.

Being nearest, Greg had simply turned as the dogs explored this apparently new tract of land, gingerly sniffing the air, glancing about cautiously.

"I don't remember a path being here – do you Danny?"

Stifling a sigh due to yet another delay, Dan stepped over nonetheless, gazing over the incredibly fertile grass, something a little odd about the avenue amidst the thick woodland now that he gazed at it.

"Odd," he mumbled, shaking his head!

"What is it," asked Harry Dean as he and Tom re-tracked their steps to rejoin them?

"How is it we've never gone down this path before," queried Dan, watching the dogs' activity closely? They were on edge, unnaturally so, neither Lady nor Harry's big Labrador anxious to venture too far up this strange new avenue. Bruiser, Tom Everly's two and a half stone small boulder of an animal hung back, almost behind his master's legs – its very attitude suggesting all was not as it seemed. Perplexed – and a little miffed some ecological team or the council; or a gang of tree-huggers had somehow created a new woodland glade, Dan marched forward, eager to explore the little grassed pathway and see what lay ahead.

The three older men hung back, only Bruiser relying on Dan's bulk dared follow on; sniffing the air warily; Lady and the other two dogs stepping with obvious trepidation as the alpha male took charge.

A little way in, dense foliage in the shape of strange flowering rhododendrons; dark foliaged buddleias and even odder-looking hydrangeas had created a complete circle it seemed, as if to encapsulate something. Annoyed at being waylaid, Dan pushed his way through, able to stamp down the tall furry grass and, lifting his chin above the shrubs – was suddenly brought up sharp by what lay before him!

Harry was the first through the leafy barrier after Dan, grunting as he pushed and pulled at the encroaching branches, the thick waxy leaves, following the small indentation – shocked to his core as he finally fought his way through, brushing himself down; checking on his dog – nearly stumbling over as he collected himself to straighten – then gawp at the vision before him, almost too much to take in all at once.

Dan couldn't believe his eyes. As he turned his head to take in the small glade, the spectacle before him was demanding attention – for resting in the sunlit arbour, in a small pocket of luscious soft green grass, sparkling as if with an inner radiance, a hunk of grey and pink granite sat, looking as if its sheer bulk and weight had allowed it to rest there for an eternity, slowly sinking into the ground, lichens and moss having nearly enshrouded the block.

"HOLY GOD," spluttered Greg! He'd followed Harry courageously; Tom hot on his heels, still

endeavouring to light yet another roll-up. He gave up as he realised he had to navigate a wall of bushes, holding back ensnaring branches as Bruiser waddled and barged his way through.

Tom bumped into Greg who was seriously considering retreating from his position near the entrance once he'd surged through, staggering about as the vision out before them gleamed and shone with preternatural eminence. *"Dear God,"* he breathed in utter disbelief, having realised what it was!

"Let's go," Greg urged his three companions – but mostly to Dan who had staggered a few feet toward the incredible spectacle.

Dan was hypnotised however, not by the pink and grey glistening hunk of granite but by the towering sword rammed firmly in it, the sheer power of the hilt and deadly blade pulsing with an energy he could almost feel.

Harry had fallen to his knees, making his dog whine beside him, Tom rushing to console him. Greg hung back with his Yorkie, too traumatised to do anything.

"It's the fucking sword in the stone," coughed Harry, not believing what he was looking at!

"It's a mock-up," spat Danny quietly – as if the gods might hear, cringing even as he voiced it, the ardent feeling of having inadvertently stepped into another world – or stumbled into another time – all around him, evident in the very air that seemed to sparkle with its own strength, throbbing with dire force and vivacity! Every breath of it seemed to galvanise him.

He found – despite his wards being frightened beyond words – that he couldn't take his eyes off the sword, the incredible bristling power surging from its metal throbbing to power the very air around them – energise the very glade they were in; the various compositions of hardened steel gleaming as if hewn by centuries of craftsmanship; the hilt and surrounding attachments appearing so ultra-dangerous they looked capable of cutting their way through time, never mind earthly materials!

"Does this look like a mock-up to you," asked Harry, having found his voice – and composure; joining Danny by his side after having scrambled to his feet. He continually glanced over his shoulder – the dogs having formed into a pack of their own, hanging back with Greg, who seemed happy with their apparent fortitude and canine strength surrounding him; Bruiser especially; who he could never completely take to due to his dour persona and bulk, now friend for life as he took centre stage in the band of four to hold his little patch of ground at the entrance, happy to watch on.

Dan had sucked in his lips, shaking his head worriedly, jumping a little as Tom, having found his composure also joined them.

"Unbelievable…" he drawled, mesmerised by the vision!

All at once, Harry realised the significance, turning to stare at Danny in sheer disbelief.

"Dan," he asked quietly, "what's your middle name?"

Blinking, Dan finally dropped his gaze, resting his eyes. He had to think about the enquiry a moment. "Erm... Arthur, why..." and then it hit him too?

"No," he breathed, shaking his head, turning to pointedly glance at Harry: *"No way!"*

"Yes way," barked Tom, wavering as he continued to gaze at the stone; the sword thrust within radiating with sheer outlandish power!

"This is your destiny," Harry revered, gripping his arm. "This is for you – it must be – it's not for any of us!"

Sighing inwardly, Dan turned to Tom, the pensioner looking up at him with the same bated breath, his pale eyes almost imploring. Still however, he baulked at the thought – the sheer lunacy of it!

"It's not right," he continued, prevaricating, putting off the inevitable. *"I'm nobody* – just a fitness instructor!" He flexed his shoulders, feeling however, the incredible weight of responsibility already gathering about the ether. Above, the blue sky of morning was allowing just one or two wispy clouds to float by, framed by the fantastical glade they had found themselves in, Dan watching one for just a moment, but inside this eco-cosm of lost time they were in hiatus, suspension, protected from the world outside; encapsulated by some inexplicable force. He was becoming part of it, he realised slowly, frighteningly, being immersed, energised.

"Your name," Tom insisted, searching for a roll-up; "King – for Christ's sake – Arthur King – it couldn't be more obvious!"

"King Arthur," Greg called from his rearguard position, having listened with cocked ear patiently.

He'd sunk to his knees to be nearer his pet Yorkshire terrier, almost cuddling him – cushioned by the soft grass.

"You know what you gott'a do," refuted Tom, eventually retrieving a battered cigarette from a pocket? "Wrench the thing from the stone!"

"No," Dan exclaimed, trying desperately to dispel the hypnotic pulses washing over him! *"It just can't be – this is unthinkable!"*

"We could be in a combined fugue," offered Greg from behind.

Harry guffawed. *"Oh, yeah – we're all really lying on the path outside, dreaming our lives away!* Get real, Greg!"

Greg simpered, ruffling his dog's coat tremulously.

"Well…" asked Tom?

"Well what," Dan persisted?

Tom raised his eyebrows in utter exasperation, clamping the unlit roll-up in his teeth to usher Danny forward toward the stone. *"Git,"* he mumbled!

Dan breathed in a deep sigh, still glancing around as if a team of camera men would jump out of the underbrush, hooting and creasing up with laughter, calling the ruse a complete wrap; but as the glade continued to pulse with power and radiant energy it was hard to ignore the lure to walk up and release the sword; incongruous as it seemed.

He let out a sharp breath, glanced behind to make sure Greg was ok, then, rubbing his hands together in a desperate show of hesitancy, stepped closer to the stone, leaving his companions behind for a moment.

"Break a leg," called out Tom under his breath! Beside him, Harry sighed, shaking his head.

"The future king of England is about to draw Excalibur from the fabled stone, change history for the good of the people – and all you can do is *joke* about it!"

Tom shrugged, still unable to light his fag from the feeble flame that his match produced. He watched the flame splutter and fade as if the very air surrounding it had robbed it of its spark and warmth, reducing it to a blackened twig. He discarded it and glanced up to see Dan approach the stone.

"Careful," warned Harry!

Nearing the Sword in the Stone; a fable he had read as a boy – even disregarding it as a teenager for what it was – now found succinct and empirical value in the legend, the power as he neared seeming to grow and swell in his being, as if building for this moment. He reached out with a hand to touch the stone with his fingertips, the radiating energy wrapping around him, caressing the smooth granite, worn by time itself. He moved around to the back, finding a step cut into the lump of stone, able to hold onto the granite as he took his place, now so close to the sword it seemed to welcome him, genuflect almost to his presence. Dan steadied himself; glanced quickly through the mists of the coruscating air, to where his three friends and the dogs waited, Tom still with a roll-up in his lips, all watching him as he prepared to change history.

Dan took a breath, felt the fetid air seep into his being, then stepped up, reached out determinedly, taking hold of the hilt firmly, arranging his body to take the full force of the sword as Excalibur released.

His fingers gripped the ages-old handle – the bound hemp twine stained a mottled brown by eons of spilt blood. He went to apply pressure, but the sword just elevated itself, drawing its awesome blade out of the stone, out from the centuries of time, out from the prison that had held it for so long. It left its granite home with a slight whine and unmistakable scrapping of metal on stone, the incredible honed shaft of arcane steel gracing the air once more. Dan heaved the destructive weapon skywards, glistening sparks and soft lightning hovering about the blade, the sheer magnitude of the sword now in rightful hands. Around him the glade drew back, allowing vistas of another time and lost continents to surge in – and from the mists of centuries gone, armies swelled, knights rising from dusty graves, crusaders emerging from the sand, sailors and privateers crawling from the shores; legions of the dead, hundreds upon thousands of the un-dead, ready to honour their king once more.

"Jeeze," coughed Tom, staggered by what was unfolding. Harry had almost backed into him, unsure of his own sanity. Behind them Greg had fainted, allowing the dogs to shelter under his coat.

With Excalibur in his hands, Dan stepped down and away from the stone, allowing the weapon to fall to his side, the steel gleaming in all its majesty, the ultimate power!

As he walked to join his brethren, shadows were forming, ages-old knights of yore were being called; all manner of soldier and combatants that had fought for King Arthur now pledged their allegiance. He was ignorant of their names or history but they marched forward nonetheless, drawing ever nearer; plodding through the vistas of time to congregate at this special juncture.

Concerned for his wards, Dan sided with Harry and Tom still wielding the huge sword. It was so long he had to hold it off the ground as he stepped, even his height not able to fully outstrip its girth. He put a comforting hand out to his friends as he rejoined them, knowing somehow things would never be the same, but vowing in his heart that nothing would harm his compatriots; moving to stand between them and place the razor-sharp tip of the sword firmly at his feet, the hilt buried within his hands.

"Way to go…" encouraged Tom!

On the other side of Dan, Harry cringed, inching that bit nearer the six-foot champion, eager to skulk in his shadow.

Around them the mists of time swirled, giving way to massed armies that were slowly but resolutely marching; converging on their spot, as if summoned by a higher force; compelled to form and do battle once more.

Dan could do nothing but hold his ground, terrified for his wards and the dogs but unable to do much about it at the moment, hoping the whole charade would play itself out.

Greg had come round and scampered on all fours to where Danny, Tom and Harry were standing, kneeling behind them to gaze around in a stupor, unable to focus for a moment. When he did, he promptly fainted again, unable to compute the hordes of battle-hardened knights and crusaders that were drawing ever nearer, flags and standards fluttering in the strange ether that passed for air; even odder looking animals caught up in the melee; horses, war-elephants; what looked like giraffes – strange winged beasts that waddled uncomfortably on wingtips and stumpy legs. *"Nooo…"* he'd mumbled before his consciousness left him!

The billows of roiling satin-white mists were tramped under foot; dispersed by hundreds – if not thousands of feet, many clad in steel or leather. Finally the legions were closing, a small detachment dismounting to begin the last approach on foot, drawing near to Danny.

He swallowed down his trepidation, ever fearful for his companions and animals around him; something telling him they'd all be safe however – something inherent in the very air; a sure feeling that the massed armies were friendly – were ready for something – *were his!*

The knights – around twelve in all drew near, Dan and his two elderly compatriots able to discern details as they tramped toward them, wispy beards on tanned and sweat-stained faces – the eyes bright and almost hungry looking. Battle-scarred armour and frayed tabards covered the combatants, heavy-looking implements of war strapped and slung about their bodies and shoulders, sheathed swords in sparkling scabbards that appeared too cumbersome to wield; doubled-headed axes and maces hanging from belts; the incredible weight of just one implement weighing down a normal person yet these soldiers were inured to it; it seemed – of another breed; one that had been weaned on combat and chivalry; the power of these beings coming not from sweat and toil now, but from another place.

The twelve stopped, forming a semi-circle; the armour glinting in the morning sunshine; torn and ripped ribbons rippling in the scant breeze. A tall knight seemed to collect himself, then, checking his apparel as he glanced down at himself, approached, holding out a welcoming hand.

Dan could look him in the eye – almost, the combatant well over six feet tall, clad head to toe in some kind of steel that appeared more like a cross between aluminium and iron; the surcoat and chain mail ripped and torn almost to shreds; dents and rents in the plates of his protective shell showing where his protection had saved the day, one or two of the scars so deep it may have been the killer blow. He seemed alive now however; Danny contemplated, still appraising the vision before him.

"Shake his hand; for Christ's sake," Tom urged beside him, rummaging in his pockets for his matches!

The knight's eyes slid from Arthur to wonder at the troubadour down by his side, continuing to hold out his hand, prompting Danny to snap out of his trance and move to reach out and take it, his mind in turmoil at holding onto an apparent ghost!

He was solid however, as his fingers touched the legendary knight, not as bulky but certainly rangy and strong, the strength evident in his eyes; eyes that shone a bright blue like his. Up close, the knight's battle-scarred face told of a life of adventure, the golden brown wisps of hair about his chin and neck unable to soften the hard chiselled features – the welts and pockmarks made up a mask of a face that he realised could look absorbed one moment but so deadly intent the next.

"Lancelot," the knight rasped in gravelly tones. The knight bent forward to cough up eons of dust and dirt, straightening again, looking Danny dead in the eye. Intrigued beyond words, Dan just nodded slightly – knowing from history the knight was one of Arthur's most trusted aides; but according to legend he'd run off with the King's wife Guinevere hadn't he – perhaps all the stories were bunk – the reality much different – *but what reality;* Dan mused? Whose reality was this?

"Where you from," asked Tom?

On the other side of Danny, Harry cringed, trying to shrivel up.

Tom had found his matches worked now and he could suck on a small roll up, the flash of the match-head drawing Lancelot's attention once again as it sparked. The smoke coiled through the air, hitting the knight's nostrils, making him take stock, as if the smell had reminded him of something.

Lancelot dismissed it, returning to the point in hand. He let go of Arthur's hand, bowing from the waist, then drawing his sword and holding it point down – not upright as if in an act of warfare, called out. "ALL HAIL ARTHUR; KING OF ENGLAND;" and with that he turned in an unmistakable act of submission, knelt in a clattering of armour, bringing the immense sword before him – as if to offer his services – and his sword, but more – his life!

Dan felt the surging energy of Excalibur race through him, the legend brimming with soft lightening, sparks and sunlight; the ether drawing around it as if to enshroud the awesome weapon, the whole multitude of assembled legions falling to their knees, banners, lances; halberds dipping, as Dan swelled to the moment, his muscles galvanising him as he gasped, hefting the incredible icon aloft, brimming with excitement, with pride, with power!

Bedazzled in a silvery hue, the sword seemed to pulse out a tidal wave of extra light, thrumming through the multitudes like a tsunami, illuminating everything in its scintillating roll, appearing to count and consolidate the hundreds and thousands of individuals.

"Well," coughed Tom beside him?

To Dan the moment had lasted forever – one he'd certainly remember for the rest of his life – the awesome power of Excalibur in his hands imbuing him with remorseless strength and vigour; the incredible energy surging through the very ether and every molecule of his being – the amassed weight of numbers seeming to fill the vast eons of time and space with a certainty that things would change. With both hands he lowered the destructive weapon, bringing the blade safely back down to earth; the knight before him looking up (and around at the strange settings), finally struggling to his feet once more.

Remembering his manners, Dan moved to lend a hand but quickly thought better of it, the impropriety not lost on Lancelot as he shot Dan a steely look, pushing himself to his feet. In a complete clamour of subdued clattering and shuffling the massed legions rose to their feet again also, preparing.

"What now," asked Danny, searching Lancelot's eyes?

The knight turned slowly, as if having only just awoken from a deep dream appraising the hoards; every manner of common man; long-bowmen; slingers; infantry; knights on horseback and crusaders; sailors and privateers who at one time had aided or sworn some kind of allegiance to King Arthur – all here once again.

"Many – if not all, will want to ingest something, allow the food to reinforce the transition from revenant to immortal and take up the sword once more. As the legions move through the countryside, they will call all to arms, those who will follow the true King – and it will of course, allow those who wish to oppose you to scarper. Who holds power over England now?"

"Queen Elizabeth the second," spoke up Harry for the first time, his whole body experiencing frissons of a truly deep-seated unholy nature, the sort that any horror film producer would be inherently proud of.

Lancelot raised his eyebrows under the brow of his battered helmet in an undeniable question – obviously having never heard of her. He glanced to Danny for clarification but he could only shrug himself, explaining the royal line had itself in its time experienced ups and downs throughout history but the English throne had managed to hang onto power since the twelfth century – this being the twenty first.

"Twenty first," muttered Lancelot with a certain amount of stupefaction?

"Aye," chipped in Tom on the other side of the knight's King. "Lot of centuries of taxation; corruption; skulduggery and daylight robbery has gone on since your time, *I can tell yer!"*

On the other side of Arthur, Harry winced, shaking his head. All around them the legions were beginning to break up, form into huge convoys and head out to the coasts – in all three directions but south, hoping no doubt to pillage as much as they possibly could en route. Their world was being allowed to shine through once more – but although the green and verdant trees of Bodmin moor were allowed to stand again, the land around them was changing – possibly forever.

"They'll ransack the place," worried Greg, having finally awoken and convinced himself it was but a nasty daydream, cringing however as the massed groups turned in their thousands to surge off in all directions, the clatter and clamour so riotous they could probably be heard in Sussex.

"You ok," shouted Harry?

Greg had nodded then nearly faltered again as Lancelot moved, calling to the eleven other knights standing close by.

"Where are you all going to stay," asked Danny somewhat bowled over by the immediate logistics of it all?

Lancelot turned back, waving the inquiry aside. "It's plenty warm, we'll dig in somewhere for today – we will however need to provide for our livestock – and we will have to liaise with you during the daylight hours – things are going to move pretty quickly from now on, so be prepared to move further up country."

"How far up country," asked Tom earnestly?

Lancelot looked down upon the old timer once more, finding a certain amusement in his bearing, the wily old knight not above his dry humour. "For our King here – probably all the way to the kingdom and perhaps beyond a little – depends on how quickly we restore power: Could be some resistance."

"You don't say," quipped Greg from behind? *"Don't suppose you've heard of an intercontinental ballistic missile – or a tank by any chance?"*

Again Lancelot shot Danny a searching glare, no doubt wondering what the terrified old boy was wittering on about, but the future King of England shook his head, even the explosive might of an A-bomb seemed a little ineffectual against the spiritual might of not only Excalibur, but the legions of the un-dead that were already massing for an onslaught.

Danny held onto the sword tightly, still mesmerised by its unyielding power, the one true eminence he reasoned. *"Just how am I going to explain this to my parents,"* he mused to himself?

"We'd better go with you," assured Harry, as if Dan might be scolded for encouraging a riot.

Chapter 2

At number six Tenby Avenue, Camelford, the homeowner, back for lunch – was somewhat distracted by the commotion passing by his front door. Through the windows of his designer kitchen overlooking the back garden, he could also witness men on horseback making their way along the small road that ran down to the scrubland towards the coast. Frowning, he left his sandwich he'd just made and hastened through to the front door to pull it open, curiosity burning up inside.

Opening up the door however, pulled him up sharp, thinking the teams of a re-enactment society were extremely good this year, the make-up especially. The man stepped out to look up and down the estate, finding the hoards were made up of hundreds of men – some young drummer boys mixed up in the crowds. *My God – this is fantastic,* he thought!

He stepped back as a knight approached, trying to step carefully around him. In doing so the armour-plated being stopped to consider the person before him a moment, studying his apparel closely.

"Bonjour friend – do you have food," he asked looking past the smart-looking man to his home. The knight thought to point to his open mouth.

"Why of course – you must be starving – hang on!"

Rory Splengier shot back into his house and through to the kitchen, taking time to notice there was still men on horseback trudging along the road behind. *Strewth,* he ruminated; *this is going to be some battle!*

Rory grabbed the plate of sandwiches he'd made, deciding quickly – due to the multitudes passing his door, he ought to perhaps cut them into quarters.

He did so quickly and returned to the chevalier hoping to garner some insight into the apparent influx of people – a film perchance in the making.

He offered the tired-looking knight a sandwich.

The fourth Earl of Sandwich – from which the culinary delight has been named had long since passed into history himself but the French nobleman – who consequently had supported Arthur in some uprising having lost his way in England at the time, was able to recognise the mixture of bread and cheese by smell alone and was thus readily tempted.

Remembering to thank the stranger, the knight reached out, plucking a quarter almost daintily.

Rory held his ground, despite hungry-looking pike-men of the fifth or sixth century stopping to gather around, watching the proceedings with interest.

Having examined and sniffed the little piece of sandwich at length, the chevalier took a tentative bite, masticating it slowly, nodding to himself appreciatively, savouring the taste. The butter was a mite odd, but even so, he could remember the coarse grain bread and tart cheese any day, even the small piece of tomato was a welcome relish.

The knight swallowed the mouthful and considered the aftertaste, sucking in his lips as he did so.

Glancing around at the pike-men and infantry, many with dusty worn out sandals of a very basic design – *very authentic,* there was a distinct worry formulating in Rory's mind that despite the sandwich being only a few minutes old, the odd film extra might well be allergic to perhaps the cheese and suffer a nasty reaction – which on the face of it, surrounded by tens of armed men of all demeanour was perhaps not a good way to go!

He watched the knight carefully, plate still in hand as he suddenly went a decidedly darker shade of grey, and gripped his stomach forcibly!

Jeeze, Rory thought, looking on in panic!

The knight's face fought with the first ingestion of food, word having passed through the ranks that at some point they would all have to eat something if they were to walk this earth again. Despite this the stomach ache was acute, giving him some jip, the knight fighting it with all his fibre. At last he could stand it no more and he faltered, easing himself down onto one knee, pointedly turning away from his provider in case he threw up all over him, his guts growling and burbling loudly.

Rory, gripping the plate before him as if paralysed, could only force his lips together and hope to god the guy survived, wondering whether to take a bite himself to eschew the food was safe. But within minutes the knight seemed to recover, finally pushing himself back to his feet.

He straightened, his stomach still gurgling, and still with a morsel of the sandwich stuck in one hand considered forcing the rest of it down, deciding to do so whilst a big crowd continued to watch on.

As he swallowed the remaining piece of bread, the surrounding men cheered and moved to pat Rory on the shoulders, many then asking if they could partake.

"Of course, of course," cried the homeowner in ardent relief. "I'll get more!"

Rory rushed back inside and made more sandwiches. *He was in,* he realised with brimming excitement – no more insurance deals – no more sucking up to Mr fucking Johnsonby – the poof! Now he was a film extra and maybe even getting a bigger part – becoming a small time actor – *brilliant! No more office work for me – I'm off to join the circus!*

Rory shot the plate of rushed sandwiches outside – then back in the kitchen decided to reach up and catch hold of an ornate china platter that he and his wife used years ago to stuff themselves on a Friday night with a take-a-way Chinese, bringing it to the sink to wash all the dust and grime off it. Once done he brought out from the fridge a half-eaten chicken, a new ham, a cheese board – ripping the lid off, and anything else he could find that could possibly pass as normal food. He carried it all outside where others had crowded around, handing out slithers of ham and chicken and salads. Most – if not all appeared to suffer the same throes of stomach ache before the food was accepted by the body – Rory supposing they'd been on the road a couple of days and hadn't eaten properly. To this end he dived back in and prepared bowls of fruit and cooked rice, opening up cans with gay abandon, rifling through the cupboards for peaches, fruit cocktails, baked-beans and big tins of meat left over from Christmas. He grabbed a table from the lounge and, setting it up outside, made the front of his home a rest point and staging post for the tired and weary actors.

By the time his wife came home for lunch at one thirty the kitchen looked like a tornado had passed through and most – if not all the food stuffs had been rifled.

The door was wide open and, of her husband there was no sign, the road of the estate looking as if an army had recently moved through.

"You're doing WHAT," cried both Dan's parents?

Danny had brought the magnificent sword inside his house – (just the thing to show your family), handling it with extreme care, the blade especially pulsing with vibrant energy, the hilt with its two ultra-dangerous knife blades protecting the operator's hands in battle one supposed as blade slid along blade, throbbed too with unbridled power almost daring anything to touch them. Standing in the living room with Tom and Harry flanking him, the incredible sword before him, Dan could only hesitate – wondering where to start?

"Where'd you get *that*," his father asked again, incredulous?

"Pulled it from the stone," Tom interceded.

"What stone," his mother practically gasped?

"On Bodmin moor – "

"Dozmary actually," Dan muttered, "just off Bluebell lane – some strange part of the wood we'd never seen before. We blundered into something – "

"It was like nothing on earth," Tom effused, brimming over with excitement. Beside him *Bruiser* sat nonchalantly, appearing rather glad normality had returned in the shape of a comfortable rug carpet. He hunkered down while the two Labradors and Greg's Yorkie trotted off to explore what was left in Lady's food bowls in the kitchen.

Dan's father reached for his atomiser, sucking on it furiously for a moment. His mother couldn't take her eyes off the gleaming weapon her son had brought home. She knew him well enough to calculate he hadn't stolen it – nor purloined or exacted it from some unsuspecting hawker for a few bob; but it was just so big – and ultimately dangerous, where on earth had he found it?

"Mrs King," Harry began again, trying desperately to explain things, "Dan legitimately pulled the sword from the stone this very morning – " he looked down at his watch and realised several hours had slipped by whilst they shifted between worlds – or to put it another way – sort of hovered between them – he dismissed it to carry on. "If you remember the legend – whoever pulls the sword from the stone *is the rightful King of England – and he did?"*

"Did what," asked Dad who hadn't been fully listening?

"He's pulled the sword from the stone," breathed mother with dire conception – the act finally sinking in, "which actually means – due to legend and folk lore – *that* Danny is the real King of England."

"Bollocks," retorted father phlegmatically! "He works at a leisure centre for God's sake and our name is…*shit..?*"

Everyone stared at father. "What's wrong with our surname," asked Dan quietly?

Dan's father shot mother a remorseful glance, a certain amount of guilt wrapped up in the rueful look as well. Mother drew herself up a bit, clasping her hands before her.

"Actually, Danny… *King* is not our real surname, father had it changed from Pendragon to King before you were born – we felt the name might draw derision from the legend and all."

"Quite a nice name, I think," put in Tom, fiddling with a roll-up.

"So you are the true king," Greg sighed – certainty evident in his words. *"There's no denying it now."*

"Danny Arthur Pendragon, has a nice ring to it, don't you thin – " A loud rapping on the front door interrupted Harry.

In the throes of expecting the police or the authorities of some kind, everyone glanced to everyone else. As the one true culprit of everything so far, Danny hefted the sword and, carrying it as carefully as he could, went to answer it.

Lancelot stood there with several other attendants, all glancing about with a certain wonderment and awe. With the sword clamped in one hand, Dan stepped outside quickly to look around, fully expecting helicopters and police sirens to be filling the air, but all was quiet, an odd kind of faint sparkling mist floating in the atmosphere, almost dampening down everything, a refulgent gleaming power that he was beginning to recognise, the very same sort of energy the sword produced – or perhaps was drawing from somewhere.

Remembering his guests Dan turned to Lancelot.

"A word," the enigmatic knight asked?

"Sure," Danny told him. "Erm, come in." He stood aside whilst Lancelot, indicating that the others should hold the fort outside, walked in.

In the lounge, a dull clunking and clinking told Harry and Tom that Lancelot was probably paying a visit. Dan's mother, already beside herself with worry, now had to contend with a ghost of the Round Table; Harry worried she might well faint. He made to try and explain further, but Dan re-entered the lounge then, followed by an equally tall and bulky (due to his armour) man dressed entirely in a full sixth-century battle-suit, complete with weapons. As Danny moved into the room, ever careful of the sparkling weapon that was Excalibur radiating in his hands, Tom and Harry moved round a bit, Tom making for a small occasional leather seat tucked in-between a sideboard and a music centre. He kept wondering – if – under the new circumstances, he'd be allowed to smoke.

"Mum, Dad...*this is Lancelot.*"

For his age, Harry moved surprisingly quickly as mother looked in danger of fainting. He stood by her side as she sought to grip something, the giant figure radiating with supernatural power despite appearing calm and collected.

"M'Lady, Sir Knight," Lancelot spoke, his gravely tones filling the room. A soft clanking and grinding of metal on metal followed his every movement.

Overcome with shock, Dan's mother nearly curtsied, hanging onto Harry, his father accepting the plaudit despite never being knighted by anyone, especially not the ruling bodies. He grumbled an acknowledgement.

Lancelot turned to Danny. "We have been offered a hall and some ground further up the road, onto which our horses can be fed and watered," he instructed his King. "Across from this hall appears to be an ale house so we'll reconvene there if that's alright – soon?"

"The Bell should be open at twelve," Tom reported with alacrity.

Dan nodded thoughtfully. "That should be fine. Have you managed to eat anything yet," he thought to ask?

For the first time, Dan thought he saw a certain worry in the stalwart knight's face – only a passing glimpse but it was there all the same, the centuries-old ghost shaking his head.

Dan turned to his mother. "All my knights have to eat something quickly, mum, to consolidate their being here – do we have any biscuits?"

"Um," swallowed his mother. "Yes, I think there's some Bourbons in the cupboard," she couldn't take her eyes off Lancelot, the former Knight of the

Round Table as bold and handsome as ever the depictions had made him. Now the fabled hero was here in her living room having tea and biscuits – *for crying out loud* – it would be something to tell Mabel that was for sure!

"Er, mum, if you have any digestives, I think they may be better," spoke Danny with hindsight, putting oatmeal before sugar.

At last mother's spell was broken and she hurried to the kitchen to find the necessary food items.

While they waited, Lancelot moved to inspect Tom's dog *Bruiser,* as he rested by his master's feet; the breed somewhat new to him. He clanked and rattled by Danny and knelt in a welter of noise as the rheumy-eyed Bulldog watched him narrowly.

Lancelot held out a metalled gauntlet, the animal not moving a muscle. Intrigued the knight bent forward a little nearer wherein *Bruiser* growled so deeply and so menacingly, Lancelot's metallic fingers curled up quickly, retracting his arm just as swiftly.

"Bruiser," Tom admonished his pet! "That's not very nice of you!" He fiddled with his roll-up while Lancelot studied the old codger, the tired old commoner somehow having befriended this boulder of an animal, taken it into his confidence. Perhaps there was some merit to this little troubadour after all?

He pushed himself to his feet as mother re-entered the room with two packets of digestives.

"Not the chocolate ones," Dan's father bleated, clearly disgruntled.

"No," Danny agreed, "the normal ones will do fine. It's just to get them started – then they can eat something more substantial."

"Them..," mother asked tremulously.

"There are twelve knights all told," Dan mentioned.

"Plus an army of around thirty thousand – give or take…" Tom added, making his mother giddy once more.

"Thirty thousand," asked his father querulously? *"Where?"*

"They arrived this morning – along with the sword," Harry explained.

"They're taking over Cornwall," Tom uttered in passing.

Dan's mother faltered.

"Mum," Dan worried. "It'll be ok. We have *'right'* on our side – and – " and he shifted Excalibur pointedly, "we have the sword!"

"And whoever wields the sword is the true King," Lancelot confirmed, moving to go.

Dan stepped over to place a hand on his father's shoulder, gripping it firmly, the sword so bright it hurt his Dad's eyes. He stepped away, but held his look, trying to impress he meant no harm but would put the country back to rights. Father nodded, somehow reading his thoughts.

Dan stepped over to his mother, bending to peck her on the cheek. He stood back to gaze down at her, a warm smile on his lips. Creaking and grinding, Lancelot watched on. "I love you, mum," he whispered, lifting a hand to caress her cheek.

"I love you too, son," mother croaked, a tear escaping one eye.

Dan sucked in a breath. "I got to do this, mum. It chose me – so I guess I got to see it through."

"I know son – just be careful – and if it doesn't work out you've always got a home here, you know that?"

"We'll take care of him, Mrs K," Tom spluttered getting to his feet. "Don't you worry."

Mom handed her son the packets of biscuits, a heartfelt sob escaping her lips. Dan took the packets and hugged her as best he could with the big sword between them.

***

Outside it seemed as tranquil as a normal Sunday morning, with the scintillating mist above dampening down the sounds of everyday life. Dan stopped to consider the day, noticing the warm sky above had disappeared under a scintillating dome, the shrouding umbrella stretching as far as the eye could see. He marvelled at this, not sure of what he was witnessing while he waited for Lancelot to join him, having also issued a cheery parting to his mother and father; Tom, Greg and Harry with their hounds following on. Now, with legions of his army spreading out across the county, Dan realised the whole of Cornwall may well be surrendering to some kind of hypnotic spell.

He handed the packets of digestives to Lancelot, who took them questioningly.

"Biscuits," Tom instructed the steely knight.

"Bis-queets," he repeated, glancing down at the packets.

"You have to open the packet," Harry pointed out, then moved to show the armoured being how to, ripping open the cellophane of one for him. Harry pulled a handful and, after issuing Lancelot with one, passed the others around, handing Tom one without realising.

"Ta," he mused, snapping it in half to munch on a mouthful, then bend to give *Bruiser* a nibble.

Biscuit in hand, Lancelot watched the proceedings as Tom ruffled the dog's ears after it had wolfed down the treat.

"He's quite fond of the odd digestive," Tom told the knight after he caught him gazing down at him.

Lancelot glanced down at the digestive in his gauntleted mitt, looking as if he might actually forgo his initiation and hand the biscuit to the dog, but after watching his other knights nibble at the round oatmeal – and then go into something of a spasm as the food regenerated their bodies, he took a careful bite himself, munching the biscuit up stoically.

Within seconds he was trembling and doing his best to hold himself together as his guts did somersaults, his whole suit of armour clinking and rattling as if his body inside was experiencing a tremor. Finally the shaking subsided and the foremost warrior was able to relax, taking another careful bite, the second going down without hiccup.

Dan, along with Tom, Greg and Harry and the three dogs had watched on in wonder as the five knights all writhed and groaned with the first mouthful, then finally they all recovered, enough anyway to take another tentative bite and then, still left with a little in their hands, tossed the rest away, or like Lancelot tried feeding the remains to either dog, all the combatants taken by Harry's Labrador.

"Well," sounded Dan. "Let's hit the boozer!"

"Amen to that," called out Greg.

"Boozer," Sir Percival asked of Danny?

"Common name for pub," he enlightened the revenant knight.

"Pub," repeated Lancelot, as they walked down the estate to where a hall presented itself, the village hall as it happened – now the centre for recruitment of the village folk and the initiation by first mouthful for the various hordes. As Dan glanced in, tables and chairs had been set up but many were being used as stretchers or seats as the first mouthful of food proving seemingly near fatal for some, had to be laid out; others finding it quite painful; while some were able to pass it off easily. It was pandemonium as hundreds of combatants milled about anxious to get their fix before the day was over, many fearing nightfall may be the deadline.

If the hall was busy, the pub was practically bursting at the seams, many a villager and townie alike – finding the day had somehow been cancelled due to some strange atmospherics, sought refuge in their drinking establishment, the chance of a pint on this fine sunny day not to be missed. On top of that several legionnaires who had been able to swallow down some fish or crustaceans at the shoreline, raiding many a boat landing with its catch –had been revived – and were now quite ready to sample the hospitality of the town, the smell of ale unmistakable as the pub opened its doors – even if it did look a little like a boudoir to them. With his retinue of twelve knights – the others joining him at the hall, Dan made his way to the bar, the way parting for him as he and his band prepared to confer.

Inside The Bell, Tom, Greg and Harry and the dogs headed for their favourite table, finding the place was already filling up fast, re-structured knights; bowmen and others mixing it with village and town people alike – there being an awful lot of catching up to do.

The knights pushed several tables together, everyone making way for them as Dan ordered two dozen pints, asking the landlord politely if he wouldn't mind putting it on his tab just at the moment. The landlord nodded sagely, having already been issued with several pieces of gold and one or two Doubloons for his ale – worth an estimated small fortune by his wife, he was now tempted to allow Danny just about anything – the obvious quiet deference shown to him by the surrounding knights (these ones all having a certain aura of a potentate) as he was ushered to the head of it, telling him things might well be in for a bit of change around here, especially as Danny seemed to be carrying a rather splendid rendition of what looked suspiciously like the fabled sword Excalibur!

As everyone took their seats and the beers were presented in glasses making many a knight stare down at them, Dan wondered what to do with the sword. It wouldn't sit by his side for fear of sliding down and slicing through the chair, and he couldn't really sit with it between his legs as it hampered his view of the assembled. He was just wondering if he should lay it down – worried that someone might catch their feet on it – when the scabbard – a most magical weapon in its own right was presented, more noble knights of his Round Table finding him.

Dan stood as the beautiful cover was handed over, a shield and spear also being proffered. He gathered up Excalibur and sheathed the terrible blade, almost silencing the volcanic throbbing the metal seemed to vibrate with. Dan looked the spear and shield over, puzzled by the hollow middle of the aegis. He ran his hands over the thick brass circumference, wondering over its design.

"The Shield of Light," the famous warrior Sir Galahad educated him, sipping on his ale. "It'll only work in your hands – and when it does, all the power of the sun is at your command. Excalibur will cut through anything including time itself but the shield will repel or swallow up anything – including time itself! So be careful how you wield it."

Danny was about to ask if he should take a quick crash course in quantum physics when a business man of some repute in the immediate southwest bustled in, carrying a large suitcase. A retinue of knights surrounded him as he was allowed to approach the tables, Dan ushering him forward, somewhat surprised to see him here.

"Hello Danny," he spoke with adulation. "Earl Mason-James. The last time we met you showed me around the wonderful new sports centre in Redruth with some of my cronies. I remember thinking you were an admirable person for the job then – and I might add a great spokesman for the centre – now it would appear I have to bow down to you – and I do so, Dan – Arthur with all the solemnity I can muster, as I see the true King of England has finally arisen – and with a formidable army to boot – which all means a whole new order may be ushered in, and – well, although I may not be the most just or moralistic of all your subjects, I hope this small token of my loyalty will prove that I'm right behind you Dan – er, Arthur in as many ways as I can; financier; politician, spokesperson or statesman – whatever you need, I'll be here for you?" Earl Mason-James hefted the big case onto the table and opened it up, revealing a cornucopia of riches, gold rings, bracelets and other jewellery that must have equalled a small ransom took up a quarter of the space while the other was packed with money. Big denomination notes; fifty to one hundred pounds sat in bundles looking like a lottery jackpot prize.

A hush fell about the place as onlookers took in the fortune.

"This is yours," Earl Mason-James annotated, pushing the case toward him. "If you are to wage a campaign then you'll need to fund it – and this will be a starting point – any funds you need immediately – I'll cover. As your campaign gets under way, then my self and other investors and bankers loyal to your cause will fall in line, backing you all the way. You have *my full financial backing*."

Dan found he couldn't take his eyes from the suitcase, that one bundle being the help he always wanted to be able to buy some quality medical care for his father, the N.HS in such a pickle due to constant cutbacks and shortages, the sick nowadays simply fell by the wayside. He felt like crying. He had all the power at his fingertips it seemed, but fix his father's ruined lungs – well – only money – lots of it could have cured him. He felt like telling Mason-James to take the whole bloody lot round to his mom and tell her to get private medical care that his father needed right away, but this businessman hadn't ruined his father's lungs, hadn't even asked him to work for him, so it was somewhat academic at the moment. Perhaps in all this spiritual upheaval there may be a release for his father; some kind of supernatural spell that would make him better.

"Thank you, Earl," he managed, almost wiping a tear away.

"What is it," Lancelot asked noting his distress?

Dan shook his head. "It's nothing," he reassured him. He brightened considerably as Earl Mason-James hovered thinking the gift was nowhere enough.

"There's plenty more, Dan – er, Arthur. Just ask away."

Dan held up a conciliatory hand, appeasing the businessman. "It's fine, thank you, Earl. I'll have the knights start up some kind of treasury. I expect we'll need money at some point.

He looked satisfied, nodding salaciously. "I do believe I'll have a drink now I'm here," and with a tap on the table as if to indwell it with an oath, he wandered off hoping to find like-minded folk. With his eyes Dan followed him for a moment, considering the expensive suit and shoes, then the assembled clientele which ranged from knights of all orders to bowmen, and squires, pike-men, strongmen, commoners as well as quite a few of the villagers and townspeople all mixed up as if in a massive jamboree.

Dan gazed again at the collection of riches, wondering for a moment how much Cornwall would have squirreled away, just waiting for ...*what*...a rainy day – or something like this – did *they* – or the ruling classes have tens of thousands hidden away knowing this might unfold? It seemed incongruous – *but then,* so did everything else right now – including his fantastical army – which appeared to be growing substantially by every passing minute.

An update by a Knight of the Round Table – a one Hector de Maris told him an emergency meeting by the privy town council was in attendance by Sir Kay, Gawain and Bedivere – who in literary history was reported to have returned Excalibur to the Lady of the Lake – with the intention of ensuring the county continued to operate as normal, any defections to be replaced immediately by appointed representatives or by any willing knights – the three standing in just to get a flavour of the proceedings – once one or two councillors had sufficiently recovered. Once other knights were up and running and could spare the time, they would approach hospitals, day-care centres; schools and residential homes in order to ensure the day-to-day running of these important places was not disturbed.

Another Knight of the Realm known as Cador who according to written works was Arthur's direct cousin and had raised Guinevere as his ward - also father to Constantine II outlined the various logistics to date, reporting on defections as well as recruitments.

"Who's holding the road blocks at the moment," Dan wanted to know, understanding that only about half his army as yet had gone through the initiation?

A huge map of Cornwall had been found – ripped off some wall by the look of it and brought to the pub, laid out in all its glory on the table, many a knight engrossed in it, logging details in their minds as they ranged over the colourful cartography.

"Not big," Constantine II mentioned, joining Dan by his right shoulder, having just joined the throng – many acknowledging his arrival. With some spiritual cartographer and two other town's people the knight had perused a motoring atlas getting a good idea of the whole south coast, realising pretty quickly that they could be soon pushed back into the sea if they didn't move outward and secure more of the peninsular. "Spit of land beyond must be annexed quite soon," he indicated sternly.

"Summer's set," Lancelot ruminated, overlooking the motoring atlas Constantine II moved to place before Arthur.

"Somerset and Devon will give us the peninsular but we'll have to move faster to secure the whole southern flank," stated the fabled Green Knight to Danny's left. "We don't have enough power yet to start the campaign – rushing ahead may well leave us stretched."

Lancelot turned in his seat to confer with knights behind him – many more approaching the table to announce their allegiance. "How are our numbers," Dan heard him ask quietly?

One knight bent low to whisper in his ear, trying to recall everyone he knew.

Something occurred to Dan just then and he voiced his concern. "Wasn't King Arthur supported and aided by a most trusted and resolute wizard, Merlin?"

Many around him nodded empathically. Others looked around and at each other as if he might have been seen somewhere. Again Lancelot, having turned quickly in his chair to address the King, turned back thoughtfully to confer once more. Again Dan heard him however, the steely knight not wanting to shield his King from the conversation as he barked orders, trying to arrange his armies.

A phone call from the regional police had to be taken, no one but the King quite understanding what all the fuss was about.

The landlord brought the phone over personally.

"Hello," Danny answered cautiously.

"Morning, Mr – erm…" a firm voice addressed him, "who am I talking to – is that Danny King – and if it is, can you confirm that?"

"Yes; this is Danny King speaking although I'm afraid my former persona is slowly but irrevocably being subsumed by another higher one – that of Arthur Pendragon, my middle and proper surname."

"Really..." the voice mumbled! "Well, Danny – er Arthur, my name is Chief Inspector Skinner of the County Constabulary here in Devon and I just wondered if you have a moment as there seems to be some confusion out on the road systems, and I wonder if you could clear this up for me? Constables on both sides of a sort of demarcation line right along the border of Cornwall to Devon are all reporting an exodus of some people, while hundreds of others are trying to get in – only one way in at the moment and one way out, and its causing quite a lot of confusion – especially out on the roads, so I just wondered if you have any thoughts on the matter?"

Dan picked up on the sarcasm right away, responding in kind. "Sure do," he called into the phone confidently. "It's like this really – this country has literally gone to the dogs, the governments and conspirators alike not only unbalancing the eco-system, but our once proud health service and also our democratic way of life – which – to be honest has been ground into the dust. Something has snapped Chief Inspector, something deep down. I can't explain it, no more than I can explain the surging life force that seems to be swarming out and over all Cornwall – but I suspect it won't end here. I hold Excalibur, the fabled sword – pulled it from the stone this morning – and following the sword is an absolute army of Knights of the Round Table – ready to take on anything the establishment can throw at them. The denigration and corruption of this once beautiful land will stop forthwith: The outright inequality that has left thousands without proper medical care and hundreds of pensioners without decent attention –

will end – *now!* Already Cornwall has given up its hidden treasures, already the coffers are coming to light, the millions of pounds and riches that have slowly but inexorably been stolen and secreted away – *and for what,"* Dan practically shouted down the phone, the suitcase containing enough money to probably build and fund a day-care centre or small local hospital, still lying open on the table reminding him of just how greedy his fellow man had become? He took a breath while the Inspector on the other end issued a sigh that could be felt right though the ether.

"I know that sigh," Danny spoke before the Chief could interrupt. "I hear it all the time, the sigh that says I really would like to do something about it but my hands are tied or I can't get involved, or I might jeopardise my job, or the money I'm laundering from the public office, or worse; but now you can make a difference – now you are being given a choice, join me and the brethren to fight for honour and chivalry, and challenge the old order, bring in a new way of life that will benefit all – not just the five percent."

"That's all very poetic young man, but challenging the establishment can only end one way – disastrously for you. Insurrection, rebellion, heresy – are all very much an updated treasonable offence – culminating in almost a lifetime of jail. So, why don't we meet around the table and perhaps discuss this man to man, just you and me. I know the system isn't perfect, I know the criminals – especially the financial type – always seem to go free, but it's the only one we've got – and to be honest when I look at other countries, I'm often reminded of how decent and honest ours is! So what do you say, lets' talk about it, eh?"

Dan thought for a moment, knowing the Chief Inspector was trying to bamboozle him, lull him into some kind of rose-tinted view where every misdemeanour – every crime and every billion pound sucked from the public monetary funds could be pushed under the carpet, shrugged at and swept away – considered with a blind eye. The greed, the avarice and damned excuses politicians gave for failing the people ignored.

"Chief Inspector, we will meet. If you're not prepared to give up your post and fight for justice, then I'm afraid we'll have to postpone the meeting until I sweep with my armies across the southern states, and begin my march on London. Perhaps you can spare a half hour or something out of your busy schedule then?"

Another sigh, this one inward – almost a groan:

"I just don't want to see any bloodshed," he voiced almost candidly after a thoughtful pause.

"Hm," hummed Danny. "Let's see who strikes the first blow, eh?"

Another big sigh; "Danny, Danny, Danny," the Chief Inspector simmered. "You don't want to do this; hundreds of people could get hurt, these re-enactment guys are really taking things a bit too far. You know in your heart of hearts that a machine gun will always outwit a sword any day – you just don't want to allow that to happen, I'm warning you Danny – any more incidents and it will be considered insurrectional and you will be held responsible. I wouldn't like to see you go to prison for the rest of your life, Dan – it'd be such a waste!"

Danny issued a sigh himself, catching Lancelot's look of concern, the phone especially taking a lot of interest as villagers and towns people tried to explain the technology. "You weren't there this morning, Chief Inspector – and I can appreciate your point – and also where you are coming from, but I've legally pulled the sword from the stone and am now – by rightful decree – lawful King of England. Now, if the rest of the morning hadn't unfolded as it has then I would have just gone home with a lovely trinket, but it didn't happen like that, Sir, in fact – something really magical has taken place – *and* I'm so glad I'm part of it."

"Alright Danny, so be it – I tried. And I did warn you." The line went dead.

"Trouble already," asked Lancelot?

Dan nodded, staring into the space before him. Around the map and atlas, pints of beer were frothing away, as if it was some kind of drinking contest; many wanting to buy the King a pint. He gulped one down almost without a breath, soothing his throat – and his senses.

He took a breath and set the glass down carefully. Fearing an air-strike of some kind, Dan asked, "how strong is this shielding – or whatever it is that's protecting us at the moment?"

Lancelot, placing a glass down on the table himself, turned to someone behind him, trying to get some bearing on how many had been indoctrinated by now.

"Shield is at full strength," came back the answer.

Lancelot looked across to Galahad, then his King. "What sort of weapons are we expecting – what's an inter-continental missile for God's sake?

Dan shook his head. For a moment the Inspector's words had rattled him, thinking he might just ring the local Air Force and arrange a strike, hitting the pub square on. He almost laughed to himself however. Anybody in their right mind would not deploy weapons of any kind right now – not until they understood the situation – calculated numbers of innocent lives and collateral damage.

Another battle-scarred Knight of the Realm, Agravain, who had reportedly aided Mordred in some rebellion against Arthur back in the day – and who had been thrust into the mix, and who wore the badge of honour proudly now, reported that he'd seen Merlin but he was having trouble digesting the bread roll he'd been given; the bacon perhaps a tad greasy. He was sitting about a mile away at the moment, still coming round, awaiting the next herd of horses to come through so he could catch a ride, his legs apparently not working too well.

"Well he's here," confirmed the Green Knight.

"Hm," growled Lancelot.

"Are there other coloured knights," Danny asked politely, his third pint in as many moments going down well but on a near empty stomach?

"A few," Sir Galahad instructed him, "there's a Red Knight no one talks about, and a black one. Boris the younger now holds the mantle for his mother Evelyn the White, who might be resurrected as well."

"Why green though," Dan persisted, glancing over to the Green entity?

"Armour is cursed," the heavily built knight croaked, reaching for his beer. "Green tinge comes from the mossy grave I was entombed in. Doesn't let me forget," he added solemnly!

Dan, staring at him thoughtfully, handed the phone back – only to be given it again as the landlord – answering it, handed it straight back. "It's the town council," he voiced warily.

The knights around watched on in interest.

"Hello," Dan spoke, trying to keep his vowels together.

"Hello – is that Danny King – or as I believe now to be Arthur Pendragon," a stressed mellifluous voice trilled. "If so, this is Madeline Crawley of the councillor's office – and I really need to get some questions answered – firstly – who are these gentlemen – who claim to be Knights of the Realm – yours I take it, and what do they ultimately want? I know some kind of strange atmospheric anomaly has shrouded our county, stopping traffic, but what's really going on – you can't be serious about taking on the establishment? My kids are at school – and they're absolutely terrified. We're cut off: The county has ground to a halt! What's going on?"

"Madeline," Dan started with a sigh, placing his elbows on the table to massage his forehead with the other hand. "I know this is going to sound real odd but something fantastical happened this morning. I was out walking the dogs when I stumbled upon the Sword in the Stone – the real article. I was with other people as well – so it wasn't some kind of hypnotic episode – and, well everything that has transpired since – me releasing Excalibur; the powerful miasma of energy that has encapsulated our county; Knights walking in from their epochs of time, the war horses and other animals as well – and I might add Merlin, who has just arrived – are all here for the sole purpose of supporting their King – me, in putting this country back on its feet – I don't know whether this is a world event, other countries having their legends but its certainly happening here, every Knight from history is reforming to do battle once more and restore order."

Dan could tell she wasn't convinced. "You're right Mr – erm Pendragon, the country as a whole could do with some sweeping reforms, but really – is swamping the streets with teams of re-enactment people really the way to go – I can see this getting very ugly if it's allowed to escalate any further?"

"Believe me, Mrs Crawley, I'll be doing my very best to keep violence out of the picture. I really don't know how powerful or battle-ready my army is – or whether spiritual or otherworldly forces will be at play – it's hard to say at this moment in time – all I really know is, I have Excalibur in my possession, and the sword seems to be drawing power from somewhere – and the pulses of energy cannot be denied – nor can my army, which is getting stronger as we speak."

Dan stretched in his seat. By now on any given work day he might well be heading for the refectory to gulp down a protein mix in readiness for the gym later, but now with three to four pints of ale slopping about in his stomach, he was feeling decidedly groggy. He took a breath, trying to instil clarity in his deportment, awaiting some kind of answer.

"Mr Pendragon, can we expect things to return to normal any time soon?"

In the background, Arthur could hear the clank of armour as a knight moved nearby – perhaps accepting yet another cup of tea, Dan visualising the exchange, the battle-ready veteran bowing regally while around a table sat the town council, all practically scared out of their minds. Its not everyday three knights in full battle regalia turn up to tell you your world is about to be turned upside down!

Dan tried to think of something ameliorating to say but could find nothing suitable save telling lies – and he wasn't about to start doing that, so told it like it was. "I'm sorry Mrs Crawley, but I really think pulling the sword from the stone this morning has ushered in a whole new change for this country – don't ask me why or how, because I don't know – its as much out of my hands as it is yours? I can no more give back the sword or call the whole thing off – than you can. Some big plan has been put into motion – and it looks all set to push to the very end, which I suspect will be the abdication of our ruling monarch and myself placed at the head of the country. I promise you, Mrs Crawley, I'll do my level best to make England a much better place to live."

"For whom," he heard the councillor ask him, a little sarcastically?

"Well," spluttered Dan. "I would hope everyone, but I suspect one or two who will have their riches taken from them might feel a little aggrieved – but once order is restored – I'm sure the country as a whole will be better for it."

The line went dead, either deliberately or not, it was hard to tell.

Dan waited for the council to ring back but they didn't.

Lancelot shifted nervously in his seat. Food stuffs of all kinds where circulating, mouth-watering aromas wafting through the pub; the landlady sparing no expense when it came to refreshments, big platters of sandwiches and rolls, hot pies and cooked snacks, baskets of sausage or chicken and chips; the knights digging in now their stomachs had settled down. Dan's right hand man ate sparingly however, he noticed, wondering if he suspected an engagement would be in the offing.

"I'd better line my own stomach," Dan quipped, tucking into a big steak baguette.

By three that day Dan had fended off phone calls from the local constabulary, several civic employees; the Director of the Eden Project whose plants were now shrivelling as the Domes fell under yet another layer of insulation; several irate farmers who had come across hundreds of footmen and cavalry messing up their fields; and several apoplectic coastguards – especially from the Channel Islands and the Isles of Scilly who'd fallen foul of the encircling power grid as it gently pushed shipping and fishing boats out of the way. To add to all this a small host of local journalists phoned continually, those who were practically beside themselves to get the first interview with the 'supposed' King of England. Power lines had been severed and telecommunications and the grid had to reroute electricity as they fizzled on each side of the sizzling power curtain. The river authorities too, were quizzical about the force field that hovered over the water like some tremulous animal, divers finding an open lattice had sunk into the water and would stop anything bigger than fish.

The unusual morning and now the intake of beer was making Danny tired beyond words. He rubbed his eyes and spoke as politely as possible to yet another journalist who had realised The Bell public house lay geographically more or less in the middle of Cornwall, and had been taken over by a complete army of re-enactment societies – all calling for Danny King – real name apparently Arthur Pendragon – to lead them on some sort of crazy crusade to unseat the royal monarch! It was a story of a lifetime and if just one journalist could navigate the cordon of men surrounding the pub – then somehow slide past an absolute phalanx of Knights of the Round Table – all apparently armed to the teeth – they'd be in for a chance.

Bill Nightingale of Devon and Somerset's Southern Chronical sat in his car and cogitated at length about this.

Chapter 3

The road he was on was littered with broken or discarded implements of an injurious kind, snapped lances and spears, jagged bits of metal, making it look as if Napoleon's army had just passed through, the leafy by-road awash with an assortment of iron.

Torn or ripped bits of clothing of another age also littered the lane; flapping about the verges; dropped pendants, discarded flags caught on bushes, a leather gauntlet, a smashed iron helmet, a cart for god's sake – that looked as if a horse pulled it – all suggesting several battalions of some sort had just passed along it – and as Bill Nightingale stared, his car parked on a verge a few miles from Trewint near Launceston, a plan of sorts began to form in his mind. Gazing out at the hundreds of milling re-enactment people – many looking as if they'd travelled miles to get here, it dawned on him that the only way he was going to get anywhere near the nucleus of this idiotic set up, was to discard his current apparel of modern clothing and don rather more basic garments. He had in the boot of his car his summer sandals, a good leather pair, and if he cut a hole in the dark-toned sheet he used for his little dog he could make a kind of tabard a lot of the dazed combatants were sporting. He was quite a way from Trewint and The Bell public house where apparently a one Danny King had taken up residence – claiming he'd pulled Excalibur from the stone that morning (causing all sorts of panic), but he had an idea he might just be able to slip through the cordon that was already surrounding him, if he looked right. As he tapped his steering wheel, staring out at the welter of people and horses passing by, many manhandling equipment this way and that, he wondered again at this Danny King and all this ensuing chaos he'd caused, the strange sea-green and blue refulgent shimmer that continued to encapsulate Cornwall – as he had witnessed it for himself earlier that morning, finding the main A30 into the county blocked – not only by a wall of shimmering energy but several knights on horseback that looked anything but approachable. He'd studied the motoring atlas thoroughly and having painstakingly followed the curve of the coruscating iron wall by zigzagging all along its boundary line found four major roadblocks, one allowing traffic to exit via the Newton Abby intersection in the south and *'in'* via the small collection of B-roads at Chulmleigh towards the north – and in and out again on the main roads exiting Barnstable; most of the traffic almost at gridlock. According to police and the motoring organisations a complete circle of *'something'* had ringed the county, only a small spit of land at Lands End left unmolested.

It had taken some organisation, Bill Nightingale considered, still cataloguing the people passing his car – many scrutinising the vehicle as if they'd never seen the model before. Getting all these people down here either by train, coach or ferry – plus all the horses and equipment, must have been a logistical nightmare – there was just too many to comprehend, not to mention the livestock. Bill shook his head and ran his plan over in his head one more time, wondering just how he was going to carry tape recorder and his other paraphernalia that every good journalist needed, to carry out a successful interview.

He glanced behind, wondering if his wife had left the canvas bag she sometimes used for the beach, the grass green body and beige strap not wholly atypical of the shoulder bags and leather satchels the re-enactment contenders used. If he picked up the odd belt or piece of chain-mail and tried to blend in, muddied up his face a little, he might just pass as a roving – *what?* Jester; salesman – did they have salesmen in the fifth or sixth centuries? What – for *christ sakes* could he be – did they have journalists in the dark ages? Sages – that was it – *he could be a sage – a town's crier,* news person. Sage sounds better; he ruminated, glancing out the window to the passers by – many looking a little confused and not at all with it. He shook his head again at the wonderful costumes, the attention to detail commendable, even if they were taking over this county.

He was wasting time, he realised. He had to get down to it, get himself immersed, become one of them. He unbuckled himself from his seat belt, made sure the car wasn't going to be rolled off somewhere – handbrake fully on, then with thoughts of where he was going to secrete his car keys, he climbed out of the vehicle, careful not to crash his door into anyone passing close by.

Once outside – the welter of noise and an odd smell in the air – probably from the livestock, stayed his hand, the area he was in quite built up with schools, shops and a business park nearby but where were the local people – had they all taken the advice of a lunchtime community directive aired on TV and stayed inside? Around him men were traipsing with horses and livestock toward the nearby woodlands and small lakes where the animals could graze perhaps (although many were taking advantage of the wild flowers and high sedge of the verges as they passed); men of all calibre, squires in gaudy tabards and leather boots and jerkins – with strange looking bonnets on, bowmen in a kind of leather or skin outer garments and huge longbows over their shoulders, quivers full of arrows on them also; other men – and some women in very basic clothes indeed – roughly stitched, practically thrown together – the whole gamut of what one might call the caravan, those people that sought quarters for all the horses, the squires and maids all preparing food or sleeping areas, all in readiness for the knights to do battle.

He'd seen mounted knights already, a few holding the rock-blocks and passing up and down the major routes, looking so resplendent in their armour and weaponry it was inconceivable that anyone would have the effrontery to challenge them. *They looked so real,* he had to conclude – wondering at the mental state of many of those men on horseback, sitting so high and mighty – scaring the absolute *bejesus* out of the locals: should he upset one such individual he might well find himself, not only outgunned but also without any friends – and quite possibly without any law and order because like it or not – the police force as a whole had been whittled down to practically nothing in Cornwall and Devon by cutbacks in the last few years – two patrol cars – and no one to service them, most of the local constabulary working from kiosks in one of the superstores due to redundancies.

The country as a whole was ripe for change, Bill ruminated glancing about – and if this lot had anything to do with it chivalry might well replace corruption. One or two passing gave him a quizzical look, but he dived into the back of his car and dragged out the dog's bed, giving it a good shake. What he needed to do now was cut a hole in the middle of it, tie a bit of rope or his belt from his trousers around it – *and Bob's your jesting little incognito journalist.*

Cut a hole... hmm...

Bill stood for a moment, sheet in hand, searching his memory. The last time he needed a sharp lock-knife he'd been on the beach, trying to open a shop bought carton of cheese sandwiches, the plastic refusing to give no matter what the family did. In the end – having searched through a hamper he'd found a small penknife and managed to slice the packet open, the sandwiches promptly falling into the sand through his fingers. *Where was the knife now, he wondered?*

Bill rummaged through his side door pockets, the glove box – finally the boot area – coming up with a blank – being considered dangerous his wife had probably squirreled it away in a drawer somewhere never to be found again – not this side of Christmas anyway.

He considered trying to rip it but knowing his luck he'd probably tear the thing clean in half and it would be useless.

Sheet in hand, he glanced about at the men passing by, realising dimly some were a kind of semi-armoured infantry, the soft clinking and clanking as the column marched, reminding him they were fully armed – nearly every person somehow carrying a knife or bladed instrument of some kind. He just had to ask someone, he concluded.

He looked the column over, the somewhat exhausted expressions; the dazed or unfocused thousand mile stare, the very quizzical gaze others gave as they stepped passed.

As luck would have it, a senior figure looking somewhat fatigued and almost ill at ease, had stepped out of the column nearby to take a knee, dropping his huge halberd like a toy – which hit the ground with a thud, then pushing himself to his feet again, having to lean against a tree next as his stomach hiccupped and gurgled away.

Bill approached cautiously, sheet in his hands like a toga.

"Are you ok," he thought to ask quietly, drawing near; the man's head dropping, body supported by the arms on the tree trunk?

For a moment the man didn't hear, or didn't answer, so consumed by his own dilemma, he had little time for anything else.

"I have a medical kit in the car," Bill thought to add, wondering if he seriously had anything for a hangover. Then he remembered a bottle of water he'd bought this morning and not opened. He walked briskly back to his car, found the bottle on the passenger seat and after shutting and locking the door again, carried it over to the flagging man.

"Here," Bill called softly! "Water, aqua:" He ripped the top off and proffered it, the prostrate combatant finally realising he was there.

"Water, aqua," Bill repeated, holding the bottle out?

The pause in the pike-man's breathing was an indication that he may have heard, Bill holding his ground, studying the costume as he did, the man cased in a kind of thick unyielding leather, almost a suit of armour in itself as it creaked, the boots heavy and well-made. Like many of his contemporaries he had kind of handmade bandoliers which held small slithers of metal – throwing knifes Bill judged, trying to catalogue his apparel. At long last the man lifted his head – and in that moment the journalist got a sneaking suspicion all was not right with him. As he gazed into his eyes a gulf opened up, a chasm that held all the coldness and frightening entropy of a long lost grave, the emptiness of man's forgetfulness; bonded by epochs of yet more loneliness – the eons piling up on one another, the incredible look of a totally lost person – not just lost in his own area but in space and time as well.

'Jeeze," Bill mused.

The look became so hauntingly eerie it seemed to pin him to the spot, those dead grey eyes unseeing, uncaring.

He wanted to back away, forget the whole thing, get in his car and head for the nearest pub that hadn't been taken over yet by more of the re-enactment freaks, this guy obviously so spaced out he was on another planet, in another place and time.

The column had passed, leaving way for yet more squires with horses, dozens of them – each, he calculated needing a knight to accompany them, thinking they were all accumulating around The Bell public house.

He decided to try the pike-man one more time, offering the bottle over once more.

"Water, aqua," he prompted?

All at once the man before him appeared to come back down to earth, finally able to hold his head up – the sickness or malady leaving him a bit.

He breathed in deep, eventually standing on his own two feet. A colour of sorts came back to his face and eyes.

"Water," he asked, turning toward Bill, holding onto the tree however for a while yet?

Bill nodded eagerly, unscrewing and holding out the plastic bottle. The soldier eyed it suspiciously.

"Sorry it's not in a gourd," Bill quipped, still proffering it.

The pike-man straightened, letting go of the tree, looking around for his huge halberd which he let fall to the ground, the grey wooden shaft looking so old it had to be an original. He left it where it was for a moment while he considered the stranger offering help.

The man, after glancing about to get his bearings then took a step toward Bill reaching out for the offered water. Flinching, Bill held his ground, the air in his lungs freezing as the soldier's mitt curled around the top of the bottle, his clothing so authentic it was hard to find fault, the linen shirt beneath the man's leather breastplate and thick epaulets having faded over time, the colour having been leeched by sun, wind and rain, a necklace of what appeared to be real bone on fraying hemp twine around a very tanned and marred neck.

His face – as Bill confronted him – held all the history of adventure and skirmishes one would want to shy away from, etched in; the deep weals and welts reminiscent of many encounters and set battles. His deeply tanned skin and black hair under the leather and iron helmet gave the combatant the quality of being of Greece or Spain perhaps, yet his diction when he next spoke appeared to be of a northern dialect of England.

"Thanks to you, commoner."

Bill nodded, letting go of the bottle. The stranger held the bottle in one hand while his eyes slid from Bill to his red car parked up a few yards away, suburbia all around despite this little patch of woodland and scrub at the end of the tributary. He looked around again – as if trying to get his bearings. He sniffed the sea air. "Southern England," he asked hoarsely?

"Hm...," Bill coughed, clearing his throat. The soldier was only a head taller than him – but by his size alone must have been almost twice his weight, his arms and legs so thick they'd have made two of his. Almost tremulous under his bearing, Bill fought to keep his equilibrium, hoping to converse and perchance take the stranger into his confidence.

The soldier indicated with a nod of his head Bill's car parked up behind him. "Red...cart," the man stuttered, finding his throat sore. "Yours?" He lifted the plastic bottle to his lips and after squeezing the container and finding it pliable – and getting over the shock of that apparently, he put it to his lips to drink, nearly draining the small half litre in one go.

The man looked visibly relieved, not gushing or gasping for air, or thrashing around, simply holding his ground stoically as his stomach dealt with the filtered liquid.

"Ok," Bill asked, hoping to god he hadn't poisoned him?

The pike-man nodded at last, glancing down at the plastic bottle still clamped in his fist. "Thank you," he muttered softly.

"You're welcome. Where you from?"

The combatant considered the topography, glancing around. He shook his head slowly unable to comprehend the houses and roofs of industrial warehouses in the distance. "If this is southern England then I'm home," he voiced with solemnity.

"You've travelled from afar to reach here again, I take it," Bill prompted.

The revenant nodded, swaying slightly.

"You sure you're ok," Bill asked with concern?

The stranger shot him a glance that said he was – just; looking down at the bottle again in his hand. He offered the small amount of liquid back to Bill who shook his head, indicating he could finish it off. The pike-man nodded appreciatively, slugging the rest down without question.

Bill watched as his very skin took on a healthier tone, his cheeks flushing and his eyes clearing still. He almost looked human, Bill thought, nodding to himself.

"Hm, well… if you wouldn't mind. I have to be on stage within the hour – and wouldn't you believe it but I left my costume behind and well; if you wouldn't mind lending a hand, I thought I'd just make a jerkin out of this old sheet, and I can be on my way. I actually just need to cut a hole here, if you would be so kind."

The stranger looked the raiment over, trying to visualise what he meant, then it came to him and he drew a dagger that looked sharper than a lancet, asking Bill to lay it out on the ground. Bill did so, trying to mark the centre where he wanted a slit to go.

The infantryman knew what he wanted however and made a cross slit about six inches either way, allowing Bill's head to slip through.

Bill stripped off his shirt laying it aside, then slipped the sheet over, loosening his belt next to lash it around the sheet making it look remarkably like many of the squires tabards and surcoats. Without another word, the soldier unbuckled his leather waistcoat and handed it to him, indicating he should put it on too.

"No, I can't," Bill uttered, completely taken by surprise.

"It's yours," the pike-man told him – *"and this,"* he spoke, walking over to heft the enormous pike shaft into the air with one hand, walking over to present it to him. Bill, trousers around his ankles, took hold of the huge pole of wood with both, the massive blade and spike on top threatening to unbalance the thing at any moment. "I don't know what to say – this thing must be worth a fortune. I'll …I'll just borrow it," he stammered, terrified the thing would collapse onto him, "bring it back tomorrow – after all you are going to need something to fight with," he stipulated.

"I don't want to fight," the infantryman issued, his words laced with lassitude. "Anyway there'll probably be hundreds of spare weapons in the opening phases of the battle so I just equip myself again – don't worry."

"Where will you be," he called after the man began his trek down the lane following his detachment.

The stoic combatant shook his head, shrugging his shoulders. He turned back to wave, a small smile on his face, looking, Bill thought in that snapshot of time, the happiest –untethered human being.

He was soon swallowed up by dozens more tramping off to the nearby coastline, many claiming the sea air would soothe their aching stomachs.

Bill, relaxing for a moment – suddenly realised he was still supporting the halberd and it came crashing down, digging itself into the ground with a wallop, missing his car by a couple of feet.

"Jesus," he gasped knowing the damn thing would be far too heavy to carry far. He'd have to hide it, he worried!

Behind his car, Bill decided to pull his trousers up and roll up the legs under the tabard instead of abandoning them, using the belt to catch the waistline and trap them as he tightened it. With his shoes safely in the boot and his socks tucked inside, he put on his sandals to then try the leather waistcoat, the thing incredibly heavy as he manhandled it.

It was about seven sizes too big, but he could at least bring the two sets of buckles each side in to their full limit, pinching the leather panels in, the stitched in shoulder flaps so enormous they looked more like bits of an arm covering on him; still, with his blond hair ruffed up and some mud and dust added strategically, he decided he did look the part, even if he had to leave the halberd under the car.

Bill filled his wife's beach bag with laptop, tape recorder, pens and notebooks – his Kindle and anything else he could think of, then locking the car up once more, headed off for The Bell, happy in his new disguise.

***

Back at The Bell public house HQ, Dan had suffered enough. So unused to all the excitement of the morning and alcohol in the day, he was ready for a nap that afternoon and asked the landlord politely if he had a guest room he could possibly use for a couple of hours. The innkeeper was more than happy to oblige and offered to show him to a suite, collecting a key from behind the bar.

Danny collected up his weaponry, dimly wondering over the mystical shield.

Upon alerting his two henchmen on his plans, Lancelot waved for several knights to accompany him, act as bodyguard, several falling in behind as he followed the landlord across the pub and up the stairs.

The rooms were pretty spartan, double bed under a prettily decorated window, matching wardrobes and fittings; a tiny sitting room, Danny not noticing – just happy for some peace and quiet – and a couple of hours shut eye. Around him however – as the landlord left him the key on a bedside dresser, knights cased the joint, inspecting the adjoining bathroom and shower, poking their noses into cupboards and sets of drawers, their fascination with their environment never diminishing. Dan left them to it, laying his equipment down or against a nearby wall, stripping off some garments to climb straight into bed curling up; whilst around him knights knelt to pray or lean against the window to gaze outside, sipping on bottles of beer: Some just flopped about, keeping an eye on the sleeping king. Along the landing knights also kept guard, one or two holding the stairs, a complete phalanx blocking the stairwell. Downstairs hundreds filled the two bars, surrounding them outside and swamping the grounds.

At the tables downstairs in the front of the pub, Lancelot and Galahad formed a council of war. Hundreds more were passing through the gate as they conferred, Merlin now on route, as were several mages and sages, the brains of any operation, the intelligentsia that could direct and organise the legions. Acting as Vice Regent, Galahad found he had to diplomatically fend off phone calls of all kinds, some very important, it seemed – especially from the 14th reconnaissance army unit that was being blocked at Exeter, wanting to know why they couldn't return to their loved ones – although a spokesperson for the renegade knights pointed out the patrol was heavily armed – not exactly debriefed and looking ready for a cosy homecoming, he hovered awkwardly as Lancelot and others pored over the map; the southeast coast in all its glory; picking out key points of Devon – their next staging post: "Let them through," he advised a very confused Knight of the Realm, "their weapons will be of little use."

***

At sixteen hundred hours British Summer Time, a small inflatable manned by Three Four Commando, plus two scientists, landed at Porthcurno Sands loaded down with equipment, ballistics and weaponry. It had been pointless trying to clear the beach as there seemed to be no one around. Acting Captain Davis had seen action in Yemen and various other parts of the far east in his twenty three years where deceit, deception and improvised explosive devices was the rule of the day for the new type of war the enemies of democracy waged. Along with all the other derogatory *D's* was Dust with a capital D – the damnable stuff getting everywhere, and dirt of course, but also *d*espair and *d*esolation that summed up the civilian plight in so many of the godforsaken dust bowls. This however, as he climbed out of the small boat and took his first look of the encapsulating dome that had settled all over Cornwall – was something completely new.

The smoke the small frigate had laid down to cover the disembarking and hasty scuttle ashore had dispersed quicker than he would have liked in a short but strong off- shore breeze, but the sandy dunes of the Penwith Heritage Coast were ideal for a rapid assault landing, his men able to speedily deploy along the small coastline. Despite this however – as he stewarded the two scientists with all their paraphernalia up the sands, he was most disgruntled to find he was being watched almost casually by what he could only describe as peasants; rough-shod villagers who – by their attire alone – had seemed to have let go of their senses.

He followed his men as they ducked and dived over the shoreline making use of the small dunes and tall clumps of sea-grass, scouting through the landscape like true professionals while all the time being scrutinised by people on the other side of the curtain, who were slowly but surely being joined by others, the disconcerting way one bowman lent against his weapon most troubling. With his updated SA90 assault rifle Captain Davis drew near the curtain of shimmering power that seemed to have enshrouded Cornwall in its entirety; the coruscating grid appearing to clear at times as if looking through a cloudy window or conversely go completely opaque at others as if a living thing, energy pulsing around the shell, as and when it was needed. Even so, as he ordered two of his men to make initial contact, he hunkered down, protecting his wards – the two scientists who might be able to make some sense of what they were dealing with.

Staff Sergeant Enders and Lance Corporal Henderson scampered up to the power curtain – making the two hundred yard dash easily; much to the curiosity and amusement of all watching, Captain Davis even more unsettled by two men on horseback who had sauntered into view, these individuals in full battle armour it seemed, what he realised a moment later were actually fully dressed knights on equally armoured war horses.

"Jesus christ," he muttered under his breath! "Whatever next, Ian," he called into his mike, "update!"

Staff Sergeant Enders and his company commander struggled out of their rucksacks, the Staff Sergeant starting by pushing his helmet out of his eyes and reaching out with a hand – relaying every movement back to his superior, reaching to touch it with gloved fingers, the section of power curtain quivering as if alive, going opaque almost immediately – as if to strengthen that small area. He pushed a little, applying more pressure, but found the harder he forced it the stronger the resistance, as if made of a superfine polymer that tightened up its molecules as it was disturbed.

Davis got an update from two military helicopters that were encircling the area, one carrying his superior who was in turn relaying the exercise back to base, trying to discover if the power curtain was indeed a dome or just a wall, initial impressions indicating the former. "It's certainly a dome," a pilot radioed in from above, "stretching from Exeter and Holsworthy in the east as far out west as Penzance."

"Ok, thanks, we'll take it from here."

"Good luck."

Davis signed off, watching the assembled crowd on the other side of the power curtain with steely interest, trying to catalogue the various ranks, hoping to ascertain their strength by the military ranks already present – something you could never do in the

Golan Heights – or anywhere else in the far-east for that matter as one towelhead looked pretty much like another.

"Preparing first contact," Lance Corporal Henderson spoke cautiously, preparing to fire into the wall with his pistol. The pistol was not any old popgun either, commissioned solely for this deployment, the powers above decided a little force right now would be the thing and had fitted him out with a Desert Eagle firearm, the gun professing a forty four magnum; hollow cap; armoured steel jacket projectile – a percussion cap of three hundred and fifty grams; capable of punching a hole clean through several brick walls – in his estimation far too powerful – a Walther PPK would have been fine.

As he prepared to fire however, trying to hide the act by shielding the big gun with his body, yet pointing it downward so any ricochet would bounce the missile off into the sand dunes, it was a bit like handling a sledge hammer to crack a walnut.

Lance Corporal Henderson, radioed into his mike – "taking first shot" – then, gripping the gun with both hands called out softly *"fire in the hold,"* and fired, closing his eyes in case of any shrapnel.

The ensuing explosion of the handgun echoed out over the sea, reverberating off the walls of an empty tea room and ice cream parlour nearby, despite the weapon having some contrived silencer on it, the noise scared half the population of local seabirds into the air. The big bullet nudged the force field and slewed off out over the dunes like a bolt of lightening, slamming into a chunk of driftwood and exploding it like a grenade, shards of wood spiralling off into the air, the projectile then racing out to sea.

"Dear god," muttered one of the hiding scientists.

Captain Davis looked up from the crouched position he'd taken to find nothing much had changed, the wall seeming as impregnable as ever, his two men mercifully still there.

He let the ringing in his ears settle, before he ordered the next phase – a small controlled explosion.

"The curtain's condition," Davis barked into radio, trying to ignore the two mounted horsemen and the small group of onlookers who appeared to be cushioned from the gunshot by the encircling wall?

"Same as ever," reported Staff Sergeant Enders, running a hand over the force field, finding it incredibly tactile, as if he was running his hand down the side of a gigantic whale. He glanced up from his position to find several herdsmen and one or two bowmen were watching their progress, two mounted knights keeping a safe distance, the warhorses looking unfazed by the gunshot.

"Preparing secondary contact," he reported, aiding his subordinate by holding the device he'd pulled from a small rucksack to plant down close by the power curtain, digging a small hole to then place the claymore deep down, hoping to force the explosive impact up toward the wall.

Lance Corporal Enders strung out a thin fishing line, the both of them then retreating with all their gear to a safe place, the soldier thinking to pause and warn the onlookers that a landmine was about to be deployed. Considering the bullet of one of the most powerful handguns in the world had little or no effect, he didn't really hold much for the claymore either, quickly forming the opinion they were up against something not of this world, something supernatural.

Still, he was just a small cog in a massive military machine and if the powers above wanted to try and blow a hole in the strange creation, then that's what they'd do – try, at least.

Thirty yards back, hunkered safely behind a thick sand dune; Enders radioed *"Fire in the hold,"* and pulled the rip cord!

The resultant explosion shook the ground, blowing a chunk of cement – that had until that time lain undisturbed for years –under the sand, high into the sky in a shower of deadly bits; the horses of the mounted knights whinnying and unsettled at the noise as it echoed through and over the land on either side of the iron curtain. Seabirds once again took to the air, squawking and screaming at the row. Having taken cover for a second time, Captain Davis peered over his sand dune to see if the landmine had had any effect, finding much to his dismay – once the dust settled and everyone had got to their feet – that apart from a small crater, nothing at all had bothered the power field, the wall seeming to have absorbed the force – if it was at all possible?

"Jesus christ," he cursed, gazing upon the small crowd beyond, watching as the knights eased their horses forward, as if to inspect any damage. "Your turn," he sighed, turning to the scientists.

Fairly confident missiles couldn't pass through the scintillating wall, both boffins stood unsteadily, sinking in the soft sand, shouldering their equipment; Davis shouldering his rifle also, lent a hand, struggling with them as they made their way over to the wall.

Avoiding the depression, the scientists knelt by the wall once they arrived, ignoring the small crowd of onlookers, inspecting the curtain at length, both eminently versed in physics and dynamics, the force field seeming to defy all known parameters as it fluctuated and shimmered before them. Once convinced it was a plasma shield however, held together by corresponding ions of a magnetic field, their first thoughts were to fire a small laser at it, the laser beam hopefully bringing the ions much closer together – so close they could fuse and burn up.

Agreeing on that point firstly they quickly adorned arc-shielding glasses.

Fearful of any kind of reaction, both knelt back a bit as well, as one fired the pen laser directly at it.

A highly condensed green light smashed into the wall causing a small thermonuclear effect to take place, the piece of wall shuddering as if mortally wounded. Sparks and smoke blistered outward; the two mounted knights coaxing their warhorses even nearer, curious as to the odd effect. The scientist snapped off the laser as both lifted their glasses, peering closely at the damage.

The section of wall shuddered, seeming to cringe internally – as if a living animal. Streaks of white lightning arced through the matrix as they centred on the affected area, swirls of what looked like liquid glass melding with each other.

"Well," coughed one of them?

Not wholly surprised at the effect and making notes, the other boffin thinking something else entirely, wondering that as the sheet of plasma coalesced when the atoms were affected or damaged, the magnetic lattice tightening up, then nitric acid may just cause as much damage as the laser – but unlike the laser could be spilt on top of the Dome to eat its way though, the acid causing a chain reaction with the matrix.

The scientist asked his compatriot to flash the wall once again, hoping to attract its atoms, the wall immediately following suit by reacting, closing on the damaged areas with deep blue refulgence, the lattice appearing to be at its thickest at this point. The scientist dabbed at it quickly with a little plastic spatula, finding it worked exactly as planned, the plasma burning freely with oxygenated air each side.

"Bingo," he called, sitting back as fumes billowed from an apparent hole.

"Christ on a rocking horse," Captain Davis groaned, watching on with cold appraisal. Beside him his radio operator was filming the proceedings, his camcorder relaying it all back to base.

"You getting this, sir," he croaked, sickened the skinny little boffins had beat him fair and square with nothing more than a pen torch laser and small bottle of acid. I'm in the wrong job, he told himself – not for the first time.

***

Rory Splengier – formally of number six Tenby Avenue was having the time of his life. From his home in Camelford he marched with the other re-enactment societies to Port William, learning all the time about life in the dark ages, turning right then, to join with hundreds of others who were making a sort of pilgrimage to Tintagel Castle, running down onto the beach at Trebawith like school kids, regaling in its golden sands and turquoise seas – although the beaches were crowded almost to bursting point by thousands of people – not all revenant fighting men or herdsmen, many civilians mixed up in the fray. Rory had divested of his modern clothing and found, begged or borrowed some authentic rags, a pair of filthy soiled leggings he'd had to rinse off in the warm sea, and a threadbare tunic that had a mysterious slash both back and front. He kept his white T-shirt with a print of a heavy-metal band on it as it didn't look too out of place with the rest of his new apparel. Rory was barefoot but he couldn't have cared less. Without a thought for his young wife, he'd given himself totally over to the event, however long or short it was going to be, just thrilled to be part of it. He gambolled in the surf, was allowed to trot along on a mule, splashing about in the waves, and join in the festivities as the weekenders spit-roasted pigs and chickens; searing fish and lobsters which the local inshore boats provided. He shared oysters with noblemen and danced his heart out with camp women, just loving their body scents and frivolity;

bowled over by the authenticity of all the fittings and equipment – but what really did it for him was the costumes, the attention to detail most uplifting, not one person accidentally forgetting about sporting a watch or modern undergarments – the whole army of re-enactment groups – and there seemed thousands of them – were as realistic as they could be. He wandered along the coast toward Tintagel stroking the horses, marvelling at the knights in full body armour; the absolute epitome of chivalry, the magnificent swords and liveries, everything harking from an age – that although brutal and savage at times, now seemed so pure and without corruption. He would be a squire, he told himself, not sure if he could wield an axe or mace in anger; wandering through the encampments in a hedonistic daze, partaking of food readily offered, everyone encouraging each other to eat and become battle-ready.

He sauntered on, on to his beloved castle, not caring if he actually touched stone as so many wanted to do, but live in the moment, soak up the majesty of gallantry and nobility, the deep sublime indulgent yearning for everything natural and untainted. He was adrift in mortal levity; walking on air, breathing deep of Arcadia's pastoral groves, relishing the energy, warmth and vim the blue haze above seemed to be exuding.

***

Conversely, on the road to Trewint and the HQ of this riotous assembly – The Bell public house; Bill Nightingale was finding the going distinctly disdainful, the reek of animal, human sweat and excrement noisome in the extreme, this journalist definitely for the bright lights of the city rather than the leafy smelly lanes of pastoral Cornwall – even if he was on the road to stardom perhaps, being the first to actually get near the centre of all this madness – for he'd heard via radio and phone messages that local TV vans had been clogged up in road jams, enthusiastic journalists who tried to make the same kind of journey on foot, pointedly halted two or three miles from the pub, the knights setting up a steel ring around the epicentre, doing a thoroughly good job so far of stopping anyone suspicious or who wanted a private audience – and didn't have a suitcase or car loaded down with money to offer, only re-enactment people allowed to pass through the cordon – many it seemed on their way to the ruins of the castle at Tintagel. As he had walked, many sort of way stations had been set up at the side of the road, where the more audacious of them had apparently slaughtered and then set about barbecuing a lamb or heifer, in order to encourage people to eat, just about anything combustible used to get a spit roast going. At one time he witnessed from afar two Land Rovers packed with men squeal to a halt on a dusty lane, whereupon everyone jumped out to ostensibly set about several groups of peasants and bowmen who were happily setting up a camp in one of the farmers corn fields; the men swarming over the field toward them.

Thinking something might be in the offing – having a distinct nose for trouble; Bill pushed his way into the shrubbery and dug out his camera; surreptitiously bringing it to his eye, trying to catch the skirmish as it developed – the first antagonism he'd witnessed so far between the invading tourists and the local people. He reeled off several shots as like chess pieces, archers formed up into a line, expecting trouble, two or three men with pikes and spears taking up a flank, protecting the small caravan of women and a young boy.

At that point out on the road to Bill's left, several knights were making their way toward Tintagel when they too spotted the developing skirmish, obviously thinking it might be a little mismatched. With only the slightest of deliberation the knights vaulted the ditch and began trotting outward, carving out a dirty great chasm in the corn.

Seeing the knights suddenly enter the affray put a somewhat different aspect onto the scene as the heavy artillery thundered into view, the crowd of farmers and workers fighting their way through the corn (who'd perhaps initially thought the caravan were perhaps gypsies cashing in on the bonanza); baulked by the magnificent war horses rolling toward them; advancing like some upgraded WarCraft machine.

All twenty men were brought up sharp by the knights – *no one mentioning armed men on horseback for crying out loud!* They quickly huddled into a tight group, conferring whilst the knights cantered to a stop, putting themselves directly in the path of the marauding men, one breaking away to approach them, the two ton armoured war horse enough to worry the most stalwart of men, never mind the knight sitting atop it.

Bill reeled off more shots; the knight plodding to a stop a few yards from the men, banners and pendants rippling in the wind, the sun glinting off polished steel armour plate; two agreeing to be spokepersons and being practically shoved forward, approaching the anachronism nervously, one looking back tremulously as if to encourage his friends forward with him.

Bill zoomed in with a three hundred millimetre telephoto lens, the men approaching the mounted knight dwarfed by the war horse, reeling off several more shots, flashes of Tiananmen Square flitting across his mind. He got a great shot of the knight lifting the visor of his helmet to converse, the men below wondering where to start. At this distance Bill couldn't hear what was being said, but by the armoured man's dour actions it was clear the aggressors had made a fundamental mistake and no further action would be taken should they return to their homes immediately, the knight pointing emphatically to their trucks. Bill photographed one irate farmer as he tried to explain his plight, most of his farmland being tramped over – his livestock cooked and eaten, several years of damage being wrought in one afternoon. Bill could sympathise with him, the numbers just too extreme to contemplate, many more piling in from the coastlines each hour, he assumed as thousands tramped along Cornwall's roads, lanes and lokes. Would the farmer be compensated? One assumed so, he mused, a film perhaps in the offing; any film director or star able to buy the county three times over.

Reluctantly the small crowd of men about turned and headed back to their trucks, but not before the young boy shot an arrow their way, the bolt narrowly missing one thug as he minced back to the Land Rovers, clearly upset he'd been outgunned – and somewhat out numbered as well, none of them wanting to chance their luck with mounted knights, not even a shotgun having much effect.

The small arrow zipping past his head was just the trigger, however – and bristling with anger – and hating the invaders with a passion, the farmhand stopped, tried to reign in his temper, failed, and about turned and raced back seeing red, ready to take on anything – even the mounted knight. Another man – seeing his actions spun on his heel and charged after him hoping to rugby tackle him to the ground.

Bill was about to put away his camera, worried his disguise would be discovered, when something had obviously transpired and a younger member of the gang had apparently had enough and seen red, turning back to charge the knight on horseback.

Futile as it seemed, the knight – who was turning his mount to rejoin the others, suddenly realised he might possibly have something to do after all, spun his warhorse in a tight circle – ready to confront anything. Seeing the two men apparently race toward him, he drew his sword from his hilt and raised it to the heavens, a soft crackling of lightning rapidly hovering just above it. He waited until it had powered up then swiftly brought it down, arcing the power in a bolt of lightning that struck both men fully in the chest, knocking them back off their feet. Bill heard the crack drift across the land, the knight not satisfied with that, encouraging his warhorse forward to make sure both were fully immobilised.

Bill zoomed in as smoke barrelled from the chests of the two fallen men, many farmers backtracking to whisk the injured away.

Back in the camp the young boy – who'd nearly caused an international incident – which actually could have been a whole lot worse, was being censored by his seniors, the small bow having been taken from him, Bill unable to fathom the full picture as he hadn't seen the arrow in flight. The farmhands gathering around their fallen, hands in the air, only worried about caring for them, the knight making sure they packed them up and carried them home. Regally, he sat immobile for a while, looking resplendent in his war bonnet and finery – watching as the crowd ferried the two men back to the trucks, then turned the magnificent warhorse and cantered back to the camp.

Bill reeled off a few more shots as the knights dismounted and partook of the food offered, others crossing the field to join them.

He stood there for a moment considering the incident, wondering just how many locals had been upset by the invasion and how many had been swept up by the tide, the way the re-enactment people accepted most of the locals commendable to a fault, as many would share or offer whatever they had, giving support or comfort, unknowing of the full picture just yet.

Bill had made one or two enquiries himself, trying to be low-key about it – just appearing to pass the time of day as they tramped, one particular woman unable to bring it all into focus as she tried to clear her head, the wench with her handsome face and head of wavy dark hair attractive in a rough sort of way; the distance in time and history so vast and so inexplicable she faltered each time he made the slightest of inquiry. The woman's candour and obvious distress concerned Bill, as they neared the outer cordon of King Arthur's head quarters, a quick presence of mind, making him aid the woman helped him pass through the first hurdle without question; his bag buried somewhere between her ragged skirts. Appearing to be common-law husband and wife certainly did the trick, the woman certainly one of them as her outfit and general state of wear gave her complete credence, Bill able to pass through several other road blocks as they neared Trewint.

"What's your name," Bill thought to ask of his chaperone?

"Fay," the woman sighed, appearing fed up with traipsing half-way across the county.

"Where is everybody going do you suppose," he asked nonchalantly, as if he was as confused as her – which – when he thought about it wasn't far from the truth?

"Do not know," she sighed again with feeling. "May I sit," she asked of him – as if he was already her husband?

"Yes of course," Bill spluttered and happened to gaze around. Without realising it, he'd wandered clean into the pub's boundaries, passing through cordons of knights as if invisible, making their way to the garden areas where bench seating was commandeered for the knights only. Bill wandered through however, stopping at one table to ask if his partner could rest awhile, all six knights immediately jumping from their seats to lend a hand.

The heavily clad warriors were at their wits end to receive the woman, no thought to her station or bearing – just the fact that she might possibly be in distress or someone important by the fact that she was already within the inner boundaries. Looking around, as the knights fussed over Fay, he found he was actually at the back of the pub and would have to negotiate crowds of knights of all denominations to actually get into the place, the surrounding grounds of the pub resembling a jousting tournament.

"I've got to meet with someone, Fay," Bill mentioned as she received yet more adulation from the surrounding men of war, water and beer being procured – and some food.

Bill gathered up his bag, thanked the knights thoroughly, then went on a scout to test the lay of the land, see if he could actually push his luck any further. He left Fay and the knights and threaded his way through the throngs of armour and livery, finding his way to a side entrance, the steps heavily guarded.

Bill hesitated, wondering at two extra big knights lounging by the door, the heads of the two bigger men looking somewhat mythical and strangely preternatural – as if they'd been in make-up for hours having extra-big foreheads and shaggy hair added. He looked around considering the hordes of other knights, the welter of iron that was protecting the front of the pub and decided this side entrance – despite being guarded by two giants would be a slightly better bet – perhaps he could bamboozle them, blind them with science!

He formulated a quick plan, then gathering up momentum surged forward forgetting himself and glancing down at his wrist where his watch should have been –implying he was already late, covering his actions by swiping at an imaginary insect instead. At the doorway steps he tried barging straight through keeping his head down but a hand the size of a dinner plate stopped him dead, almost robbing the breath from his chest.

Bill looked to his left where one of the giants had held out an arm like a tree trunk, a quizzical look on a face that wouldn't look out of place in one of Grimm's fairy tales. Swallowing down his fright, the journalist found his words.

"Unhand me young sprout, I am the sage – er, um – Nightingale and am here especially on request of the commoners of this land to represent their say in this erm, takeover: Arthur is expecting me. I must meet with him, take a statement and report back within the hour for a TV broadcast. It cannot wait!"

Neither young – nor a sprout, the giant looked suspicious. He looked across to the knight holding the other side of the door, this one of near-giant proportions too. "What do you think," he growled?

The knight nodded sagely. "Merlin and his entourage will be arriving soon. We have been told to expect some re-porters from the other side – so I expect Merlin will need all the help he can get. Ok, sage, I'll take you to Arthur."

"It's the smell," Bill cogitated as he was led through the pub and up a small flight of stairs to a landing, having rubbed against Fay more than was necessary – not wanting to smell like a harlot but at least a little more unwashed, unkempt. Here on the narrow landing, knights of all rank and file lounged or held a post of some kind, many wandering about apparently awaiting for something. His accompanying warrior led him through the maze, finally halting at a door. The nameplate read *'Suite One,'* Bill wondering just how many luxury apartments this building had. The knight opened the door carefully after he'd looked the thing up and down and decided the handle was there to operate it. Inside another big knight barred his way – wanting to know who it was and what it was about?

Arthur Pendragon had slept peacefully for a couple of hours but was now awake again and showering in the adjoining bathroom, feeling the life surge back into him; knights constantly fussing over his bearing. He had no clean underclothes to change into but they'd been clean on that morning so he wasn't too concerned, dressing back in jeans and T-shirt, slipping his trainers back on.

In the bedroom he sat on the edge of the bed for a moment gathering his wits, unable to dispel any of the morning's events due to the welter of ironmongery surrounding him. His sword Excalibur lay where he left it, his spear and Shield of Light also, many instructing him his suit of armour and other implements of war were to be with him soon, everything hopefully ready for the push forward. But fizzing in the ether and rippling in the tides of time something stirred: He felt it; something powerful and all-knowing, the essence of the man pulsing amid the lattice, pulling things toward him as if a great planet moving through the cosmos was drawing all gases, moons and planets as it progressed. Dan's muscles were being galvanised amid this, his very soul energised, the very air around him filling him with power as if – having awoken, he'd drawn a little vigour from each of the knights as they too had roused, sapping a tiny bit of each of their strength. He couldn't recognise the signature, yet he knew it – knew it to be one of the supreme powers of his court – one of mystical threats only a wizard can muster – it was a cross between a powerful knight and a master sage:

Merlin had arrived.

Dan pushed himself to his feet, ably helped by those surrounding him, making him feel eminently regal and cared for.

"Arthur," a knight asked? "A sage is here representing the commoners around about – and would like a quick word – to allay any more hard feeling."

Dan nodded. "Show him in quickly."

"Enter," a knight told Bill Nightingale.

Bill, journalist's bag on shoulder – the thing never having been checked in all this time, entered the suite, finding a muscle-bound six foot Adonis facing him, the young man having all the bulk and steel a future kKing of England would need, the powerhouse looking as if he was ready for anything.

Bill Nightingale took a breath, stepping forward to hold out a hand.

Danny took it while knights hovered, many unsure of this interloper. Remembering to only pull out a notepad, Bill started the interview quickly – knowing he'd probably only have minutes to get to the bottom of it all.

"Your real name Danny is…?"

"Arthur Pendragon – apparently; it was Danny King, but somewhere along the line my parents changed my surname – thinking Pendragon would be too fanciful – and of course Arthur is my middle name."

Bill nodded assiduously, noting the subtle change: "You apparently pulled the sword from the stone this morning, I take it," the journalist a bit foggy on this point?

"I did indeed," Dan quipped, holding out the magnificent sword for his approval. Bill couldn't help himself. Without thinking, he reached in his shoulder bag for his camera – saying. *"Look, please don't chastise me*, BUT I NEED THIS, *so… can I?"*

Dan didn't see the harm, "Sure, fire away."

Relieved over his apparent subterfuge, Bill carried on, "Could you, er, pull the sword out a little?"

Dan obliged while knights were urging him downstairs – someone waiting to see him.

Bill snapped picture after picture hoping to god the satellite feed hadn't been screwed up by the Dome, sending the pictures to everyone he knew anyway – and at the same time marvelling at the supreme weapon, the blade looking like it could cut clean through boulders or granite, the hilt and shielding knife blades that appeared to be honed from some especial blue steel looking so ultimately deadly. Laying there in his hands the thing looked like a nuclear bomb – even worse.

It brought Bill swiftly to another burning question. "All these people," he enquired earnestly – *"where the hell are they all from?"*

***

Merlin had breezed in like a warm summer wind – and headed straight for the bar.

"Your best mead," he practically growled at the female head bar manager, a rather tall and rangy – and quite handsome PT instructor. Being extra tall and rangy himself he could look the lovely woman straight in the eye and wanted no brook from the Amazonian. She lent across the bar though, leaning in close to the wizard.

"You've forgotten the magical word, your highness. Perhaps you should try somewhere else until you've remembered your manners."

Merlin's eyes narrowed. A knight at the bar tried to intercede. "Er…Good lady – if you don't want to spend the rest of your life as a mouse, I suggest you fix Merlin with a drink now."

Lindsey Cartwright had spent the last hour trying to drive ten miles and would have cheerfully biked or run it if she'd been aware of the chaos out on the roads, but to find her favourite pub taken over by a load of louts dressed in suits of armour was one irritation too much on this hot sweltering day, now, to be confronted with a monk in a brown shabby habit – well, it was just one straw too many already. She backed off, bringing herself up to her full height, trying to outstare the stranger.

"Merlin, eh," she parodied, fixing the wizard with her best evil eye? "Mouse, eh," she drooled. She leant forward again. "I happen to like cheese."

"Magical word for today is…" she added, straightening again.

"I tire of this," Merlin sighed. "Seven –maybe eight furlongs on a bloody mule, my arse is sore, I get taken to the wrong damn inn, another journey – on foot this time – and I finally arrive to find I have a half-illiterate serving wench to serve me a drink to slate my thirst."

Lindsey arched her back, putting hands defiantly on hips. "Illiterate, eh," she chirruped.

She leant forward again, menacingly this time, enough to make the knight who was about to ask for a beer – having been indoctrinated (and liking it) in the hope of getting the fabled wizard a drink on the sly – and thus avoiding any unpleasantness, cringe. "Spell it," she growled.

"Spell *what,*" Merlin grumbled having not been paying attention, the banter and surroundings making him take stock. "I take it our King is here," he asked no one in particular?

Fearing the situation was getting somewhat out of hand, the knight sitting next to Merlin rose in his seat to go get Arthur.

"Be back …in a …erm, thing," he coughed, hastily vacating.

Reigning in her temper somewhat – and a little confused over the general state of the man before her, the tanned and deeply lined face that sported the best hooked nose she had seen, the sparkling eyes beneath the hooded brow; the atypical white curly beard just tinged with brown – a real selling point; the faded runes; mystical signs and sigils adorning his clothes – making it all appear very convincing. Perhaps she should show a little compassion, she had after all been advised to take the re-enactment societies completely at their word as the boss was already booking three weeks in the Seychelles for crying out loud, so the money had been pouring in.

"We don't have mead," she decided to tell the noble wizard. "How about a nice drop of lemonade?"

"Lemon – *what*," Merlin asked?

"It's nice," she commented, turning to select a small bottle from a cool fridge, "refreshing on a day like today," she popped the top off, selecting a small glass – then spied the Tabasco sauce and decided she'd get her own back, reaching for the bottle to tip half of it in, mixing it up liberally. The brown sauce dissolved rapidly in the sweet fizzy drink, turning the lemonade into something like a red brown concoction of food dyes.

Reverently, she placed it in front of the wizard, holding out a hand. "Four pounds please?" It sounded a lot in any money!

Merlin eyed her sceptically, ignoring her hand – and comment.

He reached for the glass and took a good slug – just as the knight reappeared with Arthur and his entourage.

"I'LL KILL HER," Merlin raged, gasping for air! "Bitch poisoned me," he croaked!

As knights tried to console him – many explaining the first taste of anything was very queer, Danny led the coughing and retching wizard around to the other bar where Lancelot and Galahad were keeping the war council, runners and knights of all colours popping in to place their name, many more yet to follow, one mentioned.

"Our strength has doubled," Lancelot told his king as he took his seat at the head of the table once more, ignoring Merlin's fuming outrages over the serving wench; Galahad moving around to the fabled wizard.

Still coughing and spitting, Merlin took his seat, calling in agitated words for a decent beaker of mead.

"What's afoot," he inquired finally?

***

Sir Reginald Smyth was not gallant. He was not brave – and he certainly wasn't fearless. He inherited his father's standard and had been fortunate enough to find a peaceful way of life helping out in the fields or milling corn when his – and many other's lives had been turned upside down. But even before this strange turn of events he was not a crusading soldier, not even a jousting type of warrior, the thought of riding his destriers into someone else, terrifying – the consideration of mortal combat even less appealing. Despite this he looked the part – had all the armour and killing tools and was tall and rather good looking to boot – just no courageous heart – quite a faint one actually – never mind – in this free for all who was to know, eh? Out there somewhere, along with his horse, was his squire and knave – and for the moment anyway – they could stay there for all he was concerned – the arrival of his entourage perhaps blowing his cover as he often spoke of peaceful pastimes rather than battles – and his squire had noted this over the years and was sometimes ad-lib to voice his concerns over his master's validity, calling into question his gallantry – so his squire and his knave could stay lost for all he cared, he was in a cosy establishment, being attended by a rather nice serving wench (or he was) to pass the time of day with, and real ale to sup – what better way to embrace a new strange land?

Down on the floor – behind the bar – a pretty little black and white mouse squeaked pitifully, the poor thing in utmost distress. After a moment's consideration, Sir Reginald pushed himself from his stool to grab a glass mug from the counter and, slipping behind the bar, scooped the little distraught mouse up into it, holding it up to his eye. He looked on in sorrow as the little creature slipped down into the beer suds. He'd have to look after her for a while, he mused thoughtfully, perhaps approach Merlin when he was in a slightly better mood and perchance ask him nicely for the lady's soul back!

Outside the pub, Bill Nightingale stepped as a man in a trance, trying to bring it all into focus.

The King had been gracious – seeing him out of the room and down the stairs himself as the journalist desperately fought to classify events; the King even brushing aside the fact that Bill had obviously pulled a fast one and slipped past his best knights – something Arthur noted – almost applauding him for his inventiveness, then spelling it out for him – that one single statement that had rooted the journalist to the spot – the fact that hundreds – if not thousands of men and woman (and some children and livestock as well) were somehow walking through some portal in time and turning up here in the twenty first century – *to do what,* – take England back – that's what?

Holy God, he thought. This can't be right?

Something bumping into him brought him back to his senses and Bill Nightingale, journalist for the best part of his life, dragged himself through the crowds of fifth or sixth century beings to find the table he'd left Fay at; unable to bring his eyes or his mind fully into focus.

He found Fay where he'd left her, rather glad to see she hadn't been whisked away by some dashing knight, walking over to collapse down beside her, knights of all denomination surrounding them; one even knocking the top off a bottle of beer to hand to him.

Dazed, Bill looked up into the grizzled face of a fifth century knight, complete with battle scars – and accepted the beer, thanking him profoundly. He took a sip whilst his mind tried to bring him up to speed, thinking this all might possibly be some lurid dream and he'd wake up soon. But as he looked through unseeing eyes he realised with some certainty that things – in *Merry Old England* anyway – might never be the same ever again.

A delicate hand on his shoulder brought him out of his spell, Bill finally acknowledging Fay who had sat patiently beside him. He turned to her, issuing a weak smile, the woman the very model of the conundrum he was trying to come to terms with, his mind still stuck on the quandary that was the hundreds of knights of yore surrounding him, having walked straight from the sands of time – *so,* he thought logically, history will re-write itself, somewhere in those lost centuries there will be a deficit of thousands of people; because two events cannot occupy the same timeline. But wait a minute – those events of the dark ages were never recorded too accurately – hence they were called the Dark Ages – nothing came out –

Bill's mind stopped dead.

The penny had finally dropped.

Suddenly, it was all coming into focus – well, at least some of it. Somewhere back in the realms of time some kind of power source connected a century of time to this one – and once this timeline had reached an apogee, then – *Bang* – two worlds collide.

And the catalyst – the sword – that bloody great raptor of a blade was something to do with it surely, imbued with every magical spell and curse men could utter – maybe even forged in the heavens or hell – but wherever it was, it was here now – and ready to do battle – along with a few thousand revenant knights – *Jeeze,* he thought – he had to get his thoughts down, make a full report.

Bill Nightingale snapped out of his daydream and took stock, glancing around. He had to get home, he realised, get all his thoughts down on the computer whilst it was still fresh in this mind. He'd have to walk back to his car, somehow navigate home and get to work.

He pushed himself to his feet, banged the bottle on the table so hard froth seeped from the top making Fay giggle, mentioning he had to go – *he had a rather unique article to write!*

Fay held out a hand. "I go too," she asked so innocently?

For a moment, Bill chewed his bottom lip. "I, er…well…" He had a girlfriend of some time – a somewhat sordid affair that he really should have ended years ago, but they only saw each other once or twice a week – so what would be the harm?

The harm; Are you serious, this woman has just wandered back from time, dust and dirt and all: You can't just invite her back for tea and bloody biscuits!

Why not!: This sort of thing doesn't happen every day – and anyway she's probably hungry and tired – *and lets face it, she's miles better than that harlot from Bude!*

Throwing caution to the wind, Bill made up his mind. "We'll have to walk back to the car," he explained, "I doubt I'll be able to bring it anywhere near here."

"Back," Fay asked, confused?

"Hm," Bill hummed, making sure he had everything.

"Ok," Fay sighed, getting to her feet, "rested now."

Chapter 4

"We move in the morning," Galahad intoned, loud enough for all to hear.

Runners and knights spread the word; many making sure their personal effects were in order. "Make sure we have enough horses," one senior knight called to his squires and knaves.

Around Danny the pub was in a fizz, the late afternoon drawing into evening; many looking to get their head down somewhere.

"Might be a good idea to visit your parents this evening," Lancelot spoke in hushed tones to his king. "May not get another chance until much later."

Dan nodded, having listened to plans that would be the first expansion out of Cornwall taking over Devon in the process. He had no idea of how this would take place but the entire war council seemed to think things would run smoothly – the welter of knights having passed through, strengthening their resolve – *and* the power shield!

"Your armour has arrived," Merlin spoke having felt its presence. Everyone glanced to everyone else.

"You'd better try it on," essayed the Green knight, now a little further down the ever-expanding table.

"Right," Danny called. "Let's do it."

"Ready the King's horses," Lancelot called.

"Camera," Danny asked with exasperation! *"Someone's got to have a camera?"*

Dan stood in his impressive suit of armour, bedecked head to foot in shimmering steel and bronze, silver and gold, the plates imbuing him with yet more vigour and power, his muscles appearing to swell to pad out the brassards and palettes, breastplate and cuissards, his gauntlets and gorget. The crowning glory – the helmet was something to behold, a heavily fortified casque that held a glistening crown of gold padded out with a sort of hemp fibre. It sat beautifully on his head, Dan feeling impregnable and invincible.

"Where's that reporter," Dan continued, but no one around him knew quite what he was complaining about?

"We can see you," Lancelot addressed him, "why do you want a picture done?"

"For posterity," Dan argued, flexing his limbs within the suit. It had taken him more than an hour to climb into it, and now he was adorned with shield, spear and Excalibur, he hoped to god someone could photograph the event.

"We'll let the reporters film you as you parade down the streets to your parent's house, a local businessman instructed him. "You'll look even more resplendent on horseback."

Dan conceded the point, preparing to go out and meet the crowds of supporters and knights outside.

***

Bill Nightingale parked up in his driveway and blew out a sigh of relief. Beside him, Fay – marvelling at the car and its smooth perambulatory ride – couldn't take her eyes off the car's interior, continually stroking the satin-black contours of the facia and door fittings. Bill hurried out of the vehicle and around to her side to let her out, the poor woman now totally bamboozled by a modern bungalow. Having made sure he had everything, he led her to the front door to let her in, Fay following in something of a daze, the revelation of the homes' interior completely fazing her. "What's this place," she breathed in awe?

"This is my home," he told her, rushing through to his small office to switch on his computers and consoles to write what was probably the most important essay of his entire life. He ditched his bag in his seat, then, hovering for a moment just to verify he had all the known facts at his disposal, he rushed back to show Fay how to use the shower, dashing about to locate her a tracksuit or something similar.

"Bathroom's this way," he coaxed her, taking her arm.

"Bath – room," she queried, frowning? She allowed herself to be led through anyway, pulled up sharp by the tiled cubicle and bath, shining sink and toilet.

"What's that," she asked expressively, stepping over to inspect the loo?

"Er, toilet," Bill remarked, stepping in to turn on the shower. He spun Fay round and held her by the shoulders, implying she listen to him.

"Look Babe, I've got to work – I've got to get things down as soon as – before I forget anything. Have a shower and I'll get some clean clothes and then chill out, watch a movie or something – just be quiet if you can for an hour or two as I write down something, ok?" Bill heaved in a breath, hoping she'd get the picture. Hot water began to stream from the shower faucet, startling his consort. Bill turned to consider the running water. He moved away to turn the temperature down a little. He put a hand in then to test it, nodding appreciatively. "Just nice," he instructed her.

He went to leave, realising then Fay had not a clue where to start. "Take your clothes off darling and I'll throw – um, I mean, wash them later." He pointed empathically to the shower, nodding furiously.

Towels, he thought, rushing to the airing cupboard to find – to his relief – he had some clean ones. He brought out a big bath-sheet, his towelling dressing gown, and a smaller hand towel, explaining they were for drying herself off.

"It's nice and warm," he explained further, trying to convince her it was alright "– you can get all nice and clean." He wondered about modern soap and if it would temporarily blind her?

"Alright hun," he had to ask, burning to get down to work?

Fay nodded unsurely, beginning to loosen her top. Bill inched back towards the door, hoping to give her some privacy but Fay stripped off nonetheless, slipping out of her top and shabby skirt, slightly soiled bloomers. Trying not to ogle her shapely legs and buttocks, Bill swept up the rags to toss them in the bin, wondering briefly if she valued them.

"Shower," Bill prompted, leading the naked woman into the cubicle. Fay's hands clasped over her breasts as she allowed herself to be shown in, stepping up cautiously into the glass enclosure, marvelling at the construction; the continual stream of warm soft water spilling from the chrome faucet, lifting a hand to wriggle her fingers about in it. In close contact, Bill caught a whiff of her aroma, wood smoke evident in her hair, a slight sweet nuance of rosewater mixed up in it – and something else, a rich intoxicating whiff of the warm sweat of her skin, the smell so soft yet so feral, eldritch yet so recognisable; the very essence of woman.

"Oh, my," she gushed, thrilled at the circumstance!

Bill pulled back almost drunk on her bodily scents.

"Shower gel," he told her, pointing to the black bottle on the interior shelf.

"Shower gel," Fay questioned, getting used to the spray – and enjoying it?

"Soap," Bill prompted, "gets you nice and clean – and smelling nice."

Fay nodded, stepping a little closer to allow the water to cascade over her. Bill stepped further back, not wanting to get wet just at this moment in time, unable however to take his eyes from the ample but totally firm body, the backside, the thighs and slim calves leading down to a very delicate ankle. He noted the curve of her firm round breasts, then the dirt rinsing from her hide and, leaving the door ajar, left her to it, saying; "I'm just in the back room if you need me, ok?"

Fay, consumed with glee at the warm water, nodded – in complete rapture as the droplets rinsed off eons of dust and dirt.

"Don't forget the shower gel," he called out, leaving to get down to work.

***

The evening was warm and inviting – just the time of day, Danny mused, for a horseback ride, despite the fact that he had never been near one in his life. His destrier however when it turned up was just as spectacular as he, he judged noting the high-pointed gilt saddle and chanfron that shielded the magnificent grey shire horse's head and neck; emblazoned with polished steel and bronze. Adding to the horse's splendour was a dazzling poitrel and quarter piece covering its chest and rump, the brocade depicting the Pendragon coat of arms in metallic threads of azure; crimson, silver and gold; the satin-white flancard and underlying protection serving to compliment the steed's natural colour. Even the animal's hooves had been blackened and waxed to shine out regally.

There was only one thing bugging Dan as he greeted the cheering and jubilant crowds – how in god's name was he supposed to climb aboard?

A rickety stool was brought forward, the wood so ancient and blackened he fancied it would collapse under him as soon as he stood on it, Dan thinking a trip to B&Q would do the trick, pick up an aluminium hop-up – a sturdy collapsible stand that would take some serious weight. He had one or two kicking about the changing rooms of the sports centre so cleaners could reach the top of the changing lockers. "It's not going to take my weight," he spoke aside to Lancelot.

"There's a heavy old chest in the pub – that'll do," someone mentioned.

"Commandeer it;" Galahad uttered!

Within minutes a sturdy-looking modern chest that had previously held big tureens for any function in the pub, had indeed been requisitioned; the chinaware placed aside. It was a bit tall but someone had the bright idea of utilising a breeze block as a secondary step – and Danny was able to easily step from one to another, easing himself onto his steed, the big shire not batting an eyelid as Danny – complete with Excalibur and other weaponry including the enigmatic Shield of Light – wriggled into the saddle, a saddle that was more like a supporting armchair.

Galahad and Lancelot each made sure his feet were securely in the leather-bound stirrups.

A cart of sorts – pulled by two big powerful horses – was used to transport Danny's steps and a few archers; the shabby construction having seen much better days; still it did the job for now as his closest knights also mounted, the whole rigmarole making Dan think they'd all better get used to using a coach.

Finally they were ready and Danny, comfortable now on his massive steed, led the way –

since no one knew where they were going, apart from some enthusiastic locals who were tagging along on bicycles.

Atop the huge horse, Dan urged the animal forward, pressing his heels together as he'd seen others doing, the horse below him pricking up his ears as the command to move registered. It surged forward – to a tumultuous roaring from the assembled crowds – as if they were already off to war.

I'm only going to visit Mum, he laughed to himself, guiding the horse down a country lane from the back of the pub that could only take two fully-laden knights at a time, the whole ensemble rattling and clonking as the cart followed on.

A short way into the trip – and Dan was warming to the spectacle; the ride incredibly comfortable despite being encased fully in a suit of armour. At this height he was able to gaze out over the surrounding fields and meadows, every inch playing host to hundreds of troops that had managed to rig up some form of shelter for the evening; so many, Dan worried, sleeping rough. He straightened in his saddle to gaze over the nearby copses and woodlands that lined the route, trying to calculate the weight of numbers that had marched from the sands of time, the mishmash of men, women and children – and livestock that had been encouraged through the portal to live another day – fight for something that – in all likelihood they'd never be able to fully appreciate – or perhaps understand.

It was an incredible sacrifice – assuming one had a choice in the matter – the servitude and respect already shown to him – and other local people making him think some higher power was at work here. But why England – why now – *and what about the rest of the world – would he be able to save the entire planet?*

One step at a time, he told himself, glancing across to Lancelot who was also enjoying the trip – breathing deep of the rarefied air. With his war helmet and other trappings he looked magnificent, the blue, red and gold standards of Pendragon fluttering in the breeze: if ever a warrior had a second, he was it, dashing, thoughtful, resolute. A man who – despite bound by some supernatural force, was now living again to bring law and order to his besieged land.

They skirted Bodmin Moor, following a ring road around to the housing estates on the other side – the roads unusually quiet, just managing to squeeze through the bollards at the end of his road. The cart had to stay there, unable to pass through, four knights staying with it – keeping a rear guard. With eight more of his best knights King Arthur rode into town, the noise alerting just about everyone in the neighbourhood. Eyes peeped from net curtaining while most opened their front doors to view the spectacle, the eight knights nodding to all and sundry.

At number fourteen, Danny held up a hand – the mounted warriors halting almost simultaneously, his mother – with her friend Mabel – who was practically swooning already at the front gate, many other neighbours daring to inch down the road, over-awed by the incredible scene.

Squires raced to carry the two steps to the king's side, the riders moving round to allow them access. Beneath him, his steed stood perfectly still having understood they were pausing in their journey.

Dan dismounted, making sure he didn't impale anything with his weapons, stepping down carefully backwards from the steps. As soon as he was free, the squires moved his horse out of the way to allow Lancelot to dismount, the two then able to approach his mother.

Dan clanked forward, remembering then to divest himself of his wonderful helmet, the golden crown shining and glinting in the evening light.

"Hey, Mum."

Dan bent to peck her on the cheek, freeing up a hand to rest it gently on her shoulder. "Been alright," he asked?

His mother nodded, trying to come to terms with his attire and crowned war bonnet; everything about the boy now screaming *'King'*. "You've really done it," she breathed – as if it had all been a bit of a lark; the sword – Lancelot being nothing more than a stand-in? But now it was obvious he'd taken on the mantle of a monarch – a true king, his armour alone crying out for attention.

"It's some suit," Mabel gasped, completely bowled over.

"It took some getting into – I can tell you," Dan guffawed.

"Where's the middle to your shield," Mum asked, having noticed the empty rim strapped to his horse. Lancelot, standing patiently behind Arthur turned with him to look back at the strange aegis; both considering the thing for a moment.

"It's, er, it's a special shield, Mum...has special powers."

"You're not getting into any black magic are you, son," mother worried?

Towering above her, inches taller now than when he last saw her, Dan squeezed her shoulder comfortingly, unable however to answer the question truthfully, suspecting all manner of good and bad karma were circulating at the moment, never mind Merlin turning up.

"He'll be a good king," Lancelot decided to tell the two women. Around them quite a crowd had gathered, one or two local reporters also snapping away.

"I'll just pop in and see Dad, if you don't mind," Danny asked of his second in command?

"I'll wait here, my liege," Lancelot assured him, arching his back.

Dan walked with his mother back into the house, having to duck to avoid hitting his head on the lintel. He had to duck again to miss the lampshade in the hall, and also in the entrance to the lounge, his father almost choking on his cup of tea as his son moved into the room, unable to sit down for fear of not being able to get up again.

"Hi, Dad," Danny intoned, moving to shake his hand.

Stunned, his father didn't know who he was anymore, completely taken aback by the armour and splendid helmet, the polished steel plates glinting and throwing out rays of coloured light as he moved; the faintest of blue haze appeared to encapsulate his entire body and weaponry. "What are you," his father breathed, still hypnotised by the being in his lounge?

"It's me, Dad: I've – er – just taken on the persona of something else, a really mystical rendition of King Arthur. I know it sounds crazy – the whole county is going crazy – but its happening all the same – I'm going all the way, all the way to the top – unseat this ridiculous money-grabbing family and all their entourage and install myself as the true King of England – bring in a new order that will serve the people – *all the people, instead of just a few."*

"Very commendable," reported his now recovering father, having gulped on a respirator. He reached for a small whiskey he'd been nursing all evening, throwing it down in one belt, holding himself as if it was going to thrust him into spasms; Dan watching on with a worried countenance.

Fed up with watching his father die a little every day, Dan moved forward, making father jump with a start, stepping over to kneel in front of him, placing his helmet on the floor to then put a hand on his knee. Without knowing what he was doing, he looked into his mind and asked the question – *can you at least ease my old man's suffering?*

For a moment nothing appeared to happen, a blue haze then leaving Dan's gauntleted hand to creep very cautiously into his father's being; the ectoplasm seeming to consider the damage to the person's body before committing itself to investigate; then it swept up and around his father as if wanting to enshroud him, willing him to accept the ghostly embrace. Paralysed with fear, his father could do nothing but tense as if being slowly infiltrated.

Dan breathed deep, feeling some kind of power seep through his fingers to then infect his Dad, still totally unsure of the haze and its properties – but what harm could it do; if it could protect an entire county and resurrect thousands of lives, including all the extras, then this eminence – this energy – this god, could fix his father.

He strived to think about drawing out the ruined parts of his father's lungs, falling into a short meditative state, allowing the lining of his father's lungs to repair themselves, the alveoli spitting out the crystals that had grown there, stifling the workings of the bronchiole, oxygen rushing in to wash away the granules with the expiration of carbon dioxide. As his mother gasped, the blue haze glistening and sparkling as it embraced his father, a subtle change of colour graced his face; going from a bright red to a fleshy tan, then, after what seemed like an eternity, the mist weakened, slipped from his father's shoulders like smoke to almost disperse, tiny shrouds of it making their way back to Danny.

He breathed deep, having almost fallen into some kind of trance, then – with something of an effort, pushed himself to his feet, the armour clinking and grinding as he fought to regain his balance. Instinctively his mother had rushed to lend a hand, a delicate flower moving to support an iron war horse, but Dan was soon standing straight, the loss of energy noticeable, although once upright he seemed to be able to draw power once more from the ether.

His father coughed lightly, putting a hand immediately to his mouth, his palm when he looked down at his open hand filled with grainy speckles, inspecting them at length with the fingertips of his other hand. He found a tissue by his side to wipe away the dirt, taking another deep breath, enjoying what could be a brief moment of clarity, his lungs seeming to convert the oxygen for once. Again father coughed – not a deep chugging splatter but just a light expel of air that again brought up grains of stone and crystal, his father glancing down at them in sheer amazement. He looked up at Dan as if suspecting him of some trickery but after taking another series of experimental breaths; realised with sudden revelation that he could breathe without any discomfort, his chest having apparently cleared.

Mother and son watched him closely as he pushed himself upright from the slouched position he'd taken of late, looking almost collapsed in the chair, squaring his shoulders as he put a hand to his chest, finding the air was being inhaled and expelled at regular intervals, no serious pain anymore, no bronchial congestion, all appearing much better all of a sudden. He pushed himself to the edge of his seat, sitting up even straighter, unsure of the miraculous turnaround; appearing to wait a little while longer as Dan told mother of his last few hours at the pub, the welter of men, women and children that had been brought back from the dark ages, some fantastical portal opening up so he, *'King Arthur'* would have some kind of army.

"But son," his mother worried; having seen enough action thrillers to gain some idea of weaponry; "all the armour in the world won't stop a bullet."

"I know, Mum; but we have something else, some other preternatural force that can outwit conventional military, this –" and here Danny pointedly brought his gauntleted hand to bear, highlighting the sparkling mist enshrouding him, "is the one true power – it seems to be able to do almost anything."

Mother glanced back at father as Dan continued to consider the all-encompassing ectoplasm, the haze seeming to be a living thing as if it had been on earth all this time but been pushed into the shadows by modern living.

With a jolt, Dan found his father by his side, the tan in his face the first thing to startle him as it looked almost normal, the colour having returned to a face continually fighting with a searing chest and painful breathing. He looked down at him with nothing but love and admiration in his eyes.

His father stared back at his son, almost saddened by how much he'd grown and not taken a blind bit of notice. At his height and bulk now – with his suit of gold and silver he looked every inch a future king. "I – I don't know what to say son – only that I've been misjudging you these last few years – only because I couldn't see through my own distress – a cowardly way to look at life, I'll grant you, but it all seemed so hopeless; the pain and shortness of breath so debilitating."

Dan raised a metal hand to place on his father's shoulder, resting it comfortingly, shaking his head, waiving the last few agonising years away with a wave of the other hand, the armoured suit creaking and clinking as he moved. "I love you both, so much," he croaked, wishing he could have done more just as a mortal man, maybe a better job, more money, private health care, but when he'd put it to a health official at the fitness centre one day the consultant shook his head – all the money and care in the world would not save his Dad – his condition having reached a level of no return. Like asbestosis and certain types of pulmonary diseases – once diagnosed they were practically impossible to readdress, the complications just too immeasurable. A full lung and trachea transplant would still have left the other organs at risk the consultant stressed, knowing full well Danny was a devoted son.

"I won't let this happen to other families," he muttered in sorrow.

"We're alright, son," his mother rejoined brightly. "We've got each other, that's what matters. I couldn't live on my own like Mabel."

He drew both of them in, into the metalled arms of not a future king, but their one and only son, a son that loved them both dearly. "If for one moment I thought I was doing the wrong thing, guys, I would have thrown in the towel, but with every passing hour – and every passing action, I seem to be more and more sure of myself, more confident with each passing minute, ready to take on anything the old establishment can throw at me."

His father pulled away and looked him up and down again, marvelling at the costume. "You are a king, my boy – even if you don't make it, even if this all fizzles into dust – you are still a king in my eyes!"

"Mine too," Mum bleated, fighting back tears.

"When will we see you next, son," Dad asked earnestly?

Danny shook his head, not knowing; the next few days fraught with danger and god knows what else. "We move to take Devon tomorrow – then in sequence the rest of the southern counties – once I am sure of my strength and numbers we'll move on the capital. I just hope I can minimise the bloodshed."

"You'll do it," his mother assured him. "Everyone will kneel down by you."

Dan hugged his parents again.

"I'd better go," and Dan let go, bending to kiss his mum one more time. "Look after her, Dad."

Father raised a steady hand, putting up his thumb. Dan stepped to retrieve his helmet, striding then for the door, turning for one last look.

"Got to go – got a country to save," and with that he was clanking off down the hall, catching his head on the lampshade!

***

"'Tell me I'm dreaming – suffering from some kind of exotic fugue,'" Bill Nightingale wrote feverishly, *"'then try and tell the rest of the county – the police; civic assemblies – the army for crying out loud, who have already tried (in vain) to breach the fantastical dome that has settled over Cornwall – that I'm wrong! 'Sceptical' doesn't even begin to describe how I felt myself yesterday morning, reporting the Dome must be some kind of atmospheric anomaly, but*

after employing subterfuge and gaining access to (Danny King) – now King Arthur – I can now make some fairly reliable assumptions.(1) Danny King did indeed draw the fabled sword from the stone this morning – I know, because I've seen it – and a more magical weapon you've never seen – this is the true Excalibur – it has to be – nothing could radiate like that with such unbridled power, the steel pulsing with energy – I only hope my photos have captured the essence of the mighty blade. (2) All the combatants, cavalry, caravans of cooks and drummer boys; serving wenches and livestock; didn't make landfall this morning from the continent – or last night – off some damn ferry – they actually walked – have been propelled – or have been sucked up by some kind of portal or cataclysm of time, because they are here now in flesh and blood in the twenty first century. (3) – and this is the real kicker, like me your immediate question to all of this, is 'if several thousand warriors and all the supporting rigmarole has been transported through from another century – then where were those people in real life – because we all now know of cause and causality, no two living things can appropriate the same time line – ok, but what if they didn't, what if they were supposed to be here all along. Think about it – why are the Dark Ages so full of mystery – why is there so very little information about the way of life of the people of the fifth and sixth centuries – we know more about the Romans than we do about the legendary King Arthur and his knights. So is this all preordained; set in stone from the very beginning?'"

"'If nothing else – it'll be a massive talking point, finding out what life was really like in the fifth and sixth centuries – fill in all those blank spaces!'"

"'This is Bill Nightingale, reporting for the Southern Chronicle.'"

Bill Nightingale sat back, finally blowing out a contented sigh, his opening piece on King Arthur and the fabled sword Excalibur well and truly set in print now.

He ran through it a couple of times editing it and changing one or two details, then flashed it through, along with all the photographs; happy to see at least the internet was still working. He sipped at a glass of the ole' thought processing stimulant – whiskey and soda, then wondered just how many staff were actually working at the office. Worried the script might lay there all night and not hit the front page tomorrow, he reached for the phone to get straight through to the head editor.

"Thanks Bill," an enthusiastic voice blurted back at him minutes later, Bill not even recognising it. "This is brilliant, just what we need – and what fantastic photos – *Jeeze! Where did you get them* – Oh, I see, (I'm scanning the essay now – *Jeeze* – Arthur and his knights actually fell for it – the ol'e cloak and dagger bit – hah! Very good, this is great stuff Bill, thanks!"

"Erm," Bill stammered, for one insane moment thinking he might have emailed the wrong office," who is this?"

"Oh, I'm sorry Bill, Gerard is out and about gathering data – trying to do exactly what you have done, quite a few of the roads as you probably know totally blocked. I'm his wife Georgina. I'm holding the fort until he can get back in."

"Ah, ok, well tell him to get back as soon as and get the print schedule running otherwise we'll miss the deadline."

"Sure thing – he's not far away – has managed to interview one or two of the strange people. Anyway Bill thanks again. Have a great evening, and if of course you have any more information, please let us know. This sort of first hand Intel will push sales through the roof. Bye for now!"

Bill replaced the handset and meditated for a while imagining the set piece winning the southern journalistic award – recognition at last!

With another big sigh – one of contentment and of a job well done, he was about to fix himself another well-earned drink, when he realised he had a very special guest.

"Jesus Christ," he blurted out, how could he have forgotten about her – because if that last piece of writing didn't rock the shire counties, then having seconded a real live serving wench from the ranks of the revenant dead, he was going to have something of a book in the making if she hadn't drowned herself in the shower!

Bill dropped his glass and hurried through to the bathroom where the shower was still on, happily filling the bathroom with steam, his paramour nowhere to be seen.

Stupidly he glanced into the shower cubicle, once he'd turned the water off, waving away the steam, finding traces of the shower gel on the floor, the woman obviously managing to open the bottle and squeeze a little out. Wondering where she was, realising then he'd probably been longer than he intended, he shot through to the bedroom, finding it empty, then the kitchen thinking she might be hungry – not finding her till he marched through to the lounge to find her sprawled out on the sofa fast asleep, her dark auburn hair tussled and half-covering her handsome face. She'd discovered his dressing gown, the towelling material drying her off, her silky tanned skin glistening in the early evening light as the gown had fallen open revealing her taught stomach and full round breasts; the tantalising nipple and aurora beautifully formed. Panic over, Bill left her to wander through to the bedroom to locate a spare duvet, pulling one out of a cupboard to lay over her, the summer evening not especially cold but still the temperature could drop in the depths of the night – and he wouldn't want her catching cold having just stepped from a hot shower.

Bill laid the light duvet over her gently, tucking it in a little, wondering over the mind boggling circumstances, the inexplicable abnormality of time that had brought her here. Bending over her, her sleeping form seemed to exude enticement, the face so wonderfully formed, the eyelashes long and delicate; the skin so clear now it had been scrubbed, one or two pockmarks and tiny scars indicating she'd already led a full life. The lips were plump and so captivating they complimented her beautifully rugged face.

Bill lingered, mesmerised for a moment by her loveliness, totally taken by her symmetry, her sleeping form appearing so serene and at peace.

She was certainly some woman, he ruminated, finally leaving her to go fix that drink.

***

Once back at The Bell public house, Dan decided to go over the plans for the morning, knowing the whole army around him was preparing for a push forward. He had so many questions he hardly knew where to start. Having made sure the squires had some kind of supper – and that the horses were well cared for, he rallied his knights to gather around Merlin and discover what the sage had in store for everyone.

"The power is incredibly strong," Merlin answered when the enquiry was put to him. "So many have passed through now, we have the makings of a real army – complete with supply lines and intelligence gathering. I am sure the power curtain will exceed our expectations."

"We have information that the sages of the other side may well be able to burn a hole in our canopy," Gawain reported having returned from his civic duties with Bedivere and the heavily-built knight Sir Kay, Arthur's original foster brother.

"They used some light beam to damage it too," he added, accepting a bowl of stew!

Merlin was shaking his head. "The power curtain will know when to react to such a threat," he intoned cryptically. "It is the supreme power on earth right now, surpassing any atomic weaponry that might be brought to bear."

"You mean we could survive an atomic blast under the shield," Dan asked incredulous?

Merlin nodded. "I have been enlightened into the modern arts of warfare and realise the marvels of modern machinery – but they forget the power of the old ways, the power of the earth and all its allies."

"I'm assuming the power curtain will kind of march with us," Dan asked of Merlin directly?

Merlin nodded, experimenting with some cheese. He swallowed it down with a grimace and elucidated. "Throughout the southern sectors we should be able to secure the entire region without conflict, simply marching from one area to another, releasing all manner of war dogs as we go. If battle lines are drawn – it will most likely be at London where the seat of power lies. Here the curtain may well weaken but by then we will have such an army – of all denominations – we will destroy anything in our path."

Danny shifted nervously in his seat, accepting a flagon of ale. He sipped it thoughtfully as other knights around him joined him in his drink.

"THE KING," many quipped, raising their glasses!

"To our liege, Merlin – *and success,*" a jubilant Green knight called out, standing for an ovation! Many rose, including Danny.

"Well," he called over the clamour to Merlin, finally seating himself once more, "let's hope tomorrow brings success."

"Have faith," the old wizard chuckled: "The battle when it comes will be decisive and swift, the legions of death knowing no quarter once they've awakened."

"We're fighting alongside other combatants – from different time lines;" Dan asked?

Merlin shook his head, munching on more cheese. He wiped his whiskers: "No, there are many dark powers lurking below, young Arthur; many never to see the light of day – unless especially called for: Once summoned they will do my bidding and crush any subversive enemy; the Hounds of Hell and the archangels are just some of the retinue that's waiting to exact revenge."

"Revenge for what," asked Galahad nearby?

"Being sent there in the first place," Merlin uttered, appearing astonished no one realised this!

In one corner of the pub, crowded in by dozens of other knights ready to grab some shuteye before the big day, Sir Reginald Smyth – replete with around ten pints of strong ale, sat dozing, head supported by a corner, backpack containing clean silk undergarments and a few accessories and helmet on his outstretched legs, sword, big shield and jousting lance propped up over him, his pint glass containing Lindsey Cartwright tipped over in his lap, the few suds of beer having dried up now, the dear little mouse a little worse for wear herself as she tried desperately to lick the beer from her sodden fur. Gazing up at the sleeping giant, the little mouse wondered if it wouldn't be a good idea to climb up the knight's breastplate and gnaw into his neck letting him bleed to death – then she could scamper about the floor until she reached the sleeping Merlin and chew her way through his neck too; although – in tearful hindsight, that might undoubtedly consign her to her miserable existence as a small bloody rodent! *Goddamn men,* she cursed with rancour; *what bloody right did that bastard have to do such a thing to her* – and then her tiny mind somersaulted, rolling to a grinding stop somewhere at the beginning of her day; the full panoply of the terrible events unfolding before her – the scorching morning she emerged into due to an unnatural atmospheric anomaly covering Cornwall, the blue haze seeming to soak into everything – the hundreds (if not thousands) of re-enactment societies that had descended on her lovely town, the roads chock a block with them – having to cycle to work with a practically flat tyre – only to find the pub filled with these crazy types – *all possibly true somehow though,* she realised, scratching herself. *She'd missed something along the way, this morning,* she mused; sitting upright on the knight's lap, chin in paws. *Somewhere along the way something weird happened and reality took a nose dive whilst stupidity ruled the hour – and continued to, it seemed.*

She could not deny the awful truth however, the mind boggling certainty that some kind of dimensional time disruption had engulfed Bodmin for some reason – *but why?*

Then something else struck her; the references to King Arthur being bandied about – as if a real king had entered the pub; Lindsey remembering walking through to see what all the fuss was about and seeing an Adonis of a powerful young man wielding an incredible sword, placing it reverently into a scabbard.

Excalibur!

Jesus, Mary and Joseph what in god's name had he done – pulled the bloody sword from the stone – impossible – *No – what's impossible is you are now a tiny mouse, squeaking your stupid heart out because you couldn't rein in your temper – and now look at you – what will Mum think?*

Movement in the leather breeches beneath her made the soft material feel like an earthquake was taking shape, the mouse scampering around in a tight circle as Sir Reginald Smyth dreamt of her former shapely form, the dream getting quite steamy at times. Suddenly, Lindsey Cartwright realised what was happening and cried out in anguish. *"Nooo,"* she squealed in despair.

I'll gnaw into it, she raged madly, trying to find a level spot whilst the knight's leggings tented, then the little mouse vaulted up the revenant's breastplate and found a cosy niche between his suede jerkin and the metal.

Resisting the impulse to chew into his skin, Lindsey Cartwright nuzzled into the warm material, wriggled into a pocket of sorts – and settled down to sob.

Chapter 5

The day started early for many of the people that had crossed over; the fully armoured knights and their war horses; the lighter cavalry and infantrymen; archers and slingers; pike-men; caravans of cooks; jesters; serving wenches and young boys ready to become squires or knaves – many used to a dawn chorus. Along with the consolidated and initiated, hundreds more had passed through during the night, filling Cornwall almost to the brim, groggy and dazed knights of all rank and file; leather-clad warriors; bowmen and sages; caravans of supply wagons – the whole panoply of an army on the move.

Danny King woke early himself, stretching languidly under the sheets. He'd slept remarkably well, he realised, despite a barrage of ale beforehand, waking refreshed and ready to go. It had certainly been a time to remember though, he had to concede as the warm blue haze of the morning roused him; the sixteen or so hours that had made up the previous day; the incredible spectacle of stumbling upon the sword in the stone; the wonderful experience of actually releasing the invincible weapon – the energy surging through him, the inexplicable appearance of Lancelot and Galahad stepping from the mists of time to grace his favour once more; the complete vistas of another world opening up to reveal the shifting epochs of time as mounted knights began to emerge;

phalanxes of lighter cavalry; marching pike-men and archers – the whole assembly of an invading army.

He'd lived that day as if in a dream, the cold light of it breaking through only occasionally as he visited his parents.

And as the day had progressed, so things had steadily got worse – or more exciting, depending on whose side you were viewing the events. It hadn't been all bad however Dan ruminated, as he lay there listening to the waking hum of hundreds – if not thousands of invading fifth and sixth century men, women and children; the distant clatter of steel armour plate; the rattling of pots and pans – the strident call of esquires and battalion leaders as they tried valiantly to bring their legions together. All for today, Danny mused – all for a day that would probably be the make or break of this weird adventure – for if Merlin had it wrong, or had been given false information then the engaging force field would not extend – or if it did, may become so weakened it could not stretch the distance, leaving Cornwall undefended as they tried to march on Devon. Without the supporting shield – and despite the unbridled power of Excalibur he doubted nothing could withstand a hail of machine-gun fire; rocket launchers and tank rounds; many a war film (which his father never tired of watching) all too succinctly depicting the devastation that could leave. Yet Merlin seemed so sure of his information, so versed in future events it was as if he'd been privy to some special audition. Aside from all this the county itself had very quickly come to the resolution that what was going on was fundamentally right – and the only recourse was to back it – back it to the hilt in some cases as men, women and children threw in the towel with their former lives and swiftly signed up to join the escapade, Danny welcoming many as he'd travelled the streets the previous evening; hundreds lining the fields and lanes, many championing his return – and cause.

Civic authorities and council bodies tried their best to keep the county running as it was encapsulated by something they had no hope of understanding, finding they were cut off from the rest of England; strange men in suits of armour riding up on war horses to essentially take charge – although many found the invading knights to be above all else courteous and polite, advising rather than demanding, finding amazement in their surroundings – making many a councillor or school governess consider the state of play – and of course there had been plenty of capitulations and walkouts by many a worker or office temp, those who'd taken the strange invader's words as verbatim and many school, office and municipal buildings tried to find temporary staff.

Danny couldn't worry about any of that however as the main thrust of the army got underway; placing himself at the very head of the offence. He wished he had Merlin's presence of mind – or blind optimism but he had neither; simply going along with the flow until the shit hit the fan.

A little while later he was greeted with breakfast in bed, several rashers of bacon, three or four lightly fried eggs; locally sourced sausages;

tomatoes; hash browns – even some black pudding; brown wholemeal bread complete with real butter – complemented with mug of tea and glass of fresh orange juice, the future King of England wondering where the food had come from since just about every superstore, every shop and village store had been depleted in the first few hours of the hordes arriving. He was ravenous, he quickly found however, ignoring his entourage of knights that had slept around him all night, stomachs rumbling as many had eaten sparingly since arriving.

Lancelot made an appearance with Merlin just as he was finishing up; advising him he'd better think about getting ready; the time for the deployment rapidly approaching. Dan nodded, wiping his plate clean with the last of the bread, instructing many of his supporters to go find some food before the engagement. Two squires and three knaves arrived to kit him out, Dan slipping out of bed whilst Lancelot moved to clear his tray aside, handing it all to a serving wench who arrived – complete with white shawl and tresses – looking a bit like a latter-day nurse. He padded through to the adjoining washroom, those who were still mesmerised by running water and the toilet leaving to allow him some privacy.

Alone in the bathroom, Dan, performing his ablutions, reflected on the coming day – and all that would contain, the assimilation of Devon under his auspices; the upheaval of all those people, all the school kids and teenagers at college, the police and civic assembles – all having to make a choice quite quickly – join him or suffer the consequences as the whole country turned around. Under the present government the austerity cuts had rendered the council insolvent and tried to infer mismanagement was the main cause, despite the local audit office finding no such claims, but the pleas for more money to sustain health care right across the board was ignored and Somerset – along with Devon and Dorset – and to a point Wiltshire had to try and rally round to support their ailing partner. The whole southern counties – once proud and lucrative due to tourism and the patronage of wealthy Hampshire and Sussex had been brought to its knees; rebellion so ardent in the very air; many calling for independence. Well, if things went well they could forget the ridiculous burden of tax and revenue payments and just concentrate on looking after each other as the takeover took shape. But how would it transpire Dan worried, would there be conflict straight away or would the takeover of the complete southwest presage the march on London?

As Dan showered and lingered, despite calls from his knaves to hurry, he offered up a prayer of hope for all those frightened school kids and young people who would find their way of life suspended for a moment, whilst an invading army of irredentists marched through their streets and towns.

Back in his room, he climbed slowly into his shining suit of armour, feeling each piece of steel or inlaid silver and gold imbue him with a sense of vigour and energy – as if the suit once complete would galvanise in him a superhero cloak of ultimate power. As if the suit was not enough – Excalibur –

when he picked it up to un-sheath it for a moment, thrilled him yet again with another lifting bolt of pure energy, as if the sword was annealing itself with him; gelling with his soul, filling him with resolve and determination – the valour of a King. Those watching felt it too. With a grim smile, Danny buckled it to him, the sword no longer an unwieldy hunk of ethereal metal but a real sword he could wield with dire consequence and rigid mastery.

He lifted the enigmatic Shield of Light next and strapped it to his left arm, the mystic ring of bronze so strange it seemed an ideal counterpart for the mighty Excalibur, the aegis having kept quiet for the time being. He picked up the Spear of Destiny, allowing his squires to bring his helmet as it might catch on lampshades and fittings as he left the room.

Downstairs the pub was packed with knights, almost shoulder to shoulder as they welcomed their King, a chorus so deafening he had trouble collecting his thoughts; Merlin waiting patiently. Lancelot and Galahad and a host of his closest knights led him out to their war horses; all looking resplendent in shimmering sigils of rich aquamarine, crimson, silver and gold, the white finery glimmering in its own spectrum.

Merlin sided with him. "As we move, so the curtain will extend to complete another full circle, hopefully encapsulating this shire you call Devon. The ongoing bubbles will have to take time to fully energise but as long as we can outwit our enemies and avoid conflict at the opening stages, we will have the upper hand later on. I feel we may well fall under attack later on today as aircraft try to burn the existing dome – but I have something of a plan, which I hope will work, otherwise innocent people may get seriously hurt."

Amid the tumultuous welcome of thousands of surrounding knights and cavalry, Danny took notice of this and asked; "What sort of attack?"

Merlin hummed – as if not sure. "Acid – probably dropped from above. They appear to have an idea the screen will burn once attacked, so – although I do hope they descend on an unpopulated area, because I fear their ruse will work – the force curtain made of natural atoms, I will have to try and outwit them."

"Will you stay here," Arthur asked?

Merlin shook his head. "No, I will be able to sense the events as they unfold. I must make sure we progress as planned, otherwise we are doomed from the start."

Lancelot raised a gauntleted hand to quell the rising tide of applause; allowing Danny to say anything if he so wished.

"Thank you," he remarked, realising he should address the crowds – perhaps give some propitiation or thanks to the spirit or power that appeared to control the glowing dome above – but mostly to applaud the brave men and women who'd crossed over so willingly – especially not knowing what was to become of them.

"Ladies; friends, knights of valour," he called out over the assembled crowds causing a hush to fall over them; "Today we march on Devon and release it from the puritanical vice-grip it's been suffering under, bring down the social mores that have practically enslaved the county. Thanks to you – who have all made this sacrifice – others may live again in a much better world, one of prosperity and friendship once more. I will endeavour to make sure your commitment and valour will not be in vain, this world will change because of you. It will be a world where all of us can live in harmony. I salute you!"

The crowds erupted, banners being raised, flags unfurled; a ripple spread out over the county... the day had begun. The King was on the move.

With Lancelot, Merlin and others he stepped down to walk to his horse, stopping only once to turn back and thank the landlord of The Bell Inn, who wished him well; the look of relief on the man's face evident as he watched the mounted army decamp. His pub would never be the same again he realised, with a modicum of sorrow mixed with quiet satisfaction – enough gold coins being handed over to start again afresh in France or Spain; famed for having housed The King, infamous for having Merlin present – and overawed for having one of his staff turned into a tiny mouse, the patron wondering just how he was going to break it to her parents – better perhaps to say she'd just upped sticks and joined the merry parade.

*Oh, gawd...*he mused.

Danny thanked him, assuring him he'd have a word quietly about the bar manager, turning then to step up to his horse, mounting the blocks confidently.

Once in the saddle, feet firmly in stirrups, he accepted his helmet, waiting as the royal standard was tied to his spear, allowing a squire to then lash it to the side of his saddle panels.

The helmet gleamed in his gauntleted hands. Dan took a moment to appreciate the fine workings and goldsmithery, especially of the crown ringing the top of the protective dome, giving the head yet more fortification. It was a work of art coupled with the strength and awe of a halo; the metal and steels imbued with a thousand years of determination, grit and fortitude.

He raised it and placed it carefully over his head, feeling the tell-tell signs of the power and energy seeping from it.

Around him mounted warriors were jostling to make way, clear a path for The King and his entourage; two standard bearers with the Pendragon shield gilded on flags slotting in behind Lancelot and Galahad, Merlin riding off to his right. Before his wagon train, thousands were already amassing at the demarcation line, troops and police on the other side of the Dome trying desperately to meet the numbers but failing miserably – just not enough reserves or army units left, police numbers cut so drastically over the years there was hardly enough to go round. Still, armed with the very latest weaponry they felt reasonably confident they could handle men on horseback – even heavily armoured knights as a high velocity bullet would probably travel through several breastplates before it's lost its velocity. Armoured cars with thirty three millimetre canons would soon turn any infantry into so much mincemeat, rocket and grenade launchers would take care of the rest. It seemed an unforeseeable endgame as thousands of pike-men, light-mounted cavalry, wagons of squires and knaves lined the streets, spreading out to fill the fields and parks, gathering in lines so deep it was impossible to keep count.

***

Sir Reginald Smyth woke with a start that same morning, wondering like quite a lot of his contemporaries, where the hell he was; the pub's decor so sterile and strange he had a job collecting his thoughts. Adding to his dilemma was the misty events of the previous day when the call to arms went up; seeming a little odd and eerie – as if experiencing it from a distant land – and having answered that call with many of his friends and allies around about had found himself wandering across a mystifying stretch of sand, (complete with horse, squire and knave) into something he hadn't noticed before, to then find himself standing in some kind of street with funny-looking poles at regular intervals as if ready for a crucifixion; alien hedgerows and even stranger dwellings nestling behind them, curb-stones that many tripped over; the knight just following his feet until the pub presented itself. *Thank the gods he was surrounded at all times by many of his cohorts;* he ruminated with confusion; those he'd drunk with and fought alongside occasionally.

The impulse to stretch nearly resulted in tipping the glass beer mug he had sitting on his lap onto the floor, Sir Reginald just catching it before it bounced.

This was yet another quandary. He was totally taken by the manufactured glass tankard, finding the construction mind blowing; intending to keep it despite the bar manageress scolding him as a *'tealeaf,'* whatever that was?

It was a full couple of minutes before Sir Reginald, nodding and acknowledging other waking knights around him, realised the beer glass had kept something very special in it!

"Oh, damn," he spat out in alarm, looking about his person in panic!

"What afflicts thee," a knight close by asked, witnessing his distress?

"There was a mouse – ,"

"Mouse," repeated the knight?

"Where," shrieked a nearby lady of the realm?

"There," called another knight rousing himself opposite! He was on his knees wondering what had happened to him, when he looked over to find the warrior abreast of him had a rather attractive little black and white mouse sitting on his shoulder, making him wonder if he hadn't let go of his senses. "It's erm…" and the kindly knight pointed to his own armoured epaulet.

Sir Reginald tried to pull his head back and squint at the little rodent on his shoulder, but after hissing at him she scampered down his armoured chest to slide down his breastplate and land in his lap, rolling over in dire anger.

Having picked up his pint pot, Reginald Smyth attempted to coax the little being back into the glass, whereupon she turned and sunk her sharp teeth into his finger, the intake of breath making her cringe as he pulled his hand away. Still rankled however, Lindsey Cartwright stared around at all the big faces staring down at her – all – she noticed, taking pity on her, stepping grudgingly back into her travelling compartment, virtually spitting as she did so.

"Spirited little one, isn't she," spoke the knight next to him?

Sucking his wounded finger, Sir Reginald nodded, staring down at the disgruntled rodent. "Merlin's work," he conceded unhappily, considering the injury to his digit.

"Oh…" stressed the knight.

"Keep that thing away from me," bleated the woman. "Or she'll be in the pot!"

Confident the little creature could not scale the slippery sides of the tankard, Sir Reginald righted it and scrambled to his feet along with everyone else – the first port of call – the loos, which he, along with just about everyone else, marvelled at – *clear running water – for the love of the gods!* Something someone called a *'toilet'* being yet another revelation as many stripped off just to try it; and a *'urinal'* something Sir Reginald could associate with – what looked like a pig's trough! All in a building of their own however, quite a novel idea he had to concede. He stripped off half his armour to go see if he could gain access – the loos being an essential visit with so many a knight and lady having dodgy stomachs, plus somewhere where one could wash off all the dust and grime of the previous day, carrying his pint pot carefully with him.

A short while later, having managed to find an empty cubicle and relieve himself rather a lot; Reginald slouched back to his corner of the pub and collapsed, fully intending to sleep off his hangover a little more. It wasn't to be however, he'd only just got comfortable again, placing the glass tankard reverently in his lap, when a call from outside told him his squire and knave had finally located him.

"Ssss...pigswhistle!"

Cursing, Sir Reginald pushed himself to his feet to go meet the dawn.

***

Bill Nightingale woke with a start that very same morning, surfacing slowly but at the same time allowing his thoughts to arrange themselves in something of a hazy chronological order. He'd sunk a few whiskeys the previous evening revelling in a job well done, having flashed through the opus of what might possibly be the most important editorial of his life, but he'd not only done that in fact, but, had single-handedly coaxed a serving wench away from the invading army and managed, *by hook and by crook,* to squirrel her away in his car – then house her; allowing the lovely creature all the luxuries of the twenty first century.

The crazy events of the last twenty four hours raced through Bill's mind like a montage through a kaleidoscope on acid, the images of Danny King pulling the fabled sword Excalibur from the stone, the image a somewhat animated and Disney-related version, but later witnessing himself the legions of mounted knights; archers; leather-clad infantry and groups of cavalry; all accompanied by women – even children and livestock *for crying out loud,* traipsing through the lanes and over the fields, all trying desperately to arrange themselves despite having just been propelled through eons of time, Bill's mind still not too conversant with the mechanics but (could not doubt the validity of what his own senses had told him), having very cleverly disguised himself as a latter day sage and – with the help of a wayward and thoroughly lost woman, gained access to The King himself finding the seven-foot Adonis every inch the monarch everybody else was kowtowing to.

It took Bill several seconds after the heady slideshow, to realise someone was sleeping right next to him, the unmistakable warmth of a nubile body only inches away, the wily reporter turning ever so slowly to find the mass of glossy black hair meant Fay had left the couch in the living room and, having found the bedroom, decided to share his bed!

Well, he cogitated, *would you Adam and Eve it,* allowing an exploratory hand to slide ever so slowly over to the sleeping woman, making sure it was Fay and not his friend from Bude; the firmness of her wide buttocks and back endorsing the feeling that it was indeed the enigma of that beautiful woman.

He rolled over casually, feigning to appear half-asleep and sliding a hand beneath her delicately, wrapped her in his arms; allowing fingers to caress the wonderful firm breasts, nipples, exploring her taught belly and thighs, the thick thatch of black hair.

***

It took several hours for Danny's army to reach Dartmoor, passing through Launceston following the A30, then the slightly narrower A3072; the huge expanse of the common as they passed covered in colourful tents of all kinds; the caravan moving at a leisurely pace, stopping to enjoy lunch just passed Oakhampton before moving to the nearest major cut off point at Copplestone on the extreme edge of the Dome, putting the place firmly on the map. With the dry summer (and now the enfolding dome) drying the land out further, Danny and his team had quickly decided the fastest route was the shortest, cutting a path directly through Cornwall and heading for the minor capital of Tiverton in Devon – a fairly central point; there to recruit and consolidate yet more combatants crossing over from some place only Merlin knew of – somewhere in the woodland of Exmoor Heath, Dan was told.

From a small hill near Copplestone – and from the height of his mighty steed, Dan could just make out the town of Crediton lying only a few miles to the west, the authorities on the other side of the fence having one hell of a time trying to hold their own front lines while staving off thousands of people ready to welcome him.

"It's going to be one showdown," a local reporter had gushed having the luck to pose as a pike-man whilst strapping a microphone boom to his staff and covering it with muslin, his camera man being jostled about as he desperately fought to get a stable picture – also dressed in appropriate garb.

The way parted for Arthur and his entourage, everyone stopping for a while as Merlin consorted with some of his sages; the attack on the Dome they were still under apparently going ahead as planned, despite local people milling about everywhere. Acid was dropped from a big glass vial over Bodmin moor, hoping to reduce casualties if it dribbled through; Merlin making sure the Dome parted to let the fluid fall through harmlessly – well as harmless as possible as a tent vaporised along with a cow and several chickens.

In the helicopter, Flight Lieutenant Harper watched on hopelessly as the shimmering Dome, acting like some frightened animal as the deadly toxin was released, shrank back from the deluge as it was tipped; only to reform after it had gushed through, destroying a rather nice gaudy tent – the sort Punch and Judy might like to hang out in, and a few grazing animals, leaving a smoking hole several meters wide. He sighed into his radio; "It's a no-show guys – the force field is way too smart to be fooled by this – we'll have to try something else."

In another helicopter close by, two scientists shook their heads and went straight back to the drawing board.

With his army behind him, Dan and his immediate entourage threaded their way down to the intersection of Copplestone, the small town lying just inside the Dome's enclosure. Throughout his tour of Cornwall, runners and the local TV stations had been able to keep him abreast of movement on both sides of the barrier; things appearing pretty chaotic wherever he looked; the crepuscular wall having fallen along the main A377 as it ran its convoluted and zigzagging route all the way from Dartmouth in the south across to Barnstable in the north, crisscrossing the shimmering circular Dome many times. As it fell into place, drivers originally had to slow as the scintillating wall descended, giving people time to get out of the way. Once down, they all found they were one side of the wall or the other; some regrettably having to abandon their vehicles and hike to the nearest exit or entry.

This, along with thousands of ardent supporters of King Arthur – whether it be a complete mock-up or not, hampered the attempts of the authorities, service men and women who had been ordered into position all along the demarcation line, no easy feat when thousands of people were jamming the roads; abandoned vehicles having to be pushed aside or towed away, and a no-go area set up along the seventy odd miles of the danger zone.

They came to a halt on the other side of the town, The King and his entourage looking around as they did so, staggered by the amount of support either side of the Dome, the shimmering wall appearing like a wall of slightly opaque glass that allowed a smudged view of the countryside beyond, noting the resistance already – the authorities not standing for any more colonisation – in any shape or form.

"It's time," Merlin mentioned from his horse nearby. "We'll cut across land as the lanes seem totally blocked."

Ahead of The King's convoy; hundreds – if not thousands were waiting for the push ahead; many with railway sleepers, stolen or borrowed wheelbarrows full of wood or iron railings; car trailers (pushed, pulled and carried over the terrain) also full of materials that would ford any river or stream, leaving the coast clear for The King and his caravan to follow. Already the castle in Tiverton had been made available, many of the surrounding guest houses and premier hotels opening up their doors too, in the hope King Arthur might prefer a more salubrious stay-over and grace their establishment; although the castle with its immediate grounds right in the middle of the town would provide much needed space for horses and his retinue of knights and squires. The support was overwhelming, Danny realising the rural areas had almost been cut off by the capital and central government over the last few years, pushed under the carpet and left to practically starve to death as financial cuts deepened, and pressures put to bear that could be borne no more. Whole sections of the country were ripe for change – and now it had come in the most bizarre of ways there was no stopping the juggernaut.

At Merlin's signal the bubble began to expand. Like a cell undergoing duplication the force field slowly but surely crept over the land, inching forward to inexorably push anything not wanted backwards – cars, police vehicles, vans and lorries being edged backwards – consequently subsuming other items, leaving the telegraph poles, electrical substations; street lighting and buildings: A tank that had bulldozed its way along a B-road stood obdurate and steadfast with its nose at the demarcation line, now having its barrel bent up as the awesome power-grid moved forward, the entire metal hunk trying to resist the shimmering wall but failing miserably as it pushed the modern weapon of warfare back along the road; metal squealing as the tracks dug in. Before much damage could ensue, the occupants managed to get the thing into reverse and spin around to make a swift retreat.

As this seemed the biggest and heaviest obstacle the wall had encountered first off, it appeared to pause in its trajectory as it waited for the metal object to vacate the area. Similarly, all along the line, armoured police vehicles were also persuaded to back off, the living wall of overpowering energy coaxing them back from their position.

Guns failed to work, armaments unable to deploy, as the scintillating wall enveloped everything.

By seven o'clock that day they'd reached Tiverton, passing through the lush pastureland and countryside of Cheriton Fitzpaine and Well Town along the way, the streets lined with well-wishers until they had to funnel down to cross the big river Exe; here, finding a little resistance by a few soldiers and policemen who decided it would be a good strategic place to bar the army's progress; although it was a token effort, the Dome having rendered ballistics ineffective. By the time several thousand pike-men, archers and infantry had built up around the other side the collection of soldiers and police, they had to concede it was a waste of time and rapidly dismantled the barriers, ably helped by hundreds of Tiverton's population.

The King was allowed to cross in style, the sparkling Dome spreading out before him, being welcomed on the other side by hundreds, if not thousands of well-wishers. Devon had fallen without a shot being fired.

***

"I can't very well ride into battle without a horse," Sir Reginald Smyth was exclaiming, holding a glass pint pot to his chest as if enjoying a cool beer! Both his squire and knave were staring somewhat vacantly at the small mouse sitting in the bottom of his odd-looking tankard, both finding the sight very strange indeed.

They'd walked for hours, having eventually located him, spending a lot of the previous day getting their bearings and threading through the phalanx of knights as they formed an almost impenetrable steel ring around their king. Both had also had to endure their first bite of anything to eat, their stomachs both recoiling from roasted chicken, and something called *'hotdogs'* forcing both of them to their knees as the food roiled and churned in their guts.

It was the mouth-watering smell that alerted them to the rear garden, both totally lost at this point;

the terrace housing looking to them like a fortification to the side of some castle; Gwent and Adrian stopping to peer in, finding a lone woman performing a kind of spell on a cauldron; smoke billowing from the coals.

"Come in, come in," the slim Negro invited as she turned to find she had an audience, looking to the both of them like one of Satan's demigods.

The revenants glanced at each other, looking then up and down the sandy track they'd found themselves on. The fact that the wooden back wall to her den had been torn down and put aside didn't seem to bode well either.

Gwent was about to pull Adrian away when the mouth-watering aroma of roasting chicken and other spicy meats reached his nostrils – and despite the woman looking half-mad as she jounced about to some jangling tribal music, the squire knew he'd have to eat soon, the news of their strange transportation from their own part of the world to this new one, causing some kind of rift where to consume something – almost anything – would consolidate the arrival to keep the person intact and alive.

Still, Gwent hesitated. Black witches were notoriously devious and by consorting with her could possibly result in ending up in the pot themselves.

Shaking his head, he was about to drag Adrian away when the woman slid over to them, quickly presenting them with a platter with two big white things!

Both Gwent and Adrian had stepped back in alarm, frightened beyond words, speechless as the woman stepped nearer, proffering the food.

"Not hungry," pouted the woman?

It was the look of hurt in her eyes that stayed Gwent's hand, that softness that he recognised as sadness; the fact that she'd perhaps insulted them by offering her meagre wares.

"I have spicy chicken breasts cooking too," she cooed, hoping to interest their pallets.

Gwent studied her face, convinced there was evil in there somewhere, just waiting to pounce; the demons proving to be cruelly deceptive and have a man eating out of their hands in minutes, one only having to accede to their wishes.

He peered up and down the dusty lane again, wondering where the hell he was and what on earth was going on, that very strange and eerie call to arms early that morning seeming to come from the very air around them rather than some runner or clergyman? Then, having followed the idiot Smyth all over the place – and getting thoroughly lost into the process, he was now at the gates of hell, awaiting damnation!

He turned back to the negress and was again mollified by her countenance, those soft brown eyes having not a hint of malice, just seemed to be so warm and inviting.

Just the way they like it, he thought, then cast the idea aside and gazed down at the platter of food.

"What food," he asked as politely as he could – still fearful of upsetting the demon?

"Hotdogs, of course," she screeched gaily, making the both of them exchange glances!

"Hot-dogs," Adrian repeated, knowing some dogs didn't taste too bad?

Gwent stifled a sigh and reached out for one, his hand retracting swiftly as he touched the white bread roll.

"Mercy," he bleated, unsure of the baked item and its pulpy softness.

"How do you know my name," the woman asked – now a little suspicious of the both of them, despite their obvious candour, the plate retracted somewhat?

This had the both of them confused and Adrian was all for walking away, when the woman deliberately picked up one of the hotdogs and took a bite, munching on it for a moment before swallowing it down.

"Hm," she chortled.

Gwent watched her closely for any reaction, convinced the food was poisoned but she took another small nibble and then held out the other roll again, hoping they would partake.

In doing so, their costumes struck her as very well thought out, she realised – the suede tabards, the leather trews; right down to the last detail, the roughshod sandals a real winner.

"Where you from," she asked sweetly, persisting again with the roll?

Adrian glanced at his elder, shaking his head. "Devonshire, my lady," he told her. "I fear we've strayed from the path a small time."

Still unsure, Gwent sucked in air, hot fetid air that seemed to suggest he was very far from the coast – not wanting to trouble the woman though, he plucked up courage and reached for the roll once more, picking it up gingerly.

Hot butter dripped through his fingers, the woman despairing and rushing for a tissue, bringing it back to give it to him. Gwent took the napkin but didn't have a clue what to do with it so just held it in his forefingers – to be polite of course, attempting to take a bite of the roll in his other hand.

Adrian watched on in fear as his friend and mentor munched on the Savoy sausage and buttered bread roll, finding the combination truly magical, the spicy meat tasting great to him. Then the masticated food hit the stomach and Gwent suddenly froze, his eyes telling his partner that something was very wrong.

"What is it," worried the negress?

Gwent tried to explain but the pain was excruciating, forcing him almost to his knees as the fire in his belly erupted to sear his insides. He staggered about as two more infantry men passing by, both stopped to watch the proceedings.

Mercy had rushed for some water, quickly turning the chicken breasts over on the barbecue, then racing back to help Gwent. By the time she did, he'd sort of recovered, able to stand straight again as he glanced down at the squashed bread roll and sausage in one hand. He considered the tissue in the other and decided it was a kind of neckerchief and wiped the spittle from his mouth with it, coughing a little as he accepted without question a drop of water from a plastic bottle.

"Thank you," he gasped. "It's not the food," he managed to tell her. "It's the moving from one place to another – or so I'm told. We have to adjust."

"Can we try," asked one of the infantry men who'd stopped to look on, both completely lost too?

Mercy hadn't the time to take in the other two re-enactment people but when she did, her mouth nearly dropped open. The two thick-set men were heavily armed – not only with belts laden with knives and daggers, but a dirty great pike that looked anything but legal. It was their persona too – along with the aura of someone who had seen a lot of action, as if they were very skilled stuntmen. Their extra big hands and heads put Mercy in mind of trolls!

"Oh, god," she cried, making Adrian jump out of his skin; *"My chicken!"*

Now the two of them were staring at their knight as if he'd lost his senses, carrying a mouse around in a glass jar and seeming to protect it with his very life, evident when Gwent enquired if it was some kind of bar snack?

Sir Reginald had not found the joke at all funny and had insisted they go off on another journey to find his steed.

"No, wait a minute," he called, stopping to turn back, realising the bar wouldn't be open for some time yet. "I'll come with you. I expect we should follow the army, eh."

Gwent sighed inwardly, looking the big pub over. "Well at least we've eaten," he mumbled, the unmistakable aroma of beer hops making his mouth water again – and now his system had settled down, a pint or two of ale would be a sheer blessing, especially on a hot day like today.

"We'll get ale on the way," Sir Reginald instructed them; "Best to at least make a token effort, eh?"

"Whatever is your pleasure; Sire," his knave spluttered happily.

Sir Reginald eyed him suspiciously – never really knowing if the lad was sincere or not, or if he was picking up the snide and often vitriolic insults his squire was often partial to.

"Very good; would you please collect my lance and other effects from the bar, Gwent – and no stopping for ale or women," he added?

***

Tiverton Castle looked like a real authentic fortification from the outside but inside had all the trappings of a luxury hotel, the walls plastered, painted and fitted with stylish lamps or the odd painting, the décor definitely haut monde; the opulence not lost on all the knights as they followed The King inside and gazed around at the entrance foyer with its array of arched doors leading off – all inches thick bog oak. The manager hovered about like Basil Fawlty in full fawning mode; tripping over his own feet as the entourage filed in, all clattering and clanking – the noise reverberating off the stone of the walls where they'd been left bare. The manager tried to lead Arthur and his knights to the attendance desk to sign them all in, but in the end thought better of it, bustling about with his staff to show The King and his retinue to their prospective rooms, the finest luxury suite left for Danny. He followed the under-manager, a tall slim woman that reminded him of Lindsey Cartwright (and who he'd have to do something about once he'd had a chance catch up with the knight who'd so gallantly rescued her – and then talk to Merlin), up a short flight of stairs to another kind of open richly carpeted area where a large lift awaited to transport them up to the fourth floor, Arthur – now a little dead on his feet – and – if he wanted to admit it, a little saddle-sore, barely taking in the riotous pot plants and glassed cased ornaments as he squeezed in with his squire and knaves, Merlin, Lancelot, Galahad and the others having to wait or take the stairs, no one wanting to climb several floors in full battle armour.

Danny felt himself sink into the rich carpeting of the fourth floor, the lift opening into an expanse of luxury and high expense, everything gleaming and shining. Along a short corridor and an open door led into the suite, the rooms large enough for nearly twenty people, the place dripping with taste and opulence, something he would never have seen in his former life.

"Will there be anything else sir," the under-manager asked as they clanked in?

Arthur – a little concerned about the welfare of his horses and staff outside; asked if they would be given the same courtesy as was shown to him and his knights.

The under-manager assured him they would – and not to worry – every thing was being taken care off, many other hotels and B&B's catering for his army, parks and nearby estates being commandeered for the thousands of troops and caravans moving through. Devon – a little like Cornwall – which didn't really have much of a say in the matter, capitulating or welcoming Arthur and his army without question, the push forward so irrevocably and deftly carried out, there now was no question about the validity of the course.

"You must be hungry after your journey," the under-manager spoke, her confidence growing with every moment, watching Danny divest of his magnificent costume, the retinue of people around The King as worn out by the route as everyone else.

"Some cheese and wine would be most gracious;" Merlin muttered having fallen into a plush arm chair, looking up from his meditation.

"Grilled steaks;" Lancelot told the woman without compunction, having enjoyed one at The Bell Inn – *"and all the trim!"*

A knave dropped one of his vambraces making the poor young woman jump out of her skin, Danny too slow on the uptake, just smiled at her weakly as the rest of his armour came away. He caught her glance as she took in Excalibur and the Shield of Light, the huge aegis being rested against a wall by two squires, the rim of bronze so enigmatic being hollow, she wasn't the only one to wonder over it.

"If you rustle up enough for our little group here that would be great," Dan assured her. "What time does the restaurant open?"

"It's open now," the young woman told him; "we'll get it ready to accommodate all your staff."

"What about the other guests," Arthur enquired?

"Other guests?"

"I take it there are other people staying here," The King pointed out?

The young woman caught herself. "Erm, actually it's quite a quiet time right now, so most of the rooms and suites are vacant."

"You mean the rats have jumped ship in the face of chivalry;" Merlin jibed, picking up a magazine of yachts; the sort that needed a crew of about sixteen.

"Well…" and she smiled into the floor, not wanting to comment further.

Lancelot approached, now in leggings and leather tabard with the crest of Pendragon emblazoned on it, handing the young woman a golden coin – the doubloon worth a small fortune.

"Keep it," he instructed her as she shook her head in apprehension, not understanding the generosity.

"It's courteous to tip the bellboy;" Danny joked with her, letting her get on her way.

"Thank – you," she uttered – totally shocked. "I'll treasure it," she added, unsure of what to do next.

"Don't," advised Merlin, throwing the magazine down in disgust. "Flog it as quick as you can and run with the money. It might very well turn to dust in the very near future!"

The woman glanced to Merlin slumped in the chair and considered the golden gift sitting in her palm, the weight alone suggesting he may well be right, the coin solving all her financial problems overnight.

She practically curtseyed as she left, totally unsure as to the etiquette, racing away with her treasure.

Danny did a tour of the apartment, along with Lancelot, a squire and knave in tow, considering each room as they passed through, Dan commenting to his group that he would never be able to afford to stay here in real terms – the place too lavish by half, each room a real sumptuous set up, the ample sitting room leading to an ante-room – a sort of reading room complete with small library of the classics, two extravagant bedrooms leading off from it. The other way, a bathroom complete with golden or gilt taps and fittings was big enough to play tennis in, while the master bedroom adjoined it, the room so abundant it could have slept a dozen people.

Dan noticed the squire and knaves open amazement, unknowing before of such luxury.

"The floor's good enough to sleep on," commented one of them.

The door banged open and Galahad, still in half of his armour, stalked in, brought up sharp by the immensity of the rooms. A bellboy hovered tremulously at the door.

"The sages need to confer with you, Merlin," he alerted the numen.

Merlin looked up, nodding, having selected another magazine from the occasional table down by his side, this one showing grandiose houses and their glittering interiors. He shook his head in obvious disgust and sheer bewilderment, pushing himself to his feet.

"They're in the lobby;" Galahad instructed him, "the lad will take you."

"Thank you Sir Knight," Merlin acknowledged him. "I'll be back later, Sire" he told Danny. "I have to make sure the portal is open here now under the protection of the Dome, and that the troops can get through."

"Ok, Merlin," Dan replied, eager to fall into his now vacant comfortable-looking chair.

Merlin slouched out. Galahad stood to take in the surroundings, marvelling at the splendour. "There's room for you in here if you are crowded;" Lancelot spoke; noticing his awe.

Galahad snapped out of it. "Do not trouble yourself, Lancelot. The rooms we have are fine – and just down the hall, sumptuous they are too. The rest are accommodated all over the castle, the place quite well endowed!"

"Have you found this Sir Reginald yet," Dan asked, tiredness seeping through his body?

Galahad shook his head, falling into another easy chair he'd pulled further into the room.

The apartment door opened again, a knave immediately levelling a lance, finding a bellhop was pushing a trolley full of wine and a cheeseboard, the platter enough for thirty people. Dan waved a thank you, forgetting to tip him. Lancelot searched in his pouches but had run out of small coinage. "I'll catch him later," he assured Danny.

"Goblet of wine," a squire asked, having worked out how to cork a bottle, the attachments a little foreign. Dan nodded thankfully, smiling graciously. It had been a long day – and he mentioned it.

Galahad and Lancelot nodded. "It will be a big war," Lancelot mentioned seriously, he pulled out a map he kept with him, perusing the different counties. Two knaves pulled an occasional table over to them so Lancelot could put the map on it, Arthur and Galahad moving in to study it as well. Around them the squire and knaves flustered, making sure the wine and cheese flowed.

Dan insisted they take their share, the squire and the three knaves all comforted by their King's gratitude.

"This Sir Reginald must be in the rear of things at the moment," Galahad assumed, "so many of our knights and cavalry spread out all over the place. *Gods – if we had to hold some kind of defence we'd be in a right old mess!"*

"Merlin has things under control," Lancelot assured him. "It's going to take time to get everything in order. This takeover of Devon went remarkably well, no casualties – on either side."

Danny sipped his wine, an extra fine first-press burgundy – the sort that would cost a mortgage normally, nodding his assent. Being revived a little by the superlative liquor, he queried Merlin's next move – Somerset and perhaps Dorset combined.

"The army will probably split in two," Galahad speculated, scrutinising the map upside down, he'd found a twelve inch plastic ruler in his room and kept it on his person for such a task, pointing out key points on the map. "This place Taunton will be the next port of call for your residence; I would have thought, your highness; the main thrust of the army having to sweep across the lower part of the county to take Yeovil and Weymouth, is it?"

"Weymouth, yes," Danny applauded him.

"Glaston-be," Lancelot mentioned. "Is that the same place?"

Danny looked questioningly at Galahad.

"Possibly," he muttered, a little unsure.

"We rode there once, don't you remember, a Viking uprising?"

Galahad nodded, although his memory told of another explanation. "Not exactly an uprising Lancelot – more a festival gathering, pushing the Druids out of the way – both wanting to share the same place at the same time, anyway by the time we got there, it had all fizzled out anyway – nice trip across country though as I recall."

"Glastonbury," Danny spelt out for Lancelot's sake.

"Aye, Glastonbury. Dark forces were afoot there once upon a time."

Galahad guffawed. "Stories – nothing more."

"There were sages more powerful than Merlin once upon a time, *and evil witches and demons; God's what sorcery we had to combat!*"

"Poor Agavan," Galahad mentioned almost in soliloquy.

From studying the map, Danny looked up sharply.

Lancelot jumped in over The King's obvious lack of understanding. "We nearly ate him by accident," he told his liege.

Dan raised his eyebrows.

Galahad looked somewhat embarrassed. "He was under a spell," he explained, "running amok as a big hog."

"Percival caught him, Gwent and his squire nearly gutted him – and if it wasn't for Tristan and several other noble knights securing the other big savage hog in what was quite a skirmish, *we might well have eaten him*."

"Damned witches," Lancelot grumbled viciously.

"So the land was full of magic at that time," Danny uttered in awe?

Galahad nodded solemnly, glancing at Lancelot ruefully; "It was as well we saved Agavan," he mentioned.

"Hm," Lancelot hummed sourly. "Did not do us much good, did it?"

"Well," Galahad prevaricated, "eating the other hog probably was not the best thing we could have done, still, it tasted good."

Lancelot snorted, not wanting to even dwell on the ramifications.

"What happened," Danny had to ask?

"We all went around the next week or so looking like beasts, long hair, fingernails, breath – and everything else smelling like we'd turned into hogs ourselves, our own pigs were not safe. And that wasn't the end of it. Knights Lucan and Mordred set a trap for the witch, baiting a stew with the bones. When the demon found out, all hell broke loose, many of us having to drag Merlin back from his studies at Winchester."

"Did you beat her – the witch, I mean?"

Galahad nodded, sipping his wine almost reverently. "Merlin – with other powerful white witches managed to drive her out, but she hovered about the southern coast – literally, causing mayhem whenever she could. A squire shot her with an extremely lucky arrow one afternoon and she blundered into a tree, and that was the last we heard of her for a long time."

"License revoked," Danny joked tiredly?

The two knights nodded, not quite understanding.

"This magic," Danny asked, "is it still here, in the modern world, I mean?"

"Possible," Galahad muttered, staring vacantly over the map; "pushed into the shadows I imagine by the passing of time, the more people born the less the old ways survive; people as a whole wanting something more tangible. I suspect some people however have kept the old ways alive, perhaps practicing old magic and spells."

"Merlin will find them out," Lancelot mentioned, toying with his wine. "The sage will draw every black and white witch for miles around and get them to fight for him."

"Is he that powerful, the one true power?"

"Not at first," Galahad told Danny. "He was just a wizard like any other, but something happened to him once upon a time – no one's too sure what, but he told us once he'd come across this shaman who'd shown him the future – taken him on fantastical journeys, then imbuing him with incredible power to be able to survive them on his own, Merlin so stunned later it took days to get any sense out of him."

"His power has grown over the years," Lancelot spoke reverently, munching on a sliver of cheese – washing it down with the sumptuous wine. He smacked his lips and continued; "witches, demons, forest harpies and ground serpents, trolls; evil elves; all seemed to move away from Camelot once Merlin had come of age, he ruled the land with an iron rod."

"How come I've had to replace Arthur? How is it he didn't come through with you lot and take the sword himself?"

Galahad and Lancelot shifted their weight uneasily. Danny realised he'd hit on a sore point.

Eventually, Galahad plucked up courage and told the story. "Arthur fell under some kind of spell over Genevieve, his love for her almost consuming him. Not only that but some mystical sylph seems to have enchanted him as well about this time, drawing him continually to a nearby lake – this place apparently instilled with magic from long ago."

"The Lady in the Lake," Dan voiced with reverence?

Galahad screwed up his eyes in confusion, shaking his head. "It was just some water nymph I'm sure, but whatever happened, dark forces were at work, Merlin in the north of the country by then – on one of his pilgrimages."

"What happened," Dan had to ask yet again?

Lancelot leaned back in his seat. Dan realised the chatter of the squire and knaves as they enjoyed their snack had all but dried up, as they listened to the crux of some story that had never been fully explained.

"Besot with Genevieve, Arthur, one portent afternoon, went to the water nymph to seek her advice, but found himself in mortal danger by some witches that had set up a coven on the shore. Enraged at their effrontery – Merlin having chased everything off – he slew two of them with Excalibur and pursued the other into the lake; there to be dragged under by some leviathan that had lain in wait – the ensuing battle lasting hours, but finally the monster was too strong and Arthur succumbed; the water nymph dragging the sword from the dying creature's hide and returning Excalibur to us."

"How do you know all this," Dan asked, breathless?

"The nymph," Galahad essayed, his eyes portraying the sadness. "The power of the sword allowed her to leave her prison for a while to walk on land and carry the incredible weapon, bringing it back to Camelot. Now Arthur remains in some kind of purgatory – and even Merlin can't reach him. He knew he needed a new champion – and as luck would have it – you came along!"

"Poor Arthur," Danny murmured, "bewitched by all the magic and adventure."

"Indeed," grumbled Lancelot.

"Would it have been better if you would have had your own king with you," Dan asked, a little coyly?

Lancelot smiled wearily, glancing to his co-conspirator. "You will make a fine king Danny –

Arthur. This is your destiny, young man. Take it with both hands."

***

In the darkest fortified oubliette of Bill Nightingale's mind, a rattling sack barrow was trundling the remains of his former girlfriend's memories in a rusty trunk, to dump the thoughts, reminisces and wayward daydreams forever into oblivion; for the lovemaking with Fay that morning had been frenetic; fantastic; joyous; wonderful; exciting and crazy; endearing; and unforgettably sensuous, she bending to his wishes at every juncture; her body pliant and supple; soft yet firm, skin silky smooth, highly entertaining. He'd never known a session like it – and now, staring out of his kitchen window to the small patch of grass he loosely called a garden, it was evident their fondness for each other had grown in leaps and bounds in only the short time they'd been together. He'd made tea and stood almost quaking as he stirred the tea bags as if in a trance, the throes of the lovemaking in the early morning still seeping through him, Bill shaking his head over his performance, never in his history knowing the fulfilment and delight in managing three to four orgasms – one after the other, Fay doing everything and nothing to raise him up, bring forth a heady lust that took some time to be sated.

He realised the tea would go cold if he didn't stop stirring it into a soup, going to the fridge to add milk and a little honey – the sweetener just for her to make her feel more at home.

He smiled. The innocence and wonderment in her lovely brown eyes overriding the fact that she'd spanned centuries to be back in dear old Cornwall – here to support an army all ready to sweep across the country and rid it once and for all of its corruption and skulduggery. The conundrum still plagued his consciousness and toyed with his mind until it spiralled uncontrollably into something close to a meltdown, the sheer lunacy of it all confounding him, the inexplicable vying with everything his world had to offer; logic; common sense; law and order – all thrown out of the window as another century from the world's dark past swept into being, intending to put right a wrong he and his countrymen had no hope of going up against. It was just judgement, he minced thoughtfully, wondering with concern if he could reasonably hang on to the love he'd now found – and what about all the other ramifications – supposing he'd made her pregnant already, *Jeeze wouldn't that be a turn up for the books* – 'journalist has baby with fifteen hundred year old woman!' It was just too much to comprehend – *but it was happening just the same!*

He gave the tea one more spin, then, picking the mugs up, padded back to the bedroom, half expecting the sheets to be devoid of anybody – his mind having snapped and this having been all but some lurid fugue.

Fay was asleep however; entangled in the sheets; those wonderful legs sprawled apart so teasingly he had to bite down hard on his ardour.

Having given herself wonderfully each and every time, giggling at his first amorous advances in the light of the early morn, but complying with them nevertheless, the first coupling was stunning; she meeting him head on in the next two bouts only fifteen minutes later – her own body shaking in sheer enjoyment at the copulation, almost swooning later finding his stamina hit new heights of excitement as he went for her again, the sexual rampage finally coming to an end as he clung to her, gasping his heart out.

Now as he sat by her placing her tea on a bedside unit, he had nothing but respect for her, nothing but un-relenting admiration. She was some woman, he mused, gazing over her form, wondering at the deeply tanned skin – the bronze colour not fizzling out at the bikini line or bra, but sweeping completely all over, as if she'd never had clothes on and been exposed to some really hot summers.

She was of a different ilk, he understood, running a hand softly over a shoulder, marvelling over the tensile body, the taught breasts, firm thighs, slim calves and ankles, that beautiful round derrière that enticed him so. She was beautiful.

His mobile thrumming away back in his office demanded he take notice, and resignedly he stood to carry his tea through the house to answer the call of work.

Complimentary texts of all kinds were telling him his editorial had hit the headlines and he was being feted as the hottest journalist around at the moment having gained an audience with the famed King Arthur, the photographs speaking for themselves; the paper's circulation going into its second press already – and it was only half nine in the morning. Bill swallowed down his sweet tea and, diving back into the bedroom, dressed quickly, to leave the house quietly and rush down to the local newsagent to swipe up several copies of all the tabloids and some broadsheets, practically buying up what was left.

Back home, he spread everything out on his kitchen worktop and gazed over the reports, his own paper shining out from the rest with a picture of Danny King on the front, bedecked in a tabard of the Pendragon insignia, drawing out Excalibur from its scabbard, the pulse of energy as the blade hit the air almost evident in the picture as the flash of light blurred the edges just a little, the sheer magnitude of the moment encapsulated in that one beautiful snapshot. It was a picture to outshine all others – some not even bothering with shots of the re-enactment societies, trying to pass the whole episode off with a half-hearted report and only half a front page editorial. Hopeless; Bill's paper was out in the lead by far, a full report inside detailing Arthur's movements – even his intentions – giving the authorities something to think about, he judged, smiling grimly.

One other paper had an interesting description of how the authorities had actually attacked the Dome by spilling a cauldron of acid onto it somewhere over the Bodmin moor, the Dome apparently acting like some animal and shying away from the fizzling liquid as it tipped, opening up a hole and letting the ghastly fluid fall through. Just what the army had in mind was anybody's guess, Bill Nightingale wondered, perturbed by the thought that the powers-to-be were not going to let this charade get any further out of hand and try and nip it in the bud, although according to the report no further attempts were made on the refulgent curtain so they must have gone back to the drawing board.

Bill walked back to his office to ring in, getting through to his editor almost immediately.

"Well, Bill – ole' son, you've done it! We're on our second print run now as we speak and could be on our third by lunchtime, old Smithy from Truro having to supply us with paper this time; I can't thank you enough Bill – if you never write another piece for us again, this one will stand as a testament to first class journalism, top grade. What are you going to do now, Bill?"

Bill hadn't really got round to thinking about it yet – being somewhat preoccupied but he came back with a hearty riposte. "Actually, I'm thinking of trying to tag along with some knights I have already befriended, and follow King Arthur's progress – once I get close again – I may well get another full interview – he's nearly said as much!"

His editor nearly sounded apoplectic, "You've got my full support, Bill – anything – anything you need – just ask, expenses, car – *hell – helicopter* if you really need it – just name it my man, and we'll be right there, what a story, eh, Bill! What a story!"

"Ok, John," Bill glanced down at his watch, noting the time. If he was lucky he might well have time for another half-hour in bed with Fay, but he'd have to be quick, the train was already leaving the station and he'd have to get a shift on. "I'm connecting with people soon," he lied, "so I might be off the grid for a while as I do my incognito bit, but I'll see if I can get you another big scoop today, hang tight."

His editor had calmed down sufficiently. "Ok, Bill. I'll await your call – big bonus in the system, my boy – big bonus!"

"Cheers, John." Bill hung up, not surprised to find offers pinging up all over the phone, his place in history confirmed (in more ways than one), his loins tightening again as he recalled the sweet lovemaking with Fay.

He'd have to play this next episode very coyly, Bill ruminated, staring into space for a moment, turning to gaze out and up at the Dome that he could just see sparkling in the near horizon of his window. It was still incredibly warm outside, he knew, having just been down the shops – the Dome acting as an insulating cover. If they (Arthur's army) took over Devon, he mused as planned, would the Dome move with them or like an amoeba split into two sweeping over the next county. He had no way of knowing unless he got into the action. And he wasn't getting into the action standing here gazing out his office window. Still, he hung back however, planning – planning – it was everything right now, skulduggery being the apt word; for he planned to somehow get near Danny King again and get yet another low-down – stay in his company if possible gaining his confidence, hopefully producing scoop after scoop. But getting back through that phalanx of knights was not going to be easy – especially as they had been duped before – would they remember, he calculated – probably not, especially with Fay looking resplendent and shining like a new coin. He could perhaps pass as a nobleman with his lady.

He hadn't thrown his new love's clothes away luckily, tossing them into a bin, the bin remaining in the house. Would those rags wash, he asked himself? If they did – and didn't disintegrate in the machine he would have them dry in a few minutes, spinning them off and airing them quickly outside, perhaps allowing her to wear the leggings she'd fallen in love with – the pair obviously his former girlfriend's but hers now. He found a bra too but it was way too small, although a tee-shirt she also loved would go under her thin – worn out bodice; the rope-tied skirt equally threadbare. Still it was summer – and very warm – even warmer with the big Dome still covering Cornwall.

Bill swigged down his tea and got to work, checking the time as he did so.

Chapter 6

Late afternoon, and Danny King and his extended bodyguard of knights; squires and knaves sat in the big lobby of Tiverton's magnificent castle; conferring with Merlin and his growing pack of wizards; magus; sorcerers and warlocks – the group looking to him like the great unwashed – even if they had partaken of a bath or shower, the beards and shabby habits and hats (often emblazoned with archaic motifs and symbols) appearing decidedly dirty and unkempt; The King wondering if they had so much magic between them they might possibly be able to rustle up some clean togs. Still, he likened the dusty group to the intelligentsia who were often forgiven for being a little absent-minded, the vision of quite a few of the politicians of the day coming to his mind.

Aside from the fact that his army was now spread all over Cornwall (many still getting organised) and had successfully conquered Devon, parts of Somerset and Dorset into the bargain, reports were coming in thick and fast of knights and infantrymen being distracted by the Steam Railway as it wound its way through Devon's coastal scenery on its last trip for a while, many of the castles such as the ones at Barnstable and Exeter getting special treatment – and the magnificent 12th century Abby at Torres – a complete legion getting bogged down on the moorland – having to be helped out by the military – those that had capitulated – many more being waylaid by places of interest like the Prehistoric Show Caves at Kents Cavern; and to top it all – hundreds of his soldiers and staff were queuing up at the Model Village of Babbacombe.

If that wasn't enough, mounted knights, cavalry and supporting infantry were clubbing together to see if they could afford a trip around the zoo at Paignton – the best in the country Dan knew.

Only half his knights and infantry had actually reached central Devon, spreading out to enjoy the heath and woodlands of Exmoor, and colonising the coastal regions as far as Lyme Regis.

None of this however, was concerning Merlin as he and his group watched in consternation as the curtain kept spreading, finally coming to a halt just short of Bristol in the north and Bere Regis in the south, Blandford Forum; Shaftsbury; Frome and the major town of Bath just beyond the scintillating wall as it finally crept to a stop. Merlin blew out an exasperated sigh and turned back to his porter of wine to consult a huge map that had been laid out over a conference table, stroking his curly white beard thoughtfully. A cartographer drew a circle of the dome's new circumference, highlighting key areas – and possible weak points, river crossings, etc, everyone expecting some kind of military strike soon.

"It's almost doubled in strength," Danny commented, watching the television coverage avidly.

Merlin glanced up to appraise him from under his brow, nodding then with distinct worry lines about his forehead.

"Will it hold," Lancelot enquired?

"It'll hold," the numen averred, sounding a tad unsure. He whispered something to a sage nearby and he and several of the sorcerers stood to leave, all bidding Merlin a farewell.

Dan frowned over the covertness.

Merlin noticed it. "My apologies, my liege: I've merely sent an envoy to ensure the next portal stays open. We still need more of the army to pass through to bolster what we have already got. The legions and caravans are moving slowly so we must give them time to catch up. We need to send knights ahead to control the flow of traffic in and out of the controlled zone – if not we will have to lock it all down – and I don't really want to do that – many people I know having travelled to and from work."

"Can we afford to rest up a while or is it best to surge ahead with the vanguard," Danny asked?

Merlin considered, staring at the map, his attention however drawn again to the big TV screen set in the wall at the far end of the room, the aerial shots by drones or helicopter engrossing him. All over the south chaos was ensuing, Dan cringing as reports flooded in as the Dome had crept ever forward over the plains of Somerset and Dorset, pushing anything it didn't want aside and allowing everything it considered civilian or without threat to pass. It made simple mistakes – pushing tanks along with tractors into dikes and rivers, but the nullifying effect of its protons made sure any military installation buried underground or hidden away had their munitions rendered ineffective. The power fluctuated at times as the curtain passed through the electricity cables, but it came back on presently and nothing benign seemed damaged by the wall's passage.

"The power curtain," Danny asked? "Where's all the energy coming from?"

"Gia," Merlin told him. "The earth goddess herself: She's watched as her life force has been stripped, the forests and countryside denuded and cleared – for what – to let empty buildings rot and blot the landscape? All over the world the human population cares little for the planet they live on – now she is taking back control – now she aids our crusades – and others like it."

"So, things like this are happening all over the world right now?"

Merlin shrugged, holding out his hands. "I know little of the rest of the world but once England has been secured, we can then possibly look at cleaning up Europe, if it needs it."

"A real crusade," the Green Knight effused, "the gods should tremble!"

***

At Okehampton, still in Devon, Sir Reginald Smyth stopped to rest awhile as his squire and knave set about finding his horse or at least purloining or borrowing some other nags in the hope of getting somewhere near the front line – *not too near,* Sir Reginald thought though as he waved off the nice gentleman that had given them a lift this far in his wagon – something he had referred to as a *'truck'* having no intention of getting too near or involved in so much as a skirmish, there being plenty of willing knights, cavalry and infantrymen to take the fight to whoever they were supposed to be engaging with; this knight never one to pick a disagreement that might possibly end in a duel; life in his past existence, too hard and cruel at times to waste it on squabbles and embitterment. He'd look the part when the battle lines were drawn up, he calculated, *by the gods, he might even do a little sabre rattling,* (but actually charge headlong into battle) – *forget it!*

He sat now in his splendid armour upon a wooden seat, already worn out, his weapons scattered about him, cradling Lindsey Cartwright still in her glass tankard, the poor little mouse suffering a little as the sun beat down relentlessly, heating everything up.

Presently, as he dozed in the sun, drops of warm water splattered incoherently onto Sir Reginald's breastplate, the knight opening his eyes to squint skyward, finding small clouds were forming beneath the encapsulating Dome, water vapour collecting at the enclosures' extreme points and then dripping down as a warm rain. Drowsy, unconcerned about going any further – unlike his squire and knave who seemed anxious to get to the front line, he stretched out further, by chance catching a quick snooze.

It wasn't to be, a shrill squeaking down in his lap, told him his little friend – one the driver of the truck commented was a real nice little rodent, alerted him to the fact that water was running off his left pauldron and gorget to rapidly fill his glass, the little mouse in mortal danger of drowning as the water collected.

Fighting for her miserable life, Lindsey coughed and spluttered as a shower quickly drenched her and began to quickly collect about her paws, yelling in no uncertain terms as she tip-toed on her hind legs for her saviour to do something about it!

Blearily, Sir Reginald shifted his weight, sitting up a bit from the slouched position he'd taken, holding the mug up to eye level to find the dear love of his life was swimming about for her life – in immediate danger of drowning. *"By the gods,"* he choked, raising the glass to his lips to savour the warm water! As a bedraggled Lindsey Cartwright slid down to an opening maw, she braced herself to crash into his mouth, sinking her teeth into his upper lip to hang on, desperately struggling to avoid those gnashing teeth, hanging by her incisors as the rest of the water rushed passed trying to push her into oblivion!

Sir Reginald groaned loudly with pain as another warm liquid seeped down the whiskers of his jaw-line, mixing with the wetness of his chin. Lindsey pulled her teeth from the flesh, spitting out blood, then scrambled back down his breastplate to land in his lap, debating whether to bite into his groin or not.

Seething with anguish, the knight dabbed at his face with the back of his hand, cursing the very air, a stout woman who'd been standing at the end of her road wondering what all the calamity was about; frustrated by all the soldiers and equipment that were finally leaving her boundaries. After standing with hands on hips, watching the caravans finally depart she walked over with quite some concern, looking Sir Reginald Smyth over.

"Quite some way from the front lines, aren't you," the dour woman stated, addressing him?

Sighing, Sir Reginald glanced up to find a portly middle-aged woman – wearing a kind of green serge business suit with white blouse beneath – and despite the warm weather, frowning down at him. *"What on earth have you got there,"* she barked, making the knight start?

"It's erm…" the knight sighed again, wondering (not for the first time), whatever he'd done to offend the beautiful young woman he was so desperately trying to rescue. He daubed at the blood seeping from the wound, searching for something to staunch the bleeding.

"Here," the woman offered, holding out a dainty square of cloth.

Sir Reginald half raised, accepting the gift with dignity, bowing at the kindness. He held the pristine napkin to his face, holding his face upward whilst positioning the glass tankard on its side so Lindsey could scamper back inside. Once securely back, he hoisted the glass mug upright, trapping her once more. The woman peered closely, shrinking back a little when the reality sank in. "A mouse," she spluttered, putting both hands to her throat.

"Only in passing," Sir Reginald spoke, his attention being drawn to his squire and knave who'd managed to secure a good war horse – with a couple of sad-looking nags that would have to do under the present circumstances.

"What the hell happened," stammered his squire, noting the injury to his face?

"Domestic," the dour woman inserted, neither aide able to make sense of her input.

"We couldn't find your horse," the squire told his master – "The gods only know where he is, the fields yonder having still hundreds of people and wagons preparing to leave."

Sir Reginald collected himself, making sure the bleeding had stopped before pushing himself to his feet, making sure he had a good hold of the tankard.

"You need a good cage," the woman suggested, Sir Reginald quite forgetting about her as he looked the nags over. He stopped to look down at his captive, then remembering the small woman's graciousness, handed the soiled linen handkerchief back, most apologetically.

"Keep it," the woman advised. "You might need it again, if that little varmint has her way."

In the glass tankard, Lindsey Cartwright hissed with indignation.

"Tell you what, Mr Knight. My friend lives just over there and she keeps hamsters – and I'll bet she has a nice little cage for her, little wheel etc. If you wait a moment, I'll go and see."

Sir Reginald bowed most courteously, holding the glass mug out from his side. "You are too gracious, madam."

"Well, I," gushed the woman, never in her day having been treated so nobly. She practically curtseyed herself as she left, buoyed by the knight's deference.

His squire and knave watched her go, bemused by the conversation, the cad of a knight always one for the ladies, no matter what class or vocation.

Taking his steed by the reigns, Sir Reginald stepped with reverence over to where the woman had disappeared; finding she presently reappeared, holding a small silver cage, the bars shining with newness. The woman approached, holding the cage with the little door open so the knight could tip the mouse straight in.

Sir Reginald did so, making sure she landed as safely as possible, Lindsey Cartwright having not much choice in the matter as she slid uncontrollably down the wet, slippery chute, landing in a heap in the cage, the tin floor covered in sawdust.

The woman righted the cage, slamming the door shut; making the mouse flounder again on her paws, Lindsey finding there was a tiny section of plastic in one corner that offered her sanctuary and a little privacy – even a straw mattress as a bed. She scampered over as Sir Reginald thanked the woman effusively, offering his services should she ever need it.

"It's been a real pleasure meeting you, Sir Knight," the woman praised him, affording him a real gaze of respect and fondness.

Sir Reginald took hold of her hand and kissed it most gallantly, making the poor woman practically swoon; telling her his sword and lance were hers.

His squire guffawed, shaking his head, sighing as he tried to mount his horse.

"Thank you dear lady," Sir Reginald called out, leaving to mount his steed.

"I do hope you return," spoke the stout woman. "The local WI would love to learn of your exploits."

Sir Reginald bowed from the waist as he settled in his saddle, his knave strapping his pendant and lance to his saddle's panels, the war horse looking quite resplendent now it had a knight aboard.

The woman blew a kiss and the knight bowed his head, pulling his horse away. He waved courtly as they trotted off, holding up a gauntleted mitt as they joined a never-ending procession of infantry, cavalry, mule trains and wagons.

"Nice old crone," his knave commented as they took formation.

"Mind your tongue, lad," growled Sir Reginald still dabbing at his swollen lip, the small square of linen blood-soaked, the napkin doused in a most provocative perfume however, Lindsey catching a whiff of it as it wafted down into the cage, the mouse growling with her own discontent.

"Always one for the ladies," his squire muttered, looking the other way.

"What was that?"

***

Back at HQ Danny and a huge welter of his bodyguard of knights had congregated in a bigger downstairs conference room – the manager gleefully opened up the bar – having phoned and chatted cordially to the landlord of The Bell public house in Cornwall beforehand, hearing how courteous and gallant the knights and surrounding infantry, squires and knaves had all been, most – if not all trying to pay their way; the publican letting slip that many a knight was loaded down with a purse full of gold doubloons, or rough shod pieces of eight, one chunk worth a small fortune in today's currency!

The knights did indeed furnish the manager with a collection of various gold coins, many so old he had no idea of their worth but accepted them anyway, deciding he'd throw the lot into a spare section of the till and rush down to the jewellers in the morning to get a valuation. In the meantime, his supply of ale was running out fast and he made reparations by calling up past favours and getting delivered any beer stocks that were available, even sending a girl down to Tesco's with the four by four in order to raid their shelves. So desperate was he, he'd handed over his own credit card with the number – a completely desperate act he'd only dreamed of in a nightmare once, hoping to the sweet god of wine that she'd come back with the wares and not disappear to Spain forever more.

Food as well would have to be thought of as his castle was now catering for dozens in each room – and the foyers – and they all would have to be fed something in their time here. He sent another girl out in order to buy up as many hot pies and the famed Cornish pasties as she possibly could find, in the hope he could provide.

As Danny's surrounding bodyguard supped ale, beer, cider, wine and lager in the air of a lofty afternoon, Dan watched the progress of his armies as they continued to catch him up or surge ahead to take control of key points at the line of the Dome's demarcation; Merlin, Lancelot and Galahad, along with many other fully-fledged knights of the realm continuing to appraise the situation as the throngs of people tramped ever eastwards.

Among the seething crowds – many not bothering with paths or roads – preferring to march in a fairly straight line and stamp over field, dyke and river – through someone's back garden, in the hope of cutting down the time, Dan noticed groups of very unhappy men – one or two at first that didn't seem to be fitting in with the normal subdued look of the newly reincarnated or the happy gaiety of the wagon and mule trains, these individuals and groups of mostly men passing through the cordons unimpeded as they posed as volunteers or willing supporters, but Dan suspected, something was going on. And it came to a head only an hour later when a band of recently formed men managed to stage an ambush of sorts at Mudford using the banks of the Yeo tributary to hem in a unit of infantry that had only passed through that morning, many still dazed or coming round, several having the fabled sore stomach. Three hundred lightly armed men fell furiously onto the sixty or so soldiers, many not understanding what was transpiring until it was too late, the small legion battered remorselessly to death as they tried to form a defence.

Knights, still coming up the line, soon heard about it and rushed to put down the insurrection but they were hopelessly too late, the men having melted back into the countryside – many now disguised as true supporters of the king as they pulled the staffs from dead fingers, robbing dead and dying bodies of their leather garments. Dan's blood boiled along with other knights as the whole ghastly event was portrayed on television not long after its completion; a young woman holed up in a collapsed shack on the other side of the shallow river, filming the whole rotten episode on her iphone – the news feeds fighting over themselves to be the first to air the horrible engagement.

A battalion of knights had soon reached the site but could do little as the stripped bodies began to decompose rapidly, returning to dust, the sixty odd light infantry the first casualties of the takeover.

"Swines," Galahad growled.

A palpable tension settled over the conference room as the wicked scene unfolded yet again on the news feeds, the small detachment of revenants not realising what was happening as – from the bushes and copses of surrounding countryside, hundreds of irate men wielding only hammers and machetes charged headlong at the detachment, one or two assailants finding they fell uncontrollably onto a levelled lance or halberd, although many of the victims stood for too long wondering if it was all a ruse, not realising the men charging down on them were antagonists.

Soon it was a bloodbath, the detachment forced back into the shallows of the stream as they were bludgeoned, punched and kicked into touch, the soldiers still not wanting to inflict serious injury until it was too late.

Dan watched grimly, gripping a glass tankard so tight he worried it might shatter, as staves and lances were torn from unsuspecting hands as the two groups engaged, and were plunged without mercy back into their own stomachs, the unfathomable look of incomprehension evident on many of the defenders faces as they died – many a young boy in the small ranks.

"The gods will have vengeance," one knight in the background voiced, many agreeing menacingly.

The horrible engagement lasted for a full eleven minutes, the incredible brutality clearly shown as mankind wreaked their own vengeance – those loyal to a monarch that had served them for so long. *Diehards,* Lancelot had speculated. "They will have to be weeded out before they grow stronger, otherwise we'll have an insurrection on our tail – and we can ill afford that."

"How do you catch a thread of mist," Merlin spelled out? "These men know the lay of the land, can smuggle their way into our ranks and hide quite comfortably, even our knights not knowing one from another. They will scatter and reform again elsewhere, we must be more vigilant, perhaps segregate mankind from the army – we have no need of help anyway!"

"There are thousands mixed up with our army though," Danny knew, having talked and passed comment with many of his supporters. The streets were lined with them.

"The enemy within," speculated Galahad. "Always non-conformists and heretics," he sighed heavily – as if all his life he had a threat of insurrection to deal with as well. "The only way to stop them is to have spies of our own," he mentioned, Merlin nodding sagely with him "Recruit many of the volunteers and send them out to root out these bastards."

"Intelligence from our own spies is the only way," agreed Merlin, clearly upset at the slaughter.

"That's a real bummer," a circulating young barman spat, a tray full of empty glasses balancing precariously. "To be brought back from the dead – only to die again – that's just not cricket, is it?"

Many a knight stared down at the young lad, deciding if he was genuine or not – many giving him the benefit of the doubt however, trying to put aside what was an awful waste of life.

Dan lapsed into a moment of thoughtful contemplation as reports of other incidents and skirmishes filled the news channels, the mood in the conference room most sombre for a while as the despicable act sank in; the second manoeuvre by the invading army having gone entirely peacefully from his side of things. A moment later he was all for saddling up and calling everyone to arms, but was instructed to rest the horses and await the wagon and mule trains that had to navigate the roads and bridges.

Dan watched the news channels idly, one having followed some knights as they pushed a trolley around Sainsbury's then found themselves stymied by the checkouts, the girls wondering whether to just let them through – then attend to the backlash as other shoppers wondered why they couldn't do the same, or try and ask for some payment or other – a solid gold coin making the checkout girl's eyes pop out, or as in another case reported recently, the shifty cashier, accepting the coin graciously – stripped off her apron and dashed for the nearest porn shop, never to be seen of again!

By six that evening, ad hoc intelligence and networking spies had indeed located a ramshackled old barn at the edge of Ilchester, north east of their central position, with around a hundred men hiding out, more scattered about the land desperately trying to regroup; the revenants quickly surrounding it with pike-men; infantry and archers – a detachment of knights also heading that way. Within the hour the barn was blazing away and as the men inside made a dash for it, the bowmen cut most down by a hail of arrows before they'd even got five feet. One or two managed to dodge the arrows but pike-men ran them through and knights on horseback rode them down.

The bodies were soon thrown back into the inferno of the barn and no more was said about it, the action taking about the same time as the deceased's own dastardly act. It had been so swift and decisive the news teams had not a hope of covering any of it, nothing but a red hot conflagration to stare at when they did arrive.

Stragglers were seized and stripped of their weapons and any armour – then sent packing before the knights caught up with them.

***

Earlier that afternoon Bill Nightingale had sat in his small estate car and considered the state of play. At a miserable four miles per hour he'd crawled to Okehampton, then Copplestone, passing through the heavily fortified checkpoint on the A377, posing as a nobleman and his lady – a sage in fact who had an important mission to keep the people of the land appraised of Arthur's movements. Luckily no one thought to ask where he'd learnt to drive – and he passed through unimpeded, trundling as far as Bickleigh before the roads became so clogged it was impossible to drive any further. He'd reversed into the entrance of a field, deciding to abandon the vehicle to its fate, leaving his press card on the dashboard.

With his laptop and other paraphernalia, Bill climbed out to go help Fay out of her seat.

With her hair rinsed through again in another shower of soap suds and experimentation, she looked absolutely resplendent with her clothes washed too (as quickly as possible as it happened), put on practically wet, the hot air drying her out as the car wended its way across the counties.

Her hemp-tied and threadbare skirt was damp where she'd been sitting on it, Fay pulling the shorts he'd found and which fitted her nicely, out of her crotch, the dampness making her smile coquettishly, reminiscent of the lovemaking that morning.

"You'll dry out quickly in this heat," Bill advised her, locking up the car. He'd managed to roll a little into the field, able to leave the entrance unblocked – and to one side, the crop trodden so flat it was hard to work out what was supposed to be growing in it.

He checked his bearings, knowing he was only a few miles from Tiverton where Danny King and the heart of his army had billeted, leaving time for the rest of the wagon and mule trains to catch up, the land around seething with troops of all kind, wondering just how far the power curtain had extended. Reports from Lynton and Minehead suggested another portal of some kind had been initiated by Merlin, encouraging yet more legions of the dead to creep through, swelling his army even more. Bill would have liked to get as close to that portal as possible and see if there was any two-way traffic, but his mind was on Arthur himself and how he would play the complete takeover.

"We've got to walk the rest of the way, honey," he cooed, hoping her legs were ok.

Fay nodded encouragingly however, full of the joys of spring. She spun in a small circle, allowing the air to dry her out, then, smiling lightly, rushed to kiss him tenderly.

Bill glanced around nervously.

"Roll in the hay stack," she asked coyly?

"Later dear," Bill condescended, wondering if he'd opened the floodgates and somehow awakened her libido. "I have work to do today, Baby; we have to catch up with Arthur and get the next low-down so I can report back to my paper."

"Low-down..." Fay asked questioningly? "What paper?"

Bill consulted a compass, checking it against a small by-ways signpost, encouraging her along, then setting off, heading for Tiverton.

"I work for a regional newspaper," he explained as they walked, rubbing shoulders with all manner of troops and other people, "that's who pays the bills."

"Bills," Fay questioned?

"Hm," Bill hummed. "Something that may be amended in the future hopefully."

Fay skipped along beside him, enjoying the hot dry air, happy to meet and greet everyone. A phone call alerted Bill to the sickening attack on a small platoon of infantry that had only recently passed through the new portal on Exmoor, and were quickly heading for Taunton, when they were attacked by around three hundred Royalists, the ambush unprovoked and thoughtless in the fact that they had unwittingly given the opposing forces the upper hand as it was the first engagement – and had drawn first blood – and unluckily for them, having been caught red-handed on camera were deemed the aggressors.

Bill wasn't totally surprised, having noticed dissention and anger from a lot of farmers and landowners, the mansions and castles mostly overlooked as they had no real value – and no company of men to back up the huge defences needed, most of the staff having hightailed it out of servitude just as fast as their little legs could carry them – the chance for some real adventure just too exciting to pass up.

Now, thousands of willing volunteers were clouding the issue as spies on both sides tried to undermine each other's position. One thing remained clear however, no matter how big or ugly a mobster could be – or even how mob-handed, no one short of him was ever getting near the king, the last attempt by ten heavily-built farm workers ending in ribaldry as they were carried and then dumped head first into the nearest river.

Bill had heard already of how ordered the defence of The King had become, knights lining the walkways and entrances and even surrounding this latest encampment by accommodating all the land around the castle, searching for underground passages that may lead directly inside.

With his big satchel over his shoulder, Bill and Fay trudged on, holding hands mostly until Bill was handed a hastily cooked chicken leg and something that resembled a rice cake, although it was actually ground corn mixed with egg and milk and then fried briefly, the article reeking in the hot atmosphere. Bill handed Fay the food but even she – after sniffing both, tossed them in the hedgerow whilst no one was looking.

***

News that the large detachment of dissidents had been caught reached Danny's ear around seven that evening, no one he noticed, overtly happy with the outcome; the scenario just one more incident in the search for justice. A central table had been cleared and he, Merlin, Galahad and Lancelot sat around it with many others, contemplating the lay of the land and the exits and entrances being guarded by dozens of loyal troops who'd managed to make it across county, the land now securely in the hands of the invaders. Civic bodies were moving to try and parley with Arthur but he'd heard it all before as he took over Cornwall, surmising it would all be much of the same, so denied them access, telling the various councils and police bodies he would address them all in good time, give some kind of press conference; although Merlin – and others, advised him against it; worried not all munitions had been neutralised and one lucky shot from a firearm would end it all. Dan assumed he was impervious to any bullet or arrow but his contemporaries were not so sure – and certainly didn't want to test fate. He looked for the reporter who'd so cleverly gained access to his very bedchamber the other day, the wily journalist having dressed up in traditional garb and managed by hook and by crook to wheedle his way in, Arthur quite struck by his candour. He'd give the reporter his undivided attention – if he could ever find him in all this confusion.

He was gaining a lot of attention now, he realised as notes on pieces of paper continued to be brought to his notice, having cut the main arterial motorway in half just short of Bristol. Luckily it was still in operation for a while as people about turned and made their way back home, many no doubt glad of the interruption to the daily grind. He accepted yet another pint of ale, cringing at the welter of beer he was consuming, already missing his usual routine. Right now he'd been squeezing out the reps in the small gym the sports centre had in the basement, the half five to six thirty evening period a wonderfully quiet slot where he could immerse himself in the almost hypnotic trance his training brought about, throwing himself into the exercises like a demon. He reminisced in his brief history, having first decided he wanted to pursue a healthy lifestyle, not knowing the first thing about weight training, falling into all the usual pitfalls, torn and wrecked muscle groups, aching solar plexus and ruined thighs, the pounds spent on protein powders and vitamin pills, the tuna, eggs and steak diet. He smiled with recall, being a gangly sixteen year old, unsure of himself, totally green. Now he was on the way to becoming the future King of England for crying out loud – it couldn't get much more fantastical if it tried.

"Missing Ma and Pa," Lancelot mentioned aside, noting his vacancy?

Dan breathed in a sigh, nodding, worrying more about his parents at that moment than missing them, concerned there would be repercussions for him becoming king, knowing his own life would never be the same again, questioning – despite the galvanising power of the life force of Gia – or whatever the force was surging through him, if he was really cut out to be a monarch, suddenly having to make all those mind-boggling decisions, front social engagements and attend all those boring balls and soirée's, people bowing and scraping. He shook his head, he was sure he'd never last, it was something you had to be born to, accept as a way of life.

"We can only man an exit and entrance at the moment," Merlin was instructing an aide, sending him out to give something to the awaiting press, camped almost a mile away in a village called Cotterlands where they were allowed all the luxury of *'Glamping'* , *"whatever that was,"* the old wizard muttered.

Dan had smiled despite his nostalgic and unsettling musings, imagining the local press billeted in the wooden sheds; the constructions being one dubious step up from camping. He'd stayed in one in Wiltshire with a girlfriend once and hated every minute of it, the wooden structure not much better than a shed in his estimation as wind funnelled through gaps in the doorway and rain found its way through the curved roof. Six hundred quid to sleep on a bed that felt like it had no mattress at all, the fittings as basic as you could get – getting back to nature the brochure boasted. Well, Dan fancied he could have stayed in a hotel for less and simply spent his time walking out in the daytime.

Yet another rip-off he'd had to suffer simply because his daft partner could not see past the misty call of the wild.

He barked out a laugh making everyone look up, forgetting completely where he was for a moment, the memory of trying to get out of bed the following morning after their first night *'glamping,'* finding they were as stiff as the board of a bed they'd had to sleep on.

He shook the memory from his mind and looked across to Merlin as if for the first time, noting the face framed by the silky white ringlets of hair; overwrought with worry lines and deep concern, the archetypal guise of a wizard or warlock, his emblazoned hat pushed back off his head so the brim made it look a bit like a cowboy hat at a rakish angle. What adventures, strange times and mystic avenues Merlin's feet had trod, what curses and spells had those old deeply tanned and bony hands of his wrought, how much magic and fantasy was wrapped up in that supernatural persona?

Dan smiled at him warmly across the table, nearly always getting a good vibe off him, making others around him know he'd not only been studying him openly but admiring and wondering at the same time.

Lancelot put a comforting hand to Dan's shoulder again, feeling the years of hard slog in the massive deltoid, the muscle built upon muscle – then his eye caught a news clip on the big television screen behind them and alerted him to the unfolding story, his concern as he let go to straighten up, making Dan spin around in his chair.

Merlin sat up as a silence fell over the crowded conference room, other knights beginning to crowd in through the open doorway. At various points from Blandford Forum to Bristol – all along the dome's line scaffolding was being erected, the construction then threaded through with telegraph poles or hewn trees, an accelerant of some kind then tipped over the lot.

"What's that liquid," Galahad asked suspiciously?

"Probably diesel fuel robbed from tanks across the county," Dan elucidated for all to hear, "burns fiercely once alight."

"What's the point of burning down your own defences," someone asked innocently?

"They're hoping the Dome might possibly baulk at the firestorm," Dan speculated, watching as firemen, police, army cadets and willing volunteers – those loyal perhaps to their Queen, or simply misguided, or still under the duress and orders of the civic bodies helped others to build a spirited defence.

Merlin guffawed into his wine, shaking his head over the antics, no doubt having faith in the Dome's power. Dan noticed the scaffolding only went so far then left a gap – a big central one where, no doubt his army would be funnelled through – if they were daft enough, a hail of crossbow bolts awaiting the unlucky first wave. Danny watched the construction, the phalanxes of tubing stretching a kilometre or more in some cases having to bridge a stream, dyke or electrical substation.

Hmm, Danny thought turning back to the table, the highly lacquered wood-grained top littered with platters of food; jugs of ale; bottles of wine. He was no tactician; could remember nothing of his time in the army cadets, nothing at least that suggested an outcome of two huge opposing forces. He gazed at the welter of plates, bottles, glasses and jugs crowding the table, and the interstices, wondering how he was going to get over this next hurdle – *unless Merlin had something up his sleeve.*

"They're making it awkward for us, I give 'em that," Lancelot half-chortled!

"Could cause problems though," Danny mused, staring at the table, hoping the gaps of polished wood between all the implements would give him some idea.

"Fear not, Arthur," Merlin spoke, having waved off yet more requests for The King to show himself. "I have a plan!"

***

Bill Nightingale also had a plan – and it was working splendidly until he finally reached Tiverton, road-weary and a little jaded, the heat, tramping and jostling – not to mention being goosed up the backside once by a young boy (a human boy at that carrying a stolen harpoon to utilise as a spear, his enthusiasm showing no bounds as he clumped along in a pair of rigger boots five sizes too big for him, and a toy plastic Roman helmet that was also so big it fell all over his face blinding him half the time). Bill took the harpoon from him, before he impaled someone else, swapping it with a rather good penknife he had in his bag, throwing the bolt into someone's front garden as soon as the opportunity arose.

Fay revelled in the day out, mixing with other ladies and squires alike, chasing after lost and dazed children, and stroking the regal war horses as knights tried to make headway. But around the castle it was almost log jammed, people anxious to see or even glimpse The King, whilst a small army of knights kept everyone at bay, the phalanx of armour and muscle having doubled since his last attempt. Practically dragging Fay, Bill endeavoured to circle the castle – hoping to find a chink in the steel ring.

Around the back of the castle, spread out before them like a tapestry of colourful squares and oblongs was a wonderful ornate garden dipping away gracefully, along with refreshing waterways threading through it and bench seating dotted about. Despite the upheaval, old-age pensioners were crowding the seats, Bill and Fay having to wend through the gardens quite a way – getting ever further from the target, the reporter now resigned to just sit for a while and try and come up with some sort of plan – something a little more dramatic than the last, because all around the massive establishment, roads and small footpaths that snaked down into the bowels of the stonework, were completely and heavily guarded, some so choked up with knights of all denominations and rank, it was impossible to even slide passed, not a rat was getting through without being questioned. Bill had made inroads but as soon as he mentioned *'Press'* he was directed or told to make his way to Cotterlands where all the journalists and sound guys were awaiting updates – a small camping and caravan park accommodating the hundreds of vans; camera men and reporters. The King was taking no chances, Bill Nightingale mused, dissention and a clumsy assassination attempt already having shown their faces – although thousands of willing supporters – many tagging along as if on some kind of adventure holiday whilst the county was held in suspension, swelled the ranks of his army. It was as if the whole nation as one was following on, the readiness of refreshments; food and shelter being happily given and received. Many brought their own tent and supplies he'd noticed, crowding the fields and lanes; others simply joining the throng as if satisfying a long lost cause to join the circus; Bill shaking his head as he eventually found a seat, the small walled arbour seconded by a knight and his squire and knave already. Bill threw himself down and bent forward to put his head in his hands for a moment, wondering how in the hell he was going to get anywhere near the king ever again, despite the

Adonis assuring him he'd give him another interview. He could see the king's dilemma, but it didn't help him.

As Fay danced about the flower beds, enjoying herself immensely, Bill blew out a sigh, sitting up a little and letting his hands fall to his sides… then realised several people were eyeing him speculatively, the sort of unwavering attention one might give a hunted animal. Having noticed the somewhat hostile stares, Bill sat upright a bit more, straightening his back, wondering if the knight sprawled out on the other end of the bench perhaps needed his space.

There was plenty of space however, and it wasn't until a squire moved forward toward him, that Bill, looking down at his hands that he had put by his side, feeling some rough silks and fabrics, found – when he glanced, he was sitting on some kind of big pendant, the thing draped over the seat possibly to dry out from the small shower of warm water that fell that afternoon.

Bill stood quickly as the squire moved to check there'd been no damage, then gazing at it himself to find the symbol of the Pendragon staring back at him, the rich gold and azure, mixed with the vibrant red and silver of the crest mesmerising him for a second.

Bill's eyes slid over to the knight, who was still sprawled out on the bench, his concern for the magnificent pendant only in passing it seemed, as the squire brushed the fabric and silks to buff them up again, lifting the beautiful sigil to carry it over to where there were other empty benches.

"I can sit over there," Bill mentioned, alarmed he'd made the knight's squire move it.

"No matter," the squire mentioned, Bill's costume and the fact that he had a real revenant of a woman at his side making the squire and knave think he was one of them.

Fay bustled into the opening, making the knight open one eye as she giggled and presented Bill with a small posy.

Bill thanked her with staid embarrassment, wondering what to do with it.

Fully awake now, all senses on alert as a buxom female had drifted into his orbit; the knight collected himself somewhat, drawing himself up to his full height as he arranged himself, his sojourn in the sun having rested him sufficiently.

From a sitting position, he bowed curtly, sweeping a hand out in a graceful arc, nearly upsetting a cage he had set on his lap. The cage lurched and the knave nearly jumped out of his seat as Sir Reginald caught hold of it, stopping it from tumbling to the floor.

Intrigued, Fay took a closer look, taken aback that a fully-fledged Knight of the Realm would be caring for a small rodent, the thing hissing and squeaking in dire contempt as it peeped out from its cubby hole.

The knight tried to cover the cage his with his hands, pretending it wasn't there, but Fay was compelled and stepped forward despite the deference that should have been shown to a knight.

"Why sir, do you care for a small rodent," she asked so coyly and sweetly, Sir Reginald was quite taken by her. Meanwhile Bill had fallen back into the bench seat, content to watch his career slide into the doldrums, the one fantastical interview being the one and only. Out of the corner of his eye he kept a watch on Fay as her innocence led her astray.

Stretching his legs the squire rose from his seat again, having enjoyed a repast of cheese, what looked like some ham or other, and a good bottle of wine, the knight too having partaken of the spoils, Bill noticed, watching all with a modicum of unrest. The squire sauntered over as the knight, now squirming under the glare of a beautiful woman, found himself stuck for something to say.

"The knight likes his food fresh," the knave barked from his seat opposite, giggling raucously; the young lad a tad tipsy from the wine.

Sir Reginald glared at him but said nothing, moving the cage nonchalantly to place it at his side on the seat, hiding it almost by his armour plating.

"It's a rather especial mouse," his squire dared to tell the woman, enjoying his master's discomfort.

"Oh," gushed Fay, enjoying the attention, "how so?"

"It's black and white," growled Sir Reginald, hoping his gruff manner would put the conversation to bed.

"There's nothing unusual about that," spoke Fay most confidently, "we had a whole horde of them in our larder once."

Not wanting to especially make eye contact with anyone, Bill glanced to the knight with a sideways look, finding the knight stretched out must be well over six feet, cautious to a point of being obdurate and totally unprepared to talk about his little pet to anyone. He wished Fay would drop the inquisition and leave the poor bloke alone. "Fay," he called softly but was largely ignored as the squire blurted out the details.

"The mouse is Merlin's work," he elucidated for all to hear, an old lady sauntering through the shaded area, stopping to squeak a hello! From his sitting position the knight bowed regally, making the old lady titter, Bill smiling at the deference despite the revenant being heads and shoulders taller than anyone around – and armoured to the teeth.

"Merlin's work," Fay had asked quizzically, frowning at the squire in a most pretty way, enamouring both the knight and the knave who was listening on with a drunken ear?

"Hm," coughed the squire. "She upset him apparently and that's the result, scratching and nibbling your backside."

"Enough," growled the knight, narrowing his eyes; Bill nervously shifting his weight on the bench seat up from him.

"Calm down for heaven's sake, Reginald," issued the squire. "They might be able to help – you don't know?"

The knight drew in a breath that to Bill sounded imminently dangerous; wishing both of them would just leave the poor guy alone.

"My man," Fay, instructed the knight, turning to present Bill with outstretched arms, "important, make words for paper. Clever; he write story about mouse." She turned back with hands in a shrug, making the knight stare at her blankly, whilst Bill, the squire – and definitely the knave tried to catch up. Then Bill realised something.

He rose from his seat carefully and walked even more cautiously toward the pendant now draped over the bench seat the squire and knave had commandeered, squinting down at the sigil once more.

He turned back to the knight, taking in his dazzling tabard emblazoned with the same motif.

"You're a Knight of the Realm, no less," he half asked?

"I am," Sir Reginald uttered, wondering what the reporter had up his sleeve.

Bill walked back thoughtfully, a plan of sorts forming.

"I was supposed to give The King another interview today – asked especially by him, but I can't get near the castle, never mind enter it – but with your banner – and joining forces, we could perhaps gain an audience – and you could talk to Merlin whilst I attend The King?"

Sir Reginald eyed him speculatively, his eyes glazing over quickly as the simplicity of the idea sunk in. He could have indeed marched right up to the castle and gained an audience with someone – if he so wished – feigning some excuse or other, but had no real desire to waste The King's time, or present Lindsey to anyone but Merlin, hoping to catch him in a good mood – but he had no idea what he was going to say, *please sir, could you restore Lindsey to her former self so I can ask for her hand in marriage, or failing that return her to her former life – although first, I think I might just put her over my knee and spank the hell out of her!*

He had to do something however, carrying her around like this was getting embarrassing to say the least – if she was whole again at least he could befriend her, perhaps woo her, but if not, then letting her go would also be the honourable thing to do. He chewed the idea over again in his mind, deciding then he had to try something – at least sign his allegiance to Arthur, which he hadn't been able to do yet.

"The plan has credence," the big knight rumbled, definitely thinking about it, sitting up that little bit straighter.

"It's a good plan," endorsed the squire. "You can borrow our small pendant and carry it as Reginald's squire – and nobody will know any different."

"Thank you," Bill gushed, meaning it. He glanced down at the time, finding it was a quarter past six in the afternoon, the heat with the encompassing dome not relenting – even in the latter part of the day.

He straightened, murmuring the time to himself, then realised everyone was looking at him.

"What..?"

The knight leaned forward onto his knees, eyeing him speculatively. "You're from this time," he asked?

"I – erm," Bill cleared his throat. "I know I've pulled a few strings," he stammered, "but I mean well – well, I don't mean any harm, if you know what I mean – just need to tell Arthur's story – complete it if necessary."

"He's been very kind," blurted out Fay in his defence.

"It matter's little," uttered the knight, brushing the concern aside.

The squire had moved to examine Bill's chronograph, having espied the bright timepiece on his wrist, completely dumbfounded by it. "That small thing tells the time," he asked, inferring the obvious?

"It does," Bill instructed him, showing him the watch.

The squire gazed at it as if it was one of Merlin's creations, only better, peering closer as he caught the second hand sweep by.

"A marvel," he breathed, hypnotised by it.

"If I get this second interview, I'll buy you all one," Bill announced, thinking to push it further up his arm.

"Keep it hidden," the squire warned. "Arthur is worried over assassination attempts."

Bill nodded knowingly. "I've heard," he mentioned. "Not everybody is happy with the state of affairs."

With a deep sigh of resignation Sir Reginald Smyth pushed himself to his feet with the air of a man who'd rather be anywhere than where he was right now, glancing around at the strange land and ornate gardens with a desultory glare as he straightened, arching his back as he did so, stretching to his full height, which to Bill Nightingale standing under him seemed very impressive indeed, with his armour bulking him out and his weaponry dangling from his huge leather belt like a trumpery of collected toys, the huge broadsword that he continually adjusted, nearly four feet in length.

"That's some weapon," Bill mentioned with tempered awe!

The knight nodded with conviction, pulling the scabbard round to wrench the sword by the immense hilt, one handed, showing off the incredibly wide blade, the sort of implement that would sever armoured arm from body if it connected.

"Brave knight," Fay muttered in awe of him!

The squire coughed, turning away, collecting up his things. The knight watched him go, narrowing his eyes again, sliding his mighty sword into its scabbard once more with an audible clunk. The action made the warrior look down at himself and twist his mouth in an obvious dilemma, his armour dusty and in need of a good polish. He glanced around but with his knave half-cut and his squire in a decidedly off-hand brash mood, there was nothing for it, he had to go as he was – and hang the consequences.

Bill picked up on the quandary. "You've been on the road sometime," he explained in the knight's defence. "Battle-ready; what do they expect?"

Sir Reginald nodded, then seemed to look at Bill in a slightly different light, nodding sagely. He turned to pick the cage up wondering then what he was going to do with it, the knave usually carrying it but he was a little untrustworthy at that moment in his inebriated state and his squire was burdened down with his war helmet, and other paraphernalia, so after a moment he turned to Fay.

"Would you like to ride, mam," he asked demurely?

Fay, who'd been examining some old ladies' jewellery, suddenly perked up, turning away and skipping back to him pertly.

"Your horse..." she asked?

The knight nodded, knowing it was only a short walk back to the castle. He held out a hand courteously, helping her up and into the ornate saddle, the stirrups way down low, but at only a walk it didn't matter.

"Would you mind," he asked, handing the cage carefully up to the woman?

"Not at all," and Fay, looking like the cat who'd got the cream, sat primly, looking about regally.

Bill collected up his bag and followed on, the squire leading a somewhat deflated knave to his horse, following the knight's stallion presently. With Fay up on top of the horse and the squire and knave tagging along behind with their nags, Bill, having felt he'd gained some discourse with the big knight, decided he'd try and pick his brains for a moment as they threaded their way through the throng towards the rear of the huge castle.

"You've made quite some sacrifice, leaving your lovely homeland for this engagement," Bill parodied?

The knight seemed to be concentrating on putting one armoured foot in front of the other as his big war charger made way, the articulated plates of his sabatons clanking on the tarmac.

"The call went up – and I answered," he coughed with a short sigh, batting aside a pretty butterfly.

Behind them, the knave dropped the big pendant from his horse, the staff and metal truck atop clanging as the pole bounced woodenly. With an inward sigh, Sir Reginald stopped, glancing skyward; not looking back just issuing an order. "Get that boy drunk again, esquire Trent – and I'll have no recourse but to dock your pay."

"What pay," asked the truculent squire as he hastily dismounted to go pick up the big pendant and brushed it clean once again, deciding then to carry everything himself?

Sir Reginald shook his head and continued, making sure his charge was still where he'd put her.

"Can't get the staff, eh…" Bill joked, then realised his diction wasn't quite devolved to base level yet.

"My apologies," he mumbled, forgetting himself.

"I understand," grated the knight – "no, you're right – trying to lead a peaceful life is not always in the keeping of some people."

"You were a peacekeeper in your former time," speculated Bill, trying to fathom what life was like in the centuries gone by?

"Peace-keeper – no not especially – just trying to get through life without too much ado – if you understand."

"I think I do," Bill rejoined with a certain empathy. "Was life as brutal as we've been led to believe?"

The big knight sighed heartily. "Brutal – yes, but idyllic as well. The air clear and bright, even the winter days full of sparkle and wonder. I yearn for my homestead, and my comfortable fireside."

"Where was it," Bill asked?

On top of the horse, Fay tutted at his inquisition.

"Somers-met;" the knight answered gaily, lost in some reminiscence.

"Somerset," Bill chirped, "We are very near, in fact I do believe The Dome has clipped parts of the county. Perhaps you'll recognise the area?"

"Hm," cogitated the knight, the phalanx of King Arthur's bodyguard nearing. "Let's hope the confrontation doesn't take place in my green land, eh?"

"No," Bill spluttered, eager to put the knight's mind at ease, "I suspect the main thrust of the movement will be nearer London where the seat of power is held, bypassing most of the southern counties."

Sir Reginald Smyth nodded agreeably, stopping to take stock.

"We'll set camp here," he called, leading his horse to an indentation in the rose beds where a bench seat had been vacated by pensioners. Being let loose, the horse immediately went to inspect the flowers, chomping into one of them to see if it was edible.

A moment later the squire and now flagging knave halted. The war horse spat the chewed up rose out, deciding the green grass a few yards away would have to do.

Before he could get too carried away, the knight kindly helped Fay down, bowing graciously as he held her hand.

Bill watched on with a smile, understanding the valour and chivalry of the Knights of the Round Table, each with his own code of honour.

Sir Reginald stripped off his weaponry, sliding the massive broadsword in between the slats of the wooden bench seating, then removing a mace that looked as dangerous as anything could be, also unbuckling another leather sheath that held various knives and other stabbing implements.

By the time he was finished, he must have weighed half as much, Bill wondered, the bench littered with all sorts of archaic armoury.

His squire made an inventory as he perched the knave on one end of the bench, Fay fussing over the young boy as if her own, Bill content to leave them whilst he and Sir Reginald tried to gain access to the king.

"Be back in a while," Bill told Fay, fearing he'd lost some of her ardour to the knight and his company, siding with her for a moment. She caught hold of him and kissed him forcefully, taking him by surprise, the big knight smiling despite his favour for the woman. Bill pecked her on the cheek quickly and made to leave, joining with the tall knight.

"Guard the horses with your lives," Sir Reginald instructed his servants, the squire muttering an acknowledgement under his breath.

Bill followed on, stepping with the knight, his small charge still in her little cage. Bill wondered what sort of mood Arthur would be in – and Merlin, the two hand in hand with the development and progress of the war machine.

At the castle's boundaries Sir Reginald walked confidently through the crowding phalanx, huge pendants and flags indicating the houses and legions that made up England's military might in the fifth and sixth centuries; the colourful Pendragon motif becoming more common as they made their way forward; the tall knight making way like a scythe through thick grass, the cordon of men not batting an eyelid until they reached a main door. The big heavy door of the archway was open but guarded by knights, so heavily armed a side of beef could heave been filleted and diced up in milliseconds.

As they were allowed right to the doorway, Bill crossed his fingers and toes and tried to look as bored as any squire would be, just acting out the commands. Knights gathered around, one or two recognising Sir Reginald and acknowledging him with a cheery hello or official grunt, the big knight then having to explain the mouse in the cage – the whole escapade a little delicate as Merlin was obviously in something of a bad and dazed mood at the time – Sir Reginald hoping he might well have mellowed by now and would perhaps think better of his judgement. He had to register as well, he explained so wanted to get the whole thing done while he had the chance. One big knight bent to gaze into the cage, frankly fascinated by the story, Sir Reginald obviously embarrassed by the incident himself, somehow finding himself somewhat responsible. Bill stuck close, holding the small pendant of Pendragon, the crude wooden pole worn smooth but it still gave him splinters as he tried to manhandle it with what looked like nonchalance.

Bill and Sir Reginald were shown through the castle to where Arthur and Merlin and a host of closer, more trustworthy knights and squires kept a vigil, cramming into the conference room in the bowels of the building to keep abreast of current events.

Sir Reginald made his way straight to the table Arthur and Merlin were sitting at, many recognising him and welcoming him, his height and bearing making him a formidable-looking knight despite his peaceful intentions. Bill was brought up sharp as his mentor sunk sharply to one knee in front of the table Arthur was sitting at, taking off one of his armoured gauntlets and holding it aloft, Bill noticing even the back of the metalled glove had a Pendragon design in metal emblazoned across it. "My sword – my liege – my life is yours, Arthur," he called out regally.

Impressed, Arthur had stood, then walked around the table, the phalanx of muscle and armour jostling aside, allowing him to acknowledge the knight formally. Arthur put a hand to his shoulder, telling him to rise; Sir Reginald accepting his honour.

Whilst he'd been on one knee, Arthur caught sight of Bill behind; this time disguised as a squire to the big knight, half-acknowledging him as well, indicating with his hand he'd talk in private in a minute.

That moment came quite quickly as Sir Reginald was accepted into the family, many making way as they led him to the bar, the big knight stopping at Merlin's place to confront him.

"Sir," Sir Reginald started, as apologetically as he could. "I know you are extremely busy, but please, could you restore Lindsey Cartwright to her former person, as I fear my ministration may be woefully inadequate for such a small rodent."

"I can make her into a bigger one, if you would like," Merlin half-jibed to him.

"Erm, well, thank you Dark Lord, but really – she knows she did wrong, and I feel she has learnt her lesson – and, well, if you please, she isn't a bad lass really."

Merlin sighed inwardly, considering Lindsey Cartwright's travelling quarters, then the big knight holding the cage so reverently, the gallant knight with the Pendragon insignia worthy perhaps of his condescension. He nodded and rose slowly, deciding they better find somewhere a little less crowded as she would find herself naked and perchance the unwanted attention of several desperate men. While Merlin led the knight to his quarters, Arthur grabbed Bill and took him to his, intending to put the record straight about the attack and subsequent reprisal that afternoon.

Chapter 7

Merlin marched into his accommodation and, like a business man preparing for a relaxing evening after a summit, looked around for a bottle of wine to sink into. He found one in a hidden cupboard, pulling open a door beneath a huge oval depression that was the television; the hidden space in the wall holding a drinks cabinet the size of a double fridge, the wily old sage having a nose for hidden treasure – of any kind. He selected a rather expensive burgundy and set about de-corking it before even thinking about anything else. Sir Reginald Smyth glanced around at the opulence and reminisced – having spent the previous night camped on a pub floor, the establishment so crowded he barely had enough room to spread out his legs: the big room he was now in able to sleep thirty or more knights comfortably, never mind the other rooms leading off. He placed Lindsey carefully on a deeply polished sideboard and was about to throw himself into a real comfortable-looking armchair when Merlin approached, wanting the cork ripped out from the bottle he was holding, the corkscrew already buried and unyielding.

Smyth took the bottle, examined the label and construction then – putting the bottle between his legs, gave the corkscrew one almighty tug – the cork exiting with a loud '*pop*'. The tall knight regained his balance and raised the bottle neck to his nose to smell the bouquet, as Merlin fussed about finding some glasses.

"Hm," Sir Reginald hummed, agreeing with the aroma heartily. Merlin brought two fine glassware flutes over and, handing the big knight one, proffered the other for him to fill, Sir Reginald complying readily. He tipped a little into his own glass – just to taste it, but Merlin tut-tutted him, so he filled it up, supping the wine as the two of them stood there admiring the grandeur of their surroundings.

Over on the sideboard, Lindsey Cartwright squeaked her disapproval, having awoken and scratched about her cage for some water. It brought Merlin's mind back to the task in hand and he glanced over with a mixture of rancour and contempt, ameliorated however by a little exoneration, the inward sigh as he sipped the hundred pound bottle of wine, mellowing him somewhat.

"The advance going according to plan," Sir Reginald thought to ask?

Merlin nodded, taking off his wizard's hat to look around then for somewhere to toss it down, rubbing his forehead testily as the day's events settled around his shoulders. "Some resistance was foreseen but I think we have the advantage. My army is almost complete but if I need more I can summon dark forces if necessary. We'll win – one way or the other."

"Can we go home then," asked the knight wistfully?

Merlin nearly choked on his wine, coughing as some of it went down the wrong way. He spluttered, wiping his chin on the sleeve of his voluminous smock and looked up at the weathered knight, shaking his head sorrowfully. "We've been dead thousands of years, Sir Knight," Merlin instructed him. "Brought back only for this especial time: Once completed we will once again disappear into the dust."

Sir Reginald contemplated this, frowning heavily. "But I was alive," he stammered, not wanting to believe all this was for nothing.

"It was an illusion," Merlin stated.

The tall knight considered this. "It didn't feel like an illusion."

Merlin sighed, sipping his wine liberally. He held the glass up, contemplating the dark liquid within, completely bowled over by the sumptuous taste, the wine like the finest port and softest fruit juice he ever enjoyed. "It was worth it," he essayed, "even just to taste these wonderful beverages." He sipped again, proffered the glass for another refill, then whilst Sir Reginald complied, told him they were memories, just memories, transient whispers in the wind.

The knight considered this.

"We're not going home," he repeated sadly, having gulped a big mouthful of the superlative wine?

Merlin glanced up at him speculatively, wondering at the warrior's gestalt, this knight not so concerned with the here and now as the future – as if they had any.

"Do not be disappointed my fine warrior, there's a place in the warrior's temple for you, I'm sure, along with all the Knights of the Round Table."

Sir Reginald took another sip of the thick burgundy, sighing deeply. "I'd swap it all for another day in my home, watching the fire die down, being waited on hand and foot by a beautiful wench. What more can a man hope for?"

"Fair comment," Merlin agreed, taking the bottle from the tall knight to empty it into his own glass, discarding the bottle as if it were worthless over into a chair. He threw back the last of the wine and immediately went to look for another one.

"Erm…" tried Sir Reginald.

He followed Merlin over to the drink's cabinet, the huge opening displaying bottles of all manner, racks of glasses and tiers of smaller bottles that looked only big enough for one mouthful, the knight completely forgetting about Lindsey as he peered into an Aladdin's cave of escapism.

"What's that pink one," he asked as their eyes roved over the glittering array?

Merlin shook his head, reaching for another bottle, this one a ruby port of some distinction, the bottle radiating with pomp and grandeur. "Let's try this," he insisted, while Sir Reginald reached for the pink gin to peruse the gaudy silvery label and square bottle?

"Looks like water," Sir Reginald posed, twisting his mouth in a question mark.

"Do the honours, dear boy," Merlin asked, falling into a chair nearby while Lindsey Cartwright did somersaults and hissed and threw herself at the bars in agitation.

Completely taken by the cornucopia of drink on offer, Sir Reginald threw off his gauntlets and sat down opposite Merlin, admiring the chessboard inlaid in the table top before them, Merlin finding the pieces in a drawer beneath. The knight pulled the cork for Merlin, then, having inspected the gin bottle enough, twisted off the top and took a big slug straight from the bottle, finding the liquid was anything but water.

"Mercy…" Sir Reginald coughed, holding the bottle from him! He glanced at it again, while Merlin scrutinised it from the other seat.

"It's gin," he laughed, asking for a taster before he filled his glass (a bigger one he'd found in the cabinet) with wine.

"Definitely gin," coughed Merlin a moment later. He rifled through the chess pieces and sorted through the back line, placing the castles and bishops in the right places, filling the front lines with the pawns.

Sir Reginald supped some more – straight from the bottle again, letting the firewater slip down into his stomach, the warming sensation thrilling him. "By the God's," he wheezed, drawing in a conjectural breath!

In her cage Lindsey Cartwright seethed, watching as the both of them chatted amiably and sank into a drinking game, whilst she died of thirst. She wanted to throw something but nothing would fit through the bars – and she had very little save a tiny bowl into which she suspected food was supposed to be put. She waddled over to it and, after turning it over in her paws, was able to pick it up to drag it over to the front of the cage.

"I had a dog, geese, cattle, sheep – you name it – a complete homestead," Sir Reginald was telling Merlin, lost for a moment in pure reminiscence.

"Pawn takes knight," Merlin espoused, smiling broadly as he reached for his grog.

"What," Sir Reginald, stared at the tabletop, dumbfounded? He did a rough calculation and brought out his second knight to advance the attack.

***

"Give us the room, please," Arthur asked of one or two knights who were engrossed in the TV or having a bath or shower and were still milling about his apartment, all experimenting with the toiletries and shower gels; the rooms littered with armour of all kinds. One – completely devoid of his clothes and protective suit, wearing nothing but a shower cap, was using an electric toothbrush as a scrubbing brush, having found how to operate it.

"Erm," Arthur called out, but the knight had already done the inevitable and shoved it between his backside before he could advise him further.

Beside him, Bill Nightingale could only smirk, shaking his head.

Arthur dragged a chair over to an occasional table near a window, Bill doing the same with another – the two sitting across from each other to converse, Bill already sensing the overshadowing and overbearing worries of the campaign settling about the Adonis' shoulders.

"I don't feel like a king," Arthur blurted out before he'd even got settled properly. "I'm not of that kind of material."

It was such a blunt statement it made the reporter pause in rummaging in his satchel for his Dictaphone and notepad, bringing out his laptop slowly in a deeply thoughtful manner in order to plug it in somewhere. He tried to make light of Dan's admission however, assuming throughout the decades many a layman had been thrust into power totally unsure of how to wield it – the second world war being one of them where many a dictator was brought to power to use it unwisely. Bill made this point as he arranged his stuff.

Arthur nodded, deep in retrospection; warming to the reporter's savvy. He thought to ask the wily member of the fourth estate if he wanted anything, and Bill nodded eagerly, his thirst building as The Dome had heated the county up just like the last one. It brought about a few questions Bill had about the gestalt of The Dome itself – and if Danny had any more evidence or knowledge about the strange power curtain?

The King shook his head wearily, obviously as confused as anyone else. "I thought it was acting independently of everyone else, but I'm not so sure now," Arthur explained. "Merlin holds all the cards but is unwilling at times to show them – which – when you consider it, is probably the best thing, the less people know about anything of our defences the better for all concerned."

Bill nodded tactfully, surreptitiously turning on the voice recorder. He brought out his digital camera and asked if he could take a shot, a nice casual one of The King at repose. Arthur smiled at the request and acquiesced, simply leaning back for a moment.

Bill took a couple and checked the lighting; then happy, got down to the interview, stating the time, date and location.

"My first real question Arthur, *is* – pertaining a little to your very first statement, how are you feeling – now that the second advance and enclosure of The Dome has taken place – and extremely rapidly and without much damage or loss of life; is this another Dome or did the first one simply move over."

"No, this is a new one, generated by the power of the earth itself – it seems – Merlin is channelling the energy through some kind of portal where more of my army and support columns are coming through. We obviously need to encapsulate the whole southern peninsular before we move on the capital, make sure there can be no rear-guard offensive."

Bill nodded, having realised as much. He reiterated the first enquiry.

"Oh, I'm alright," Danny King sighed. "It's just all the carousing as we move across the counties. I'm not really used to drinking so much. Of course I'm worried over attacks and skirmishes, losses on both sides, but this is bigger than all of us, so I have to roll with it – as much as I hate even thinking of a conflict."

Bill made notes, empathising with The King's apparent compunction, already knowing of the ambush that morning by an armed group of men – the retaliation swift and decisive, supporters of Danny as numerous – in fact, overwhelmingly so in his favour – against those opposing him. It seemed to show in every press release and talk show discussion, the fact that Danny King, aka King Arthur, had come from humble beginnings and had not even gained so much as a reprimand in his six years at the sports centre where he previously worked. He was a law-abiding, courteous young man who loved his family, and due to some inexplicable set of circumstances had blundered into something one morning that was going to change not only his life forever but the country as a whole. He was doing well to hold himself together, Bill considered thoughtfully, never mind an entire army.

A crash of glass from the busy bathroom sounded like a mirror had detached itself from a wall, a knight a few seconds later, appearing from the apartment's bedrooms with shards of plastic that had perhaps been an ornate vase for some plastic flowers, or work of art perhaps, but was now in a dozen or more pieces, Dan waving the incident aside.

The knight put the collected pieces on a chair and returned to his ablutions, his cicatrised hide glowing red from over-scrubbing.

It brought another raft of questions from Bill's mind as he continued with his interview.

"Assuming you take control Arthur, what then – will all these revenants find a new home here – in this time?"

Danny held out his hands, blowing out a sigh of complete ignorance – that bridge so far in the distance it wasn't worth considering yet. "I have no idea, Bill. It's just one more conundrum I'll have to think about at one stage, I guess."

"I see from a news channel this morning, there are significant defences going up all along the perimeter line. How's that going to play out do you think?"

Again Danny smiled a shrug, not knowing. "Merlin has a plan," he issued enigmatically.

"But you're hoping for a peaceful takeover of the next county or counties?"

"I would sincerely hope so."

"Is it possible to stay close to you, Danny – get the low-down every day?"

Arthur nodded. "I'd like that, Bill. It'll give me a chance to set the record straight and clear my conscience a bit."

Bill nodded knowingly, relaxing a bit as he sat back in his chair, collecting up his thoughts; Danny being treated like a true king and not troubled with detail. He really needed to interview Merlin, but reasoned that might be pushing things a bit too far just yet. One wrong word and he could be snuffling around in sawdust for the rest of his life.

His mind spiralled off to the knight who accompanied him and his little cage – and the mouse inside, who he'd discovered was a one Lindsey Cartwright from Bodmin who'd somehow fallen foul of Merlin and been transposed into a mouse of all things – as the county found itself encapsulated by a strange atmospheric anomaly; Bill cataloguing that there could be one hell of a story there aside from the main one, a story not dissimilar to his own.

He would have to give this Reginald Smyth and his chaperone one full interview as well, before the night was through.

He prised a few more heartfelt answers from King Danny, then left him in peace, going to the in-house phone to order a light lunch and something to drink – plus the password for the castle's broadband as he needed to get the interview away as soon as. Once done – and before Danny could disappear back to his Round Table, he asked him a rather delicate question.

"Danny would you mind bringing my consort into the castle, please, she's my secretary and proof reader – and I need her expertise if I'm going to keep submitting the interviews. She's also got some more of my equipment."

Again Dan nodded agreeably, telling him he'd send someone out to collect her.

"What's her name?"

"Fay," Bill instructed him. "She'll be with Reginald Smyth's squire and knave only a short walk from the rear of the castle."

"We'll find her."

Dan left to put the thought into motion, intending to check on Merlin next door.

***

Having lost the first game of chess to a rather reckless approach, Sir Reginald played a much shrewder match afterwards, narrowly beating Merlin – who'd succumbed to his port, only to find the table and board had begun to swim about a little as he succumbed to the bottle of gin he'd polished off himself – unsure now of which side he was on, black blurring into white.

They were still discussing the en-passant move with a castling one, having got totally confused over both, when Arthur minced in, having successfully shown his now in-house reporter just how much of a pacifist he was. A shrill squeak from a deeply polished mahogany sideboard next to him, alerted him to the fact that the small silver cage still had Lindsey Cartwright in it.

Dan stopped and peered into the cage finding the mouse was sitting on her backside, apparently seething as her little arms were crossed, her small teeth bared.

"Want some water little one," Danny asked, noting the upturned food bowl, his voice booming over her.

The mouse unfolded herself and squeaked loudly.

Dan walked to the small kitchen to get a glass of water as Sir Reginald tried to acknowledge his King by getting to his feet and failing miserably, Dan waving the subservience aside; Merlin – still engrossed with the intricate moves of the game, ignored his liege as he swept past to furnish their little guest with some much needed liquid.

Dan came back into the room presently with small glass of water in hand, reminding Merlin he had a task to render – as a one Lindsey Cartwright needed salvation.

Merlin muttered something, pulling himself away from the game as a rather blotted Sir Reginald tried to fathom his move from the other side, neither having much of a clue anymore.

"Let's get your woman back shall we," he spluttered wearily, fully intending to return to the game as soon as possible? He pushed himself to his feet and wobbled over to Danny who was patiently dribbling a little water into a bowl. Once the rodent had slaked her thirst, Merlin picked the cage up and set it in the middle of the floor, indicating to his king that the woman may well be in need of a towel or sheet with which to cover herself.

Dan caught on immediately and went to rip a sheet from a bed, thinking to look in a cupboard or two for any clothes. He found a new pair of jogging pants someone had left behind in a drawer – and on a hanger a new T-shirt with a kid's flower-power design, large enough to fit an adult. He threw the items on a bed and walked back with the sheet, fully intending to wrap her in it.

When he got back, Merlin had overbalanced trying to open the cage's small door and nearly collapsed over it, flattening it. Sir Reginald, sensing that something was occurring with his loved one, made a point of standing for the occasion, staggering over to hang onto the sideboard for support, trying to focus on the small cage in the middle of the room with Merlin draped over it.

A knight blustered in, wanting Merlin or the King, but was told to wait while the wizard performed one of his miracles.

Ruffled, Merlin got to his feet to stand back, composing himself, telling Dan to encourage the little rodent out of the cage.

Sheet in hand, Dan knelt to put a hand tenderly at the cage's open door.

A tense Lindsey Cartwright climbed out, scaling the bars of the cage to stretch carefully across into Danny's open palm. Dan carried her to a spot on the floor, setting her down with tenderness.

Swaying, Merlin tried to focus, finding the task a little arduous, the mouse very small on the mottled carpeting. Nevertheless he gathered himself up and thought hard, closing his eyes as the magic coursed through him, his fingertips soon coruscating and igniting with shards of static and small yellow flashes. He murmured something unintelligible and seemed to hold an invisible football out before him as power seeped from his hands and rushed toward Lindsey, hitting the mouse full on.

Dan scuttled back on his haunches, awaiting an outcome. Opposite, Reginald hung onto the sideboard, fascinated.

From nowhere, a woman appeared from a sparkling mist, tendrils of smoke drifting through her orbit, the air wild with static and magic. As the smoke cleared it was obvious it was her, the wild black hair, the nubile body – slim legs, her tanned skin glowing with an inner radiance.

Sir Reginald had forgotten just how nubile she was, her pert breasts the first thing that hit him. Dan scrambled to his feet while Merlin snapped out of his spell, ruffling the sheet to place it softly around her shoulders, the woman unsure of where she was. It was only when she turned to thank the Adonis supporting her that Danny realised her nose was not quite as it should be, the black protruding snout not entirely in keeping with her lovely persona – nor the black whiskers.

"Erm, Merlin…" Dan asked?

Merlin turned back from having looked for a drink, finding his king was indicating that the spell had not worked completely. Sighing heavily, he slouched back as Sir Reginald weaved over to inspect her himself, finding she looked fairly good to him. He raised a hand tenderly but Lindsey swiped it away. It was then that she discovered she still retained some of the previous magic. "My face," she almost shrieked!

"Merlin," Dan insisted: "Do something!"

"I like it," Sir Reginald Smyth was squawking, falling all over the place whilst Lindsey cowered in The King's powerful arms.

Merlin neared, squinting as he looked Lindsey's face up and down. "Hm," he muttered. "Needs a little tweaking. Stand back Arthur."

Arthur stood back but supported the shaky woman by retaining his hold of her. Merlin gathered up his force once again as Sir Reginald fell into the sideboard, aiming a handful of magic onto Lindsey's face, letting it go just as another knight barged into the room.

Lindsey's face returned to normal.

As Merlin relaxed, she put her hands to her nose and lips; finding all was well, her features had returned. She turned to thank Danny and he acknowledged her but found he couldn't let go – his hands somehow glued to her shoulders and sheet between them.

A Knight of the Realm approached. "My Liege, Lady Fay at your service."

"Who," Danny had to ask, confused, struggling with trying to let go of Lindsey?

"You asked for Lady Fay to be found and brought to you, Sire. She is here."

A buxom wench approached, a lovely strong face, thick ebony hair, overawed that The King himself had asked for her. She curtseyed and murmured something, as Danny implored Merlin to undo the spell.

Clearly flustered, Merlin searched his last incantation, unsure of what went wrong. Convinced she'd been ushered in for some kind of service, Lady Fay hovered, wondering over the semi-naked woman in The King's arms. Perhaps she was a prisoner trying to escape?

Merlin, having shaken his head over the misguided magic, summoned up yet more power and threw a spell toward the groping couple, just as Sir Reginald Smyth stumbled forward again to inspect his lady's face, falling over his own metalled feet and tumbling into the woman Fay, pushing her into Danny and Lindsey as he fell over her – the four now locked in close contact as Merlin's spell backfired once more.

"Hello, my love," slurred Sir Reginald, now in very close contact to his charge.

"Well, if it isn't you," hissed Lindsey? "My saviour – a nitwit who very nearly drowned me, ate me; starves me of water the next minute; throws me about as if I'm some worthless piece of luggage – *God,* I'm going have great pleasure in super-gluing all your armour together."

"Stay away, *you hear me,"* the angry woman spat, struggling to get an arm free with which to clout him!

"Miss," Danny tried to soothe!

"I'm stuck," someone called sweetly from the middle of the scrum!

"Hush, the love of my life," cooed Sir Reginald, deaf to her insults, stumbling, dumbstruck due to his lovely barmaid who was back in one piece.

"Piss off," Lindsey growled! "Come near me and I'll tear your balls off!"

"Merlin," Danny cried with frustration!

"I'm trying my Liege," the drunken wizard spluttered, trying to coax other knights who were trying to help, out of the way.

In a moment of clarity, Merlin suddenly realised where he'd gone wrong and gathered up his wits once more, just as the besotted and rather squiffy Sir Reginald, towering over everyone, overbalanced again, and pulled all four people to the floor, Merlin missing with his spell and turning a sleeping knight in a chair to the back of the room into something resembling an ogre. The semi-clad knight woke a minute later, realising something was seriously wrong, then having looked down at himself, stood to bellow out a war cry, rushing from the room, taking the door and lintel with him in the process.

"Erm!"

Merlin cringed as the clattering of armour and fitments resounded; a Fortean menace surging through the corridors like a monster possessed. He shook his head, then whilst all four were still thrashing about on the floor, roused up yet another hex and threw it at them, hoping it was the right one.

***

Lindsey Cartwright sat on the edge of the bed, dressed in black jogging pants and garish T-shirt, tears welling in her eyes. Having rebuffed the knight Sir Reginald for more than a dozen times, he'd collapsed in a chair and passed out, leaving Merlin to cogitate over the chess game.

Dan had returned to the command centre, reuniting Lady Fay with Bill, a thought in passing that the woman didn't seem to be of his time, more medieval, making him frown as he wended the corridors with a retinue of bodyguards in tow, putting it down to the subterfuge the reporter had first employed to gain an audience.

It was the horrifying thought that Lindsey Cartwright may well have been a mouse for the rest of her miserable existence that had brought on the weeping – now alone with her thoughts, abandoned probably by her drunken mentor just as soon as he tired of her – although she had to concede (amid sobbing) that this Sir Reginald, although liking his beer, had been thoughtful enough to at least carry her along on his peregrination – with the intention perhaps of righting the wrong Merlin had wrought on her. The shock of her return – the transition from tiny rodent to full womanhood in a matter of a few seconds had been traumatic and as harrowing as a road traffic accident, the distressing wrench from one being to another an unholy jolt of pure occultism that tested her very sanity and personality; the residual furry snout just another kick in the teeth that had all the threat and terror of a sudden amputation until it was rectified.

She wiped the tears away with the back of her hand and sniffed away her sorrow; adamantly grateful to the Adonis Danny King for his intervention, although his mind seemed anywhere but seeing her for what she really was; the memory of his powerful hands on her shoulders, those rugged arms about her; it made her shudder in a nice way. Still that other witch was probably his Guinevere, her big firm breasts pushed into Lindsey's stomach as that idiot Smyth dragged them over, Danny leaving with her – although she noted he left with his hand on her arm, not arm in arm as if lovers.

"Whatever," she mumbled! "I gotta get home, safe with ma and pa for a while. I've had enough adventure for one lifetime."

***

Dan sat in the conference room having tucked into rib-eye steak and tinned tuna, naturally sourced fresh vegetables, polishing it off with a big cheesecake which he portioned up with as many as it would go round, garnishing the sweet with tubs of natural chilled yogurt.

Lancelot and Galahad and others looked resplendent, having finally broken away from being fascinated by the news channels and how the whole networking of satellite feeds kept them abreast of events; or experiment with a shower, safety razor and soap or bath gel; many redolent with various aftershaves or bottled lotions. Danny had spun around in his chair to watch the news via the massive TV; witnessing many a soldier and recruit on the other side of The Dome – again either pushed into servitude, or encouraged by loyalty to their Queen – or simply beaten by sheer peer-pressure – lined many a dyke and hedgerow, hunkering down along the road systems of Bristol, Bath, Frome, Shaftesbury and Blandford Forum; intent on using any weapon to hand to ambush the crusading march – the whole idea that they were not going to let another county be bulldozed over without so much as a fight, high on the agenda. Dan knew the conquest of the southern hemisphere of England wouldn't go entirely smoothly – however fast his armies advanced. He'd made a heartfelt plea with Bill Nightingale to print his wishes that he intended no one any harm, would rather the activists took a softer approach and simply awaited an outcome, instead of trying to stem an inevitable tide, but tempers were obviously running high and he sympathised with the die-hards – knowing if he'd been pushed into the same situation he might feel honoured to do the right thing and fight for his county – although the injustices that had ravaged the country – not only here in the south but in the north too had reached critical – and something had to give whether the population's patience or the infrastructure itself crumbling, it was ripe for change, however it came – England on the whole only a hair's breath from open revolution.

Dan sipped at an ale and wondered, watching idly as knights and cohorts of infantry began to open up the railways again at the first demarcation, having checked the freight carriages for weapons or incendiaries, ardently wary of a build up of arms of any kind amassing behind them. Wizards and warlocks opened and closed the junctions allowing commerce to continue, Danny himself outlining the need for food stocks to be replenished – even farms denuded of their supplies as the armies had coalesced and then marched outward. He worried especially for pensioners and young families who might not have large stocks of food with which to fall back on, hoping the national spirit might shine through – as so many financiers had already, so that no one went hungry amid the upheaval. It was yet one more plea he'd sent out with his reporter, Dan mildly happy he'd made the connection and now had a reliable source at his disposal.

"My liege," called a sentry from the front of the castle, "Earl Mason-James with a group of financiers bequeathing treasure!"

"Who," Danny wondered looking up from the table?

Earl Mason-James was smiling broadly as he was led – along with some rather striking people into the conference room, many a crowding knight making way for them, one woman looking as if she'd stepped right from the cover of a magazine, her skin radiating with a bottled and rather plasticized glow.

"Danny," Earl Mason-James called over the table, immediately accepting a brandy and coke from one of the hovering barmen. "I convened a meeting this lunchtime with many of the financial leaders of the counties of Somerset and Dorset – and a good seventy five percent have aligned their allegiance to you – having heard of your exploits and intentions. We want to further finance your campaign." Two svelte young men hoisted suitcases onto the big conference table, opening them up, knights making way for them. There was a general hush as the cases revealed their wealth, a huge solid gold cross, with chain – looking like it had been purloined from a church once, nestled in amongst other riches in one case, whilst the other was crammed full of one hundred pound banknotes. Danny had never seen a hundred pound bank note before, the big bills looking like treasury notes.

Dan nodded. "Thank you Earl." As he rose to accept the group more cordially, he wondered seriously at the apparent altruism and if it wasn't a bit misguided, the belief that Danny and his armies would be victorious – and thus be dripping in riches, was not his plan at all – as soon as he took control most of this wealth would be used immediately to rebuild his country from the bottom up, plough every cent into re-establishing the infrastructure and realigning some wealth to the workers who had, after all, kept the country going. As he stepped round, his Pendragon crest emblazoned across his white silk tabard, Earl Mason-James glanced up at him askance, finding the young lad seemed to have grown in stature, not only outwards – if that was possible – but in height as well, his persona now dominating the entire room. Nevertheless, the shrewd moneyman shook his hand warmly, turning to introduce just some of his more prominent backers, the enigmatic lady first.

"May I introduce, Lady Mystique Cross-Beydon, first lady of Taunton and only heir to the Pink Gin franchise – her pledge is most generous."

With enormous plastic sunglasses and a white scarf trailing down each side of her expensive business suit covering her lush auburn hair, the young woman looked anything but a philanthropist, Dan turning to her anyway as she held out a slim manicured hand that barely moved from her side.

Concerned knights rose from the table as Danny stooped to take the dainty digits, not for one minute thinking to sink to one knee, despite her bearing, instead just squeezing the small hand gently.

"Thank you," he remarked, trying to gauge her demeanour by catching her eye through the dark shades. She said nothing, simply shifting her weight as if already bored to death.

Earl Mason-James cleared his throat, saying, "And this is Paul Tyrone-Channing of Bude of the International Banking Fraternity. His very generous donation of four million will certainly help finance your movements as you consolidate the southern states."

"On his shoulder is Byron Dempsey of Weymouth, Danny and this," he stated pointing to another well-heeled young man, "is the computer giant Kiefer S Jones, yet another wonderful donation of a block of gold bars worth an estimated eight million."

"With these four alone, Danny, I think we can continue in the same vein, eh?"

Dan nodded thoughtfully, his eyes roving over what he considered the very elite of the south western states, those who'd never even consider giving over a pound to a good cause unless there was some kind of substantial return or kudos for the act. *Why now,* he wondered, what was it that pushed so many of these rich people to donate anything, why not just sit back and watch the country go to war, await an outcome – or was there some worry over the fact that the outcome may not to be to their liking – better play ball now and be in with a gesture, rather than have the whole lot taken away at a later date?

Dan led them to the bar, the way parting for them, condescending to allow the financial backers a little of his time, passing pleasantries.

***

The ogre had run out of steam. He'd surged along the corridors of the upper castle, bouncing off walls and knocking masonry asunder, stumbling and tripping down several flights of stairs until he found himself in the main entrance lobby, flanked by hundreds of knights and their big shields, all hoping to guide the eight-foot being out the back and into the gardens where it was hoped less damage would occur, the beast heading for the open sunlight of the doorway anyway and falling down the flight of stone steps that finally led to the outer courtyards. Beyond lay the ornate gardens, overrun now by thousands of knights, cavalry and infantry – not to mention hundreds of wagon trains and all the supporting logistics. The ogre had run the gauntlet then petered out as he continually fell over his own big feet, flattening a few pigeons into the process.

Now, having sat on the grass in a secluded spot – sucking the last of the meat off the bones – he happened to take in the scenery; the ornamental box hedging and topiared yew, although he didn't recognise the pheasant or dog's head for what they were, the giant wondering at the structured walkways with their powdered stone, small paths radiating out through beautiful gardens from each central point. He stretched over to gather a little of the gravel in his fingers, wondering how mankind had pummelled the stone so finely, all at once staring down at his thick gnarled digits, the transformation stunning him into a moment of sheer dismay. He looked down at himself next as he sat with his legs out in front of him, trying to recall what had happened to transmute him into such a hideous monster.

The knight put a hand to his forehead, wondering over the last hour or so, trying to remember what he was doing, a fragment of memory telling him he was an important person, charged with protecting The King – part of The King's own bodyguard. The momentary flash of insight stunned him, making his arm drop into his lap. He wiped blood from his mouth, rapt in introspection, more of his memory returning as the beast in him subsided.

"Who am I," he asked himself at length, shaking his head over the conundrum?

Then another memory returned, one so ingrained and so important he'd never forget it, being fitted for his armour after becoming a man and finally finishing his basic training, the thrill of at last being presented with a broadsword to replace all the wooden ones, the last so full of nailed on metal discs it weighed a ton, but he was a strong lad, fated to be one of the knights of the shire.

I'm a knight, he told himself – in no doubt of his patronage, *but what in heaven had happened?*

He pushed himself to his feet and glanced around, noting the grandiose castle in the background rising high over the surrounding land, turrets and minarets, the absolute welter of tents and camp fires surrounding the outer boundaries – thousands of flags and pennants fluttering in the light breeze. His memory spun like a carousel lamp only allowing various frames to shine through.

Resignedly, he came to a decision to return, the upheaval of finding himself in a strange land originally, only hampering a confused and bewildered mind. He put one foot in front of another as he slumped back to the castle, passing through dozens of camp sites all preparing for an evening meal, the mouth-watering aromas of chicken frying and bread being warmed, the gaiety and razzmatazz. He was ravenously hungry but felt determined to find out what happened to him first, before he caused any more pandemonium.

Half-way along the ornate path, he hit a heavily guarded check point and tramped to a stop.

Consternation galvanised the troops as they realised the ogre was returning, although it seemed a whole lot calmer than before.

"My word," called a young recruit getting to his feet: "It's Petersbury Dean from Claw Cross!"

The other knights looked him up and down, the ogre realising he was now head and shoulders taller than anyone – had in fact – he supposed, the strength of ten horses.

"It is you," the young lad insisted coming close, having dropped the cooked ham he was cutting up, you've changed by God, but it's you, I'd know that face anywhere – best swordsman in the county!"

"Petersbury," the ogre rumbled, dropping his head, frowning over the name – and the fact that the lad seemed to have it backwards.

"I know you too," offered another halberd's man, standing from the sitting position he'd taken. "You're a good man, loves his wife and children; Squire of the glade!"

Petersbury Dean glanced over at him, thanking him with a nod of his head. He raised a mighty mitt to look down at it, realising a broadsword would now be like a toothpick in his hands, the strength oozing through him filling him with vim.

"Well pass, friend," one watchmen called. "If these people can vouch for you it's good enough for me." The checkpoint opened up and Petersbury Dean wandered through, rumbling his thanks.

Not ten yards into the outer perimeter, a woman nearby screamed ***"OGRE,"*** nearly dropping the small child she had in her arms!

Petersbury stopped to hold out a hand warmly, trying to calm the woman, the cook taken aback at the revered stance, somewhat stunned at the action. Staring bolt at the giant she appeared to get a hold of herself and issued a curt nod of acceptance, as if she'd mistaken him for someone else.

He moved on, reminding himself he was no longer a Knight of the Realm but a ten-ton man of iron that could tear down trees if he needed to. By the time he reached the castle he was almost enjoying himself, the way the crowds stared at him, the celebrity, the respect.

He reached the castle and had to run yet more checkpoints as knights, obviously wary of his bulk barred his progress nonetheless, braving up to the giant even though he could crush a man's skull with one hand.

"What do you want," called a sergeant from the safety of the steps leading up to the rear castle entrance?

What did he want? Right then he wasn't sure. He was twenty times stronger than he'd ever been – and if he was to survive this nightmare he'd found himself in – then surely he might well survive it much better as an ogre than simply a knight. *'Hm,'* he cogitated, flexing his shoulders; get another suit of armour made, or some heavier weaponry and he could rough it for the rest of the campaign?

"Where's the armoury," he called?

"You need armour," someone remarked from the crowd that had gathered?

Petersbury Dean thought for a moment – no he didn't really – but a nice big mace might come in handy!

"Alright – forget the armour. I just need some heavier weaponry – and something to eat – I'm starving!"

"Come on," called out a woman far to his left. "We're roasting a pig over here, and there are tinkers and metal-smiths close by."

The sergeant at arms nodded; rather glad the ogre's interest had been pulled from the castle. Someone at his shoulder mentioned The King's own knight may well want his armour and weaponry back, but for now, the watchman was all for letting the beast go, better if he guarded from outside now.

***

Lindsey Cartwright slumped through to the living area and stopped to consider the unconscious knight Sir Reginald Smyth. Across the room Merlin was also sleeping – having passed out in the big wing-backed arm chair, the chess table awash with pieces.

She checked the other rooms for any suitable clothing, finding nothing but a pair of brand new flip-flops that she could cram into but nothing else save a new pack of child's knickers that were a mite too small, deciding she could use a drink. She retraced her steps – and after one long look at the slumbering knight, his broad head tilted onto those big armoured shoulders, his dark chiselled features in repose, left, stepping over and through some workmen and their tools, busy putting a new door and frame back in the hole the ogre had left, after he'd bulldozed his way from the room.

She padded through the corridors, being scrutinized by groups of knights as they lingered, no one thinking to stop her however, having come from the upper echelons. She tripped down a couple of flights of stairs, hearing the unmistakable babble of noise and chatter from a large conference room yet another floor below.

Lindsey followed her feet, finally entering the big open room, wending her way through the phalanx of knights to the bar. Once there she realised she had not a cent on her and stood crestfallen as around her pints and drinks of all kind flowed.

A huge meaty hand to her back made her jump and, having glanced around found the Adonis King Arthur looking down at her.

"I could use a drink," she explained dumbly, imploring him with her eyes.

Danny nodded, calling over a barman to issue a tab. "Knock yourself out," he had remarked, smirking.

Lindsey sipped at a very large vodka and coke, glancing around, finding The King was entertaining some very influential people, those who'd sought to finance his enterprise and perhaps make a buck or two into the process, those types in her estimation just one rung below a full-blown predator, her attention then drawn to the big TV screen.

It was constantly being updated by various news channels, one displaying the build up of men and arms on the other side of the new boundary line, army men swarming over the Wiltshire Downs and Salisbury Plain digging in. She cringed at the imagined outcome; the conflict of one massive army meeting another, Arthur's warriors vested in sword, lance and mace whereas the opposing side had probably never picked up a sword, never mind wield it in anger. A contingent of light cavalry were also highlighted – having no doubt sworn allegiance to The Queen, but going up against heavily armoured knights would be nothing short of a massacre, Lindsey moving to consort with The King in order to avoid terrible bloodshed. She sidled around to his side of the table, trying to inveigle her way in, everyone making way for her – as she seemed to have The King's ear.

"This build up of men," she spoke quietly, squatting on a small stool beneath him. "They will be meeting a grisly end if you don't do something about it."

Dan sighed, nodding thoughtfully. "I'd hoped a conflict would come later rather than sooner but there seems to be more royalists in the southern counties than I assumed, misguided as they are."

"They're doing what they feel is right," Lindsey countered.

"True," The King sighed. "I've put a plea out on TV and the newspapers, but I doubt anyone of them will take any notice. I can no more stop the juggernaut than hold back the tide – am really just acting as a figurehead."

"It's going to be a massacre," Lindsey observed coldly.

Danny gritted his teeth, saying nothing. Around him the knights were preparing for battle, the lines apparently having been drawn. *'Not ten minutes into the campaign and already they were facing their first real encounter. Damn,'* he thought, *'if only they'd see sense.'*

"Has anyone tried to talk to them, from this side, I mean," she asked, amazed that The King was apparently just going to let this happen?

"I can't very well send an emissary, I don't have one – and I wouldn't want to gamble with anyone's life either." He frowned, his eyes sliding over the young woman who'd wriggled in beside him.

"You're welcome to have a go," he added at length. "I'll send some of my best knights with you."

Lindsey thought for a moment. It would be a diplomatic role for sure, and one very worthy of its merit, a heartfelt plea from a young woman who'd seen the build up of Arthur's army from *this* side, knowing the opposing forces were totally unprepared, sporting conventional weapons but finding at the last moment they would have to rely on basic hand to hand combat, as they must know The Dome as it expanded for another time, would render any explosive dud. It was an ace move for sure, bringing things down to The King and his army's level, Merlin having all the necessary power and magic. It was a contest the other side couldn't hope to win. She could explain this, having been a recipient of his powerful spells. She could also get her own back on that idiot Smyth by asking him to be her consort – rather than taking a big troop and probably risking their lives – just take one fully armoured knight – in all his regalia and with luck they'd let her go – but lock him up – *brilliant, it couldn't fail.*

I've got to go now, she thought, throwing down her drink. "I will take just one knight," she assured

Danny. "My saviour," she parodied. "I'll have to wake him."

Dan turned in his seat to take her in his big powerful hands, clasping her shoulders tenderly. "This is a big thing, I ask," he intoned, looking into her eyes. "You could be taking a big risk." She shook her head however.

"I served in pubs up and down the south coast – and am well known. I'll make them listen."

Dan thought for a moment. "Taking a knight might not be the best thing after all – they, those on the other side, may think you've chosen who you are going to support."

"Don't worry Danny, Smyth will protect me. He owes me that at least."

The King nodded, finally releasing her. "I'll ready the horses," he then added, "– or will a car be quicker?"

"Probably."

"Ok, I'll see what I can do. Safe journey,"

Back upstairs Lindsey sought a small bucket or vessel to fill with cold water – hoping to rouse her knight. In one bathroom she found an ornate vase full of tasteful synthetic flowers and emptied them out to fill it, letting the water run cold.

Back in the lounge area where Sir Reginald Smyth and Merlin were sleeping it off, Lindsey tipped the full vase over the slumbering knight's head, standing back to see what happened.

He didn't move, just burbled something inaudible as water dribbled down his face. His jet-black hair was plastered down around his ears and forehead making him look almost comical, like a latter-day pirate sweating after a victorious scramble: But he didn't stir, his intoxication knocking him for six.

'Another vase full," she fancied, tripping back to the bathroom.

By the third attempt, Sir Reginald seemed to surface. "Wha…frome jicket – pu… .half penny…?"

"Evening," an amused Lindsey Cartwright called sweetly. Water had gushed down the inside of the knight's breastplate, soaking his groin, water dribbling from his armoured waistline. The unsavoury premise that he might have inadvertently pissed himself, brought the knight back to some sort of semblance. He opened his eyes fully, finding his love standing over him, ornate vase still in one hand.

"My love," he chortled, still semi-conscious! "What ails my love?" He held out a hand, but Lindsey ignored it.

"The King has asked for you," she lied. "He wants you and me to carry out a very important diplomatic mission."

This got the knight's attention straight away. He stiffened in his seat and sought clarity. "King," he muttered. "ME… – *You?* Where..?"

"I didn't say where – we've just got to go now – before it's too late."

"Too late for what," Sir Reginald's mind tried to untangle?

"The battle tomorrow," Lindsey stated flatly, "– *not that you'll be in any fit state!"*

"Battle," Sir Reginald muttered, confused?

245

"Yes, if we hurry we still might avoid it."

Sir Reginald considered this, taking his first long look at his consort from under his brow. "Running away is very commendable my dear, but I don't need The King's permission for that!"

"I'm not running you idiot, far from it, we're going across into enemy territory to hopefully dissuade them from engaging – in what will be a bloody massacre if we don't intervene."

Sir Reginald shot up straight. "Enemy territory," he muttered, looking even more confused?

"Yes, we're crossing the border to try and mediate, tell the forces on the other side it will be a waste of time; The Dome will neutralise their weapons, and hand to hand fighting against a fully-prepared army is not going to fare well – not at all!"

Sir Reginald thought long and hard about this, not at all impressed. "Why us," he blurted, wondering what he'd done wrong – for as far as he could see it – it was a suicide mission for any of King Arthur's knights?

"I volunteered – and as you are my shining knight in armour – I volunteered you as well – *my honey*!"

Sir Reginald Smyth eyed his lady love especially shrewdly, wondering just what he'd done to be saddled with such a nitwit. All through his life he'd avoided trouble whenever it reared its ugly head, and as luck would have it, he'd been fortunate enough to retain some sort of valour despite having never raised a hand in combat. Now he was courting with danger, taking an outsider into enemy territory without a hope in hell of getting back alive. *God's teeth!"*

Still, he cogitated, he was doomed anyway according to Merlin, so what was the big deal? He was in a dead end gallop whether he liked it or not. Might as well rot in a cell rather than face mortal combat.

Sir Reginald wrung water out of one ear and ran a hand over his face, feeling decidedly uncomfortable.

A knight banged in from the door the carpenters were trying to hang. "Sir Reginald, Lady Cartwright, your carriage awaits," and with that he about turned and whisked himself away – as if escaping a doomed couple. Sir Reginald looked to Merlin for some kind of help but the wizard was dead to the world, snoring peacefully. He sighed inwardly and pushed himself to his feet – wavering alarmingly as his balance disinherited him, the only incentive, not wanting to upset his king, or appear unwilling. He shook water from his armour and clanked to the bathroom to freshen up.

He sat in the car, having climbed in with rabid anticipation, overawed at the long vehicle's interior, the plush seat into which he sank, the strange reek of plastic and foam and the unmistakable whiff of diesel as they sped off, windows opening as if by magic. In the front seat Lindsey appeared to take it all in her stride, climbing into the conveyance as if she'd been born to it (which, when he thought about it – she probably had) the knight gazing out of the window hoping to heaven that fate would somehow intervene and save the day.

As the car threaded its way through the abandoned vehicles and lorries of the M5, many simply parked up on the hard shoulder, verges or entrances to the fields of the surrounding landscape, Sir Reginald noted horses galloping to and fro, taking word from the armies massing all along The Dome's demarcation line, tramping over field and lane, moving inexorably toward an inevitable conclusion, banners and pennants denoting the many houses of Southern England – thousands of knights, squires and knaves not only from his time, he noted, cataloguing the many sigils but also from times gone by. He shook his head at the armoured detachments, the wagon trains trundling behind, keeping the supply lines open, and wondered with dire despair why such an occurrence should take place, why couldn't this time take care of its own problems? Was it something to do with Merlin, he pondered, trying to make sense of his predicament, that old sage was probably going to come out of this all right, maybe even settle down in a nice cave with hot and cold running water – *an in-house toilet for the sake of Zeus* – while the rest of them dissolved back into the dust – once Merry Old England had been given back to the people.

The people, he mused, tutting audibly. By his estimation if that had happened in his time the uneducated urchins of the fields and shires would have made merry with all the riches; stayed drunk for a week and then wondered what to do with the coming sabbath. There was no substitute for learning and common sense he'd asserted many times, one going hand in hand with the other. He had become a knight through his father's patronage and welcomed the classes and teachings as his right to take up the mantle. There just had to be order and class division in his time, without which the community as a whole could not function. It had just one flaw in his esteemed view, monogamy – the chaste and often almost pious reverence with which a knight had to live his life. *Yeah, who said?* In his estimation a little slap and tickle made the world go round, and if knights wanted to get all fired up over virtuous celibacy all to the good – more for him.

Idiots, he chastised out of hand, all that praying and sanctimonious braying – and for what – to get hacked to death in the next engagement with the bloody Visigoths! God's teeth, it was enough to make you spit! And here he was, he told himself angrily, heading for sure destruction – or worse a public flogging or hanging, all for the courtship of the lady in the front. *Ye, Gods, he was getting soft!*

He eyed the back of her head now, with just a touch of scorn – and quite a lot of anger, her silky black hair cascading down her shoulders and back like tresses of a horse he'd once had as a child, the small stallion a more lustrous ebony you'd never find. He would have lived out a peaceful life in the shires if the meddling wizards hadn't dabbled in world events.

By eight that evening, having spun off the M5 just after Taunton, heading due west, they raced through Glastonbury then Shepton Mallet, joined the A-road to Frome, then, ten minutes later, found The Dome suddenly and irrevocably looming up before them; scintillating like a gleaming planet.

On the road a huge checkpoint existed, a group of wizards, warlocks and grubby-looking sages hanging about off to one side amid a welter of knights and infantry, appearing like a group of dissidents pedalling dirty little tricks. The car skidded to a halt and the driver climbed out, a man of this time, Sir Reginald realised, unfolding himself to exit the vehicle along with Lindsey, pulling out a staff to which a pure white pennant of the Pendragon house was attached, its silks glittering prettily in the evening glare of The Dome's wall, his driver comically attired in a cotton tabard with some lurid design on it, made all the more hilarious by his jeans and big trainer boots.

The knight climbed out and stretched, glancing about stealthily, as if he could suddenly claim car sickness and scramble for salvation, but even as he looked around for possibly somewhere to disappear into, he knew he had to see it through, the shame of being dragged back to face Arthur a crime he'd rather not even contemplate, better to die quickly in mortal combat than face that kind of humiliation.

It was a balmy evening – made all the warmer by the enclosing power shield.

Helmet under his arm, Sir Reginald went to meet the wizards who were preparing to open a doorway in the power grid.

Lindsey sided with him, taking a moment to openly appraise him, even issuing him the briefest of smiles. Towering over her he could only sigh inwardly knowing this woman had deliberately brought him to a swift end. *God's teeth,* he swore again under his breath!

Sir Reginald watched the wizards with idle interest as several raised their hands to the air, almost outlining a small doorway in the glistening curtain. Within seconds the scintillating wall of shimmering energy drew back, leaving a small doorway through which the knight could just look – standing just off to one side. It was as if a dirty pane of glass had experienced a section of it wiped clean, allowing clarity to peep through, the small window showing a snapshot of undulating countryside, bristling with men and armaments, many looking ultra deadly.

Noise and clamour seeped through as well, calls of '*Hold your fire,*' echoing over the land!

In the far distance mighty machines rumbled about, looking like big robots as they manoeuvred into position.

Sir Reginald sucked in a breath. A crack rang out and a bullet twanged off the macadam of the roadway and skittered down it like a banshee, causing the knight to turn in its direction, calculating the velocity and realising with dire consequence that a piece of metal travelling at that speed would pass right through his armour, probably his body too, leaving a gaping hole.

"Mercy!"

His stomach did a flip, grumbling as the latent alcohol made its presence felt.

"Good luck," called the driver, quickly moving back to a safer position.

Sir Reginald nodded, hefting the spear, hoping to something that they'd realise this was a mission of peace and mitigation. Telling Lindsey to get behind him and stay there, he marched forward – forward into the valley of death!

At the portal he had to duck, fearing the power curtain would laser his head in half, waving his white flag about as if it were some kind of talisman.

On the other side, the smell of mankind, the sweat and fear seemed to permeate the air, rising up almost like a tide; wood smoke, charred grass and diesel fumes choking the atmosphere. With Lindsey tucked in behind, Sir Reginald walked resolutely on, clanking as metal hit macadam.

Still yells of, '*Hold your fire,*' rang out!

No one seemed to have control. Lindsey looked behind to see the shimmering wall close its door, the impervious glistening goliath of power like a living thing as it loomed above, radiating with supremacy. Now on the other side, she shivered, the drop in temperature adding to the feeling of dread sitting in the pit of her stomach.

She turned back to cringe somewhat under the impressive back-plate of Sir Reginald's armour, the bar manageress taking a quick second to appraise the sixth century workmanship as she put a hand out to it unconsciously, the moulded steel hammered and wrought into shape, then polished and oiled to such a high degree no rust was visible despite being out in all weathers – and the water she'd recently thrown all over him. It was pitted and had obviously seen action – *unless he'd fallen off his horse in it.* But it was impressive all the same, all the little dents and rents testimony to an adventurous life, one she could only guess at. He may have had a family once, been a doting husband, dropping her hand, a father and knight all rolled into one, living out his pastoral dream – *until fate took a hand!*

Sir Reginald had stopped, overawed by the scene unfolding before him, men in all manner of combat gear, supported by what looked suspiciously like some form of light canon and monstrous lumbering machines of the like he'd never seen, manoeuvring and belching out clouds of blue smoke. A team of people had emerged from a kind of dugout and – having climbed up and onto the roadway they were on, approached, an elderly gentleman in olive green pulling on a peaked cap, seeming to take charge.

The tall knight had stopped dead, catching Lindsey off guard as she bumped into the back of him, her mind totally on the soldiers and recruits that had obviously camped overnight, hunkered down in ditches and dykes riddling the land, many a young lad enjoying the excitement. *They had to be told the truth,* she worried, *had to know that their weapons and artillery would be useless once The Dome started its advance. It would either push things out of the way like an immense bulldozer or subsume them, rendering them useless. She had to make them listen!*

Plucking up her courage Lindsey Cartwright stepped forward, around her brave knight who was standing so proudly with helmet under one arm, the Pendragon sigil on a white pennant grasped in the other, taking a step from him to take charge, a loose handful of soldiers approached.

Lindsey pulled herself upright and waited.

"Brigadier Lance Warner-Barouche," a man in front intoned as he drew near, holding out a hand with peaceful intention. He took her hand politely. "On my left is Staff Colour Sergeant Geoff Tiptree of the second and third light armoured division, while to my right is Lieutenant Nigel Horrocks of the thirty first southern infantry battalion. Also in attendance is the eighty fourth tank regiment, supported by a light field gun deployment. We have several divisions of reservists and national recruits – all armed. This charade has gone on far enough – the buck stops here – with me!"

Lindsey Cartwright caught the inference straight away, the stiff upper lip of a military background, a life in servitude to the ruling monarch. One tiny cog in the echelons of the war machine that existed somewhere between the nobility and the nouveau riche, and the up and coming middle classes that sprung from the rise of the computer and software industries, being pushed irrevocably down the social ladder by all these up and coming socialites that cared little for a national deterrent.

"Your armaments, Captain," and here she spread out her hands to include everything she could see, "your canons, tanks, guns and ammunition – all useless – all null and dud. *Void!* Because when that Dome starts to roll, it will do one of two things; either push everything it considers a threat out of the way, or subsume it and render it ineffective, somehow dismantling the molecules of gunpowder and other inflammables."

"How is that possible," asked Staff Colour Sergeant Geoff Tiptree?

Lindsey blew out a puff of air. "I don't know," she gasped! "All I know is that I've seen the power and black magic of Merlin and his sages – *of which there are many,* and I'm telling you now, once that Dome has expanded to encapsulate yet another county, the armies of revenants will sweep forward – and if your want to engage with them with just an ineffective rifle and bayonet be my guest – *but don't,"* she impressed "drag young civilians into this slaughter who know nothing of mortal combat, they will be hacked down like straw dolls."

The three lead men glanced at one another. At nearly seventy but still standing at a slightly stooped six foot two, Brigadier Lance Warner-Barouche normally enjoyed looking down at people but the knight standing behind the woman was a head taller than him, and in his bulky armour looked indomitable. He rolled his shoulders, wondering if the knight was a participant in some re-enactment society – or the real thing – as he'd heard all manner of rumour that sixth century knights of yore were piling through some portal that had opened up in time – the whole upheaval due to someone actually pulling Excalibur from its stone – all complete balderdash as far as he could see, but the man accompanying the woman certainly had an authentic feel to him. "What's your name son," he barked up at the young man?

Sir Reginald – who'd been gazing about the land as if hypnotised, snapped out of his spell to stare down at the officer coldly.

"I, sir," he growled, straightening, "am a Knight of the Realm, son of Horace the younger and first in line to his seat at the Round Table. I am not – and never will be, your son!"

In front of him Lindsey sighed, turning to address him. "It's a term of endearment, Reginald. He didn't mean anything by it."

Sir Reginald sniffed and blinked water from his still dripping wet hair, trying to make sense of what she'd just uttered. Seeing his blank look, Lindsey tried to explain further as the three men suddenly walked out of earshot for a moment to confer. By the time the idea of 'endearment' had sunk in, the three men had returned, having come to some kind of agreement. As they sauntered back, the Brigadier ran over the key points one more time.

"So if he's real – we nab him and find out what is really going on – and if he's not, bang him up anyway – right – and retain her too, because others are going to want to talk to them surely."

The other two nodded thoughtfully.

"Are you," started Lieutenant Nigel Horrocks once they'd confronted the two again, addressing Sir Reginald directly "from some nutcase re-enactment society or the real thing – you know – from the sixteenth century."

"Sixth century," corrected a private guard that had accompanied them with rifle in hand.

"My apologies," Lieutenant Nigel Horrocks mentioned, "sixth century."

"Yes," Sir Reginald stated, then relaxed somewhat, throwing caution to the wind. "I was happy in my shire – not far from here actually," – he reminisced, glancing about; "had lovely wife, housemaids too – went fishing and hunting daily – even helped in the fields sometimes – had it all in fact – then got dragged halfway through time to come and sort all your problems out! So don't blame me, it was none of my doing!"

"Would you," and here old Brigadier Warner-Barouche raised a hand to indicate the both of them, "like to explain yourself further to our superiors who are actually setting up a meeting as we speak? You could explain yourself and perhaps put us in the picture a little better."

Lindsey Cartwright nodded, knowing hostages could be used as bargaining chips, although she doubted The King would be able to negotiate, the inevitable tide that was Merlin and the incredible army stopping for nothing and no one.

"You'll be free to go whenever you like," the lead officer told Lindsey.

She nodded curtly, suddenly very concerned for her chaperone, who'd willingly accompanied her. "You'll of course show every courtesy for my chaperone," she called out rather loudly, hoping the news vans that had been kept back could hear her, "who – after all, only accompanied me to keep me safe!"

The three stooges looked embarrassed, staring down at the ground. At length they nodded, looking them straight in the eye. Then they turned to go, holding out their hands for Lindsey and her knight to follow.

More intrigued by the landscape than his own safety at that point, Sir Reginald walked on, his eyes taking in the soldiers hunkering down in the muddy ditches, the army tents that had sprung up much like the caravans of his own, the organisation and logistics of a vanguard operation.

"They've been taken into custody," called out a young knight who'd been watching the news channels on a regular basis. Dan turned from the bar and listened as the chatter in the big room died down for a moment, a young anchor-woman reporting from a hotel where Lindsey Cartwright and her accompanying Knight of the Realm had been sequestered.

"They'll be ok," mentioned Earl Mason-James. He was a little worse for wear, having enjoyed the trappings of the big bar for several hours, seeing off all of his contemporaries. "If they don't let them go tonight, we can pick them up tomorrow."

By ten that night, knights had begun to settle down, the floor as good a place as any, many stretching out in groups, utilising anything the hotel had to offer. Somewhat squiffy, Earl Mason-James waved a goodbye and headed for the door.

Danny followed him, helping him up the stairs and walking him through the foyer where dozens of knights were also camped, several wondering why they couldn't light a camp fire.

"You'll burn the place down," a hotel manageress was trying to implore.

"It's a stone castle," they retorted flummoxed.

To meet them half-way, the manageress cleared out the fireplace to the central lobby, tossing the ornamental flowers and fire stand aside, then – after throwing in paper, cardboard and some plastic bottles, lit it, adding some wood that had been donated by the visiting carpenters earlier. Happy, the knights gathered round, many falling asleep immediately.

Danny had walked with Earl Mason-James to the front of the castle, stepping down the grandiose semicircular entrance steps where more knights were camped out, many holding a dense checkpoint. They parted for The King however who watched his new benefactor weave his way from the gatehouse and through the environs of the nearby town to his own hotel, where he'd billeted himself for the night. The roadway and castle entrance was crowded with a protective palisade of knights, cavalry and armed infantry, camps fires abounding as night closed in, although it was much warmer under the enshrouding Dome. Still the air was fresh and Dan breathed deep of it, able to smell the river banks of the Exe as it ran close by, finding he was missing the fresh morning walks with his dear friends. Only a couple of days had passed but it seemed like a week, The King not even trying to catalogue the upsets and incidents. Sometime during the afternoon heavily armoured drones had made a sweep of the castle grounds, trying to ascertain in which part of it The King was staying, he reckoned, making a reconnaissance for perhaps an organised commando raid, but archers shot all of them down – a metal bolt loosed from a longbow about as deadly as a high-velocity bullet, and even so, Arthur had been careful to pull any curtains and blinds in most of the rooms, leaving only a few open at any one time, minimising the threat of being seen in any of them.

He could sleep soundly, he knew, the nearby river acting as a natural boundary – which was probably why Merlin had advocated it rather than the bigger castle at Taunton.

Yet another happenstance occurred not yards from where he was standing on the big tarmacked entrance; a man in his late forties or so, had somehow skirted through the outer defences and managed to get quite close to the castle unmolested, but appeared to fall foul of fate himself as he somehow tripped up – despite being totally alone and – as it happened with dire consequences. Having fallen, the man began to pick himself up, only to be stricken down suddenly by some kind of convulsion as his body went rigid and he was again knocked off his feet, thumping back to the ground in a writhing heap.

It took only seconds for a crowd to surround the man, a warlock taking charge – and witnessing foam and spittle bubbling from the man's mouth, blood oozing from his nose and ears, assuming he'd fallen from a great height, but upon being told that he darted through the defences, became suspicious. He had bent over the man carefully and sniffed at his mouth, suspecting some kind of poison, but then finding no mendacious odour, sat back puzzled. Then he noticed a wet stain down by the man's waist and groin, the wetness alerting the warlock that he may have had something in a pocket.

He searched the man carefully, finding a small plastic container in his trousers, removing it gingerly. Between forefinger and thumb he placed the container on the man's chest, noting it was smashed through the middle, a glass vial within also broken on impact. The dark sage had lent forward and taken a whiff of the liquid that had dribbled all over the dead man's trousers and recoiled immediately, rubbing his nose furiously. The acrid stink, still viable despite being exposed to the air for some time, made the warlock suspicious of a deadly poison. The man was obviously an assassin – but had somehow tripped in his haste and fallen on the deadly container of vials, one leeching its deadly toxin.

He pulled out a rag and carefully wrapped the smashed container, intending to show the council as quick as possible.

Dan had viewed the container later as Galahad and Lancelot and others gathered round, the very design suggesting it was a military operation, also thinking Merlin's power may have intervened, cutting the assassin down before he even got to the castle, but the wily old sage was still fast asleep upstairs, comatose by intoxication. Still, having listened patiently to all the facts it was inconceivable that such a high professional would simply trip and stumble at the last hurdle as it were, The King unable to put it down to just sheer fate. Something other than Merlin and all his other sages appeared to be looking out for him – the very elemental milieu he was living in, almost every molecule ready to protect him.

***

"So let's get this right," a leading politician sighed angrily, mobiles and tablets binging and trilling around the room, enchanting Sir Reginald. "You claim to be a sixth-century Knight of the Realm transported here through some fantastical portal of time and space to help this one Arthur Pendragon to take over England – I don't think so, ol'e son, not for a minute."

"Why does everybody assume I'm their son for heaven's sake," Sir Reginald Smyth retorted? "As I've quoth before, I'm not your son, nor will I ever be. I've already told you, I've lived a life – had a mother and father – and am in no way related to you – Moor."

The coloured politician took offence at this and nearly confronted the knight yet again, having already tried in earnest to discredit him. Around a big ornate table sat an array of council members, police chiefs and a military attaché, all trying to make sense of what was going on, the next morning turning into a debacle unless some semblance of truth could be agreed on. Opinions varied on what people and council leaders alike took for verbatim, the evening papers running the story that a one Bill Nightingale had thrown together, continuing his reporting of the take over of the second big area by the incredible Dome – the army attesting to its power by having already tried to overcome it. *It's like a living thing,* the army specialist conferred.

"So we just roll over, is that it," the leading politician cried in disbelief?

Lindsey Cartwright jumped to her feet. She'd patiently spelt out the danger already but most of the important people here had been sent down from London to get an idea of what was going on, whilst the army units had consolidated and finally gathered together enough forces to perhaps make a stand, the rapid expansion of the domes surprising everyone. "We are dealing here with fantastic magical powers – a concerted energy flow that can't be underestimated, each and every wizard and warlock having been imbued with a power source of his own – or is drawing it off The Dome itself – it's hard to know which – but *believe me,* if just one magician has the power to turn a normal person into a mouse or a knight into an eight foot ogre, than just think what a hundred can do!"

"Who got turned into a mouse," asked a lady politician doubtfully – "these are just stories surely!"

"No," stressed Lindsey Cartwright. "I – er, well!"

She gulped for breath, still upset – near terrified over the ordeal.

She started again while everyone sat patiently.

"I upset Merlin," she almost murmured in a small voice, "by mixing him up a cocktail of hot spices when he asked for a drink and… well, I suppose he did warn me – but like you – I dismissed him as a nut."

"He turned you into a mouse," laughed the military specialist?

"It wasn't funny," she barked, glaring at him so forcibly he had to drop his vision. "This – er knight, Sir Reginald, saved me, scooped me up in a beer mug and carried me to safety – well nearly."

Suppressed titters echoed around the room.

"What happened," someone asked? "You're obviously not a mouse now!"

Lindsey Cartwright sighed, putting a hand to her forehead. It was obviously a hard story to stomach but with everything else going on, they had to at least believe that The Dome's expansion would nullify the armaments and leave the men of the assembling army devoid of force and without any form of defence. "It will be a slaughter," she continued. "The infantry and pike-men – all versed in hand to hand combat will overrun your forces and knights will run them down. They'll give little quarter."

"We have commandos and battle-hardened veterans, miss – we don't intend to lose."

"How many," Lindsey Cartwright asked? "Because there are thousands if not hundreds of thousands massing on the other side – not hundreds – thousands – all battle hardened and all as fit as Sir Reginald here."

Many glanced at the impressive knight as he sat in a chair, plumed helmet on table, the sigil of the Pendragon castle clearly visible on the staff he still carried and emblazoned on his chest. He was so authentic – it was impossible to deny his presence.

"Why," a leading female politician asked, clearly flummoxed over the whole escapade?

"You have to ask," stated Lindsey, although she had had to pose many a simple question when first presented with the invading army? "It's a sign of our corrupt times, the complete breakdown of our social system – it can't go on – no-one having the stamina to take on the establishment and bring it down themselves; The Sword in the Stone is part of our heritage – it exists in our very legend and psyche, its part of the code we all subscribed to once!"

Several burly policemen – all in riot gear – suddenly banged in through the door of the small conference room – not waiting to knock or pass a discrete word, offering a memorandum to the police chiefs. Having digested the note, one put his hand to his eyes in a clear act of exasperation. The riot police moved pointedly toward Sir Reginald, ready for anything. "Will you please come with us, sir," one asked politely?

Having just sat down, Lindsey now jumped to her feet again.

"Do not hurt him," she yelled uncontrollably! "I'm coming too!"

The policemen looked to their chiefs. One nodded.

"Where are they being taken," asked the female politician?

"Further questioning," the police chiefs told her, standing to leave.

"I'll make sure you have a lawyer," she intoned, standing to leave as well. "I want legal access," she instructed the police chiefs. One groaned audibly.

***

At Tiverton castle all was well. Having done the rounds to make sure the grounds were heavily guarded and would stay that way during the night, Sir Lancelot and Galahad and various others retired with The King to their chambers. It had gone ten and Danny was ready for bed, the routine ingrained in his soul, the early morning – when ma and pa were still dozing allowing him time to collect himself, reflect on the training session of the previous day and throw down a big protein drink along with various vitamin supplements – a special time, the county as a whole not woken up just yet, the commerce and trading still in abeyance – the sun just peeping over the horizon, ready to warm it up again as the coolness of night receded. A nice herbal cup of tea with honey would give him a few minutes of grace before having to let Lady out for a sniff about and join his older friends for her little walk. Now, tomorrow held all the anticipation and worry of a day in court, the apprehension and anxiety of an early morning conflict as unsavoury as answering for a guilt-ridden transgression. The weight of the outcome felt like it lay entirely on his shoulders as he climbed the stairs with the others and made his way to his rooms, just one casualty a burden he hated to contemplate. He had to hope his emissary had made some sort of impact and that the powers to be had listened and would act accordingly, pulling their troops back to a safe distance while The Dome itself sorted out its new boundaries. By considering the various maps most of Wiltshire and Dorset would fall while parts of Gloucestershire and Hampshire would be affected, the very affluent shires also the breadbasket of England, cut off rather swiftly. Parliament had probably worried about this and hence the presence of a military build up, but despite letters and pleas from the castle, Danny was not going to allow a meeting outside of the domes. Straying too far from Merlin and the seats of power might only result in capture and worse, treated for treason and hung, drawn and quartered before the campaign had even got going.

Aside from that, he doubted his knights or Merlin would allow him out of their sight, The King in every sense a figurehead to be guarded at all costs and protected with one's dying breath.

As Arthur Pendragon allowed the trusted squires and knaves to see to his armour and kit, Dan climbed into bed quickly afterwards, calling out his goodnights to all and sundry; Merlin still fast asleep in the big wing-backed chair. Bill Nightingale and his lovely woman had commandeered the tiny box room beyond Danny's main master bedroom, several knights having to find other accommodation; Galahad not happy with this as it left a weak link in the chain that surrounded his king, but on the third floor and with just about every other avenue blocked solid, it was unlikely the room posed any real danger. Still, knights stood or sat on guard his side of the door, putting his council's minds at rest, Danny asleep even before they'd finalised arrangements.

Just before he'd retired however, a nuance in the firmament found its way into his mind, alerting him to the fact that someone important had passed through the nearby portal, someone with deep spiritual meaning and power. He had no more energy to contemplate the feeling though – could only store it for future reference, hoping tomorrow he could make sense of it, surrendering to sleep almost at once.

***

In cell number four, deep in the bowels of the new Reading police station, Castle Street, Sir Reginald Smyth was relieved of his weapons and armour, finally allowed to stand in his bare feet, even his leather straps and inner boots that protected his skin from abrasions and lesions taken from him. His silk under garments were dirty and worn through, his bloomers – soiled and washed in streams and even a deep puddle – threadbare and decidedly unhealthy. He was asked for these too, having been given a towelling gown that was several sizes too small.

"This way," barked the Desk Sergeant D Clifford of the area's police force!

Sir Reginald followed him out of the cell where two other burly constables fell into step, the tall knight being led to the showers. There they were met by an extremely young constable who handed Sir Reginald a bar of soap.

The big knight looked down at it in complete puzzlement. "What's this," he asked?

"Soap," explained the young trainee – a little perplexed himself.

The small brick in Sir Reginald's hand felt oddly strange and heavy. He hefted it slightly, as if it might be a support for something. "What to do," he asked?

"Stick it up your arse," grumbled the desk sergeant darkly!

Sir Reginald shot him an equally dark look.

"When you get in the shower," the young cadet explained, "it will moisten and lather up and get you clean."

"Really," extolled the knight, raising it to his nose to sniff it? He then ran his tongue over it, finding it most disagreeable. *"Yuk!"*

"You're not supposed to eat it: *Jeeze,* get him in the shower Davy and I'll be back in a minute!"

The Desk Sergeant left, taking the two bodyguards with him. Sir Reginald was led to the showers and shown how to operate them, the cadet, actually reaching in to lather up the soap for him. Sir Reginald stripped off his towelling dressing gown and handed it to him as if he was some knave, holding a hand under the warm water.

He was soon enjoying himself, finding the small brick did what the cadet had promised and lathered up into a froth of bubbles with a rich soapy spume that washed the dirt and grime away like magic. Forgetting he was naked in a big sparse room, Sir Reginald nigh hummed as he cleaned himself, washing what seemed like eons of dirt and filth from his hair, face and body. The cadet had to push the button in again half way through the operation, the big knight finding his eyes didn't like soap in them, but enjoying himself none the less, then spending some time rinsing himself off. The young trainee policeman had found a towel and handed it to the strange man, finding Sir Reginald took a moment before he realised it was to dry himself off with.

"Where are you from," asked the young cadet quietly as Sir Reginald towelled himself dry?

"The Shires," the big knight responded gaily.

"Shires…" enquired the trainee doubtfully?

"Summer's set," the knight responded.

"Ah, not far then."

Sir Reginald paused to think for a moment. "No," he assuaged, "since we appear to be in the southern lands of England, not far at all, although I lived in a time of plenty, a rich landscape of woodland and forest – game in abundance. That all seems to have gone now – in this time."

"This time…" repeated the cadet dumbly?

Sir Reginald handed the uniformed young man the towel back, the trainee stepping over to simply toss it into a plastic basket behind him. As the knight climbed back into the ill-fitting dressing gown, the young policeman couldn't help himself. "What do you do – you know – for a living," the officer asked, re-joining him?

"I'm a Knight of the Realm," blurted Sir Reginald bluntly, straightening with pride as he tied the small belt around him. "I hold the crest of the Pendragon castle, my father being a knight of the inner circle."

The deep frown on the young man before him puzzled Sir Reginald, the knight taking a moment to appraise his uniform – which, when he studied it, did seem to be of a thick and dense nature – almost a suit of armour in its own right. "Are *you* a soldier of this realm," he asked the young man in all honesty?

The raw recruit shook his head, looking back up at him with a certain warmth. "No – not soldier as such – more a peacekeeper."

"Ah," reminisced Sir Reginald. "A sheriff."

"Well, sort of. I'm just in training at the moment. Take my final exams in the new year."

Sir Reginald nodded, although he had no hope of understanding fully.

In the following pause the knight realised the young man before him seemed to be wrestling with some internal problem, appearing to be dying to ask some fundamental question. While they still remained alone, he blurted it out, almost shaking his head in denial as he spoke. "Have you actually come back through time," he asked with bated breath, unsure of his own words?

Sir Reginald shifted his weight, unsure himself of his predicament. "I suppose I have," he posed, knowing he'd left whatever he loved far behind, unsure even, if he could ever return.

"Can you go back?"

The tall knight shrugged.

Once back in his cell, he was handed an armful of blankets and other stuff and told to make himself comfortable as it would take a little time for senior MI5 and 6 representatives to race down from London, but they would be here – along with other senior politicians and the prime minister no doubt, so he was told to just wait a little while.

They needn't have worried on his account. Sir Reginald hadn't slept in anything resembling a bed yet since his arrival – hadn't even slept lying down – been mostly sitting up or propped up against a wall or bench. Now, with agreeable heat and a cosy room, with even a bed – and mattress, Sir Reginald smiled with satisfaction, thanking whatever gods were smiling down on him at that moment. He moved to sit on the raised platform at the back of the cell to look over all the little presents he'd been given, a toothbrush in a plastic container that Sir Reginald frowned over, another smaller bar of soap – which he recognised quickly as the same cleaning stuff, some soft paper on a roll which he at first thought was for his pillow, and a small comb – again in a clear plastic sleeve. The knight dropped everything else and examined the comb closely, something in his memory linking the object to an item of bone that had been crafted in the same way and was used to untangle women's hair. He pulled the thin object from its scabbard and held it in his fingers testing its flexibility and texture, finally understanding a little about the strange material they all called *'plastic'*.

Sir Reginald placed everything on the mattress beside him and, with comb in hand stood to step over to a toilet bowl and wash basin set in another wall that had a polished piece of metal as a mirror, the knight able to see his reflection – a rather frightening figure that he decided needed some serious refinement. He looked at the thin comb in his fingers and then tried to comb through his hair, finding it had matted together like daubed straw, the comb sinking in and sticking fast – even though he'd washed his hair a couple of times with the soap.

Sir Reginald forced it through, braking off teeth as he did so, partially managing to create a central parting and relatively neat sides, standing back with much satisfaction.

"One for the ladies, no doubt," he chortled, although the comb now had several teeth missing. "Ah, well…time for bed."

He tossed the comb into the basin and headed for the platform that he would make into a nice *flat* bed, clearing all the other bits and pieces away to the end and throwing out the blanket, using another as a pillow. He climbed in and stretched out, revelling in his cleanliness and the faint aroma of the soap still clinging to his body, feeling the muscles of his back and legs relax as the weight sunk into the soft foam. He had one fleeting hope that Lindsey was being treated equally well, then falling fast asleep before he had hope of formulating another

In the wardroom Desk Sergeant D Clifford and Sergeant Frobisha were examining Sir Reginald Smyth's armour and weapons, everything, including the silk undergarments having the essence of authenticity; the armour and weapons being especially heavy.

"This dagger," Sergeant Frobisha was extolling, "is nothing short of one entire piece of hewn metal. You can even see where the forging has left little blow holes in the steel – and the hemp surrounding the handle. *Jeeze,* it must be eons old" (he sniffed it again) "smells like a mixture of animal and human sweat; but look at the blade, honed to a scalpel's finish!"

Sergeant D Clifford, ever the sceptic, hefted the dagger for himself, finding on closer inspection the quillion was expertly folded in over the handle before a wound grip was fastened, the tightly bound hemp giving a soft texture for a solid hold. He examined the diamond-shaped pommel which had been finely engraved, running the fingers of his other hand down the beautifully inlaid blood vane, then the scabbard; a rich velvety red leather held rigid by a bronze locket and chape, the workmanship exquisite. He slid the knife (which was more like a small short sword) back into its housing and glanced over the armour and broadsword one more time, finding his effects remarkably life-like – although in his book metal could be made to look old and authentic just by leaving it out in the garden for a week. He shook his head and sighed over the inventory, leaving his compatriot to find a place for it all.

"How many goddamn times do you want me to tell the same story," Lindsey Cartwright raged?

In yet another big conference room, in a lavish hotel not far from the prison where Reginald Smyth was incarcerated, the prime minister and many of her leading government figures crowded around a polished walnut table, rubbing shoulders with the MI5 and 6 agents; police commissioners and civic representatives, all trying to make sense of what had happened – and more poignantly, what was going to happen?

The female politician who'd first encountered Lindsey now stood by her side, having been won over by Sir Reginald's attitude as she made it her duty to accompany them, the knight in no distress at all over his apparent incarceration, taking everything so much in his stride, and finding obvious wonder and pure amazement over the simplest of things: he was either a brilliant actor or the real thing. Add to this Lindsey Cartwright's apparent involvement – which – on the face of it seemed truthful enough – even if you discounted the transformation from human to mouse and back again, something Davina B Macleod put down to a trance-like state, drugs, or fugue perhaps – or all: but still – there was something in both the couple's deportment that rang suspiciously true. Why for instance surrender yourselves to the opposing side with such a ridiculous story if it didn't have a semblance of truth about it – the two miraculous domes in themselves – and the men – mostly mounted knights in splendid armour and weaponry attesting to some Fortean occurrence. Spies and journalists that had managed to slip across these enemy lines, on foot or motorcycle, evading any serious scrutiny while bringing back photos and video clips galore, ratified yet more information, although the authorities to date had discounted the whole escapade as a load of re-enactment societies creating something of a rebellious stand – possibly along with several other activist bodies all joining forces to bring down the government or worse, change the Civic Charter. But who or what had developed the encroaching domes, a technology that so far had evaded the top scientists: And what about this Danny King, aka King Arthur Pendragon? Did he really stumble across the fabled Sword in the Stone, and wrench it from it's moorings one fateful morning? What in god's name brought the thing back into our time?

In her thoughtful sojourn Lindsey Cartwright had fended off yet another load of quick-fire questions – on her feet yet again in an endearing plea to call back the amassing army of soldiers and volunteers congregating along the second Dome's boundaries. Nearly all however were still determined to trip Lindsey up or discredit her, the general feeling that by doing so would ameliorate the apparent terrible power of The Domes and leave the government to round up all the dissenters and bang them to rights – no matter how many – the story of Danny King and the Sword in the Stone just too fanciful for anyone to believe at that moment. But as the arguments raged and Lindsey Cartwright stuck to her story – however implausible – and by continuing reconnaissance and video footage, it was obvious the opposing armies were outnumbering the ten to twelve thousand or so veterans and recruits hunkering down all along the roads and river banks on the other side, three or four to one; the whole of Exmoor and Salisbury Plains turning into a war zone if something wasn't done soon.

The prime minister had the last call – along with several of the senior intelligence agents – and by the way a video clip showed the advancement of the secondary Dome as it pushed a heavily armoured tank back along a road, bending up its barrel as it did so – not to mention the discharging of firearms after The Dome had swept by, well, here then was concrete evidence that something was amiss, The Dome proving to be a sticking point that no-one could disprove. Add this woman's testament – and the knight who'd been brave enough to cross over enemy lines – and you had one compelling argument – if you wanted to believe it. If you didn't – and you left things to fate – with the lives of nearly twelve thousand men (and counting) – young and old ready to be put on the line, it put things succinctly into focus.

"I feel," the prime minister spoke quietly, once everyone had exhausted or vented their feelings, "that – with all the evidence we have at hand, it certainly would be unwise to risk the lives of so many men. If the reports are true and this Danny King and his followers want to march on London, well…" and here the prime minister faltered for a moment, knowing her next encounter would be with The Queen and royal family, where she would have to explain her actions, "then I'm afraid we'll have to pull back and try and ascertain what action should be necessary – and when. How many men and armaments opposing us, did you calculate Professor Crosby?"

Until now, the Professor of History and Antiquities from Reading University had been looking over a hastily arranged document that had various pictures and scientific printouts describing The Domes' structure and the combatants and their apparent history – everything centred around the enigmatic fifth and sixth centuries when the fabled King Arthur and his knights were supposed to have been prevalent – also calculating for himself the weight of numbers amassing on the other side. It was simple rule of mathematics if you considered the basic age of a warrior to be around twenty five or thirty – apply a somewhat dubious deed poll from around that time – say three generations to one century – put the population of the southern shires into the mix – and to his estimation there was possibly six to eight thousand fully mounted and battle-ready knights. If you then added perhaps another few thousand men from the fields and forges you could possibly swell the numbers fractionally –

but not by a lot. So – if there were hundreds of thousands of men – where were they coming from – Europe? The professor shook his head and gave an appropriate answer, giving his prudent calculations – although it was obvious from the television reports that despite his estimation – even if you considered two centuries – it still did not account for the hundreds of thousands that were swarming towards The Dome's edge.

"We've got to stand and fight," attested a politician with a military background. "If we let this go any further the next Dome could feasibly stretch all the way to the outskirts of our capital, the next swamping London and all we hold dear."

"The Royal Family have already been moved," a senior figure in government advised.

"Be that as it may – if we simply let this thing bulldoze its way over us – who knows what will happen – it could well be a foreign power after all!"

"The RAF is on standby," a military attaché commented, appearing nonplussed about deploying any air arm.

"All leave has been cancelled," a military spokesman added, "and battalions are reforming as we speak, moving in convoys from all points of the country. It has to be said however, that many are believing this to be a formal turning point in our democracy, a call to arms for the working man as it were to make a stand. *And* many are already forming into a kind of home guard – but not for The Queen – *oh no* – for this bloody King Arthur!"

"Hundreds – if not thousands have done the same throughout Cornwall, Devon, Somerset and

Dorset," Lindsey Cartwright confirmed. "The British people have been pushed and railroaded over enough. It's time to re-adjust the monetary sphere, realign the pay grades. When people do not have enough to live on, they have nothing to lose!"

"And throw democracy, fair trade and enterprise out the window I suppose," jested a portly politician who perhaps stood to lose ill-gained off-shore accounts among other assets.

"I don't assume to know how it will work," Lindsey Cartwright sighed heavily, "I can only attest to what I've seen – *and let's face it,* there's been revolution and rebellion all through our history – you only have to subjugate a nation for so long – and sooner or later the straw is going to snap. All I'm worried about right now is averting what I can see as one almighty slaughter!"

"I'm afraid," spoke the prime minister solemnly, "that I have to agree with Sir William here. If we allow things to continue, we are in danger of losing everything – who knows what this Danny King has in mind – he might well turn out to be the worst despot we've ever seen – or worse, he could be working for some third-world country – How soon for the regiments of cavalry and support units to arrive, Sir William?"

The portly politician glanced at his expensive chronograph. "Two hours, prime minister. We have other detachments arriving as well – various mounted divisions from The Met and Household Cavalry – many skilled horsemen, Ma'am!"

"Thank you Sir William." The prime minister looked deeply into Lindsey's eyes. "I am sorry dear lady that your entreaty will not be upheld, but we'll take it on note that you did your best. But truthfully – despite having dire misgivings about this whole set up, I have to agree with my colleagues, in that a stand must be made here before The Domes reach the capital. If there are hundreds of thousands as you say – then we will have to match them and fight it out here, before it goes any further."

Swayed by the thought of mounted police and the Household Cavalry joining forces, Lindsey had to slump in her chair, finally beaten by the sobering mental vision of columns of mounted guards and plenty of regimental foot soldiers from the palace climbing into wagons and trucks to hurtle down to Salisbury. By the time morning arrived, perhaps King Arthur's army may well have met its match.

Lindsey gave up. "Where's the bar," she asked?

Chapter 8

Drowsy – and not at all sure of what was going on, Guinevere found herself pushed, pulled, coerced by some unearthly force, out of an abandoned castle and over empty fields to a swirling portal of bristling energy that stood at the bottom of the valley like a celestial event, calling her through every pore of her body – her whole embodiment being sucked into the epiphanic whirlpool. As if in a dream she'd stumbled, dumbfounded, unsure of her own mind, driven by some otherworldly power, encouraged to step up and through the encompassing portal like a person possessed; released only when she fell through to the other side, virtually on hands and knees, to find she was in some desolate part of the country, the castle, manors and shires gone, the land stark and bare as she gazed out over what was now Exmoor.

There had been some time dilation as it had been late afternoon back in her shire, the freshness of early morn now revealing itself. She'd travelled not only in space but time as well.

To meet her were a complete detachment of knights on horseback and foot-soldiers, lining what was the only footpath that led directly to a country house that had already been completely taken over; knights and caravans in attendance for the last twelve hours.

The Queen was helped to her feet, Guinevere frowning over the men she should have known but were not her own knights, shown to a wooden carriage and made comfortable, the whole regiment then moving off to first freshen up at the nearest facility – then move rapidly towards Taunton where hopefully Arthur would be waiting.

Guinevere held her head as the carriage bounced over the land, glad she had at least dressed accordingly, her emerald green silk gown abraded where she'd fallen to her knees. She tried wiping the torn silks away with a little spittle, tutting, but in the end gave up, knowing her king would hopefully understand. *Why,* she had to think, sitting back, why all this rigmarole – *for who, for what?*

She remembered talking to Merlin about this, hoping the campaign would heal the rift between them, but Arthur's attentions had been drawn elsewhere, some saying he'd been bewitched, but he'd always had an eye for the girls, despite having the finest in the land, something in his lapses of detachment pointing to a life outside of the shire – one of a spiritual nature perhaps – one where only kings could go. Merlin had also prepared her for the fact that he may well have changed in their separation, perhaps been overwhelmed by some beautiful water nymph, wood seraph or witch, his persona warped by magic and subterfuge, allowing his very essence to be sucked dry. It was unlike him to dabble but something had lured him to Bloodmere Lake, the waters always tainted by some cruel witchcraft, the shores oozing with slime and treacherous deceit. There her King had been seen cavorting with an invisible mistress, the she-devil having wheedled her way into his fancies somehow, a temptress so strong even Merlin could not intervene.

Guinevere wrung her hands together, anxious over the meeting, annoyed over this ludicrous campaign, drawing the complete army away from the shires; it was madness when danger lay across the sea.

Could she coax him from his bull-headedness?

***

Arthur woke early.

Surrounding him was the unmistakable snuffling and light snoring of his personal bodyguard, forty or more encamped throughout the luxurious apartment.

He craned his neck and tried to find the time, an electric display – just visible through the plume of an elaborate steel helmet, showing it was a quarter to five – almost dawn.

In his powerful firmament there were ripples – disturbances of a kind he'd not felt before, odd feelings and strange reminiscences that didn't belong, visions that hovered about his subconscious but were not his. From somewhere he was being called; far across the eons, far across time and space – the filaments and raiments of a love he'd never experienced.

Dan eased himself from the light duvet to sit on the edge of the bed, arching his back in an early morning stretch; trying not to wake anyone.

He gazed down at a body he barely recognised, a deeply tanned and taut goliath of a man whose years of bodybuilding had been a template onto which the powerful energy forces had welded and forged yet more muscle, bringing with it more definition. He had the strength *and* fortitude of twenty men, had been built up and then honed down to emerge as a colossus amongst titans – a King amongst Kings – a saviour.

Around him however, the atmosphere continued to invade his thoughts – his very mind – an effervescent roiling mist he couldn't see but could feel with every fibre of his body; each and every nerve attuned to the signals; but unlike Merlin's arrival, this persona was totally different... purity – honesty and elegance threading though the pulses. It had to be a woman, he mused with abstract wonder – unable at that moment to put two and two together.

Frowning and shaking his head, Arthur found his feet and dressed quietly, slipping on a tabard and thick leather belt. Although warm and balmy he also stepped into a pair of soft suede slippers, to ward off any cold surfaces from his feet – or protect from standing on anything sharp.

He was ravenously hungry.

Down in the bowels of the commercialised fortress he found a large refectory bustling with activity, the room big enough to hold twelve to fourteen trestle tables along the opposite wall of the kitchen, knights already enjoying a hearty breakfast – the unmistakable aroma of frying bacon and grilled sausages waking many from their slumber. There was a small queue along a chrome serving counter, but once the crowding knights had been alerted that The King was in their presence, all melted away, bowing courtly, allowing him access. Dan, still a little groggy from the continual miasma of his encroaching ether (someone's persona wrapped up in the deft signals and nuances) acknowledged the deference shown by his body-guarding inner circle, nodding cordially.

"Monster breakfast," asked a young girl who already looked stressed out by the workload?

For one long second the word *'monster'* put him in mind of a prehistoric steak served up with dinosaur trimmings but he was quick enough to nod dumbly, assuming *'monster'* was the epitome of a super large serving; bigger perhaps than extra large. He hovered for a moment, then, not thinking, he wandered over to an empty table, trying to slide into the bench seating.

He couldn't get his big thighs in under the table so thought to move the padded bench aside, finding it was stuck fast.

'Damn', he reasoned, *'it couldn't be that heavy?'*

Thinking the seat was jammed somehow, he gave it a forceful tug – ripping out anchoring bolts as he did so, the screech of metal as they were torn from their moorings waking everyone up, especially the kitchen staff – who – up till then anyway were working completely on remote control. Accompanied by the acting head chef, the young girl who served The King now scampered back to the counter to see what was happening.

By the time they got there Dan was sitting peacefully, conversing with a Knight of the Realm who'd thought to keep The King company.

The kitchen staff stared, realised dimly Dan was this fabled King Arthur – and shrugged and got back to work, catering for the first initial rush.

Dan eyed the big knight standing over him, encouraged by the way he had approached, overriding his concerns by considering this an unofficial time of the day – when his liege might well be in need of a little light relief.

"May, I ..." the knight had asked, bowing suavely from the hip?

Dan looked up from his bowed head and nodded with a weak smile. He watched idly as the knight arranged himself opposite, taking care not to let the huge hilt of his broadsword dig into the flooring tiles. He wedged himself in with a clinking and clanking that made Dan smile. The action caused him to consider the mess he'd made of the bench he was sitting on, having ripped the bolts clean out of the concrete. There was a cloud of dust and debris around each stanchion.

The knight ignored the mishap, leaning forward to enquire if The King had enjoyed a good night's rest, placing his war bonnet and gloves down the table.

"Yes indeed," Dan spoke genially, placing his huge forearms on the table in front of him. "Since last night however, I have this – erm..." and Dan waved a semaphore hand in the air indicating he hadn't much of a clue about what he was experiencing, "some kind of feeling that someone special is coming through the portals, someone that may well be a woman."

"Guinevere, my liege."

"Who?"

"Guinevere – The Queen, your wife, sir – well, Arthur's wife actually – that's probably why there's some confusion."

Dan stared at the knight. Probably five foot ten in his stockinged feet, he had no neck to speak of, just muscle and sinew – a body as hard as the steel it was encased in. The term *'bull'* kept drifting through his mind, Dan fighting with the derogatory idea to stop him using it as a name for the knight. Then the penny dropped. *"Holy shit,"* he breathed, his worry broken over the arrival of his breakfast – a meal served on several platters – too much to be put on one plate. Dan stared down at the sizzling bacon, eggs and sausages, gammon steaks and mushrooms, hash browns and beans, not seeing them, unable to take it all in at that point in time. *"Guinevere,"* he mouthed in ardent reverence.

"Any condiments," asked the young serving girl?

Dan didn't hear her. She looked at the knight accompanying The King, but he just shrugged – not understanding. She sighed with a *'humph,'* and flounced off to get them anyway!

"We got word late last night, my lord," the knight advised him in a lowered voice. "She awaits your arrival in Taunton some time this morning – before what I think might be something of an engagement."

"Don't remind me," muttered Danny wondering where to start on his breakfast! He looked around for some utensils but finding none, began loading a plate he'd been given with his fingers.

"May I," the knight opposite enquired of Danny?

The king looked up. "May you..?"

"Join you," the knight hesitated, fearing he may well have overstepped the mark?

"Oh, of course, dig in – erm..." he looked around for another spare plate.

A minute later the serving girl banged yet another tray of sauces and vinegar, doling out a series of serviettes, asking if there was anything else.

"A spare plate for my companion please, and some utensils, thank you?"

"Prap's you'd like me to eat it for you," she murmured as she flounced away yet again?

"Feisty," remarked the knight!

Dan smiled, finally catching up with the early mornings events.

***

After a lengthy breakfast – in which Danny munched and gulped his way through a repast fit for not only a king but several of his bodyguards as well, he wandered through with a complete entourage of heavily clad knights, finding there was already a thoroughly attended war council in the making; Lancelot, Sir Percival and Galahad conferring thoughtfully with a resurfaced Merlin; many taking note of the news channels that were making much of the fact that some kind of stand would be made in the southern heartland – newsclips educating the masses on the historical bearing of Salisbury Plain – not least for the Neolithic construction of Stonehenge. More army units (made up of those who hadn't defected) had moved from the British Army Training Unit at Suffield to support other collaborations as they headed south – and from other parts of the country. Numbers had increased steadily through the night, making Danny rise from his seat to walk forward and see for himself. Regiments of the famous Horse Guards and Blues and Royals had been ferried down from London and were forming up as he watched; lancers, pike men in modern ballistic armour were marching in serried ranks as the helicopter swung over the area, huge swathes of the chalk grassland covered now with white tents.

Dan put a thoughtful hand through his hair as the weight of numbers continued to swell.

"They're making a go of it this time, no mistake," mentioned Bill Nightingale, down by his side. With him stood his beautiful consort Fay, the woman from the sixth century looking resplendent from modern cleaning products and hair shampoos. Dan acknowledged them both, but hastily made it back to the big central table where Merlin was conferring with several of his ilk. The King's own inner circle were kept abreast of the increase in combatants on the other side of The Dome, sending runners out to bring the rearguard and main armies forward as quick as possible. Merlin had wanted to get the morning over with as soon as he could, but now, with the increase in the enemies' ranks he was having second thoughts, arranging for some heavy artillery to come through the portals and ensure him of victory – at any cost.

When The King asked about this, Merlin explained that war elephants might be needed – or the odd ogre or dragon.

"Dragon," Dan coughed out!

"Extinct in your time, I know," Merlin countered, trying to whisper in his ear, "but not in mine! That's the beauty of medieval Britain, many secrets!"

"By the numbers massing on the other side, we're going to need all the help we can get. We're probably matched man for man now."

"Man for man, they will still be no match for us. Worry not my liege. I will win this battle for you because we have to – they know if we win this one, our next venture may encroach on the capital and then the country will be broken. We'll subsume the other southern states but move on London just as quickly. With their forces depleted in this confrontation they will be reluctant to fight again – the path to the capital – and your rightful place on the throne – will be assured."

Danny placed a meaty paw on Merlin's shoulder, glancing back to the big television screen, hesitant over the massive build up on both sides, the welter of regiments Britain still had to offer, despite cutting the national defence budget in half every subsequent year in the last two decades, still many were ready to fight and die for their Queen and country.

Countermanding this however was something that lifted his heart and spirits greatly, the Republican Army – Oliver's Republican Army was finally and resolutely gaining strength and numbers as it too had marched and campaigned across two counties, groups forming into crowds as they thronged through the streets, hundreds then turning into thousands as they brought up the rearguard. There were so many, standing out from their fifth and sixth century counterparts by the cameo outfits and coloured body armour, by the union flags and socialistic banners.

Arthur watched the news coverage, vans slowly creeping with the gaily clad throngs, many singing and chanting that this was the coming of the age – the coming of Aquarius.

"We should prepare, my lord," a squire mentioned meekly by his side.

Danny nodded, "We ride to Taunton," he called out to his war cabinet.

"Your lady awaits," Lancelot called back.

"My lady awaits," Danny parodied to Merlin, having pulled him aside for a moment, "but she's not my lady – *not at all* – *'I've never met her?"*

"Every king needs a queen," Merlin stated poetically.

"You're not helping, Merlin. What the hell am I going to do with her?"

"She's really here for moral support," Merlin explained cautiously, anxious to catalogue the welter of heavy artillery that had stumbled and lumbered through the nearest portal. It was important to protect his flanks as the army advanced with the dome to meet the entrenched army awaiting them, the artful sage unknowing of ballistics and other projectiles of this current century that could maim and kill – those that needed no combustible powder or paste. To advise him of what he might be up against, he'd been shown that morning a modern-day crossbow, the cased weapon clipped together within seconds and loaded and ready to fire within the next, the bolt when released cutting clean through plate armour. Merlin had seen catapults in action and knew of the principles of kinetic force such as a fulcrum or bent piece of well-oiled wood, but these new plastics and resins could harness that power and triple it in their composite design. He had handled the weapon with reverence and respect, considering the strength within its jet-black design, the item so small and light – yet deadly when in range – which wasn't great, he had to admit, merely the length of the hall, but what about larger versions? One mounted on the back of a truck could feasibly knock down a knight at full gallop. He'd enquired at length if there was anything else he should be aware of, but apart from lethal-looking catapults that had some range and could fire a deadly coin or other small object, and plastic rounds that still had a gunpowder charge of some description that The Dome would recognise and detune, he was assured there was no magical force such as lasers or proton-canons to worry about.

"I really don't need a woman to get under my feet at this stage," Danny was still extolling as Merlin tried to extricate himself, her arrival just complicating matters as he saw it – having enough on his plate. "And to top it all," he insisted nearly following Merlin as he desperately edged away, "she's obviously someone else's wife! What do I do about that?"

Merlin stopped dead and spun round to place his hands firmly on Arthur's chest, stopping him dead. "My lord, she is here merely to be by your side, the original king long gone – she needs you at this stage – as much as you need her. Now saddle up and go to her and comfort her – she's not taking this too well, I take it?"

"I'm not taking this too well," Danny nearly shouted back! "I've got an absolute army massing ahead of me – a right battle royal bearing down on us – and now I have to cosset a woman – a woman I don't even know!"

"My liege," Merlin sighed, trying to fend off his war council and other sages, "she is a powerful ally – an angel sent from heaven – she is all but divine – the power she will afford you when she sits by your side will be a hundred-fold – *do not shun her away!"*

"Holy god..." Dan sighed – and gave up, allowing Merlin to return to his ministrations! Soon he and the others would be making tracks, and he ought to as well. With a fatalistic sigh, he headed for his apartment and the squires and knaves that would be waiting to dress him in all his finery, a golden and silver suit of armour and weaponry that would gleam so; it would outshine the very sun above and probably blind the oncoming army. He strode through the hotel

and skipped up the stairs, his bodyguard trying to keep up.

***

The journey to Taunton was aided greatly by the largely abandoned M5. News by now of the two encompassing domes and King Arthur's apparent takeover, had reached all parts of the British Isles never mind most of the entire world, many allies of the United Kingdom wanting to lend a hand but unsure of how to, since the incredible power grids simply knocked out any ballistics as they advanced, rendering tanks, cannons and firearms useless – the operatives undefended. America and Europe would send troops by the thousands if needed, swelling numbers, but worried that unarmed they'd simply be at the mercy of an unnatural invading army – one that seemed to have a preternatural power all of its own. Sovereignty too, was being called into question, many world leaders immediately being appraised as to the legend of King Arthur and wrangling over who exactly should retain the crown?

With his heavily armed bodyguard, King Arthur surveyed the land of Somerset and Dorset from the gilded saddle of his magnificent charger as they set off, joining the big open roadway quickly; the motorway unnervingly quiet as they clomped, thanking the team of the fortified hotel heartily before they left, then clanking and snorting their way forward.

As they wended their way through Tiverton to engage the main M5 to Taunton, well wishers crowded the streets, many merely curious, but others making a show of supporting this new monarch, hastily made banners and flags endorsing his rise to power. As they moved swiftly into open countryside, to each side, over dike, river, railway, field and town, the caravan of his armies, the hordes of revellers – those who'd simply taken time off work to join in the spectacle, mingled with those who had a more ardent feel about the campaign – those who'd taken up arms alongside their new King, convinced of his worthiness. Trudging along with them were divisions of foot soldiers who'd passed through the portal the previous night, bolstering an already heaving army, Merlin obviously taking no chances as mortal conflict seemed the most likely outcome. As the glittering cortege followed the motorway, giving way occasionally for the lone truck or car, Danny spotted an unsightly company of ogres, the beings – straight out of Terry Prachett's imagination – waddling across the land, making him stretch in his saddle as they moved in a tangent to him, heading for the demarcation line thirty or forty miles towards the historical and much loved town of Frome, stopping just short of its conservation areas. Dressed in hide-leather bib and braces, toting a spiked club that looked like it could knock down a house with one foul swing, the ten-foot beings looked anything but lenient. Dan bit his bottom lip and worried, staring at them and at even heavier war elephants that were moving slowly in the distance, all having to navigate obstacles in the land. Having studied the maps extensively Merlin and his war council had decided to try and divert the armies away from the populated areas, instead pushing the battle lines to the Mendip hills and open spaces of Wiltshire, a massive detachment slipping around behind the town of Frome to perhaps ensnare the opposing army. The magical sage had advised Bill Nightingale and others of the press to make it clear to the politicians and military chiefs that he wanted no harm to come to civilians within the combat area – and the prime minister agreed wholeheartedly that battle lines should avoid the bigger towns and cities at all costs. It didn't stop the revenant armies trudging through conurbations however and by the support they got when pushing through the streets and avenues of Dorchester in the south and Cheddar in the north you'd have thought The Queen herself was passing along, many again throwing caution to the wind to, if not lend support, then just tag along for the excitement. In Glastonbury many of King Arthur's resurfaced army appeared to recognise or feel something special about the place, Merlin even making a detour to visit the town, the tor and Magdelene Chapel steeped in old magic. Towards the wonderful town of Taunton however, where so many a rebellion had taken place over the centuries, another now beckoned, fifth and sixth century knights and foot soldiers encamping for a while on the famous cricket ground just under the auspices of the tower of St James' church, many a knight crowding in for salvation. They were received well – as was The King as he neared.

Just shy of the river crossing of the Tone, Danny had to pause as a detachment of ... well; he hadn't much of a clue what they were save a basically human shape, neared the bridge, the horses and accompanying herds of domestic animals shying away as the golems awaited their turn to cross. Dan halted his entourage to allow the beings to pass unimpeded, allowing himself a better look of these unsettling combatants, the men apparently swathed in a leather of some kind, each individual well over seven feet, even their faces covered in a brown leather mask. When one turned to stare at the gaudy collection of horses and knights, its eyes blazed a coal-hot red, those orbs chilling everyone – and thing – to the core.

"Who in God's name are they," Dan whispered hoarsely across to Lancelot?

"Mor-men," the knight answered at length, apparently uncomfortable with the beings himself. "Live underground or within a lake, harmless unless you anger them."

"Why are they fighting for me," The King asked?

"They're not," put in Gawain, calling across; having caught The King up to fill a gap by his flank. "They are a law completely to themselves – a race of near giants that live a solitary existence – they care little for the concerns of men."

"Then what are they doing here?"

Gawain shrugged. "Probably been encouraged by the ogres – a chance to live and breathe again – well, live anyway – perhaps they think there'll be some remuneration or reward. They've a real sticking point for anything shiny!"

"They'll love me," Dan muttered in detachment.

"We'll make sure they do their job – worry not my liege," the Green Knight called from out front, watching the Mor-men with interest however.

Watching the detachment of around three hundred of them plod over the bridge, even battle-hardened ogres giving way, Dan had to hope someone would point them in the right direction and that they wouldn't decide to run amok and start attacking his forces.

"They know whose side they're on, I take it," Danny commented, geeing his charger on once the bridge was clear?

"Debatable..," worried Galahad who seemed to have old scores to settle.

The King moved on, crossing into the Tangier district, wending his way around the old historic town, greeting cheering crowds. The sight – the first big crowds he'd seen since his inauguration was heartening in the extreme, giving him more purpose than ever before. It didn't matter that Taunton was the home of the 40 Commando group, housing around six or seven hundred able-bodied men at any time, the olive green of the modern army uniform evident among the crowds. Dan sensed the age-old rebelliousness in the Cornish and Taunton psyche – the mindset that harboured deep resentment over social injustice and corrupt values: A determination that had festered for a millennium or more. As he clip-clopped around the town stopping at the wonderful Tudor buildings in Fore Street; the County hall where office workers spilled out to welcome him, he was then guided onto the Victoria Park where Guinevere was waiting.

The setting couldn't have been better. With the sun beaming through The Dome's structure, making it a lot warmer than usual for summer, many an insect on the wing, King Arthur's retinue moved toward taking over a big field opposite Priory Park, Guinevere and her heavily armoured bodyguard of around four thousand knights and foot soldiers having stationed themselves all over the other end blocking the A358 completely. The King's entourage surged along Taunton's streets to finally emerge through the sparse trees at the other end, thrilling the crowds that ringed the big field, the whole area from the Priorswood Road in the north to the conurbations of Holway Green in the south, thronging with his armies, many simply passing through to join with the main contingent massing at Wincanton, Shepton Mallet and just short of Radstock.

For Arthur, the journey from Tiverton had been filled with enthrallment – and a touch of unease, the armour-suited war elephants – many looking as if they'd seen several engagements already, along with the ogres and Mor-men – beings that looked anything but human, and legions of the dead that would not care if they lived or died – just here, it seemed for the combat – and if by chance they could take another to the grave with them – all appearing to him to be outweighing the flimsy lances of the Horse Guards and other regiments that had joined in the opposing army the previous evening; swelling the ranks immensely; the excitement of the pageantry lost amid the dust of the bloody bulldozer opposing them. No matter how many men the royalists mustered behind the line, even The Dome advancing forward would cause damage, never mind the armies following. If only he could call it off, he remonstrated with himself, sitting regally, call for some kind of cessation to the hostilities, make the other side see sense – or did he need to see sense himself?

As sweat trickled down from under his gleaming war helmet, Arthur strained to see ahead, his knights and foot soldiers ringing the field ten deep, protecting this meeting between two super gods.

Knights led him forward as Guinevere was hoisted into a saddle from a small wooden carriage, her glistening white and golden Merovingian silks flowing around her, a subtle aura of white also encompassing her svelte frame as she settled. A diadem of radiant gold and gems graced her head while a simple pure white wimple was draped around her head, neck and shoulders, affording a little shade. Even at distance, she appeared radiant and beautiful, as graceful as a swan and as alluring as sapphires.

Arthur was guided forward on his magnificent charger, the grey Percheron war stallion prancing gaily as mares abounded in the close vicinity. The cortege crossed the open centre of the field like a King from a fairy tale, crowds on all sides cheering and hollering as banners and flags fluttered; the air thick with expectation.

They met in the open ground of the field, butterflies filling the air, Arthur's horse being led to her side, the two sitting opposite one another. Guinevere moved an inquisitive bumble bee on from inspecting her glittering crown, raising her head then royally as she met The King's eyes.

Danny was transfixed. He'd seen many an air-brushed photo of beautiful young women – and it was true, there were many pretty and alluring females in the reaches of the southern shores, but Guinevere was truly remarkable, not just beautiful but radiantly stunning, her profile the accolade of symmetry, the wisps of hair a silken blonde; the eyebrows a wonderfully delicate and subtle arch that encompassed two mesmerising blue eyes. The nose was small but slightly aquiline, giving her a strong yet compassionate pose; the parted lips so lovingly crafted – not so full as to detract from her beauty, but just perfect with brilliant white teeth glistening behind. She was all things beautiful, wrapped up in one bushel – embodying every gorgeous woman that had ever walked the earth.

Dan closed his open mouth, and took a breath, realising he'd been holding it, pinned in his seat by her stunning looks, paralysed by her persona. He straightened in his saddle, dimly realising he'd been captivated by her, his eyes roving over the slim but shapely form, cataloguing the tanned forearms, the dainty fingers holding the reins, even her little riding boots – which seemed trim and sweet.

Lancelot, clearing his throat beside him, brought him out of his reverie and King Arthur licked his lips, saying: "Welcome, Guinevere to England. I'm...er, glad you are here."

The queen smirked, a very delectable smile that immediately sent Danny's pulse racing, The King knowing he'd already made a daft faux pas as she evidently already lived in the southern shires – albeit a long time ago, probably not far from this very spot.

"Sorry," Dan spluttered. He waved a massive gauntleted mitt in the air vaguely. "It's just... well, we have something of an engagement pressing and this all seemed a little...erm, out of the blue. I really didn't expect The Queen to attend me, since...well...since I'm not your real husband."

Guinevere eyed him from under her brow, almost scolding him. Dan, worried now he'd miss the engagement altogether, hoped to press the fact that he really ought to be heading east – and in a hurry!

She seemed to read his mind. "We need to go!"

She glanced out at a truly alien world and, trying to rein in her shock, nodded thoughtfully.

"We'll ride together," she spoke in tinkling tones, the harmonious words reminding him of sparkling water from a brook.

"That would be lovely," he concluded and readied his horse. "Onward to Frome," he called out.

All along the way, Danny tried to make conversation, eager to keep his queen entertained, explaining the railway lines, the routes of commerce and trade that had been the arteries of the southern counties for so long, the arable and husbandry of farms and small holdings, the common land of the Somerset Downs and Mendip Hills. When asked, he tried to explain the feudal times that had followed the medieval – the centuries after the reign of King Arthur, and how the countryside had been broken up into its prospective shires, many a field and meadow being subsumed in the grab for land. Guinevere became enthralled by the modern day cow and sheep – those that were left after his armies had surged over the land, many still having to eat their first initial meal. The livestock was being decimated, but Arthur could do little about it now, planning to restock after the takeover, spend some time rebuilding and restoring the southern shires. The buildings, cities and towns in the distance took even more careful explanations, and Danny found, for the first time in his new role as usurper, that he was a little proud of what his fellow countrymen had achieved, the engineering; the bridges, tunnels and shipbuilding; the revived historical sites, Avebury and Stonehenge; the magnificent churches and monasteries dotting the land. All by the sweat and toil of the common man, The King reminded himself as they passed close to the original county town of Somerton, the legions having explored and stopped to marvel at the buildings – running water especially, as well as the cars, motorbikes and pushbikes – the latter gaining much interest as the roads were chock-a-block with foot soldiers, pike-men and knights of all ranks, the caravans as well beginning to catch up with the main army.

A way was cut out for The King and his retinue, finally catching up with Merlin as they rested for a while in the grounds of the Church of St. Mary at Chesterblade; the historical setting a wonderful place for Arthur to show his Queen around the twelfth century Anglican building.

Thinking he suddenly had something of a congregation, the pastor raced from Evercreech to open up the doors and Arthur received him well, many a knight looking for confirmation amidst the pastoral setting. The horses were allowed to munch on the rich grass – and while the priest took the beautiful Guinevere into his patronage, somewhat astounded by the re-enactment societies, he found inside he was surrounded again by an absolute welter of knights and a heavy bodyguard – all looking for redemption.

Outside, Arthur strolled the gardens with Merlin and his war council, able to look from a vantage point across to the village of Wanstrow and the glistening power curtain of the second dome, able even at this range to see the incredible multitude of men and machinery that had massed beyond, riders and signalmen bringing the divisions and detachments into some sort of order.

The sight brought The King up sharp, able to gaze over the lower Mendip Hills and witness the ranks and files of army and specialist forces that had dug in for the coming engagement, laying their life down for Queen and country. Helicopters and heavily armoured drones swept by, keeping abreast of the opposing armies. To counter the massive build up, Merlin had brought much of his heavy artillery to the fore, allowing his war elephants, rhinos and ogres to front the attack. A massive column of knights, pikemen and other combatants had amassed further up the gleaming power grid, to sweep around the back of Frome and charge into the Wiltshire Plain, hoping to push any conflict away from the big town.

Lancelot was captivated by a pair of binoculars he'd been given, Galahad too, deploying a birdwatcher's telescope – complete with tripod, marvelling at the technology, despite the devices showing the massive build-up of men and arms on the other side of The Dome. Dan looked himself, bringing the whole disaster in the making into focus as he adjusted the lenses, the whole of Salisbury Plain covered in army tents and platoons of men, American, French and NATO forces evident through the pennants and flags flown. He swung his binoculars around, bypassing the church in the near distance, cataloguing the masses of soldiers and knights readying themselves as far back as he could see – almost to Glastonbury. The sea of men – and women – and other worldly beings – all determined to meet the aggressor head on.

A distant yelling, hooting and general clamour reached his ears. Everyone stopped to glance around, wondering at the noise. Dan raised his glasses again and swept the undulating countryside to the west, where the caravans and stragglers were still making their way to the front, a huge number of civilians coming into view, moving as one as they began to swarm over the small hills.

"Oliver's Army," Dan mused cataloguing the numbers.

Out front a man dressed completely in an old suit of armour was jigging along before the main crowds, entertaining them immensely; shield and a steel-tipped wooden pole deployed as a lance. No horse.

As Dan shifted his weight, the runner suddenly lost his footing as he cantered down a hill, tumbling over and over in a cascade of bits of armour, his shield and helmet lost too, his lance digging into the ground with an almost audible *'twonk'*.

As the giggling crowds caught their mascot up, many stopping to help strap back on an errant piece of armour, his shield and lance picked up and also handed back, Dan noticed several platoons of army men, many deciding to dress for the occasion, the olive greens and cameos standing out starkly from the usual dress code: Many – faces daubed with black and green – toted weapons, Dan wondering if they thought The Dome might release the hold it had on firearms once it had passed. They were the *'rear guard'* he realised, stopping dead any thoughts of insurrection from within: Thousands, he calculated as yet more surged into view, forming into something of a territorial army.

Dan blew out a sigh, dropping the glasses from his vision, shaking his head imperceptibly, wishing again there was some way he could avert this slaughter. He was about to turn to Lancelot nearby when his eyes caught a small piece of graffiti scrawled on the church walls, hidden by shadow mostly. The day-glow yellow paint – the type that had intrigued many a knight and foot soldier out on the roads had been very carefully daubed, and now as the sun moved around, the full import became clear.

King Arthur has risen, pulling Sword from Stone,
tramping o'er farm and field, a plan all of his own.
Razing town and village, and never looking back;
Well, don't you worry my kinsfolk,
cos, my Dad's after him, with his big baseball bat!

'Hm,' Arthur smiled, wondering what the small crowd of knaves and squires standing underneath it thought. The poetry was crap, written, it seemed by some village idiot, but the sentiment burned deep into his brain, reminding him that not all were devout republicans or reformers.

Dan tried to dismiss it and return to the issue at hand, worrying he'd heard nothing from his emissary Lindsey Cartwright and her noble knight Sir Reginald – that warrior – in his estimation the very epitome of valour and courage his army stood for, the fortitude all his legions displayed, revenants or not – it would take a lot of stamina and bravery to front an army of modern times, the fear of the unknown weighing heavily amidst the alien psyche.

Dan looked heavenward, searched the skies for the fabled dragon, as Merlin sided with him once more, trying to explain the various sections of the armies and how the vanguard would push forward – followed quickly by the main body, The King's and

Queen's own contingent buried somewhere in the middle. He was in no way to be encouraged to join in the fighting, Merlin stressed, knowing Danny's bulk would protect him anyway, but just to be safe he was to hang back amidst the second legions and keep abreast of movements and counter-thrusts. An absolute welter of hand-picked knights would surround the royal couple, Merlin confident they'd be spared – even if the opposing armies gained the upper hand.

He couldn't see how? During the previous evening – as it became clear the stand would be now, before they could advance any further – he summoned many an eldritch demon and supernatural creature, many in folklore now, he knew, modernisation having snuffed out their need – but now – in his time of crisis, these beings and fabled beasts could walk the earth once more, terrorising and stamping out all that was rotten.

The war elephants and rhinos were in place, the strange Mor-men and ogres standing shoulder to shoulder with them, the legions of the dead following – those combaters that had been hexed by witches and demons and stirred uneasily in their graves ever since. Now they could fight once more – and be repatriated – allowed to rest easily once they had fought for King and country – and liberty.

Merlin checked the position of the sun and called together his sages, instructing the war council to prepare.

"I await further news, my liege," he spoke to Danny, taking his hand. "I have a meeting shortly with some informers and will know better the situation – please follow on Arthur – I may be in need of your knowledge." He turned to go, but then turned back, taking his big hand suddenly. "I sincerely hope we will win the day and can then move onto the capital and crown you King."

"Amen to that," chorused many around him!

"I'll follow on shortly," he assured his wizard.

Dan saw Merlin off, turning to a knave to instruct Guinevere to ready herself. She was still deep in conversation with the modern-day priest as she stepped back into the sunlight from the sanctuary of the church, catching up on eons of history and culture in something of a crash course, marvelling at the mores of today against the challenges of the church as a modern-day Dissent – (pushed by the space race and advances in just about every discipline of science) vitiated every sermon and reading to the point of ridicule. *'A new day was dawning'* the clergyman had offered in sad repose, as they greeted the warm afternoon, meaning the incredible rise of computers and artificial intelligence, forgetting completely the upheaval unfolding around him.

"My King is here to right many wrongs," Guinevere instructed the preacher as they ambled from deep shadow back into bright yet muted sunlight. The clergyman blinked several times in order to bring himself back to the present, pausing as they took in the upheaval around them. He nodded thoughtfully looking around himself with something of awe – and a little disbelief, as if he might be experiencing an epiphanic fugue or psychotic episode, unable to take it all in at once. In the confines of his church all seemed rather quiet and calm, despite heavily armoured knights wanting to be blessed, now – outside, back in the real world – *if he could use the term*, all was confusion and mayhem as thousands of flashes of white and yellow glinting off suits of armour almost blinded him; suffusing the very air; the razzmatazz of an invading army, the crashing of metal on metal, the gaily attired warhorses whinnying on the breeze; the soft hazy sunlight muting the chaotic spectacle he had found himself in. *"What..."* he tried to convey?

A knave, dressed in dark green – and looking like he might well have stepped right from the making of a Robin Hood film, bowed regally as he instructed Guinevere that the cortege was about to take its leave, many a knight climbing aboard their prospective warhorses as the priest again tried to put two and two together.

"Thank you, boy; could you ready my horse, please?"

The knave bowed again, deeply this time, displaying almost devout reverence. "M'lady," he acknowledged; then spun off.

"God above," the clergyman fretted, forgetting himself for a moment. If only he could find some of that respect nowadays.

"I thank you," mistress Guinevere addressed the preacher, turning to him. "Perhaps we'll meet again in a more peaceful time?"

He nodded dumbly, almost bowing himself, trying to rein in his amazement, although as he gazed around, having taken her hand in something of a dream, his eyes alighted on the mounted King Arthur in the graveyard on his magnificent steed, preparing to take his leave – a huge detachment of Knights of the Realm surrounding him – and his sanity wavered yet again as the full panoply of what was happening hammered home, the priest almost taking a step back in shock.

"I...er, hope we do, miss – erm, Lady Guinevere," he mouthed in dazed bewilderment!

Sensing his confusion, she smiled sweetly, putting a hand out to him.

Her horse was brought round, a striking grey mare in gleaming gold and silver silks and armour, still munching on a tuft of grass he'd just ripped from around a gravestone. The knave helped the lady aboard, making sure her reins and tack were in order, leading her over then to Arthur and his retinue of knights. Arthur acknowledged the clergyman – then they were off, leaving him alone almost amidst the pastoral setting of his church.

Chapter 9

From the back of the church at Chesterblade, the royal cortege clomped down a rough sandy stony lane, joining hundreds of others still catching up; overland to the small village of Wanstrow. There, they had to stop, as they couldn't progress any further due to the multitudes of knights and foot soldiers standing a hundred deep all along the power curtain, from beyond Radstock in the north to Gillingham in the south.

"Hell," Danny breathed, drawing in a breath. He stretched in his saddle to glance up and down the power grid, marvelling at the entrenched army, hundreds of flags and banners from a bygone age fluttering in the breeze, a colossal weight of men and armour, all awaiting the order to move forward and engage the enemy. He shook his head in dismay as he strained to look over what was now the vanguard, the unruly collection of war elephants and rhinos bellowing and buffeting – everything in a rage to get going, a cloud of dust rising from the stomping of hoof and foot – the frightening animals having neither an attendant nor mahout guiding them, just seemed to be there to run amok, trampling anything in their path as they were let loose. Following them would be a detachment of beings so bewilderingly scary and shocking, that even a battle-hardened soldier would not want to engage – setting the seal for what was to be a battle of un-paralleled times. *'Where,'* Dan worried, was Lindsey Cartwright and her knight Sir Reginald? *What had become of them?*

In the expanse of someone's big back garden, amid the azaleas and roses, his maps spread out on a large garden table, Merlin – including several volunteers, held his war council; the knights Sir Galahad, Lancelot, Hector de Maris, the Green Knight, Mordred and Sir Percival his generals.

The surrounding crowds parted for The King and Queen. A garden chair, quickly draped in fine linens and a rather glitzy shawl was presented for Guinevere, the lady of the small manor house beside herself that a real queen was visiting her humble abode. The Queen accepted the courtesy with gracious sociability, asking for the lady of the house to join her – wherein the mistress was brought forward to spend a little time talking to a real life legend.

Arthur had approached the war cabinet, acknowledging everyone he knew, Earl Mason-James, and Bill Nightingale especially, nodding his thanks however to two informers who had been scouting the Salisbury plain in order to keep Merlin abreast of troop movements and any build up of defences.

"How goes it," he asked as he was led to the large garden table, a chair draped in fine regalia positioned as a makeshift throne? Arthur sidestepped the chair and, by the stony and thoughtful silence that greeted him – realised rapidly nothing was going too well.

"They've had time to prepare," Merlin versed unhappily, casting his eyes back and forth over the big maps. Arthur looked himself, easily finding the demarcation of the massive power grid by a thick yellow line, the land beyond riddled with thick red blocks and big black rectangles which could only be defences thrown up by the defenders.

Merlin elucidated, pointing out key features with something that looked like an extremely old wand, the blackened twig appearing to have all the seasoned black magic of eons.

"Here, here and here, deep ditches have been excavated by machines, other big machines lifting big containers into place to create command centres," he instructed his King, picking up quickly the jargon of his modern day helpers.

"These are storage containers, yes," he asked of a spy – a thick set man who had all the hallmarks of an engineer, his hands worked and strong, his eyes steely bright.

"Indeed," he replied. "All day yesterday and all night the work has gone on, the powers that be determined that this is the end, the buck stops here."

Danny nodded, resisting the urge to say he'd heard that before, nonetheless, with deep ravines to negotiate they wouldn't be able to deploy their ace card – the heavy horse cavalry, the knights and their chargers floundering in the wide gullies which – from other reports were full of stakes, sharpened and designed to impale horse and rider – which also thwarted Merlin's idea of using the elephants and rhinos as a preliminary assault weapon, flattening everything in their way – they'd simply fall foul of the trap as well – all stumbling to their deaths as they ploughed headlong.

"Any suggestions," Dan asked, glancing around.

"The only way I see it, is to somehow get the ogres into the middle of the battlefield and dismantle the stakes either side of the central gap creating a bigger middle ground, maybe utilizing the wood as a kind of bridge. We could then create a corridor of fire to lead the animals through and do their initial damage. If they can charge into the defences behind… well, that could prove advantageous…" the big engineer tapped a carpenter's pencil onto the edge of the table, many an eye intrigued by the big red implement as many a farrowed brow met The King's gaze.

"We were slow to move this morning – now any chance of a surprise launch, is lost." Another spy, this one more rangy and circumspect, stood with arms folded defiantly.

Earl Mason-James elbowed his way to the front, having listened patiently for the last twenty minutes or so. He reached over and tapped the middle ground of the huge expanse of Salisbury Plain with his finger. "Trucks," he issued, having thought about the plan himself.

"Trucks," Arthur asked?

"Yep – load the ogres – and other beings into trucks and drive them out, dump them and then shield them with the cabs."

"The enemy is camped only a short distance from the power grid, holding most of the ground either side, any movement will be riddled with arrows.

Dan thought for a moment. True, trucks would have their tires shot out but if the ogres created a kind of moving shield, a *'turtle'* he thought the Romans called it, then that might work very well – soak up any arrows, and make it quite safely. Once in middle ground they could form a defensive position and work behind the barricade, creating that all important bridge.

It might just work. "We need to form a turtle," he asserted, making everyone look up.

"Turtle," Merlin asked?

"You may have something," the engineer spoke, studying him thoughtfully. He then looked around himself pointedly, cataloguing something.

"You mean form a moveable shield," Earl Mason-James spelled out, having kept up with the conversation?

"An old Roman trick," someone in the crowd elucidated.

"Roman," Merlin enquired searching his memory?

"Clever blighters," the engineer observed. "And I think it could work, there's a welter of fence panels, galvanised sheets from shed roofs. We could soon bolt together a few dozen and create a sort of tunnel. The ogres and other things could simply lift it and trot safely up to the excavations."

"We could also – by the same measure," pointed out Galahad, "create a corridor of fire, funnelling the beasts (when let loose) to be corralled into the central gap and then charge headlong into those armoured trucks and other defences."

"Good point," Danny observed.

"What about the other trenches here and here," Mordred pointed out. "These have effectively stopped us flanking the battle with heavy horse."

"Can't we go around them," Arthur asked?

"Possible," the other rangy spy mentioned. "There's a big build up of men and arms on the other side of Frome, trying to countermand the army that has marched to creep around the back. And here – just before the crossroads of Deptford, I fear there will be heavy fighting at these points as well – despite the intention to keep it away from the towns."

Everyone thought for a moment. "Pull them back…" Lancelot asked? "Splitting the army will do no good now. They want us to front the engagement; hoping weight of numbers will win the day so we must be equal in battle-hardened warriors. I see no recourse but to meet them head on, throw everything into the middle and fight with fury until the last man stands."

Many nodded, although Merlin considered.

"Let's just try to even the odds a bit first, eh, Lancelot," he coughed politely? "That corridor of fire you talked about Galahad," he asked, "good idea – let's put that into motion too!"

By the time they'd got the first tunnel/shield built – having raided garden fences and tin sheets off shed roofs, it was four o'clock in the afternoon – and the power grid hadn't even been woken up yet.

Eager to create a corridor of fire to further protect the advancing teams of ogres and Mor-men, Merlin asked for volunteers to run out with tins of bitumen, petrol and oil cans – again, found in nearby sheds – and hunks of wood, employing the same tactic utilizing wooden fence panels to protect their progress.

Before any of this could happen however, Merlin and his sages and warlocks would have to engage with The Dome and command its expansion.

"I must take my leave again, my liege," Merlin addressed his King. "I have to encourage The Dome to give birth, continue in its expansion. I'm hoping this will level the playing field just a little more, perhaps confuse and disable our enemy until we can deploy our forces. I do think however Tristan, Sirs Sagarmore and Kay can make their way around the back of Frome and still keep the town safe. Do your best to keep to the plan!"

Dan nodded.

"Again," Merlin entreated, "stay safe – and protect The Queen at all costs."

"I will Merlin – and thank you for everything!"

He nodded, smiling up into his King's eyes, then he was away, hurrying with his retinue of sages and wizards to perform yet another miracle.

Ready to do battle, The King prepared himself, mounting his magnificent charger. Within him, a power like no other was burning, challenging him almost to dare unleash the unholy vigour, galvanising and emboldening him like a thousand bolts of adrenaline, his whole body flexing and buzzing with unbridled energy. He wanted to fight, he dimly realised, strike a blow for liberty and the protection of the poor and suppressed, despite his protestations against this crazy battle; yet his mind was being overruled by the might flowing through and around him; the need for action now – deliberations all but exhausted.

A loud series of horns and bellowing erupted. Down from the main ungainly head of the army, steam rising from snorting nostrils and clouds of dust from impatient hoofs – the war elephants and rhinos chomped at the bit to be let loose. Astride their horses, Arthur and his cortege were able to just make out Merlin, his sages and warlocks creating a semicircle in front of the inner Dome. They watched as he raised his gnarled hands high and seemed to invoke the power of the cosmos as he and others commanded the power grid to give birth.

Having witnessed this before, Danny knew what was coming, but still it didn't detract from the awesome spectacle as The Dome around and above them began to quiver – then shake visibly as if it was about to sneeze, then – incredibly it began its germination, the new bubble spouting from its mother like an infant, tremulous at first as it took its first baby steps, then gaining in confidence as it shuddered and vibrated into the new world.

Ten feet out it stopped to examine the first obstacle; modern-day heavy plastic zigzagging bollards that were designed to block tanks and trucks, nudging the antitank measures with interest, wondering it they might explode in its face; finding a moment later they seemed to be benign so just pushed them along with it for the moment, tumbling them over and thrusting them straight into the first ranks of soldiers encamped in the small trenches off to one side.

"Christ, pull back," a sergeant yelled in panic, scrambling from his fox hole!

From horseback – and with a good pair of field binoculars – Arthur watched as The Dome picked up and spat out various blockades in its advance, throwing the scaffolding, pallets of wood and nailed together structures aside in a cataclysm of lightening and violent showers of sparks, unsure of the metallic nails and screws, shattering even the wood into shards as The Dome grew in strength, shivering with energy as it flexed its might.

As soon as they had room to manoeuvre the first rank of three *'turtles'* began their ponderous advance, wobbling and stumbling as the ogres in the middle tried to run the gauntlet – holding the construction up, while the shorter Mor-men to the outside held onto improvised handles – keeping the panels roughly in shape.

Half-way across an absolute hail of small arrows and darts found their mark, many thudding into the wood and tin of the shielding with audible twangs and bangs.

Still, the first three contraptions marched forward, the Mor-men struggling to keep up with the giant steps of the ogres as they headed for their target. From his rear-guard position King Arthur watched grimly along with his war council as the three *'turtles'* – now followed by another rank, crossed the ground without incident – one so pin-pricked with harpoons, arrows, crossbow bolts and catapulted spears it resembled something like a porcupine when it arrived, deploying marvellously as it turned to present a flank and at the same time allowing the Mor-men and ogres to jump into the ditch and tear apart the wooden rows of stakes, piling the timbre up at one end to widen a rather small bridge in the middle.

The two other *'turtles'* found their mark but one somehow managed to overshoot the wide gulley, many jumping clear as they realised their mistake, the big contraption having to then wheel around and – with just the Mor-men to the outside, jiggle forward to join up with the other. It might have looked comical, Danny mused had not the whole scene been drenched in arrows, one or two impaled by the hugely inaccurate spears that were launched from trucks arranged in front of the command centre, the improvised catapults nothing more than thick bands of elastic or a piston-driven machine that worked on gas.

Dan eyed these contrived weapons until The Dome crossed the half-way line, obscuring his vision. He did however witness the third *'turtle'* reach its conclusion, where it simply imploded, the front end collapsing into the big deep ditch like a lorry falling into a hole, dozens of legs flailing in the air as ogres and Mor-men avoided the arrows and vicious darts loosed from longbows and modern crossbows.

As Dan continued to watch, the three other *'turtles'* following caught up with the lead ones and began their assault on the ditch, two crashing into one another as the lead ogres lost their bearing slightly, cringing as from hidden ditches and foxholes marines and army recruits poured, rushing to undo the plan.

In amongst the mêlée, the knight Sir Petersbury Dean – now bona fide ogre due to a wayward spell the drunken Merlin had launched the previous day, had got the strap to his war club caught up on a protruding screw, bolting the shielding together and could neither move back nor forward as the two *'turtles'* tried to manoeuvre amidst a hail of arrows.

"BACK," rumbled a lead ogre as his feet lost traction and he floundered in mid air, hanging onto the roof of the aegis. This was pulling the wooden and tin house down into the ditch while pushing the other *'turtle'* they'd inadvertently bumped into over, delivering a clear broadside. The wooden house toppled, having completely lost traction, crashing over the ditch in a splintering of wood and beings yelling, exposing another untidy collection of legs, while the nose of the other promptly crumpled, pulled apart by the incredible weights applied inside.

"GODS TEETH," yelled another ogre, pinned by stakes and a collection of bodies, "get off me!"

Petersbury Dean helped clear the debris, heaving out the buried beings, then urged the Mormen to create a shield around the floundering ogres as crossbow bolts fired by an advancing wall of enemy soldiers (getting braver by the minute, he realised) zipped by, the golems quickly understanding. The knight scrambled into the hole, following the work of other ogres as they collected up the stakes and then piled them up at regular intervals to show any advancing cavalry where exactly the ditch lay, working from the middle to create a much bigger bridge. Out behind, teams of volunteers were creating a funnel from dragged logs, bits of timbre, many falling as an arrow or crossbow bolt found its mark.

It took a moment before Petersbury Dean worked out the plan, the corridor of logs and timbre, once set alight would corral the war elephants and rhinos and send them gambolling through the middle, avoiding getting bogged down in the ditch. *They could use some help,* he thought and having just uprooted a collection of bolted together stakes, awaiting for them to be sent down the line, thought they might be better served creating part of the corridor.

Shielded on all sides by the wooden structures, he climbed out again, dragging the structure with him, then asking a Mor-man to shield him as he carried the section to where it ought to go.

The golem nodded and together they set off back out onto the sandy plain, quickly joining with another team who'd nearly completed a large section. Archers from his own army had collected behind small barricades of their own, back at what had been The Domes original resting place, the whole army now exposed – the bubble extending to its full potential. Arrows shot back and forward as skirmishes broke out all along the corridor's parameters; teams of black-suited special forces men trying in vain to pull apart the wooden runway, chased and harried by arrows and Mor-men – who with improvised shields of wood and galvanised tin lumbered out to protect its flanks. Still more recruits and soldiers loyal to the crown poured onto the field, eager to thwart the opening gambits of the opposing army. The ogre Petersbury Dean really hoped he wouldn't have to use his big war club, but when push came to shove, and he found himself and his hapless golem surrounded, it was every man for himself – and he had no plans of simply rolling over. With his back to the section of stakes he'd just dumped – and the Mor-man flanking him with his hand pushed through the thin wood, utilising it as a shield, he swung his club as four or five black-suited men (who seemed to be protected by some kind of plasticized armour), tried to rush him; brandishing machetes and a honed halberd that had either been taken from a museum or stolen off one of the opposing footmen. Petersbury Dean let them come in close, then moved quickly to launch an all out attack, swinging his club with devastating effect, catching one man completely unawares as he moved to engage, the club swinging loose of its strap – extended for another foot or so, delivering a vicious blow that, although glancing, dug into the man's helmet with a bolt or protruding snag of metal, twisting his head so violently it practically broke his neck. As the club continued on his trajectory it caught another on the shoulder, knocking him for six, while smashing into yet another as he tried to jump and avoid full contact, the metallic head smashing into his midriff like a steam train, knocking the wind completely out of him. Petersbury Dean smartly reined in his weapon and raised it again in a warning as the fourth member of the team, now very much alone as the fifth had found the golem advancing on him. The fourth recruit was scared half to death, not in a million years intending to try and take on an eight foot monster all on his own, the big *zombie attack knife* that looked so dangerous in its box, now pathetically denigrated to a tooth pick as the ogre loomed over him. "Fuck this," the young recruit stammered, tossing his big hunting knife to the ground; the vicious saw-toothed blade landing at the monster's feet. Beside him, his friend, both reserve special boat service personnel did the same, almost handing the frightening being the sharpened instrument he was wielding.

"It's yours," the raw recruit told the Mor-man.

In the blink of an eye following – and as Petersbury Dean was just going to see if the injured men could make it back to the safety to their own ranks, a spear, loosed from a cannon way back and on a deadly tangent, spiralled through the air to impale itself clean through the golem as he turned to head back. The dusty thump as the pole of wood arched through the unsightly being, took the ogre's breath away, the whole panoply of the battleground appearing to shrivel up into this one point, the unfortunate being compromised in a heartbeat. The two recruits stood helpless as the creature stumbled, his whole body shuddering. A greenish goo bubbled and oozed from both the entry and exit wounds.

"Oh, christ," uttered the recruit who fronted him only seconds before, finding the being seemed to realise the kid was only young and didn't know any better. It had relented as soon as the young lad held up his hands, so there was no bloodlust or dull anger, just understanding – and now the creature was dead, impaled unbelievably by a loose spear! "Let's go," he called to his fellow recruit, helping the others to their feet.

Petersbury Dean rushed to grab the wooden fence panel and shield the stricken Mor-man, kneeling with him to lay the panel over them as the golem faltered, his knees buckling, grasping the wooden shaft with both hands. It had speared him through from chest to middle of back, falling through the air like a rod of steel. The golem coughed up blue-green phlegm, a foamy spittle dribbling from a scar of a mouth.

It appeared to heave in a breath, then, looking up into the ogre's eyes with coals that had put the fear of the unknown into men for decades, nodded contently.

"I go home," it grated, then with an exhalation that seemed like dust from the depths of the deepest grave, it died, its head dropping heavily.

As a knight Petersbury Dean had always feared the Mor-men, hoping he'd never have to cross swords with them, but now he felt he understood them a little more, more perhaps of their psychology. Now he had nothing but respect for them, would in fact greet one civilly – if he ever got the chance again.

With chaos reigning all around him, Petersbury Dean collected up his club and wooden fence panel, wondering which way to run, back to the army that was resolutely surging out towards him, or back to the ditch and await further instruction. With arrows from both sides zipping around him, he made his way hastily back to the middle ground, jumping for safety as soon as he got there.

***

"See the warning signs," Galahad asked of Lancelot?

Lancelot nodded, bending to advise a runner. "Message to advance party. Be aware, trap half-way across land."

The runner sped off, but the main body of foot soldiers, pike-men, slingers and archers had already begun to swarm around and through the massive detachment of heavy cavalry laid bare by the advancing Dome, eager to engage. Pretty soon a hail of arrows left the knights' flanks, archers peeling off to both sides. The accuracy was devastating. Loosed from a longbow, a metal-tipped shaft could travel a quarter of a mile and impale an unprotected chest or neck – or leg, inflicting a terrible wound; hundreds of soldiers beyond the midway stumbling as the showers of metal fell from the sky.

The battle had started in earnest, both sides trying desperately to undo the other's efforts.

From his vantage point, King Arthur watched with his war cabinet as horns and what sounded like someone's trumpet signalled for the animals to be let loose, runners with fire sticks setting the corridor alight. Mor-men and ogres, protected by tin sheets and wooden fence panels aligned the corridor, keeping it open, harried always from attacks from both sides, as the fire took hold. The beasts, now allowed to run loose, bellowed out in fury as they broke from the ranks, a herd of armoured elephants and rhinos that knew little of war and belligerent feelings, simply worked on the instinct that somewhere out before them might lay salvation but before they reached that pastoral calm, they had to bulldoze their way through a collection of barricades and perhaps beings that would try and thwart them.

Fighting, thrashing teams of archers, men, ogres, foot soldiers and the occasional Mor-man suddenly glanced up from their fraught stances as a distant shrieking and bellowing reached their ears, the sound meaning only one thing, the beasts had been released. Amidst the clamour of steel on plastic, the grunts and curses of the sixth century against modern, ululations of panic and despair – there was a new threat as the very distant thunder meant only one thing.

"MEERRGGG," hollered out a Mor-man fighting in the middle as he realised the danger they were in! He turned awkwardly. Someone had managed to stab him in the small of the back with a short sword having been knocked off his feet by a flying elbow. Now as both assailants looked eastwards, a sand storm of animals moved their way.

Amid the chaos several side-stepped an engagement to glance up, finding when they did, a distant rumbling and huge cloud of dust meant something eldritch was on the move. Now the combaters had something else to worry about, as the collection of war elephants and rhinos thundered outward, flattening everything in their path, the fighting armies no match for the stampeding wall of meat, tusk and metal.

"Holy Christ," yelled an injured marine, his knees shattered by a flaying mace. "Jonesy, *please – GET ME THE HELL OUT OF HERE!"*

The fighting faltered, then came to be temporarily suspended, as ogres, dimly realising the new danger, pulled dart and arrow from their hides and tried valiantly to drag *all* wounded soldiers out of the way as the corridor to each side of them burned bright. The yellow conflagration ate hungrily into the wood and soaked rags of incendiary liquids. Knights, pike-men and soldiers at arms – who only a moment ago were desperately trying to kill each other – now joined forces to limp, hop or be dragged to safety as the juggernaut surged from its enclosure, the bellowing and screaming of the elephants and rhinos – and any hapless lone soldier trampled beneath ringing in their ears.

"I'll kill you later," ranted a huge butcher loyal to his queen, his cleaver still grasped tightly in one huge mitt.

"MEERRGG," hollered a Mor-man pushing him out of the way.

Arthur moved forward slowly as the main army surged outwards following the stampede of beasts as they thundered forward, men, lightly armoured knights, ogres and foot soldiers scrambling for safety as the herd surged toward them. *'Get out of the way,'* Danny breathed as his binoculars swept the open plain, thousands of dead and dying littering the ground already, the bigger bodies of ogres and Mor-men easily seen as they laid or cried out for salvation.

He spotted a lone mounted policeman in amongst heaps of his comrades, all in black, his polished saddle gleaming – sitting hunched astride his horse, immobile as the wall of destruction thundered toward him *'Move'*, Dan muttered, but something was terribly wrong as the horse too seemed oblivious to the wall of chaos charging outward. King Arthur stared at the lone rider, wondering what had happened, but then he fell forward as the horse – perhaps dazed by something appeared to suddenly wake up and realise the danger they were both in, staring straight ahead with ears pricked: But the man was dead, an arrow buried deep in his back, either from a longbow or modern crossbow, it didn't matter much as the horse – now skittish – tried to wake his rider up and alert him to the threat. No response came, the rider slipped further forward, the weight of his body pulling him out of the saddle.

Suddenly the horse bolted, rearing up in agitation, leaping over bodies in its haste to get out of the way and arms crying out for help, caring not of orders from his pillion – just concerned now for its own survival, heading away from the burning wall off to one side, its dead passenger sliding from the saddle to land mercifully softly on the only tuft of grass left vacant, the horse running wild for a moment before it decided to head for the apparent exit to this hellhole.

A tear escaped one of Danny's eyes as his compunction, raging with his adrenaline, won over for a moment, the wanton cruelty and savagery of close combat brought home succinctly by that surviving horse. According to someone nearby the engagement had lasted only a matter of forty minutes, but it had resulted in the deaths of all those beings. *And for what,* his mind cried out, *how many will die just to crown you King?*

As the unruly herd continued in its destructive course, funnelling toward the centre of the battlefield, leaving an awful trail of dead and squashed men and foot soldiers in its wake, he tried to tell himself he'd been coerced into this, had been hoodwinked almost – knew nothing of the impending battles that would take place, not prepared for this mass slaughter.

Ogres – one or two with burning sticks of wood bravely tried to herd the animals into the channel that was the middle bridge, away from the deep and wide gully that would ensnare them. The trumpeting, thundering elephants followed suit, allowing the ogres to steer them through the fire and to safety, the creatures slowing in their charge as they realised they'd have to rampage through a smaller gap. Still hundreds were trampled to their deaths, nothing able to stop the surging juggernaut. Several horses, one or two with imperial saddles joined in the stampede, hoping to escape the fighting.

Dan took the binoculars from his eyes, shaking his head as a tear filled each of them.

No sooner had the stampede passed by the middle section – then men and beings resumed their fighting – many trying to take advantage of the lull to regroup or make a surprise attack. He'd watched hopelessly as soldiers – many who'd been helped by the ogres, now hoped to kill the creatures as their backs were turned.

'God, stop,' he mouthed in soliloquy…, but out front, the fighting resumed – just as bitterly.

Now, with the corridor burning out, more cavalry divisions and mounted police galloped into the affray, endeavouring to take the centre ground again, vaulting over the burning embers, creating a small stampede all of their own – lances lowered as they wheeled and charged at the remaining ogres, survivors and Mor-men huddled in the big central ditches. King Arthur's knights became anxious, watching on from a distance, but Merlin didn't give the signal yet, allowing his ground forces to swarm onto the field, thousands more in the wings as many divisions had quickly followed on from the stampeding herd.

Corralled by the fire and lines of Mor-men and ogres the beasts had thundered through the main bridge, a massive cloud of dust following, rumbling through the small island like a sand storm, the bellowing rising up with the steam.

As soon as the beasts cleared the battlefield – from the outlying dykes and foxholes each side of the Salisbury Plain, the opposing royalist army of soldiers poured, retired, young and old alike, resembling a black tide of rats as they emerged from hideouts to intercept the opposing army of footmen, the remaining ogres and Mor-men trapped as detachments of cavalry harried them. More mounted police joined their ranks, having also been kept back, filing from around hillocks and small gorges to engage the enemy.

With the beasts out of the way – and the coast now clear, the battle could start again; weight of numbers perhaps hoping to decide the day.

The last of the wild herd negotiated the small bridge in the middle, one or two animals floundering as they fell through the wooden supports, the herd surging on relentless flattening anything in their path. The big catapults – the last line of defence, realigned their sights and tried desperately to bring them down but they were advancing too fast, it was impossible to get a bearing.

They fired wildly anyway, reloading as fast as humanly possible, the advancing wall of hoof and ivory impregnable as they stampeded on, the vicious spears and alloy arrows like matchsticks as they bounced off or dug in without any effect. Fifty yards from the command centres, a barricade of fire was lit, but with no kindling or accelerant, it spluttered and failed to catch as the herd raced towards them, many deserting their posts already as the inevitable stared them in the face. At twenty five yards the stampede just trampled through the stacks of wood as if they weren't there, the creatures bulldozing their way through by tossing the pallets and barricades aside, creating a big hole through which the rest hammered.

At ten yards the catapult trucks had been abandoned – as had any defensive positions, and everyone from the command centres were crouched in the metal containers, the doors slammed shut from inside. A moment later all hell broke loose as the creatures slammed into the trucks and barricades, smashing into the welfare islands and containers as if they were mere pebbles, shunting them about as if they weighed nothing.

Tiers of offices that had been stacked up to give a good view of the battlefield, now wobbled and teetered on the brink of collapsing, as massive war elephants and wild rhinos slammed into them, barging them out of the way, the air filled with the roaring and squealing of enraged beasts.

In his command centre, Brigadier Lance Warner-Barouche hung on for dear life as he and other senior generals tried to keep their balance, the war offices in danger of collapsing if the animals didn't push off.

"It's no use," a Staff Sergeant Grant Holby yelled, glancing out of a cracked and broken window, the courtyard of ringed offices, each weighing two tons or more being punched and pushed about like wooden cubes by something he'd seen only in fantasy films, the war elephants able to look him in the eye as he glared outwards, a look of hopelessness on his face. Then, before he could utter another word, a massive beast butted the office and the units were toppled over – and everything went black.

Even from a distance, the sound was incredible as a screeching and squealing of metal filled the air, the snorting of beasts and the bellowing of the elephants adding to the tinkling of glass and cries of wanton despair as legs got trapped, or men fell from upturned containers and were trampled in the crush.

From an even greater distance, Danny watched with growing anxiety as his forces followed the ungainly herd of animals, the way laid bare in the centre now for an all-out attack, his ranks of foot soldiers running out to take the centre ground, another huge detachment edging around the back of Frome, although – even from this distance it was obvious they'd suffered heavy losses, lances broken and shattered, many slouching in their saddles as the ragged army moved to engage once more. Still, Danny feared the worst, the terrible losses, the galling waste of life, knowing every combatant on either side had some strange but unyielding sense of duty. As he watched the two armies finally meet in a hell of a clash in the middle, ogres and the enigmatic Mor-men centre stage as they protected the bridge they'd erected; banners and pennants clearly visible as divisions of men fought with huge detachments of Horse Guards and mounted police.

***

"Anywhere but here, now," moaned Private M Mosley. He was with the 10th Light Armoured Division – Territorial Reconnaissance, but had just seen his brand new armoured car pushed up a slope and rather ignobly tumbled down the other side – causing all manner of damage, the advancing power curtain acting like some kind of living organism as it rolled thoughtfully over each and every building or structure – looking, he supposed – for hidden armaments, exploding some warehouses, leaving others virtually intact, but on finding a tank or similar vehicle would push it along until the crippled truck crunched into something else and became permanently stuck, or (as in his case – and just before they could vacate the thing), pushed up a hill and over it.

They were fighting a losing battle here – they just didn't want to admit it, he mused to himself, having watched mounted police and detachments of various guardsmen charge into the battle, only to be impaled against an absolute phalanx of pikes and halberds, wielded by men that looked like they'd just risen from the grave. And worst of all, they – their superiors, were expecting inexperienced crews and recruits to join in their war, with God knows what, zombies – the bloody living dead *for crying out loud?*

It just wasn't cricket, this wasn't!

"Come on, we're moving," stage whispered his Lance Corporal.

From the small outbuilding they'd taken refuge in, five recruits of the 10th Light Armoured Infantry pushed themselves to their feet – one or two stamping out a roll up. They'd been lucky they all realised, having been sent forward on a *'recce'* as the incredible Dome surged over the land, the army already versed in the danger of leaving tanks and big guns in the way as the domes seemed to know what was dangerous and what was benign – so the half-track was a sure bet, but the massive thirty millimetre machine gun on the back, although covered – and in all likelihood unable to wreak any damage since someone had misplaced the firing pin, deemed the vehicle unsavoury and whilst The Dome's intelligence was elsewhere at the time – the power shield having to deal with many obstacles in its expansion – they legged it – deciding it was far better to be safe than sorry – *which in hindsight was just as well.*

Outside, as they assembled, hell was surely and irrevocably in the making as legions of the dead swept over the land from the east, followed hotly by all manner of foot soldier, armed combater, and semi-armoured knights; the whole of the Salisbury Plain, plus the Mendip Hills further to the west, covered in divisions of horses and men, so many detachments of cavalry the young recruits had no idea who half of them were. "Looks like the Wild Western Appreciation Society," mumbled a private as men dressed in beige fatigues, jodhpurs and regimental clipped back barmah clip-clopped by – armed with nothing more than a big machete and a home-made lance.

"Who the hell are you lot," called up one private, obviously amused by the outmoded garb?

"Hundred and nineteenth Continental Horse Guard," replied a rather wizened and heavily whiskered rider.

"Just the job," jeered the radio operator, "most of the invading army look like they've come right out of *'Land of the Living Dead'*. You'll fit right in!"

One or two stately riders eyed the small platoon narrowly as they rode past, looking – it must be said – none too happy to be engaging with such an unqualified foe. Still they rode on, into what would surely be the valley of death for many of them.

"Let's go back inside where its nice and quiet – and sit this bloody catastrophe out," whined the youngest of the group!

The corporal – who'd only recently been promoted, summoned up all his resolve and tried to instil some valour. "Come on guys – this is for Queen and Country – we can't let other – older guys fight for us, can we – *or get all the glory,* eh?"

"Fine by me," mentioned the driver, who'd grown rather attached to his new vehicle, having been designated as official driver. Now it lay crumpled and quite possibly broken at the bottom of a small ravine, (having rolled into someone's front garden) – and although it was a tough and strong half-track, it certainly wasn't designed to roll down a hill sideways, the cab and sides buckling in as if made of matchwood. "I say we try and rescue our vehicle," he stated morosely. "Try and at least get it back on its feet."

"You kidding," spat the youngest! "That things weighs twenty tonnes – and she's well and truly wedged herself in by the look of it – its going to take a tank to pull it back out."

"Fuck it," spat the driver! "And now we're supposed to follow those fools and get ourselves killed by Mr Zombie out there – no way – *no fucking way! And what the hell are we supposed to fight with – a fucking penknife?"*

The young corporal sucked in a breath. "We can't *not* fight," he implored – what will our sergeant say – *court marshal probably* – and how do you think our families will take it – knowing we hid away in a bloody shack while all the rest fought the good fight."

"There's nothing good about fighting," remarked the most belligerent of the group, a muscular deviant who was facing a recrimination all of his own later.

"You might very well gain a medal of honour, Bret," the young corporal mentioned slyly, having spent months kowtowing and cajoling the bully in the hope of superseding him.

"Medal," Bret asked doubtfully?

"Possibly – or at least a note of commendation – *'fought bravely on the field, sir, he did – cut down many a zombie soldier!'*"

"That's if you live to tell the tale," commented the driver.

"If we stand here much longer we're going to look idiots," the radio operator pointed out. "So we either dive back in the shack and make like we've got important work to do within, or follow on – slide in behind one of these horse brigades and hope to keep to the edge of things."

"We're unarmed," the driver again pointed out.

The corporal thought for a moment: "Let's look back in the shack, maybe there's a spade or fork, or machete or something?"

"What about a lawnmower," the youngest recruit blurted out, making a Blues and Royal Horse Guard who was passing with his brigade burst out laughing.

"Mow 'em down, boy," he laughed.

"Got any decent weapons," Bret called out to the passing soldiers.

"You'll be just as well armed with a spade as an axe," someone called back.

"See, told yer," the corporal spoke. "Let's have another look."

They bundled back into the crofter's shack; having already smashed the padlock off in a fit of panic, thinking the power grid might deem them antagonistic as well – as it had picked on their vehicle – and evaporate them into the process. As it was they took cover as best they could – only to find the thick wall of plasma passed right through the shed as well, stopping briefly to examine a rusting rotavator and a clapped out strimmer, a feeling of pure dread passing through all of them as the sparkling curtain of light neared and then passed through them as if they were paper, all collapsing in a heap afterwards.

"An axe," Bret marvelled, having pulled some dusty sacks from an old chest and pulled open the lid. He plucked it from the rusty old spanners and pipe wrenches, holding it with reverence.

"Excellent," the corporal commended him.

Bret nodded, wiping off years of dust and cobwebs. The staff was wood-wormed and a tad loose, but the blade was still reasonably sharp – and swung in anger could do some serious damage – if the handle didn't snap in the process.

Someone else found a sharpened spade, while the corporal hefted a heavy pickaxe, dragging half the collection of rusting and unused implements with him, all clattering to the floor in a cloud of dust. He dragged out the item, holding it in his hands for a moment, testing its weight. It was solid – made entirely of rolled steel, a mite too heavy to wield for long, but if he could impale just one outlaw with it, then he'd be made – *a hero for life.*

The radio operator dragged from another corner an extremely old and rusty railway bar, the nineteenth century implement as heavy and as solid as anything could be, the raw recruit hefting it onto one shoulder in an exaggerated show of strength he didn't have. "You watch me run one through with this little beauty," he called out, swinging it down so it hit the floor with a clump, burying the sharpened end, *"Shit! Hey Baz, help me out here, eh?"*

Baz helped his friend pull the heavy bar back out of the wooden floor, while the corporal took stock. "Excellent work, boys," he called. *"Now we're ready to take 'em on!"*

"I ain't got a weapon," moaned the youngest.

"Here," another recruit remarked, these broken shears are pretty sharp. Make good sword too," and he swung one around his head dangerously, nearly catching the corporal!

"Yes – erm, great work. Right – let's get into this war, eh."

"After you," called out the driver!

Standing back outside – even the corporal's vim deserted him. The vision – if he'd been anything of an English literary student – was one straight out of Dante's Hell – the whole of Salisbury Plain embroiled in the most fantastical battle he'd ever hoped to witness.

"Fuck my old boots," he whispered, completely forgetting where he was!

"Erm, that a technical term," the driver essayed, beside him; "or perhaps some covert operator's jargon we haven't heard yet?"

The corporal breathed in a deep breath, his eyes for a second sliding down from the incredible mêlée out front, to the solid metal pickaxe he had grasped in his hands, the industrial tool so bleeding heavy he'd be exhausted by the time he'd trotted down into the action. "Erm," he coughed.

"That another implicit technical command," the laconic radio operator wanted to know? Down below, regiments of horse had charged headlong from various locations into the confusion that was the main battlefield, thousands of individuals fighting it out viciously as to his left an absolute wall of steel and heavy horse awaited the order to advance, the glittering army looking so resolute – even at this distance, he didn't want to imagine the carnage as they began their trot onto the battlefield.

"God – what a mess," the driver breathed!

Out below, cavalry units tried vainly to corral and then decimate the legions of zombies, archers, knights, pike-men and others wielding halberds forming into phalanxes and wheeling left and right in order to impale a rider or his horse. Throughout the main centre ogres and some other terrifying monstrosities were fighting for their lives, as dozens of army recruits tried bravely to hack them down, going for the big targets in the hope to disable them before running out of energy. Surrounding them however were the legions – discernable – even at this distance by the mottled grey green or metal breastplates and helmets, the numbers at the moment – on foot anyway, almost equal.

It could go either way, the corporal considered, cringing as axe split cranium and bayonet ran through peasant. Then from apparently nowhere, swarms of black-suited men emerged from the southeast, lorries bringing up yet more specialist forces – somehow having survived the Dome's passage. They ran onto the battlefield in groups, as if on a live exercise, their lightweight rifles useless, but with bayonets quite a good club and dangerous as stabbing implements. Many however – as brave as they were – were obviously not experts in the type of hand to hand combat they were being asked to engage in. Up against a man or youth of the opposing army, they quickly found they were totally unmatched by power, speed and strength, the knights and foot soldiers born to the sword, mace and flail. All around, the ground was soon becoming clogged, the dead or the dying falling like flies; many, it appeared from his standpoint, the soldiers of his own regiments and counties. They fought valiantly, he catalogued – but up against a man with adze or axe or something resembling a short scimitar they had no defence, one or two getting into a challenging knife fight that ended in a short scramble where usually the knight or pike-men came out on top.

"Let's go home," the youngest opined softly.

Deflated, the corporal let the pickaxe fall to the ground where it promptly dug itself in, almost daring the owner to try and wrench it out. He gave it a half-hearted tug – then gave up. He was about to agree with his youngest recruit – when – from nowhere, a small detachment of what looked like boy scouts – complete with tan shorts and green shirts – with nothing but implements much the same as they had, ran passed beneath them, having probably raided some old dear's shed en route.

"Well… I'll be jiggered," snorted the driver.

"They can't be much older than us," a recruit observed.

They all watched stupefied as the scouts ran in column into the fray, dusty legions of revenants parting as they ran, then, trotting still, they seemed to vanish in the haze, subsumed by the flailing weapons, steam and dust.

"Fuck it, that's it then – we can't go home – not when those guys are willing to lay down their lives?"

"Let Raymond go home," the corporal suggested and moved to relieve him of his broken shear blade.

"Oh, no you bloody don't," he snorted! "I'm not bloody running away when kids from my own block are practically trotting into the battle. I'm coming with you!"

"Fine," spat the corporal! "Let's just all stay close together, eh; Safety in numbers!"

"Hm," agreed the driver phlegmatically. Down below another massive army of mounted knights, running archers and pike-men had just entered the fray, making him jump despite being far away from the action – entering from the northeast – having circumnavigated Frome, it appeared, pushing the unholy mess away from the main town, completely surprising the NATO and French Foreign Legion divisions as they tried desperately to hold the northern flank, the south just holding under the onslaught – as was the western approach as a juggernaut of heavily armoured knights – having already waited long enough it seemed, now began to trot as one onto the battle field, clearing an almighty swathe in their wake. Horns and signals alerted the men on the ground to get out of the way – and many – including one lone ogre fighting his own battle near the enlarged dyke, still with a brazen army recruit on one arm, dived into it to take cover, pulling a big tabletop over the both of them. Now the advancing wall of steel broke into a steady canter, the colourful plumed helmets and household sigils creating a deadly mosaic, the three thousand or so joining with the other two or three hundred as they had entered from the north and wheeled round, the whole heavily mounted divisions intending to charge headlong into the remaining fortifications and detachments of cavalry still holding the eastern flank. The noise of clashing steel and heavy horse filled the air, rising up over the screaming and yelling out front.

"Fucking Christ," blurted Bret – "this can't be happening!"

"I've never seen anything like it," voiced a recruit, the unbelievable bringing him almost to tears.

"Even the films aren't like this," commented the youngster.

The corporal wiped his nose on the sleeve of his tunic. "That's because you can't appreciate the smell and reek of sweat and faeces," he sniffed, shaking his head.

"BACK," a grizzled old ogre ranted, pushing a whole contingent of army recruits off their feet as they tried in vain to flank around what was left of the ogres and attack from the rear!

Petersbury Dean – knocked almost senseless by one of his fellows' clubs, (swung rather ruthlessly); pin-pricked by half a dozen small darts – fired by scandalous youths who ran in to loose the infernal weapon, but then scooted away again before they could be apprehended, was beginning to feel his emotions bounce from one extreme to the other, having successfully maintained an air of calm and – to a point, nonchalance – he now found his anger getting the better of him as he watched in horror as his fellow Mor-men and ogres were hacked to pieces or impaled by swarms of attacking mounted soldiers, many falling victim themselves as they engaged the lone survivors. Now as savage hand to hand raged all around them, only a handful of Mor-men and ogres were left, valiantly defending the bridge the royalist army would have to cross if it was to avoid getting trampled again. Mounted detachments of household cavalry and divisions of mounted police formed up, trying to mount a determined counterthrust to the main contingent of knights moving menacingly forward.

The huge wall of mounted steel had been let loose, walking at a steady pace to warm the horse's legs – the beasts having stood for several hours while adjustments were made to the order of play; also in order to allow the foot soldiers time to get out of the way – and clear the field a little. The battle lines had been drawn once more as Household Cavalry units and gleaming ranks of Blues and Royals merged with mounted police and equine volunteer groups forming up a four thousand strong detachment. The Blues and Royals took the lead, asking many others to form into a diamond shape to spear through the advancing wall of steel. Many horses, already jittery from an instinct of what they were facing, began to panic, shy away, pulling the riders to apparent safety. It was a disappointment, but these horses hadn't seen combat, the reek of blood already filling their nostrils. The ranks broke and reformed, several riders unable to control their steeds as they bolted, others stumbling as the horses tried desperately to vacate the area, faltering as bodies tripped them up.

Despite the distant clatter and rattle of steel, a massive battle to the centre ground was not going to finish until each and every man had fallen, some huge fellows fighting with all their might against knights that seemed blessed with an eternal strength and vigour.

Sirs Tristan, Kay and Sagarmore had arrived finally, war-weary – their forces already denuded by almost half, having fought quite a battle themselves as they tried to creep around the back of Frome and then Westbury, a huge mob of royalists emerging from the nearby towns and villages, having camped overnight. They'd marched in a ten mile semicircle in order to circumnavigate the two big towns – also having to ford a river, only to be confronted by a large force as they swarmed across the land.

Halted directly north of Westbury, awaiting to cross the boundary line of the Chippenham - Warminster A-road, the small army was confronted by a large force that poured from the hamlets of Hawkeridge, North Bradle, Heywood and Yarnbrook, supported by the surrounding towns of Trowbridge, Bristol and Bath, Newbury, Swindon and as far away as Southampton. Vicious hand to hand developed almost immediately as a volley of spears – thrown – it must be said, somewhat amateurishly by attacking groups failed to make an impact, many foot soldiers simply picking them up to examine them and then sling them back. They were soon overrun, the foot soldiers and ranks of pike-men forced back into the streets and avenues of the nearby town.

Tristan wheeled around with his detachment of cavalry, having the room to make an initial charge into the crowds of royalist supporters, many armed with nothing but improvised pike or sword, none versed or competent with either, the knights running many down with broadsword, mace or axe, the horses themselves armour-plated and extremely heavy and powerful; able to command a field and stamp out their authority. Yet the numbers showed as thousands pushed the revenant army sideways back into the suburbs of Westbury, various villages caught up in the struggle as the fighting merged into the streets and houses. Sirs Sagarmore and Kay held their ground, not wanting the two cohorts of heavy cavalry boxed in, men able to jump from garden walls and the roofs of small buildings to unseat them. They watched uneasily as their infantry and rows of pike-men got swallowed up in the tide of royalist fervour, almost disappearing from view.

For a solid hour men harried, beat, bashed and kicked their assailants into avenues and cul-de-sacs, a riot ensuing as Arthur's reserve army was pushed further back into the town, the fighting furious, ferocious and utterly frightening for the poor inhabitants, many loyal to the Queen, some supporting the new regime – others completely neutral. The army's backs were against the wall – the walls of quaint cul-de-sacs and manicured gardens. There, a stalemate occurred as men fought savagely ripping shields from arms, pulling armour apart, swamping the legions until bodies were piling up in each quarter. Then, when they could go no further, the revenant army dug in, able to control the close quarter fighting, versed with shield and mace or short sword, the unarmed rabble finding they were unable to deal with the weaponry of an organised army, the daggers especially lethal in experienced hands.

Big shields made improvised shelters, as archers regrouped and took position. Eight or nine deep, knights and infantry closed off streets to control the flow, bringing the fight into a zone where a man could swing a sword properly. Faced with the blockages the crowds pulled up sharp in some instances, took stock, then with a snarl leapt at their adversaries, falling headlong onto spear and sword, having skulls split as mace or axe knocked them senseless. Here, weight of numbers meant nothing as bodies simply piled up on top of others, the knights pushing the piles over to allow more in, attacking hordes unable to easily climb a small wall and then launch an attack.

All through the suburbs of Westbury the battle raged, the clashing of steel augmented by the crash of breaking glass, the yelling of crowds accompanied by shrieks and screams of the fallen. Pushed onto the back foot and almost fragmented, the second army had to regroup, Tristan edging into the streets and avenues with his lighter cavalry, trying to fight without being drawn in.

By the time another hour had elapsed, Arthur's army had begun to bludgeon their way back, the crowds finding they were faced with an impenetrable phalanx of shields.

Men, fighting with lump hammer and hunting knife, eventually tired as the fighting continued apace – wielding weapons an exhausting task, especially if you were not used to it – even if you were fighting for your life. Not so for the revenants however – not so for Arthur's legions of the dead, the opposing army somehow imbued with a zeal that was hard to ignore, the hardest glint to the eyes, the furious craving for victory, the undying brutality of strength and determination, all strove to make one opponent worth ten ordinary men. It couldn't last; exhaustion soon gripping the youngest of pugilist – the strongest of farm, iron and road workers. Hilts slipped from sweat-soaked grasps, heavy implements too much to bear, faltering, the gangs and crowds were eventually forced back along roads they'd only chased their opponents up a short time ago, now firmly on the back foot themselves.

Falling back in droves, they found a wall of metal awaiting them, the whole contingent of cavalry having blocked their retreat.

The mounted knights moved aside, allowing the exhausted crowds to collapse into the fields of Heywood, many injured crying out for attention. Tristan's reserve army tramped back out of the avenues and streets of the town of Westbury like a football crowd that had watched their team grind eventually to a one all draw. Legions reformed, knights counting the cost.

***

"Oh God..." breathed the corporal of the 10th Light Infantry Territorial Reconnaissance, still perched with his five recruits atop a small knoll – all too transfixed to do anything. He could tell from the very schematics that there could only be one possible outcome, the mounted home guard hopelessly outnumbered and on steeds that were not prepared under any persuasion to confront the armoured-plated war machine striding toward them; horses panicking – even as they gawped. It was going to be an absolute slaughter and without any cavalry units left the battle would be won, the conflict finally over.

Beside the corporal, his driver watched dumbly as the wall of steel to their left paused to realign themselves, the field out front still not clear of the huge battle, another small army of archers, pike-men – and volunteers, streaming onto the field after them, another complete part of the army, it seemed, ready to do battle with anything left.

"I can't watch," muttered the radio-operator.

The chaotic morass that was the bloodiest battle he'd ever have to witness was now pulling itself irrevocably over and through the main ditch, leaving the ground empty for the mounted units to fight out the last part. As the recruit's eyes slid over the nearby detachments of Horse Guards and mounted police, rider upon rider fell from his horse, the animals frightened beyond sanity, the heat of battle, the ghastly reek of blood too much for them.

"They don't want to fight," observed Bret, fidgeting with his axe.

"Would you," asked the corporal, incredulous as the war machine to their left began to move more determinedly?

"Guess not."

The incredible spectacle of the mounted knights got nearer, the rustle and clinking of armour rising in an almost sibilant whisper; pennants fluttering, gleaming embroidered flags rippling, plumed helmets glinting in the muted sunlight, the combined weight of horse, rider and armour ready to gallop headlong into anything that threatened it, the immobile faces behind those frightful helmets portraying a diehard dismissal of any opposing force. The great wall of metal trotted a little more, then broke as one into a faster gait, gaining momentum.

"Oh, fuck!" grunted the driver as the inevitable began to play out!

"This is going to end badly," groaned the radio-operator. "Don't the police know what they're up against – *Christ!* Do they want me to go down there and spell it out for them! It's impossible – there's just too many of them."

"It's all over," muttered the youngest, spellbound.

The Salisbury Plain began to clear; remaining ogres and Mor-men pulling the injured out of the way, fights still raging even as they worked.

The driver grabbed his corporal by the arm unconsciously, hanging on, as all six recruits huddled together.

At two thousand or so paces the formed diamond of Horse Guards and mounted police moved cautiously forward, skirting around crowds still fighting it out as they continued to edge toward the safety of the middle ground.

At fifty yards the gleaming wall of steel picked up the pace even more – lances and spears of both sides lowered as the attacking force galloped irrevocably toward them, nothing on earth now stopping them.

"This is it," Bret sighed.

"God help them," sobbed the youngest!

At twenty yards history glared into the eyes of modern day as the gallop turned into a tremendous thunder.

A shire horse reared up in the ranks of the Blues and Royals, virtually unseating its rider, the Horse Guard struggling to remain upright as the huge animal tried to climb over another in its haste to get clear.

Those that could had scarpered and been pulled or crawled for all they were worth out of the way, what was left of Sirs Tristan, Kay, and Sagarmore's bedraggled army sweeping round to encapsulate the field, blocking any retreat; the war-torn mounted knights forming up to bolster the approaching wall of cavalry. The remaining NATO and French forces were whittled down and nigh exterminated as they tried to form a rear guard action and fall back over the main bridge, giving themselves some breathing space, but they ran the gauntlet of the remaining ogres and Mor-men and many more were killed as Arthur's forces joined up to corral and then decimate the remainders.

At ten yards more horses amid the mounted police panicked, rearing up.

Men braced themselves.

"Nooo," cried the driver, cringing as he shied away.

The sickening crunch when it came was all the worse as the six recruits, knowing many taking the punishment were their fellow army units, the awful row as the mounted knights slammed headlong into anything daring to stand in their way, jangling the nerves.

The driver opened his eyes, wiping a wall of salt water from them, to recoil as the ten deep wall of mounted steel smashed into the lead guardsmen, one or two having slid forward a long pole with a deadly knife taped to the end of it. But as the chargers bludgeoned their way into them like an anvil slamming into a pencil, the poles snapped, aluminium lances bent; men yanked out of their saddles – as thick wooden shafts impaling their victims won out –

the outcome already forged – the body of knights pressing home the advantage.

Horses became wedged, stabbed by shards of smashed wooden shafts, gorged by the spikes of the armoured chanfrons as they struggled furiously to get free, bits of plastic, shards of steel and gouts of blood flying into the air; the scene chaotic and depressingly horrific as head was torn from shoulder and lance lifted opponent clear into the air.

The corporal's knees buckled. Around him his five recruits shook their heads, the youngest throwing up.

The armoured warriors rammed home and kept surging, the horses behind lending support, pressing home the advantage, grinding the enemy back. The diamond formation imploded, falling apart as the dead slumped in their saddles, horses rearing as many an impaled rider relinquished control. Still the war machine ground its opponent down, the big chargers outweighing the smaller modern horse, forcing them into a frenzied retreat. The knights corralled their quarry, encircling the Horse Guards and mounted police, charging again – having enough velocity to wheel round and thrust in a murderous flanking manoeuvre, many ruthlessly skewered as an all out edict to trample and decimate the enemy pervaded the knights.

In a matter of hellish minutes, the fighting was over, the mighty steel war hammer having delivered a devastating blow, the whole mounted detachment in shreds, horses whinnying in helpless pity as they still fought to escape. The flanking knights pulled back, having smashed into their enemy like steam trains either side, practically meeting in the middle, the welter of dead and dying as they extricated themselves galling, many winded horses faltering as they pushed their way back to their feet. A small core of Horse Guards fought valiantly on, trying to bring as many of the enemy down as possible, but having delivered the killer blow, the knights pulled further back, allowing archers to take aim and finish it.

***

Having watched the whole nauseating spectacle, each thrust, each blow and parry experienced, Arthur's whole being fizzed with anger. He relinquished his grip of his reins to follow the war council as they trotted out onto the battlefield, all manner of territorial reserve swarming around him as the conflict appeared well and truly won. To each side thousands poured, many in costume, many a small company of soldier or re-enactment society. Close by a legion of Roman Infantry marched looking magnificent with their big sanctum shields, looking also to The King full of self-importance, as if a film producer would suddenly pop from around a corner and shout *"hold it – that's it – perfect!"*

Despite an effort by the ogres and Mor-men to clear the field for the cavalry charge, it was still littered with corpses, royalist army men in black fatigues hanging over fox holes – their heads trampled flat. Many of his foot soldiers lying in crumpled poses, arms and legs bent and twisted, rags and broken bits of armour scattered throughout – flags and pennants flapping where they'd been dropped. The reek of blood stained the air, held in by the encompassing Dome above.

Tense, appalled at the loss of life, The King winced as his entourage of horses, squires and knaves entered onto the battlefield, every nuance, curse, punch, split lip and stab still echoing in the ether; the odour of battle seeping up from the ground – the sandy soil drenched in plasma. Half-way across, the colossal stain of blood in the central plain told of the immense conflict, the savage and brutal hand-to-hand, the frantic struggle for survival.

Still many a crumpled and trampled body laid, a ragged surcoat here, a ripped and torn jerkin, a smashed piece of body armour, watches, scarves, knives, clubs, every scrap and broken implement having a jaded story to it. Bodies were enmeshed, piled up in places, set at unholy poses.

Arthur stopped, dismounted to stand by a young peasant boy whose only weapon had been a kind of twisted pitchfork, the shaft broken in two, a metal crossbow bolt through his neck. His death might have been agonising, Arthur reflected, yet the lad's face was serene, one arm stuck up in the air as if celebrating a great victory, his knees under him, his back rigid – his whole stance as if his football team had just won the world cup.

Dan moved round, watching where he put his feet, anxious to take in this young man, as if to connect with him, a little perplexed by his exuberance in his death throes. Where had he come from, he wondered, studying his physique, his tanned skin, straw hair and watery blue eyes that seemed to pale even more now that he looked? What part of history do you belong?

He was too young, The King judged, noting his apparel, suede trews and shirt.

"Thank you," Arthur muttered under his breath, keeping the words to his addressee and himself, as if mentally taking him by the hand to walk him home. Sighing deeply, he let his eyes slide from the young man to catalogue the tonnage of death, the abysmal waste of life, holding back a sob with each passing vista. The landscape was one of misery, desolation, despair – one neither God nor Satan wanted any part of.

Guinevere had dismounted, moved to join his side, squires and knaves surrounding her, knowing the wretchedness and melancholy of the battlefield was impinging on his sensibilities, The Queen ready to lend support. Arthur took her hand as she approached, studying the dead young man herself, saddened by his strange repose.

"He was so young," The King mentioned, trying to rise above the agony of such a titanic struggle. He pulled her close, as if to shield her from the ghastly panorama, watching as the huge territorial army swept over the battlefield, one or two bending to retrieve a weapon or trinket.

***

Back out on the knoll, the driver released a hand he'd put out to grab hold of his friend and gripped his shoulder tightly as the clash and splintering of wood and metal died away, only just smothering the clattering and yelling that had ensued back out on the battlefield. They watched with tears rolling as the medieval war machine bludgeoned their way through what was left of the mounted Horse Guards, cutting through them as if made of papier mache, the crunching snap of bone, the wrench of muscle and sinew, sickening; the bulk of the mounted detachments pulped in a matter of minutes.

"What do we do," asked the youngest tremulously? Down below, sporadic fighting still broke out as groups – detached from the main army – met in open conflict, weight of numbers telling as thousands more of Arthur's army swarmed into and over the battlefield, the archers also targeting anything that looked remotely aggressive.

"Jeeze, will you look at that," gasped an old boy who'd crept up on the six army recruits having scared the living daylights out of them!

"Holy Christ," cursed the driver, thinking a scout from the invading armies had somehow slipped around the back of them: "Who the fuck are you?"

"Ah, nobody really – just some guy who's had his shed busted into and half his tools stolen." He eyed the recruits with a steely but forgiving frown.

The corporal looked down at the pickaxe, still half buried in the soft ground of the knoll, and breathed in yet another fatal sigh.

"Who's in charge," the old timer asked, his voice suddenly carrying some form of superiority –

changing from the soft Irish lilt to a more English baritone?

The driver simply pointed to the young recruit beside him, continuing to stare out at the unfolding chaos below.

"Well," started the old boy once more, giving all six young soldiers the once over. "Now you've ransacked my old shed – and armed yourselves – I suppose you're anxious as hell to get down there and crown a few heads, eh?"

Immediately the radio operator tried to swap his iron bar with something less conspicuous but neither the youngest recruit nor his friend wanted it. "We're, er…thinking of giving it a miss, actually," he intoned, shifting his weight awkwardly "Our vehicle got overturned – our weapons ruined into the process."

"Aha, that's your truck, is it, lying in Peggy's front garden?"

"Hm," voiced the driver, hypnotised by the blood thirsty fighting that had ensued not far from where he was standing, the unholy clash of metal and plastic still reverberating in his ears: Of the scouts who rushed passed some time ago, there was no sign – which – in his estimation was probably just as well.

He watched for a while longer, suffering the scenes like his friend beside him, then, suddenly seeing many a young rider fall under the sword or be clubbed to death – or struggle very valiantly against god knows what, his verve was up, his faint-heartedness at an end, his anxiety all but spent. Now he felt cool, reserved – ready to do his bit.

He hefted the spade with an exaggerated puff of air, taking one last look around at the recruits he'd spent the last couple of years training with, reaching unparalleled heights in his estimation to be the driver of a three-tonner – even if the cannon was defunct. "You're all a good bunch of guys," he told them without rancour. "But now I feel I ought to take my leave – even if you want to skip this one."

"I'm with you," Bret vouched, manhandling the axe.

"Me too," piped up the youngest.

The radio operator glared down at him with disbelief. "I don't fucking Adam and Eve it," he complained, then hefted the iron bar, nearly toppling over with it.

"Let's go," called another recruit. "We've wasted enough time as it is!"

The corporal yanked the pickaxe out of the ground and looked around behind himself with unparalleled pride. "My boys…" he simpered, then let out a raucous battle cry. The driver joined in, "At 'em," he yelled – and with that the whole six charged down the hillside as if racing to dive into a pure blue ocean!

"Be sure to bring my tools back, yer hear," called the old timer behind them?

At the bottom – breathless – they all faltered to a halt, each brandishing a garden implement across their chests, which most promptly dropped.

"God in heaven," gasped the driver, catching his breath!

"We've missed it," gushed the youngest, incredulous.

Out before them, the complete open scrubland of Salisbury Plain – all three hundred square miles, was awash with bodies, the ground stained red with their blood, Wiltshire never ever being the same again.

"No way," stammered Bret.

The corporal imploded, along with the driver who'd stood and watched the unholy spectacle for some considerable time – and eventually having summoned up enough courage to actually want to get involved. Now, incredibly as it seemed – and whilst they'd been deliberating and arguing over this and that on top of the knoll, hundreds of thousands of people, mostly human, were dead – or close to it.

Despite it being a warm sultry day, steam rose in plumes as split stomachs and piles of intestines lay in pools of warm blood and bile, bodies – and parts, piled up in places where desperate struggles had ensued – survivors having built small defences of corpses. But the numbers had proved decisive. Although Britain as a whole had poured as many men as it could muster, supplemented, or been press ganged, it still hadn't been enough, three massive armies of King Arthur's encapsulating the plain and taking control right from the start, cavalry of all types making a huge difference as the ground was ideal for a mounted warrior. Now, as the young cadets gaped, battalions of foot soldiers ambled by, many never having drawn their swords – a whole army of territorials – men – and women, that should have been fighting for Queen and Country, fighting for King Arthur instead.

Having spotted The King and Queen earlier, the driver now looked again, finding the royal cortege parked right in the middle, the monarch being surrounded by an imperial collection of knights, to stare over the battlefield, looking visibly shaken. *'Prap's this guy wasn't such a bad person after all,"* the army recruit reasoned, watching from an extreme distance as hospital teams were allowed to filter over the morass.

"How many," the corporal whispered to himself, hardly being heard?

"Thousands – tens of thousands – " then the driver nearly jumped into his friend's arms as a nearby corpse came back to life!

"Holy Shit," the radio operator gurgled!

Down to their left a right skirmish had ensued as it seemed a detachment of riflemen went hand-to-hand with a large group of lightly armed peasants, the fighting raw and bloody – but again, not only weight of numbers showed but brawn as well as heavily swung adzes and flails, both deadly in experienced hands tore through modern day armour and thick clothing. Bodies lay haphazardly, many suffering caved in skulls as a result of a heavily swung instrument. Having to resort to hand-to-hand, there weren't many cold-hearted killers amongst the home army divisions. Sure they could kill at range – and of course there's always a specialist or two – but in the main, if today's soldier couldn't kill by pulling a trigger, hand-to-hand was out of the question.

"Holy Christ," cried Bret as a revenant – now fully conscious once more and on his knees, pulled himself from the pile of bodies he'd fallen into. He

put a hand to his head as he rose – an open wound from the butt of a rifle perhaps having brained him. He pulled his other arm from under a horse's corpse, untangling a halberd with which to aid him as he struggled to his feet.

Bret hefted his axe while the driver gripped his spade forcefully.

"What do we do," hissed the radio operator, huddling further into a tight group?

"Erm…," spluttered the corporal?

"I still can't find that order in the manual, you know," jibed one recruit.

"Shut it," Baz, "will you?"

The driver turned to his superior. "It's your call, Darren. If you're going to dispatch him, now's the time, while he's still groggy."

"Dispatch…" the corporal murmured, lost somewhat in the wholesale death and destruction laid out before him. "I think," he added weakly, "that anyone – thing – lucky enough to be able to survive this mass slaughter, should – under military law, be allowed some consideration…"

"Take him prisoner," enthused the youngster?

"Erm," mentioned the radio operator. "For one to apprehend prisoners – it helps a lot to have actually won the war, young sprout. Taking him now might very well end in an all out diplomatic incident none of us are capable of handling."

"Could hide him in me mum's shed."

"For fuck's sake, Neil, we're not kidnapping him – he'd probably kill us all!"

"Ask him his name," Baz proffered?

By this time, the revenant's head had cleared, and having pushed himself to his feet, looked aghast at the terrible vistas, the whole sea of violence and destruction visibly shaking him.

"This is all your own doing, you know," spat the youngster, shielded by five of his comrades?

For the first time, the peasant became aware of people nearby, his bleary eyes searching the piles of corpses for survivors. He rose unsteadily to his full six feet and pushed a thick heavy fringe of brown dusty hair off his forehead, revealing a broad flat face that wouldn't have looked out of place in a horror movie.

"Ho, christ, nice one, Neil- now he'll probably eat us for supper!"

"Ars longa," the squire huffed ruefully, "vita brevis Casus.belli; dies irae!"

"Is that Latin," the radio-operator queried?

"Speak English," the driver called out!

The soldier nodded, glancing down at himself, his tabard in ruins, his trews ripped and torn.

"My mum's pretty handy with needle and cotton," the youngest spoke up!

The corporal sighed deeply. He plucked up courage and, leaving his pickaxe where it had fallen, walked over, keeping an eye on the rest of the crowds filtering over the battlefield, the whole massive detachment of heavy cavalry now drifting away for some serious rest and recreation, he didn't wonder. He drew in a deep shuddering breath and – sticking his hands in his back pockets in what he hoped was a highly relaxed pose, returned his attention to the revenant foot soldier. "Where…um, do you come from," he asked, noncommittally?

"Arrest him," hissed the youngster!

The corporal ignored him.

"South of England," spoke the squire, his accent so deep and exotic it seemed laden with adventure and mysticism.

The corporal couldn't drag his eyes from the horrible scenes virtually all around him, faint cries of *'mercy'*, *'mother'* and *'medic'* drifting over the morass. It must have lasted nearly three hours, one of them spent sitting in someone's shed, another stood debating the whole incredible spectacle – and by the time they'd brewed up enough vim and determination, the vast encounter had finally wound down, any last fighting consigned now to the far hills of Devizes and Upton where knights were running down any enemy dissenters. As he'd stood there, wondering what on earth to say, he realised he couldn't even begin to describe the wanton savagery of what had transpired, could not even scratch the surface; the horrific clash of men and arms, the frightful struggle for survival, the brutal hand-to-hand in which so many of his compatriots had given their lives.

It nigh brought a tear to his eye.

The dusty revenant studied the young kid. Somehow his olive green uniform didn't seem to fit with any of the enemies' garb, many dressed in blue jeans or overalls, or black.

"Friend or foe," he asked suspiciously?

"Erm," coughed Darren?

The driver walked to catch his corporal by the arm. "I think its time we took our leave. They were being surrounded by inquisitive crowds – all from King Arthur's retinue.

"Let's get the fuck out of here," the radio-operator called, near panic in his voice!

"Well," the corporal spoke – steadying his best authoritative voice! "Congratulations on a solid victory. I, erm… should be going," the driver tugging him away before a keen eye realised they were – or had been – the enemy. They scampered back up the small knoll from which they'd all descended.

At the top they rushed passed the old boy who was asking why they'd left all the tools down where they'd dropped them, legging it for all they were worth?

***

In number four cell, Reading Jail, Sir Reginald Smyth – Knight of the Realm, defender of the laity, *miles gloriosus*; intrepid courtier, judicious milquetoast, had been given an aerosol can of shaving cream – with disastrous results!

It has to be said, that Desk Sergeant D Clifford had the odd good day – the sort of day that started with Jenny (Mrs Wheatly of number ten opposite) smiling and calling 'good morning' from her door as he drove to work; the paper arriving early enough for him to actually peruse a few pages before having to leave; and a quiet day at work as it ensued – when things ran smoothly and the sun shone brightly for just an hour or two. Then of course, he had mediocre days – those when he felt he might well have been on remote control for all the good he had done – and then, naturally there were the off days.

Today however – as he pulled open and stood at the cell door of number four (one of only two inhabitants) since the world as he knew it – had not only been turned upside down but ripped apart as well, the petty criminals having found better things to do with their time – like try and decide which side they were on – the Royalists – as the media liked to call them – or the Republicans – King Arthur's rebel army – his day was irrevocably turning in to one of those that demanded he go home feigning a headache, brain tumour or heart attack – or something equally debilitating.

The news that finally reached him late in the afternoon, after everything had stopped to watch live coverage of the battle and subsequent charge of the Heavy Brigade, decimating the Household Cavalry and divisions of mounted police like they were stuffed with paper, settling down as if it was the bloody World Cup, sickening him to the very core; tens of thousands dead – and still they lost. It was inconceivable – but worse was to come as he was ordered to let his prisoner go – without any charges, backed up by the fact that heavily armed knights and foot soldiers were moving through the county like a storm, a big contingent – including the royal party – King Arthur himself descending on Reading Jail as if to level it. He'd been advised that late afternoon – just when he was seriously deciding to go home – feigning any ailment, that Sir Reginald Smyth should be allowed to go free, especially as a one Lindsey Cartwright – and a retinue of politicians (with possibly the prime minister) – and solicitors were heading his way as well.

'For crying out loud,' he had mumbled, sorting the keys to the knight's cell: He'd interred him on the advice of the Special Branch – now the Senior Chief of Police was telling him to get rid of him as fast as possible – *'drop him like a hot brick,'* the authorities advised, as if holding him would cause a political nightmare!

He pulled the heavy door open fully, finding the tall knight standing against the washbasin, his broad back to him.

"Well, Sir Reginald – I trust your stay with us has been restful and courteous – your rag – er, clothes have been cleaned and repaired – and your armour is gleaming. Is there anything else I can do – slippers perhaps – " and then he stopped as the knight turned from the mirrored steel panel on the wall to face him, his head, chest hands and arms covered in shaving cream.

Some idiot had also handed him a safety razor during the morning, and now – having obviously been versed in the gentile art – had decided to have a go himself – with, shall we say, not too much success!

Amid the copious amounts of suds, trickles of blood oozed – the safety razor slicing through his wispy beard – and a few boils and swelling blackheads as well, creating a mess rather reminiscent of the battle that had just ensued.

"Jeeze," the Desk Sergeant muttered – visions of prisoner brutality slicing through his cortex: *"DAVEY,"* he hollered, sticking his head back out of the cell, "here – NOW!"

Half an hour later, Lindsey Cartwright arrived with the prime minister, senior politicians and a high-ranking member of the police commission, all to meet the fabled knight Sir Reginald Smyth in the hope that something might be salvaged from what had been a frightful day.

Clad again in his armour, his face smothered in antiseptic cream and pieces of tissue paper, the knight clanked and clinked back to freedom, meeting his entourage in the foyer with a stout bow.

"How goes the battle," he immediately asked in earnest, appearing eager to join his forces again, yet hoping to his gods it was over, having been kept fairly up-to-date by the sympathetic young recruit Davey, he was sure – due to the late nature of the day – that the conflict was well and truly decided?

"King Arthur was victorious," Lindsey called out joining him. "Are you alright?"

"Concern yourself not, dearest. My stay here has been much enjoyed. I've slept peacefully, eaten well – and even been pampered, showered and shaved."

"I can see – what did they use – a broken piece of glass?"

"I am well, nonetheless – and how are you, my dear, looking radiant as always?"

She nodded, appraising the tall revenant, a twinkle in her eye as she stared up at him.

"Can you sign for your belongings," the sergeant called over, having resentfully relinquished all of the knight's weapons, bringing them to the desk with a loud clatter?

Sir Reginald walked over to collect them, buckling up his broadsword, mace and war axe, shouldering another shorter sword that looked more ceremonial than combat effective, knives, daggers and the odd spike concealed about his person. When he'd finished, the Desk Sergeant pushed a clipboard towards him.

"Sign here, here and here," he pointed out, running a fingertip over the page, "for the return of your belongings – and here for your release form."

Sergeant D Clifford spread the forms out while Lindsey walked over to lend a hand where necessary. The knight however signed all the allotted spaces with a flourishing set of capital letters, all inked in Old English.

"Sign here for the release of offensive weapons," the Desk Sergeant sighed heavily, watching on with resignation, "and again here."

When he was finished Sir Reginald stood upright, handing back the sergeant his biro, the enigmatic knight having studied it at length during his signing fest.

"One last form," the policeman sighed, pulling yet another clipboard from under the counter.

"Is this really necessary," called the prime minister, itching to be away from the county as fast as her car could possibly carry her?

"Protocol," the Desk Sergeant murmured.

"What's this for," asked Sir Reginald suspiciously?

"It's a form to prove you've signed all the rest," D Clifford stated brightly.

The knight set him a steely gaze.

The Desk Sergeant stared back.

"I'll sign it," he admitted, tossing the clipboard back beneath the counter.

As the knight turned to leave, the prime minister approached, steeling herself for something of a plea bargain.

She cleared her throat as her lackeys crowded around.

"Sir Reginald –" she held out a hand, "I'm the prime minister of the United Kingdom and as such – have to make several dire decisions every day, in this – a very unsettled time, so please bear with me if I sound a little vague. Tell me please – from where do you come?"

"Summer's set, my lady." Sir Reginald gave her a small bow, holding onto his huge broadsword by his side.

"A lovely part of the country – but please – from what period of time?"

"It was late in the afternoon, dear lady – when we got the call."

Lindsey Cartwright, proud now to stand by her champion, realised her knight had not grasped the full import of the question. "She means, dear, the age – what year was it back then."

The tall knight thought for a moment. "Five forty six – the reign of King Arthur Pendragon," Sir Reginald straightened with pride.

The prime minister put a hand to her forehead, closing her eyes for a meditative second. When she opened them, Sir William of the senior government and ear to the Royal Court had joined her by her side, wringing his hands in a sorrowful attitude.

"I'm afraid we must accede to your superior weight of numbers at the present time young man – the battle lost for the moment, but the war is not over yet – I would implore you, dear knight, to do all you can to dissuade your king from going any further – many, many innocent lives hang in the balance."

"Our monarchy has reigned for over six decades and has been loved and respected for all this time, despite rebellious factions rising every so often, The Queen holds the very fabric of what our nation is as a whole – and it cannot – will not be subjugated. So I hope you can intercede on our behalf – and make this King Arthur see sense."

Sir Reginald raised his hands in an act of hopelessness. "I am but a vassal of the King, Sire. A foot soldier; I have about as much sway with the King's Counsel as my consort here does. In fact, Merlin has more to do with this than The King. The young contender is of this modern age, selected by rightful decree – simply a puppet king. Folklore and magic have finally put paid to all the injustice and inequality of this time – and decided to realign everything – its more than mortal men can judge!"

Sir William sighed deeply, the terrible loss of life exacerbated by the fact that despite nearly thirteen thousand swarming to defend the monarchy – it was not enough, hundreds – if not thousands fleeing in the opening hours of the battle, the magnificent Household Cavalry decimated – the modern-day man no match for a hardened warrior of yesteryear.

"Do what you can," Sir William called as a parting shot, news that The King was on his way, putting the fear of finding themselves in possible internment, adding flight to their wings. The prime minister was bundled away as Sir Reginald and Lindsey Cartwright watched in bemusement.

Sir Reginald turned to acknowledge the Desk Sergeant in a parting nod.

"Mind how you go," the policeman called out resignedly, on the verge of shutting up shop and going home?

Outside, the muted sunlight and warmth – and the subdued cacophony of a normal busy town appeared hauntingly strange to both of them; Lindsey, now abandoned by her chaperones – and limousines – finding the streets eerily quiet.

She searched the business suit the female politician had brought for her, finding she had been kind enough to place in one of the pockets a small purse, with forty pounds in it, a small token of her respect.

"Hungry," Lindsey asked of her knight?

Sir Reginald nodded thoughtfully, looking around and back at the prison he'd just walked free from, the towering building of metal and glass sparkling in the morning sun.

Lindsey followed the signs to the Abbey, wondering if The King and his retinue would prefer settling in Forbury Gardens to give the horses a much needed break to graze. She followed the signs to a small collection of shops however, to purchase a couple of rolls and a drink for the both of them, judging there would be a little time before the army began to regroup and move towards London – where the third dome would probably end up.

Walking through the streets, she got the oddest of stares and comments; some bemused and shocked to see a fully-clad knight strolling down the avenues, one or two – having just witnessed the terrible slaughter on television openly hostile while sympathisers championed his King and army, hooting and celebrating the army's victory.

At a local store, Lindsey led Sir Reginald in through the front door – ignoring open stares from the shop girls, leading him through the aisles and shelves until she found what she was looking for. She selected two big filled baps with crisps and drinks and headed for the tills, realising a moment later her knight was transfixed as he took in the rows upon rows of shelves, all stacked to the brim with food – food from every corner of the world it seemed as he eyed tins of fruit, cheeses and eggs, hams and fresh cuts of meat; milk, biscuits, bread by the bushel, something called pasta, packets of rice, cakes, more tinned stuffs – *"Ye Gods,"* he breathed out, "all this food – who's going to eat all this?"

"Your army when it arrives," Lindsey instructed him.

An old woman sauntered by, pushing a trolley with a few miserable items in place. The knight looked askance, wondering why – when the shelves were stacked so high with every conceivable food stuffs – she was only grabbing a few?

"Dear lady," the knight began, getting over his shock – thinking the little old crone could not reach the high shelves. "Here – allow me!" And Sir Reginald began loading her trolley with all manner of items, scooping up many packets and tins, filling her trolley with many she couldn't hope to cook.

By the time Lindsey intervened, the staff had too – and Sir Reginald was escorted off the premises, despite searching for and finding a small golden coin which he tossed to the old woman.

Lindsey was amazed she caught it, despite fumbling over her shopping.

At the park, all was quiet, the late morning giving way to early afternoon. For the first time Lindsey felt terribly alone and abandoned, as if by mankind itself, alone with no home or roof to hide under. She looked around for a bench to sit on and finding one, settled with her knight as he clanked and clinked into the seat beside her.

A few joggers and dog walkers were scattered about, none seeming to take any notice of her accompanying Knight of the Realm.

As Lindsey played mum and un-wrapped the big flat rolls, slapping Sir Reginald's hand away as he tried to inspect and sniff the cellophane, a battle royal was raging inside as reality fought with her emotions over her feelings for the big knight; the time away from him – the injustice over his incarceration and his apparent reassurance, all giving her the space to realise he meant her no harm – far from it, the revenant seemed wholly respectful and courteous as always – an innocence that was hard to dismiss – a charm and debonair that was hard to ignore – the time spent with the politicians, flunkies and toadies enough to teach her there was more to life than avarice and greed; the simplicity, the careful, thoughtful nature of her hero a breath of fresh air when compared.

However – no matter how graceful and dashing, Sir Reginald; Knight of the Realm and obvious champion of his own people was in fact a ghost from the past, a living anachronism – not real – and could, in all possibility disappear in a cloud of dust once order had been restored.

As she munched on her roll and slurped at her drink, watching her knight out of the corner of her eye as he experimented with all the food stuffs – smiling inherently as he inspected at length a packet of crisps – she knew her feelings had gone from one of rancour to annoyance – from annoyance to irritation and from irritation finally to acceptance – and now something else, a deference and warmth that she never knew could exist between her and somebody else – having never really taken the time to look or even evaluate the possibility.

'Ridiculous,' her mind told her, but as she felt the cold hard steel of his armour through her thin slacks there was a nascent ardour building in her subconscious, a tremulous dire feeling that if she didn't take the initiative she'd perhaps miss the only one true love she'd have a chance at.

'Don't be stupid!' her conscience raved at her, *'don't throw your life away on some* dandy, this fine coxcomb – *this time-thrown* flibbertigibbet. *You're better than this!'*

'Shut up!' He's polite, suave – gallant and above all thoughtful. *All rolled up, he's more than any man I've ever met at the local pub – or anywhere else!'*

'Yeah, but you just wait – come the judgement – he'll be back in his shire, and you'll be left cuckolded.'

'Hm, well damnit; if I've known true love for just a few days, I'd be better for it than have never loved before *– so there!'*

By the time she half-choked on her roll and spat out some crisps in huffs and puffs, Sir Reginald had given her several questioning glances and even wrapped a massive armoured arm around her shoulders, his body actions telling her he'd fight for her life if necessary.

She shook her head at the accusing thoughts and threw caution to the wind, nuzzling into his armour-plating.

Beneath pounded a heart of gold, she knew, nibbling sorrowfully on the last of her roll, pigeons chasing after the leftovers.

Sir Reginald shifted his weight and threw the last crumbs to the birds smiling broadly as a robin, chaffinch and starling squabbled over the treats, the knight feeding them yet more remains of his packet of crisps that tasted decidedly salty.

"Ok…" she murmured; safe in his arms, content to let the world go to hell?

"The bread," he commented, "tastes like something has been left out – if I may be so bold. It smells wonderful but there seems to be something lacking – as if the dough's all wrong!"

"You're right darling, its white bread – all the goodness has been extracted – all the bits and pieces and stuff."

Sir Reginald thought for a moment: A moment in time, when she could almost hear the cogs turning.

"It's a simple mixture, I'd thought, having seen it milled in our shire. Granted there's no husks or rats droppings but still, it seemed a little bland, if you don't mind me saying?"

Lindsey shifted deeper into his cold armour, not minding the coolness, just revelling in the strength and security it exuded.

"Your opinion is a statement of our time, I'm afraid – as everything harmful or unwanted is discarded, I'm afraid the baby was thrown out with the bathwater – now we're in a state of denial wondering where we've gone wrong!"

"Gone wrong," the knight worded in a small voice, looking out at a truly alien world?

He breathed in, almost sadly. "I really don't see a crushed up world, far from it, everything seems orderly and just so, people seem friendly – even to our army, and I must say – despite being here only a couple of days I've been welcomed as if royal – " he shook his head in solemn dismay, "I'm afraid I can't really see the sense in it, bringing the whole bleeding army here just to meddle in someone else's world?"

"I'm glad you came," Lindsey Cartwright issued in a terribly small voice.

The knight stiffened in his armour, she sensing it despite clad in inches of steel. He shifted his weight extra carefully – not to disturb her too much, but trying in his endeavour to look down at her, obviously not believing what he'd just heard.

He straightened again, relaxing, still admiring the strange scenery, ardently amazed at the buildings – the surrounding industry, the hustle and bustle – yet here – here in this little glade – only a short walk from the jail – was tranquillity and peacefulness, the pleasantness of green grass, flowers and trees – and wildlife – and the odd turnaround of his mistress, who had somehow decided that he was not all bad, could perchance be a credible person – if only she took the chance to look.

"I'm glad I was able to save you, m'lady – it would have been a miserable life to have ended up as a mouse!"

Her knees up on the bench, Lindsey shuddered and pushed the horrible thought to the back of her mind, so much having transpired of late even her own incredibly terrifying ordeal had dwindled into insignificance against the battle and the unholy clash of war – the incredible loss of life – especially human!

The knight again glanced down at her. "You are cold m'lady. I need to secure a room for you."

Lindsey considered the thirty pounds she had left, and knew in an instant it wouldn't even get her a tent in a garden – then she thought of something. Amid a distant clattering and clamour of voices, she coyly asked if Sir Reginald had any more gold coins on him.

"Indeed mistress," he answered immediately, rummaging about his person for his purse. "I should still have a solid gold ingot; several doubloons and coins and a few shekels – all gold or silver."

As the distant clamour, hooting and hollering got nearer, it became evident that part of Arthur's army was approaching, heading for the green suburbs of Reading as they resolutely marched westwards. The whinnying and clip-clop of horses followed up on a breeze, Lindsey hoping she and her knight had gained favour with The King.

She unfolded herself as battle-weary foot soldiers and light cavalry units drifted into the Abby's grounds, many liking the soft green grass and enclosed position. No sooner had they drifted in than they flopped down – anywhere – stretching out, one or two setting up a skillet or preparing a camp fire to bed down for the rest of the day. Soon hundreds were pouring in from all points, collecting bed rolls from wagons – commandeered trailers; brightly coloured tents were springing up, many a soldier being shown how to erect a modern igloo.

A knight on horseback trotted near. "Sir Reginald…" he asked in earnest?

Sir Reginald pushed himself to his feet.

"I am so," he replied.

"The King wants your ear – in fact he's a bit worried about you. Are you well?"

"I am. Where is our liege?"

The knight glanced behind him. "Should be here shortly; they are taking over the Grand Lodge hotel; some squires are bringing your horses. You are to meet him there."

Sir Reginald nodded. "The Grand Lodge, we'll find it!"

"It's across town," the knight advised. "Best follow the others."

They acknowledged each other and then the messenger left, wheeling his big charger around in a wide circle. The horse's armoured flank was splattered in blood as he did so, a dart of an arrow buried in a leather hasp.

Lindsey watched the knight stroll out of the Abbey ruins, a young man – from the look of his face – the sheer lunacy of the last few days encapsulated in that one small incident, the war-weary horse and rider having been engaged in the bloodiest battle England had ever known yesterday – and he'd survived. Perhaps his innocence had saved him, despite charging headlong into the fray, the angel of mercy riding with him. As the young knight wandered out of the grounds, she cast her eyes over the war-weary survivors – many now encamped in the Abby grounds. Pennants and big flags laid to rest. Among the foot soldiers, pike-men, archers and lightly clad warriors, Amazonian-like women also mingled, finding a spot around a camp fire. She glanced up to find The Dome that had passed over some time earlier, glistening prettily, having made the driver of the limousine she was in screech to a stop and almost curl up in his seat as the fiery wall caught up with them, the curtain of power pausing as it inspected the big car, then without apparent concern it simply passed through, Lindsey unable to feel anything despite closing her eyes and fearing the worst. Once it had passed, the engine of the big armoured vehicle started up again as if it had a mind of its own, the driver by this time totally scared out of his wits.

She shivered, despite it being warm, her knight looking around for something perhaps to close around her shoulders, but as Sir Reginald was worrying, a small group of squires and knaves led over four horses, one decked in an ornate saddle with the silk Pendragon sigils and sparkling armour-plating; lances and spears tied to its sides.

The tall knight recognised them straight away; Gwent and Adrian his stalwart and often disrespectful squire and knave. Seeing him with a woman however saved him from ridicule at having missed the battle; both being aware that he'd been asked to go on a diplomatic mission.

"Sir Reginald." Both squire and knave bowed regally!

"Gwent, Adrian. I trust you are well." He walked forward to acknowledge his horse who bowed his head playfully.

"Very well Sire," Adrian burst out, eager to be in proper service again, especially with a lovely young woman in tow.

Sir Reginald noticed the glances they were giving his mistress. He stepped over to make formal introductions. "This is Lady Lindsey Cartwright of the Shires, by decree my consort so if you would show her the full courtesy and respect, I'll be very appreciative."

They both bowed again in her direction. "My lady," Adrian murmured loyally.

"Yes, well – we have to meet with The King quickly, so if you know the way to the Grand Lodge Hotel, lead on."

"The King's train is spread out over a couple of miles; it will not be too hard to track him down." The squire led the horses over to his Knight and Lady.

"Erm..," Lindsey coughed politely, standing to brush crumbs away, then look up at the big horse being presented to her. "I, erm…"

"Fear not, m'lady. Janxy here is the sweetest of all rides – very safe." Gwent put a hand out for Lindsey to put her foot in, and holding on for dear life she was hoisted up into the saddle.

Once astride, she eased into the hard leather and took up the reins, not having a clue what to do.

Gwent made sure her feet were snugly placed into the big leather stirrups, then – happy she was safely aboard, left with a curt bow.

Seeing her distress, Sir Reginald coaxed his war-charger over to her and threw a leather strap over to link up the reins. "You'll be fine," he assured her.

They waited for the squire and knave to saddle up themselves, then they were off, following their noses and immediately asking directions.

Chapter 10

After the battle, The King had found the knight turned ogre Petersbury Dean in amongst ghastly piles of the dead or dying that evening, the last handful of the brutish beings surviving along with only three Mor-men, counting the cost – mourning the loss of brother or father or kindred spirit. Having walked the battlefield with his entourage of knights and wizards – the complete reserve army swarming over the Salisbury Plain around him as if to inure themselves against yet more bloodshed, he'd been lost in the ferocious hand-to-hand, the incredible fight for victory, both sides a worthy opponent. Yet the Plain was covered with dead soldiers; many a black-suited Special Forces combater or veteran, the army flashes and different uniforms denoting NATO or Foreign Legion supporters. So many dead, some carcases hewn almost in half, an axe or broadsword weighing anything between three to five pounds, only having to connect once to smash or cleave muscle and bone. Many appeared to be sleeping, having just been knocked silly by a glancing blade or pommel – and countless times, Dan had knelt down, hoping to instil new breath into the corpse, almost willing the man to open his eyes, see the light of day again. But closer inspection often resulted in the cranium being smashed in at the top or back, or a small stab wound anywhere on the torso; a nine inch dagger – thrust with the power of a gauntleted fist – razor sharp, slicing through woven fabric and annealed fibre like it was tissue paper, renting internal organs asunder. His army had fought with the wanton drive to win at all costs, the thought of bending or crumbling in battle unthinkable. Some knights, he'd noticed earlier, had seemed to glow amid the battlefield, somehow drawing power from the power shield above, standing out above all others as their chargers beneath them snorted and stamped out in fury, a big circle of dead and wounded surrounding them before they too were engulfed in the melee – their light going out finally.

By the time he'd reached midway, where the ogres and Mor-men had saved the day by sacrificing themselves for the greater good – hauling the *'turtles'* across the arrow-strewn land and actually managing to build a more substantial bridge for the animals to charge through, many a knight and lady had a tear in their eye, the savagery combined with the awful waste of life too much to contemplate.

Heartened to find surviving members of the eldritch beings, The King immediately stepped over to greet them, his eminence shining out like a beacon amid a sea of tragedy. In his gleaming gold and silver armour he stood a mammoth seven feet and could look the Mor-men in the eye – not only as an equal but as a loyal friend and ally, a staunch leader and confidante.

The remaining ogres gathered round, intrigue mixed with pure speculation. Back in the day, The King was still The King, despite the ogres and Mor-men living on the fringes of society – now they all seemed to meet on hallowed ground – where one was equal with the other.

"I'm not your king," Danny started, checking his voice as it felt like cracking at the appalling loss of life – many an ogre or Mor-man hacked to death in the scramble for victory, "But as acting regent I can only thank you from the bottom of my heart for the valiant sacrifice you have made. It virtually won the war…" Here The King paused, unable to keep his eyes from the piles of dead, steam rising from split stomachs and deep lacerations – severed limbs. Here and there – along the bloodiest trench he'd ever have to look down, the two metre by quarter of a mile was strewn with corpses, horses mingled in with the contorted bodies. Ogres, soldiers of all types and Mor-men had been viciously impaled on the remaining stakes, pushed back by weight of numbers at one time, there to thrash about helplessly as around them the fighting increased until it reached fever pitch. They'd taken the brunt of it; the heavily built bodies able to withstand some punishment before eventually a lucky arrow or bolt from bow or crossbow ended it for them.

Dan heaved in a shuddering sigh, bringing himself back to the present. "I'm not sure how I can repay you – only that your bravery and selfless fight for victory will not be forgotten. I will erect plaques and obelisks to honour your commitment and a day will stand in history forevermore for the sacrifice you have made today. I – I can't thank you enough…" He felt like sinking to one knee, but in the end could only hold out his arms as the Mor-men and ogres moved close to commiserate. "May the cosmos favour you," Dan murmured, tears flooding his eyes.

"Home, go now," asked a young Mor-man, so young in fact he'd probably been protected throughout the battle?

"Yes of course you can go home," Dan assured him with a sniff. "I'll tell Merlin to send you all home – with my blessing."

"I'll stay and see it through – if it's alright by you," Petersbury Dean spoke up, pulling a small dart from his shoulder, the smallest of the twelve foot monsters flanking him. One of the ogres planted a mighty mitt on his other shoulder, rumbling: "I'll stay too – might as well."

One surviving Mor-man looked to the other. "You take Manx home, Erd. I'll stay and help finish up. The demigod nodded sagely, his arm already around the youngster. "He's seen enough," he opined.

King Arthur searched the red hot coals behind the leather mask and found compassion there, despite the horrifying head. About the leather-clad body, welts and stab wounds abounded as if he'd been dragged up and down the fields by cart horses, his huge gnarled hand by his side, bloodied and almost trembling with angst.

The King spread his hands to encompass the small group, Guinevere finally stepping over, making an appearance with her entourage to wish the small group well.

Dan smiled, despite his heartbreak at the young Mor-man who'd nearly swooned as the radiance and stunning beauty neared.

"You are all welcome to stay with me at the nearest accommodation. Please, be my especial guests tonight, we'll drink to our fallen ones – but also to a resounding victory!"

"We can't miss that eh, Erd," rasped the young Mor-man, turning his head to the elder?

***

'This can't be happening,' remonstrated Lindsey Cartwright with herself! *(Not 'Mouse Woman' any more, but 'Lady Lindsey Cartwright' – it had a distinct ring to it too!)*

Astride her lovely bay mare she held her head high as they clip-clopped though Reading, Lindsey finding she was actually waving to the crowds ringing the streets in a most peculiar way? Realising she was emulating royalty she quickly and nonchalantly reversed her hand and waved normally. Astride her big charger she could see further than in a car, the whole of Reading it seemed, coming out to not only welcome the hero King Arthur, but his resident army as well, despite them tearing up the countryside and commandeering everything in sight. At the New Town intersection they were met by legions of Arthur's advance army, thousands of knights and footmen swarming though the town to bunk down somewhere near the demarcation of the third dome – which had ended up just shy of the boundary line of Windsor and Maidenhead, cutting through Henley on Thames in the north and encompassing Basingstoke and Winchester in the south. All along the blocked A4, knights on horseback tried to encircle The King who'd already taken up residence in The Great Lodge Hotel in Sonning, the area lush and open and set in acres of green woodland, tents and caravans already starting to colonize the big green spaces of the nearby golf courses, recreational parks and sports grounds, the Caversham lakes being surrounded by resting soldiers – many having been transported by coach, bus or car, setting up shop as soon as they arrived – much to the consternation of the farmers and civic authorities. Hundreds of thousands more were pouring through the towns of Newbury and Thatcham on their way to their new destination, crossing the fields and villages of Berkshire in order to catch up, battle-weary and injured, many limped by the big metropolis of Basingstoke, sightseers bringing out bottles of water or bandages which many a knight or squire showed their appreciation for. By eight that night many had crossed the Thames at various points and were encircling the area of Sonning, camping all along The New Dome's edge.

By six that evening Lindsey Cartwright and her noble knight Sir Reginald, plus a squire and a knave, had made it to the Great Lodge Hotel, having sauntered up the A4 and then the big B-road to the hotel, able to stable their horses in a nearby private school that had all but been abandoned by the staff and pupils, the revenant vanguard moving in swiftly to commandeer any available space or lodging.

At the hotel the big banqueting hall was rapidly set for an all-out feast and festivities – something that would run into the night if the victory was anything to go by, the staff in absolute awe of the ogres and surviving Mor-men who showed up with the royal party, the survivors bestowing the transfixed people the utmost courtesy. With hundreds of others, Lindsey and Sir Reginald had made their way toward the Lodge, finding several makeshift bars were opening, the owners, predicting a thirsty army after the heat of the encompassing Dome had crept over, immediately setting the temperature soaring, having spent the afternoon ordering in hundreds of gallons of ale and real beer, buying up nearly every microbrewery in a thirty mile radius. The hotel owner had made it a sure bet some hours previous that his lodge may well be earmarked, being one of the last great hotels before encroaching on the grounds of Windsor or Maidenhead, but runners and sympathizers racing ahead anyway, beating even the royal party or the heavily armoured vanguard surrounding it, had warned of the approaching army and asked politely if various hoteliers would play host to the legions of King Arthur's army as they would be encamping just short of The Dome's sphere.

The owner had agreed heartily, having just been out to view the glistening power curtain himself, overawed by such an event – but if that was not enough, he had now to play host to the actual King himself – it was something of a fairy-tale come true.

Having an immutable barrier between him and the capital – and all that implied, the owner of the Great Lodge Hotel was encouraged to throw up his recent lifetime's obsession with the toadying, sycophantic attitudes of his imbibing flock, and throw caution to the wind to accept The New King – in all his glory – stories abounding of his magical wizard Merlin and his fantastical zombie army, the generosity of the glittering knights, the immense stature of the golden King Arthur. It all seemed to be ushering in a new age where he could be himself at last and stick his fingers up to all the obsequious charlatans who he'd had to put up with these last four years – half of them owing him in credit wavers – and tabs left unpaid.

***

Finally in his quarters – a suite fit for a royal dignitary or visiting VIP, Arthur called a halt to the proceedings, placing his glistening crowned helmet carefully on a sideboard and divesting himself of his weaponry, most of the knaves sent on their way once his armour was partially removed. He was surrounded yet again by regal and opulent décor and trappings – the smell always invading his mind – the freshness of new paint, linen and polish something he'd never forget; the world of the rich and elite, into which he'd been thrust most unexpectedly, the irony never lost on him that just a snippet of this wealth could probably end poverty – in England anyway – overnight.

He fell into an arm chair, needing a moment to himself to unwind before the festivities of the evening began, to reflect on the calamitous engagement, collect his thoughts and prepare for a closing speech – something he didn't want to dwell on but needed to be done.

Guinevere was being shown around the rooms of the apartment in something of a daze, taken down a short hall to the sumptuous bathrooms to freshen up, leaving The King in a meditative state. Here, Guinevere was finally exposed to the modern world, practically bowled over by the magnificent corner bath – big enough for five or six people easily; running hot water and the power shower another revelation; fragrances and soaps – a futuristic world of ceramics and chrome, opening up a universe that she could never have even dreamed of.

Having removed her silk gown and headdress in an adjoining bedroom, she was ushered back to the lavish bathroom to soak luxuriously in the warm bath for a while; then experience a small hot-tub, giggling furiously as the bubbles caressed her. She stepped into the shower for a few minutes, marvelling at being shown an array of soaps and gels that smelt heavenly and vibrant! She sneezed over the fine powdery talc later, and coughed over the heady fragrance of a rich perfume, recoiling at the reek of a superfine hairspray – finally emerging hours later like the goddess she was.

In the expansive lounge area, Arthur had accepted a superlative glass of first-pressed burgundy – the wine having a quality of liquid velvet and a palate that inspired the taste buds – and then the thought processes, reaching parts the quart of grapefruit juice he'd been gulping down earlier never could. He sipped at the grandiose drink, listening as squeals of delight rang out from the bedchambers and big bathroom as the hand maidens and ladies in waiting fussed about their Queen.

In her haste, she'd only managed to pack a small portmanteau, he knew, with essentials and two rather eloquent dresses, hoping her stay was only going to be transitory, but now she'd been put in the picture a little, it seemed her and her new king might have to endure some days of negotiations before calm could be restored.

The battle had been ghastly, he had reiterated during their ride, the losses to the opposing forces horrendous, this modern world unable or unresolved to stop Arthur's advance; The Dome's destructive tendencies equalling out the battle lines by ameliorating the firearms and ballistic weaponry.

By the time his Queen had been pampered and washed, rinsed down and pampered again, suffered explanation after exposition, her head was swimming so much she was glad to join Arthur and sit, and just let it all roll over her for a moment or two.

The King moved so he could join her on a modern chaise lounge, marvelling at her beauty; the faint smudge of expensive lipstick that had been wiped off in something of a hurry just visible on her cheek.

"May I…" he enquired softly, raising a hand to wipe away the smear with a fingertip?

He smiled to himself in doing so, realising you cannot improve on something that is already perfect in nature.

The Queen acquiesced to the clean up, stupefied yet again as her eyes slid from him to her environs, a small shake of the head over the strange and enigmatic world surrounding her, casting her vision around the expansive lounge area. He noticed the wonder and amazement.

"It's all a bit over my head too," he confided to her, patting her knee with a huge hand.

The Queen seemed to recoil somewhat over the brazen familiarity and Danny checked himself, forgetting who she was for a microsecond. He coughed politely and, forgetting himself again as he went to put his arm along the chaise lounge, fidgeted awkwardly as he sat perched beside her.

"This is not your world," the Queen asked, slightly confused?

"Yes – yes it is," spluttered the king. "It's just that I was only a normal person, working in a fitness centre – I – er, wasn't born into riches or royalty – or anything like that, simply a working man."

"You are King now," his Queen noted with some authority!

"Yeah, I know…" Dan heaved in a sigh. "The thing is, I just happened to be passing by when the Sword in the Stone presented itself – it could have been anybody – lots of people walk the fens."

"Not just anybody," the Queen spoke evenly, knowing a little of Excalibur and its immense power, of how it seemed to seek out truth and justice on its own – and as soon as a King abused it, then the powers surrounding it would soon correct things; it was staggering how easily a King could be deposed. She shook her head with a fatalistic inward sigh, staring into space, having lost her King to some enchantment (not all of his own fault *perhaps*) – and now – having been transported far, far in time to this crazy new world, they were supposed to right a wrong that had suppressed the right of the people of this merry land for so very long. And yet, the more she dwelt on the meaning of it all, the more pieces appeared to fall into place – the Sword having the quality to survive eons of time, almost shrug off elemental parameters and travel vast distances, without moving at all. *Mordred had a hand in this,* she mused shrewdly.

"I must admit," King Arthur started, breaking her reverie. "All this magic and mysticism – it all seems a little strange – especially in a time like this when science is moving on at such a pace, men travelling to the moon and Mars, quite a lot of the awful diseases wiped out."

"And yet poverty and hardship exist – even in your country – which I must say – seems at odds from what I see around me."

Dan nodded with a certain amount of sadness. Not for himself but for the short-sightedness of those who'd inherited wealth and power, only to abuse it and squander it, spend millions of pounds buying that piece of artwork – that in all probability looked as if it was made in someone's back garden – wouldn't look amiss in some rubbish tip in fact – when thousands of children were still going to school hungry in the mornings, simply because the wages had been cut and cut until people were forced onto the breadline. When an emergency hits – some banking fraternity goes rogue and causes a world-wide monetary crash – who do you think helps the banks out once they've recoiled from the seizure – the tax-payer of course – austerity – a word that hasn't been bandied about since the war years, now thrust upon the people like a pogrom, instructing them to knuckle down and tighten their belts – *as if* they could be tightened anymore – and the old adage *'we'll get through it together'* – *meaning* you foot the bill while we sit here and enjoy ourselves.

"It's got to end," Dan spoke with remorse. "Excalibur – with all its magical power – has always been England's supreme power – and now it has resurfaced to readdress the injustices once more. Other countries may have their own *'Excalibur'* maybe in the form of a saviour or animal – but England had The Sword – *and The Sword has finally come home!*

"You are ready to be King," the Queen asked suddenly?

Danny looked down at her. Her light silver-blonde hair seemed to sparkle and radiate with some of that magic Merlin surrounded himself with, tiny suns of glistening light that created a halo almost as it encompassed her head.

He chose his next words carefully. "With you beside me, Guinevere, I could achieve anything – what man couldn't. I just worry that with all this gone, the old ways will quickly reassert themselves – and we'll all be back to square one."

The Queen was shaking her head. "The whole point of this, I think, is to give the power back to the people. The Sword's power is only for the people it serves – its purpose is to galvanise those in power to protect those without."

Danny nodded thoughtfully. "But what's going to happen," he worried, the bulk he'd put on, the incredible power seeping through him, would it all just disappear once order had been restored?

"I think, dear," The Queen addressed him formally, "that the people – having taken control will then surround you with their loyalty. You'll be surprised at how forceful that fealty can be – and you will reign supreme, needing no crawling government or toadying lackeys to soak up the limelight – you can form some kind of civil council to help run things but other than that, the country will run itself. People know how to work – how to fend for themselves – they've done it long enough – it's just those few who are going to be put out – those who have ridden the system for so very long – and who have become complacent."

"There's quite a big royal family," The King mused thoughtfully. "Somewhat fragmented now – but still receiving billions in royalties – something that will have to be addressed."

"When they see it's for the good of the country, I'm sure they'll agree. No one person can possibly account for so much wealth. If money is suppressed and hidden away –"

"Or splurged in dodgy off-shore accounts," Dan cut in!

The Queen caught herself, not understanding.

"Yes, well… it cannot benefit anyone. There must be a steady flow – like the stream. Yes, one man may work harder than the next and do better for it –

that is our way of working, but I was taught from an early age – that for a community to survive, the taxes must be met, but fairness and kindness must always prevail, above all else. If a man dies in battle or protecting his land, then the family cannot die with him, no – that family must be cared for, nurtured even – for those children are the next generation of knights, squires, tradesmen, knaves, or genteel folk."

"Genteel folk," The King parodied, smiling over the diction, lost for a moment in The Queen's own sunlit world – a world where black and white magic also played a part.

After a moment he found his queen staring up at him, studying him.

He shifted his weight embarrassingly.

"I – er, apologise my lady – I meant no offence – it's just the meeting of these two worlds – yours with all the magic and mysticism, those wonderful ogres and Mor-Men, incredible beasts, noble knights, and mine with all the glitz and glamour, it all seems so unreal – as if I'm experiencing a waking dream!"

"You should see it from this side!"

***

'A Time For *Real* Change' read the title for Bill Nightingale's ninth episodic literary quest – the scoops gaining in readership and notoriety each and every time, having the readership of the people now by still keeping as close as humanly possible to The King, gaining his confidence with each new report;

detailing the mood and demeanour of the regent-in-waiting; giving each and every article a sense that The King was speaking verbatim.

Plenty of room for artistic licence however – and Bill Nightingale had been no slouch when creative writing was called for.

In covering the battle though, the reporter found a wall of salt water clouding his vision – and the emotions, the incredible loss of life, the sickening reek of death – made ten times worse by the encapsulating Dome, heat encouraging swarms of flies that crawled about the blood-soaked ground, millions crushed underfoot as Arthur's reserve army – of which he and Fay had been part, (and which hadn't even drawn their swords) plodded over the strewn battleground, stripping many a recruit or foot soldier of their arms or armour.

The pillaging went on all afternoon and way into the evening; but Bill could not find it in himself to abhor the acts; merely commenting on it – sensing almost the desire to emulate their fallen heroes – step into their shoes – take up the mantle that would release the county from the strangle-grip that was bleeding it dry. Bill touched on the *'mob psyche'* but knew there was something more than that occurring – a national cooperative impulse that soared way above the *'collective intelligence'*.

He found it hard to describe it in full, mesmerised by the full national feeling that was venting itself further up the country. If the scenes in the south hadn't been bad enough, riots of all kind had broken out in major cities all over the midlands and northern Britain; Newcastle, Sunderland,

Manchester seeing the worst as hundreds of thousands crammed into trains and coaches, trucks, vans, motorbikes, anything in fact that would race them down to London and witness the crowning of a new king; a King that would liberate them all. Skirmishes, bloody and – in the light of it, pretty futile – broke out as Royalists tried to intercept the hundreds leaving the housing estates, towns and cities, embarking on some kind of lunatic crusade, dragging logistics with them, streaming through road and lane, tramping over field and dale; all desperate to be part of something their psyche told them would be a change for the better. In Scotland, Bill noticed, glued to his laptop, they were slightly more reserved, gathering in hundreds at the border, almost waiting for The King to be crowned before committing themselves. It had been the battle, Bill reminisced thoughtfully – had Arthur lost the day – the whole episode would have fizzled out: but he hadn't – far from it, despite thousands – hundreds of thousands in reality, forming into something of a Home Guard, ready to lay their life down in a heroic struggle to contain the juggernaut that was King Arthur's revenant army – two, maybe three massive detachments in reality won out the day – The King's forces having been big enough to split into two and circumnavigate the back of Frome and sweep round – and, despite meeting stiff opposition, winning the day, pushing ever forward to emerge out onto the battlefield just when things could have swung either way, the incredible beasts and fantastical beings met with a grim determination that fought against anything in order to protect all they held dear – but it hadn't been enough, certainly not the mounted divisions, no match for the armoured war horses and riders who'd spent a lifetime gaining their spurs. The unholy tangle in the middle later was the defining cataclysm, Bill watching on from several vantage points as news drones and helicopters continued the live feed, the whole four-hour long spectacle a real travesty to behold, so many Englishmen and their steeds – the very pride of the Household Cavalry steamrolled over as if made of balsa-wood. The god-awful scenes were still vivid in his mind as he tried to quantify it all, spelling out the very dire wishes of King Arthur that he had no intention of engaging in such a terrible fracas. It had gone ahead however, Bill, despite himself, somehow swept up in that thrill and splendour when the British Cavalry units trotted into their formations, earlier on, looking so regal and grand, even a Colonial Horse-Guard detachment, he noticed, looking resplendent in beige uniforms. All the pomp and grandeur of a prestigious ceremony of Trooping the Colours, yet the mounted police probably had more experience with unruly crowds than ever the Blues and Royals did; their duties ceremonial at best. It was sickening, he had to tearfully admit, his fingers hovering over the keyboard, trying to find the right sentiment, but try as he might he had but an inkling of the modern wanton savagery and bloodlust – no matter how ardent, finding it was not enough for even one of Arthur's foot soldiers, his army versed in close combat from an early age, capable of wielding a four to five pound hunk of metal for many a long afternoon, the vigour and sheer brutality winning out – even as the war machine that was the heavy horse putting paid to the closing pieces of the battle, it was obvious the Royalist army was beaten. It might even have been won without Arthur's army – Bill cogitating on just how many republicans existed in these islands?

He finished off with a small dissertation on the rights and responsibilities of Man as directed by Thomas Paine, then closed with a testament and heartfelt obituary for all the battalions and infantry divisions that had given their life for their country – misguided or otherwise.

***

The King and Queen looked over their congregation. Copious amounts of ale flowed, two to three litre beer steins that until now had gathered dust on shelves as ornaments, found new employment as the ogres and Mor-men supped eagerly.

"You can keep them," the landlord chortled; happy they'd eventually found a use. Having hired more staff, he'd also lined the outside of the banqueting hall with yet more tables, allowing an extra two or three hundred of Arthur's best knights into the inner sanctum, the big scenic windows and French doors leading out to the grassed lawns that in turn led down to the river; opened fully to allow more revellers to crowd around, the Great Lodge now surrounded entirely by King Arthur's heavily armoured vanguard. Yet more of his army surged through Berkshire, amassing all along the demarcation line burnt in by the resting Dome.

The King stood to raise a stein, his golden armour glistening and throwing out beams of radiant light, his straggly blonde hair framing a chiselled and tanned strong face: The Queen beside him, radiant as well in silken white gowns looked like an angel beside her titan.

"Fallen heroes – of both sides," he called out, although there were no survivors of the Crown's regiments present, most licking their wounds back in their barracks or at home, "I wish to convey my thanks and everlasting gratitude for those that have given so much – have without question travelled the eons of time to be here and fight the almighty fight that would bring the day of reckoning. Well, thanks to you and the fallen, this day has come, the battle is won – and we can all rest easy." He raised his big tankard to take a long draft.

Sir Reginald Smyth and his *Lady,* Lindsey Cartwright, made their way to the front, being recognised almost immediately by The King. His smile of relief was evident as he welcomed them, ushering them in close to his counsel. "You're safe," he rejoiced amid the banter and uproarious babble!

Lindsey nodded, the both of them working their way to his side. Choosing her words carefully, she tried to practically shout over the din. "Sir Reginald was incarcerated but shown every courtesy," she called out, "– as was I; but I'm afraid that – despite every request and demand, all our aspirations fell on deaf ears, the ruling bodies swayed by the military bigwigs. My knight here is crestfallen not have engaged the enemy with his fellow laymen but intends to be by your side whenever needed."

"I can't thank you enough for your efforts," Miss Lindsey – The King acknowledging her knight gratefully. "Pull a chair up will you," King Arthur called to some hovering knaves, wanting the two stalwart supporters close by. "Sit close and revel in a battle well fought," he called over the noise!

They did so; finding it difficult to get swept up in the fanfare and general gaiety.

Sometime later, having partaken eagerly of plenty of food and drink, Lindsey managed to scrounge a heavy-duty sleeping bag from the staff of the hotel as she wended her way to the toilets and back, set about finding a warm spot by the river, camping out for the night, the extra-warm air from the enclosing Dome making the venture a rather romantic affair. Encamped foot soldiers and knights made way for them, showing them every politeness, no doubt thinking Sir Reginald may well have been in the thick of it. He shared out a cooked and still hot chicken he'd grabbed on the way out, to anyone that was hungry and some wine – also nabbed, reminiscing on the battle and the charge of the war horses that put a deciding coffin-nail into the last vestiges of the ensuing chaos. Luckily, he wasn't asked too pointedly about his part in the conflict – and as the late evening approached, he and Lindsey snuggled down for the night, Sir Reginald's armour and weaponry, laid out neatly beside them.

***

In the Royal suite that same night, The King – a little squiffy if truth be known, tried vainly to keep up with the discourse as Merlin and his sages conferred with Sirs Galahad, Lancelot and Percival; Constantine II; The Green Knight and other generals – the meeting also attended by Guinevere and her ladies in waiting; the potentate and financier Earl Mason-James; Bill Nightingale of the Southern Chronicle with his lovely consort Fay – a complete team of other civic leaders who were doing their best to ameliorate the really terrifying ordeal The Reigning Queen and all her royal family were going to have to contemplate, handing over the realm and standing down. In doing so, of course, several subsidy payments would end, offshore accounts seized, the Civil List would be totally rewritten and any sovereign grants annulled. It was all too much, except for those who could keep a cool head – and more importantly – feared little from the outcome. While Merlin considered his next move – the complete takeover of the capitol – namely Windsor, Buckingham Palace and Westminster – where he hoped some kind of ceremony would take place to eschew Arthur's rightful place at the head of the New Throne, others tried desperately to bring everyone together in the hope of some kind of arrangement – the big room packed and split into two camps, but it looked increasingly unlikely as news broke of the aging Queen and her family (who had already been whisked from London earlier) that, on the advice of several of their diplomats any meeting would be out of the question. However – public support for King Arthur was beginning a domino effect that was rippling right through the country, millions marching on the capitol from the north; nearly as many from the south, so many in fact, no-one could deny the overwhelming support King Arthur had generated. Government moved quickly to issue an emergency public holiday – but already millions had decided that's just what they'd do – and bugger the consequences – because when it came from the top – as it had officially been decreed, then who could be wrong?

Trying desperately to engage – and hold his head together – wondering why it all couldn't have been sorted later, The King wavered and spiralled out of focus as soon as he endeavoured to confirm or contemplate something.

"The King looks weary," more than one knight advised.

Merlin continued to harry the visiting royal emissaries – wanting some kind of confirmation of a meeting the following day, the rush to crown his liege and nip the situation in the bud foremost in his mind, adamant as he and his sages and armies rode the crest of the almighty wave, a tsunami that was rushing toward central London – from all four quarters, he was informed.

"Your Regent must bow to the situation," he stressed as men and women sat at desks conferring with laptops and mobile phones, one whole half of the room looking like a huge office in the thrall of an election campaign, while the other resembled a scene from an historical Hollywood film studio!

Many shook their heads, knowing of the skulduggery forming around the denial and obduracy of those loyal to the monarchy, many not even considering the predicament – hoping in fact – if they waited long enough, it might possibly just go away – or creep back into the dust whence it came.

"We're not going anywhere until Arthur is crowned King," Mordred announced raucously, his temper getting the better of him as beer addled an already tired body and mind! The envoy sucked in his lips – unable to comprehend the thick-set legend of a war-weary knight confronting him, wondering, not for the first time in this short post, if this was really a good position or not, success bringing upheaval and chaos in unparalleled amounts, while disappointment might possibly result in a hanging or public flogging, neither in his estimation being a good way to end a day. He looked around hopelessly in the late evening light, at the other consuls and officials who were all desperately trying to bring both sides together, but at the moment meeting a stoic brick wall from most of the immediate royal families' attendants and diplomats.

Then, quite suddenly, many of the emissaries clustered around the tables held up a premonitory arm, silencing the babble. Merlin paused, wine goblet going to mouth: Arthur's taut and largely incoherent conversation with Bill and Fay coming abruptly to an end. Going to sit down, even Sir Percival froze, all staring across the room as one consul after another – apparently getting some kind of good news – sat or stood, rooted to the spot.

Finally, the story broke.

Pressurised from their younger members it appeared; troubled by the loss of life and any subsequent engagements – plus the undeniable amount of support – from north, south, east and west, (and hoping they could strike some kind of monetary deal) the royal family had to capitulate.

A former senior palace spokesman sat back in his seat and relayed the final decision. "They've set a meeting in Green Park at the back of Buckingham Palace," he sighed heavily, "at two thirty tomorrow afternoon. It will have to be official – a full declaration from the ruling monarch to abdicate and relinquish The Crown and all her territories and estates to King Arthur. You've done it…" he breathed in barely audible tones!

Chapter 11

"The next dome will extend to incorporate Green Park where the meeting will take place," Merlin muttered amid a welter of excited babble, his eyes glued to a huge map that had followed them all the way from Cornwall. With the help of a highlighter – in vivid yellow – a much smaller semicircle had been inscribed over the contours, its centre poised over Reading, cutting through Hampton, Barnet, and St Albans in the north, breaking into the neighbouring big brother dome at Stony Stratford. Sweeping south it would pass by Camberwell and Croydon, separating Reigate and Redhill, finally ending up somewhere near Southampton again, slicing through the busy M27 once more.

"That will give us plenty of wriggle-room in and around the centre of London," an aide pointed out, "allowing our supporters and your vanguard to encircle the palace and surrounding parks. Take full control!"

"The capitol is already getting crowded," another mentioned, keeping one eye on all the live news feeds. Red flags were everywhere, symbolising a kind of rebellion.

"We will have to completely enshroud our liege and Guinevere's party," one knight mused, hooked also by the continual colourful aerial shots of the city and all its suburbs.

Merlin rested his goblet down thoughtfully. "We'll proceed as we always have," he intoned, "a heavy fighting force before us – soaking up any threat or insurgence, a steel-ring around The King and Queen, The Dome allowing us plenty of room either side of the palace to manoeuvre once there."

"There may be attempts on either life," a palace spokesperson uttered, not at all convinced of the apparent abdication, "– once you drop your guard to engage with the proceedings. A high-velocity bullet will slice through armour and flesh like a laser. You won't know what's hit you until it's too late."

Amid the still raging babble, Merlin stared at the palace spokesperson – as if entranced; always amazed and beguiled by modern warfare. After a moment's pause, he made a decision, turning to Arthur. "I will have to guard you with the power of the Domes – somehow," he versed. "I will energise your shield which will in turn merge with the aegis above, creating a kind of small impenetrable dome around you, but – its true, I can't protect everyone. Some of us will have to trust to luck."

"This will protect me," Arthur slurred – having drunk yet more wine, thumping his golden breastplate with a clenched fist, "it'll shrug off any ball-is-tic slog – *hic* - slug."

Merlin was nodding confidently. "With your armour, the powerful Shield of Light, and the power of mother earth pulsing through from The Dome above, you'll have plenty of protection Arthur – if others have to engage with the abdicating party (for whatever reason) then we will have to do our best with shields, etc."

"Will The King reform parliament," someone asked?

"That's my intention," Arthur blurted out, having just heard the question over the continual rush of hushed conversation. "There'll be no more of this, *'old school tie retinue'*, the government from now on will be by the people, for the people – votes on anything from disability payments to roads or civic duties. Anyone will be able to have a say and make decisions – there will be no more, *'them and us'*.

"How will that work," another aide asked?

Arthur waved an ambiguous hand in the air – it was the wrong time to get into heavy democratic concepts. "I'll work it out somehow," he assured his audience. "Somehow we'll have a rolling government – like jury service – anyone remotely interested can sit in government for a week – and vote on anything from green issues to defence."

"You can't expect people from all over England to travel in for one week," someone blurted, having not thought the question through?

"Politicians do it all the time," the former royal palace spokesperson piped up. "Haven't forgot the *'expenses scandal'* have you?"

"They have a hierarchy even in your times, don't they," a young female aide pointed out quietly?

"We do," stressed Constantine II, "you may have called it a rule of decree by a sovereign but really, despite there being something of a nobility; The King was more of a patrician – able to be approached by anyone, there was little or no distinction from our foot soldiers to knights – we all fought together for the common good."

"But if The King fell in battle – it was all over – yes!"

"Well, if The King fell – who – let's face it, was heavily guarded at all times, it normally proceeds that the battle *is* lost – might as well call it a day!"

"You're saying there were no serfs or slaves in your time," yet another supporter asked?

"Certainly not," Hector de Maris gruffly commented, having lent an ear to the conversation – and, partially affronted by the thought! "Should anyone feel hard done by, through his actions or commitment; a knight or any part of the nobility was deemed to help out, there was local accountability and responsibility by the Knight or Lord of the area to ensure the welfare of their populace. The money was circulated as freely and as openly as one could hope for."

"Seems pretty idyllic," the female aide fantasised.

"It was," sighed the Green knight, still polishing his weaponry from the engagement. "Somewhat brutal at times – shown more, it has to be said, by the invaders from across the seas – rather than ourselves, but pastoral – and fresh – and very beautiful at times – even in winter, yes, so peaceful!"

"I'd love to see it," she simpered, lost for a long reverie in the romance of chivalry and gallantry.

***

"Arthur, let me just undo your breastplate, please!"

"Urgghhh…"

Somewhat inebriated, the three-hundred and forty pound war machine found it hard to focus, his armoured legs taking on a life of their own as two mutated into six and merged and mingled as he tried desperately to undo his cuisses, poleyns and greaves!

It had taken some time to get The King to bed, close knights, his own courtiers, squires and knaves – those he'd come to trust with his life in such a short time, all manhandling him up three flights of stairs and to the one and only guest suite situated on that floor; nothing but the attic above (which was inspected and thoroughly searched – and occupied) and another two small apartments that Merlin and his sages quickly commandeered; his Generals and The King's own Guard also trying to squeeze into the other, many crowding the stairs and landings.

Even the guest suite had a heavily armoured guard on just about every door – Merlin not daring to take any liberties now he was so close to his goal. He further studied the layout of the city they were soon to invade, going over the approach roadways and parks and – most importantly – the river crossings, so many in such a small space. The bridges would all have to be held and guarded while the ceremony took place, he had instructed the generals.

There would be a moment of pure exhilaration and anxiety, he had tried to instil in The King, worried, as the decree was read out – that his shields would be down for a moment, Merlin hoping it would be short and sweet – and Arthur could accept The

Crown – and they could all get on with handing the reins over to him. His new supporters were growing in number every hour, many now gaining his confidence as aides and diplomats, bowing to the new positions they found themselves in – many using a fairly quick presence of mind, prepared for the transition, encouraging others to do the same, so much so, the whole country it seemed, was ready for the overhaul.

In the guest suite, Arthur had divested of his armour – and had been shown to the loo – twice – and was now ready for bed, the retinue leaving him, Guinevere waiting.

The room was sumptuous. Oiled and highly polished wainscoting rubbed shoulders in the subdued light with the gold-plated and brass fittings, rich ruby-red drapes, the luxurious silk bed covers and eiderdown; the carpet so thick it made The King stumble over his own feet as he weaved his way to the huge oval bed, just managing to save himself as he fell headfirst into the edge of the valance.

"My king," cried his lady as he disappeared!

His head resurfaced over the edge, the befuddled brain behind the bleary eyes, peering over the big expanse – huge arms trying desperately to grapple with the idea of getting him into it. He heaved and tugged, his legs refusing to work, and finally made it onto the covers, throwing himself uncontrollably, sinking immediately as his bulk weighed him down. *"Where are you my love,"* he crooned, unable to fight his way over?

"Rest easy, my dear. You've had a long two days."

"I haven't done anything," The King mumbled, slowly being suffocated by the memory foam. He struggled onto one shoulder to gaze longingly at his beautiful surrogate wife, wishing with all his heart – at that moment in time, that Guinevere could be with him for all time, show her off to the whole wide world! "You're beautiful," he tried to enounce, just able to make out her silky blonde hair framing a pretty face gazing down at him, but he was slowly sinking into the mattress, probably finding equilibrium further down!

***

Much, much later as it happened, King Arthur sat with his head in his hands.

Around him the enormous breakfast room was in full swing, as if many of the celebrations of the previous night were still being upheld; knights still toasting this or that fallen hero, pints still being swilled as if there was no tomorrow, many still coming up the line or finding their way to the front. He was in no mood however for frivolity, his head and stomach for some reason today not too good, the drain on the overhead domes, the ensuing battle and all the other commitments possibly taking the strain on the preternatural power source; unable to repair and restore him to his full potential. He'd slept extra soundly however; the stresses and strains making it feel like he'd personally taken part in the enormous conflict that took up most of previous days. By early evening he and his accompanying queen had been installed in the luxurious Great Lodge Hotel's finest accommodation and he'd slept soundly once ensconced!

"We move on the capitol as soon as you are ready my liege," a young knight instructed him, having brought the news from a recent war council held somewhere outside in the grounds. "Merlin has already left, my lord – is there anything you need?"

Arthur looked up. "Just my breakfast – then I'll be raring to go. *I hope,*" he added under his breath.

The young knight hesitated, then looked about, no doubt wondering if he could speed things along a little. He nodded to his King and made his way over to where a manageress and her team were holding the fort. The King realised then he'd simply plonked himself down, expecting to be waitress-served.

He waited expectantly, watching the young combater as he instructed the manager and waitresses.

Looking over, the manageress soon realised her mistake in not noticing the goliath entering, and made to come over herself, smoothing down her uniform as she did so.

Arthur, having twisted in his seat, welcomed her with a beatific smile as she crossed the crowded floor, greeting him cordially; a lassitude evident as he heaved in a speculative sigh. He was nearly always confounded by the look of people, he realised in the small moment that passed, finding a dour, upright *'stickler for the rules'* kind of woman who may have been moulded from a young age to grovel and serve, could conversely be so adamant about her fealty for this usurper king, having perhaps made her mind up as his vanguard moved into place. It wasn't so for everyone, he knew: large parts of Kensington had decamped to take residence anywhere, other than what would become the main route for this army, once the last dome had encapsulated the palace at Westminster.

"My King," she simpered, almost bowing in reverence, catching Danny completely off guard.

"Erm...my lady," he spoke, half-raising, then realised he'd addressed her completely wrong.

"I'm sorry... mam...I – er..." He was saved further embarrassment as a big retinue of his friends entered the dining room, Lady Guinevere with her ladies-in-waiting, the reporter Bill Nightingale and his beautiful consort Lady Fay, while accompanying them was the tall brave knight Sir Reginald with the radiant Lindsey Cartwright.

"My friends," King Arthur called out, jumping from his seat.

"Breakfasts for all," the manageress called out cheerily, back-pedalling to arrange yet another run of food.

"Thank you, lady," The King called after her. He put a reassuring thumbs up as she spun round with a small grin on her face.

"My Lady," Danny voiced breathlessly, overawed yet again by Guinevere's spectacular beauty. She positively shone, he mused as she sauntered toward him, flowing silks embodying a full stature.

The ladies-in-waiting practically formed a steel ring around their Queen as she greeted her King, many knights making way as The King's own retinue finally caught up with him, many having slept in a tad. Sirs Lancelot, Galahad, the Green Knight, Mordred and Gawain having attended the war council earlier, now filtered back into the breakfast refectory to safeguard their King. Quite soon a soft clanking and grinding of metal on metal filled the large room, Arthur making the rounds as he welcomed everyone in turn, stopping to spend a moment with Sir Reginald and Lady Cartwright as they found a secluded table to enjoy a hearty breakfast.

"How did you sleep," The King had to ask, knowing they'd had to rough it out in the nearby grounds?

"Wonderfully," retorted Sir Reginald, with an air of a man who'd enjoyed perhaps the very special kind of company only a pretty young woman can give.

Elbows casually on manicured tabletop, Lindsey Cartwright hunched her shoulders in a coquettish extended shrug and devilish grin that displayed a warmth Danny recognised immediately – a nuance that shouted out that her and her saviour had enjoyed a very special night under the stars – the night air warm and inviting, the cosiness of a secluded spot – perhaps under the shadow of a wagon; wrapped up in a big sleeping bag. He put a tender hand out to both of them, leaving them to it as Sir Reginald experimented with a tailored cigar someone had obviously bestowed upon him.

Back finally at his table, Guinevere had not waited on ceremony and dug in to a sumptuous breakfast of grilled succulent steaks, gammon and pork loins, hash browns, thick bacon, eggs fried, poached and boiled, tomatoes – tinned and fresh, olives and feta' cheese, beans of every kind; complimented with fresh bread rolls, toast and tea by the gallon.

The King watched as his Queen shared out several portions – making sure everyone of her ladies had a meal of sorts before tucking in herself. In the next moment a complete platter of grilled fillet steaks, eggs, beans and freshly fried potatoes reached him, Arthur unable to comprehend sharing as he wolfed down everything placed before him. He ploughed through two helpings before he realised he was being watched.

At last he sat back with a satisfied gentle burp and sipped at a giant mug of tea with ardent relish. Replete with food, he was now feeling much better, able to look the day in the eye and prepare himself for the final ordeal, marching on London and securing his place as the rightful King of England. If yesterday held a magnitude of anxiety and worry – today was just as bad – only in a different way – a more taut and speculative concern invaded his soul, pressing down on him like a set of concrete stocks.

"Can we get the morning's spiel out the way, Arthur," a soft voice implored down by his side, Bill Nightingale sliding his chair over from a nearby table. At various times of the day – and here Bill had used the utmost of decorum, knowing the last two days had been full of woe for him – had encouraged The King to one side to get his innermost thoughts down, building a complete picture of the man over the days by exposing his worries and fears, and trying to instil in the public a vision of a man who'd been completely thrust into a totally incomprehensible situation; asked to carry out a multitude of tasks – acting as regent and usurper all at the same time. It was a fantastical story – yet full of compassion and enduring legacy that meant the very fabric of Britain's sordid and corrupt, reckless present regime was finally coming to an end. On the news channels that very morning, in England's merry island, an old war veteran who'd been punched and kicked to death by a gang of youths as he walked home with his dog was named and honoured by those who knew him – and Dan picked up on the small incident – despite it having been massively overshadowed by an army parked just outside the capitol.

" – and I'll tell you something else, Bill," Danny promised wholeheartedly as he slurped more Earl-Grey from a pint stein, "This country is going to find it has an un-corrupt and user-friendly police force – one we can truly be proud of! I'll throw out all the self-serving leaders and create a new police force from the ground up, volunteers will help in the main instance by creating groups that will police our streets and make them safe for everybody to walk – not just gangs. That will end. We will create a force worth joining – with an up-graded wages and pension scheme, proper training – and vetting – and much better equipment and vehicles. Before long we'll have instilled respect back into our young – and I will personally make sure all have something to do – no more lounging about on street corners – there'll be something of a work-share system for the time being, places where retired electricians and plumbers can impart some skills and knowledge, start to rebuild our social fabric. I envisage some sort of fourth military parallel to teach community serving skills, which can be deployed worldwide to help in disaster struck areas, give them self-esteem and decent wages to boot."

"With all this money pouring in you'll be able to build all those new hospitals we've been waiting for – reopen old ones that have fallen by the wayside and perhaps retrain social care workers – put the system back that crumbled so drastically a few years ago."

Danny nodded empathically. "There's so much to do, so much to put right – why oh why did it take something like this to happen before people woke up?" He shook his head – the murder of the poor old-time soldier just one more nail in a coffin that was bursting with them.

"We move on London," Galahad called out, as runners brought news that Merlin was about to create the last and final dome!

Before anyone moved however, a television on a wheeled stand was pushed over to him, the manageress setting it up so the news and proposed route as worked out by reporters could be shown: Merlin planned to cross at West Kensington, keeping the aperture small but allowing enough of his forces to quickly swarm around Kensington Gardens, spreading out rapidly to circumnavigate the serpentine, hopefully commanding the Bayswater

Road system and the A316, while the royal party with the heavily armoured vanguard would emerge to trundle up Cromwell Road directly toward Hyde Park Corner and Green Park where the ceremony of handing over Sovereignty could take place. (The auspicious naming of the route The King would take was not lost on many, a saviour of the people in times gone by remembered in so many ways.)

The reporters and a logistics cartography team at the news desks quickly realised the same, knowing another kind of ad hoc rebuttal of Arthur's army would be pointless and pretty futile – not to mention disastrous for the nearby residents – and any possible collateral damage. As the royal party had already capitulated, the country as a whole had done so as well, many shattered by the demise of the Blues and Royals, Ceremonial Dragoons and Horse Guards – without mentioning the thousands of mounted police and military. Hundreds of thousands dead – and still King Arthur moved inexorably forward, his incredible army unscathed by the titanic struggle! Now, before even the battlefield was stripped completely bare, politicians were debating whose head would roll as to the catastrophic disaster.

Arthur waved for the TV to be wheeled away, needing to climb into his armour once more, and again confront the world as he had known it – with all its corruption and vice, all its derogatory contempt for the poor, old and feeble, with all its greed and vile hatred that rose from obsessional malfeasance, government-generated poverty theft, and a host of other palm-greasing knavery that ran like a toxic lava flow through the veins of the country – from the very top to the middle ground where it petered out from lack of currency. He would turn it on its head he vowed, as he left the table to escort his lovely queen back upstairs to dress – for what he hoped would be the last time.

***

~~e!~~

~~*~~

~~As the big breakfast room finally began to empty Bill Nightingale, having shown his lovely Fay how to operate his laptop, swiftly~~ –As the big breakfast room began to empty, Bill Nightingale, having shown his lovely Fay the rudiments of his laptop, slid his chair over to Lindsey Cartwright and her consort, the redoubtable Sir Reginald Smyth. He quickly placed a small Dictaphone on the table as he rummaged in a big satchel for his notepad.

He held out a quick hand to Lindsey.

"Bill Nightingale… The Southern Chronicle: Could you both possibly spare a few minutes, Lindsey?" He glanced at both of them, knowing there was quite a story here unfolding – if he could just get the chronology into place.

Lindsey, pouring more tea for her and her accompanying knight, nodded, pursing her lips – having quite a bit she'd like to get off her chest.

"Ask away," she intoned with solemnity.

"We actually met briefly a couple of days ago," Bill remarked casually, "when you were about to embark on the diplomatic mission. For the readers, I like to ask Lindsey – how were you treated – you obviously made it back safely – and, I might add, unharmed?"

Lindsey replaced a teacup daintily, having drained the contents. "We did, thank you – and Bill, if you could thank all those people who wished us well, both before and after the event, I'd like to especially send a heartfelt thanks back. Sir Reginald here was incarcerated but – honestly, having slept in nothing but park benches, he was all for a good night's rest… in a cosy cell – with mattress, and hot and cold running water – plus his own loo!"

"And – I take it, you were shown every courtesy?"

"I was thank you, Bill. But – as you know, my entreaties all fell on deaf ears. The prime minister – and especially some of her lackeys were hell bent on sending scores of young men to their deaths. Not one of them, I noticed ,even had the guts to bolster the numbers themselves."

Bill shook his head, somewhat soulfully, heaving in a big sigh. "They could have thrown another ten thousand reservists into the mix, but in the end, Merlin was determined to win – one way or the other. The incredible power he wields is just too much for mortal men."

Bill paused, wondering just how to broach the next subject – one he really wanted to get down on paper – the goddamn awful transmutation of Lindsey into a dear little mouse – and back again, intact with all her thoughts and senses – it was just one part of this incredible fairytale that had to be told; but he needed to approach the incident carefully.

Lindsey Cartwright however broached the subject herself, alluding to Merlin's incalculable power.

"It was my own stupid fault," she chastised herself, watching her knight carefully as he lit up the small slim cigar to puff it regally, experimenting with the tailored pleasure meditatively. Many years ago now it seemed, smoking in all its guises had been blanket banned totally by the government – without really any consultation with the general public – or even landlords and clubs etc that stood to lose the most. Despite not being a smoker herself even she, in the day, railed against the ridiculous all-out ban, knowing smoke rooms could have easily been built, pubs and clubs that didn't serve food could have become somewhere where one could enjoy a cigarette with a pint, leaving the public as a whole to make up their own mind as to what pub or restaurant they wanted to frequent. A compete blanket ban was just non-sensible – and downright stupid as pubs, clubs and other venues fought for their existence after the drink-drive campaign – yet another nail in the coffin of free speech and liberty.

"Is there any way you can explain or relate your experience Lindsey," Bill asked softly, knowing the absolute terror that must have accompanied the event.

Lindsey nodded with some dented pride. "It was sickening really – not just the horror of being turned into a mouse – and all the fright and dread that entailed, but... it really highlighted the sad person I was really. I mean, thirty two and living with my parents again, after a disastrous failure at a marriage; working as a bar manageress – hoping against hope some nice guy would walk into my life – and let me tell you, I've talked and mixed with a host of these invaders – *and you know,* I wouldn't swap any of them for their modern counterpart, with all their foibles and hang-ups, all the effeminacy and bloody five minute health drives – and then when they drink they become the most obnoxious person going, god its enough to make you sick!" She reached for some more tea from the pot to then gulp it down, while Bill scribbled down her words in shorthand.

He stopped to gaze at her, asking again about the true abject terror of becoming a small rodent.

"You're right – horror – damnation, fear like I've never known – or am likely to again; looking up from where I stood to realise at any moment someone could walk through from the front bar and stand on me – and they wouldn't have even known it was me, just a dirty little rodent that needed to be stamped on. It chilled me to the core. But dear ol'e Reginald here – my knight in shining armour, scooped me up and carried me to rescue – I owe him my life – and I just hope I can repay the debt." She stopped to take a breath, watching as Sir Reginald puffed contentedly on his slim cigar, no one attempting to stop him as hundreds of knights and infantry of all ranks congregated outside – all awaiting their King and Queen.

"To be honest, I would really like to relay to you Bill, a real sad story that I was immersed in around a year ago – and which pointedly shows up the broken society we are all forced live in. Around the time I've just mentioned a real devoted friend turned up on my parent's doorstep, having driven all the way down from Norfolk, spending two or three days trying to locate me, desperate to just get into the warmth for some moments. As it turned out, Trudi had managed finally to extricate herself from quite an abusive relationship with her partner, to spend several nights sleeping in her cramped car before approaching the county council for help – perhaps temporary accommodation – even a garden shed would have been better than her small car, in which she could hardly lay down in, but do you know what the town council told her in all their belligerent wisdom: 'You've got a car, haven't you – well, it's a roof over your head, isn't it?' And this was just after they'd housed sixty or seventy migrant refuges in a holiday camp, footing the enormous bill of something like four thousand pounds – per person – per week – and they couldn't even put her in one of the hundreds of empty houses they had laying about.

"'Go to your parents,' one housing officer told her."

"'Don't have any – would yours do' she replied, rather cheekily?"

"Was she working," Bill asked, frankly sickened by the story?

"Yes, of course, great job in Telecommunications, tried desperately to hang onto it – all she really needed was a helping hand to get back on her feet – but the council just didn't want to know – no money in helping just one sad woman is there –

despite the move being practically illegal – placing a young woman in harms way telling her to sleep in a car – barbaric – and they call this lot uncouth. *Ha, just take a good look at yourselves!"*

Sir Reginald smacked his lips in a relaxed way, taking a long look at the small cigar he'd been enjoying, the aromatic fumes smelling delicious to Bill; the knight appearing to him the most contented man in existence!

The tall knight, noticing her anger, lent forward to put a hand out to pat Lindsey's, telling her not to worry, everything would be alright.

"I really would like to believe that Reginald," she sighed heavily, making Bill pause in his jotting and look up again. "but somehow, I fear this is all some lurid dream and I'm going to wake up sometime soon."

"I know exactly how you feel, Lindsey."

"Just one last question, if I may…I take it Merlin restored you – can you just for the readers, tell us exactly what happened?"

While Lindsey tried to fill Bill in on the escapade that was the drunken Merlin's calamity a day or two previous, Arthur and his Queen were getting ready to make an appearance.

***

Outside on the expansive lawn area that stretched in all directions, sporting a gorgeous river bank with swans, sail craft and cruisers motoring by, crowded by hundreds of fifth and sixth century infantry, the ogre Petersbury Dean rested easily; not far from where Lindsey Cartwright and her stalwart knight had spent a rather steamy and romantic tryst beneath the towering structure of big wagon wheels, the mammoth wagon getting ready to accommodate the royal cortege of awaiting ladies. Together with one other ogre and three rather battered Mor-men, he'd spent the night carousing and enjoying himself immensely, continually having to remind himself he was not a true ogre, being probably the smallest of all the monsters, despite being over eight feet tall and probably weighing in at around four hundred pounds – give or take a stone. He had however, forgotten largely about that fact – reminiscing more on the incredible fate that kept him more or less out of serious harm's way; sure he had more bolts and arrows in him than a pin cushion (mercifully removed over the course of the evening when the beer (4 gallons – approx – amongst five of them; wine, around three barrels; spirits, around seven or eight bottles) by which time, he couldn't have cared less whether the nurse attending him, removed his head, his befuddled brain mired in so much alcohol he'd lost any power of speech, and was so bandaged when the medics finished he resembled a tottering mummy.

As he sat by the river bank now, allowing an all-encompassing hangover to subside, he realised dimly the other surviving ogre was just as badly injured, as were the Mor-men – the youngest of the three having to have half a dozen cruel bolts eased from one thigh and two from the middle of his back. No bandaging necessary, the creatures just needing the holes plugged, cotton wool or a ripped up towel, then covered over with gaffer tape; the doctors and nurses in absolute awe as the beings accepted their medical expertise.

Beside him sat the remaining true ogre, the being a real giant of his race: contemplating the strange new world he'd found himself in – the awesome battle – and now solace. His left arm (the size of a tree branch) was swaddled in torn up sheets and bandages – a pillow case tightly wrapped around a huge mitt; a corrugated tin sheet he'd used as a shield stitched to his forearm by bolts loosed from small crossbows and the odd arrow, finally prised from him sometime in the early morning as medical teams of doctors and nurses moved through the huge crowds. Where they could, medical tents sprang up, many who were able limping or being helped towards them.

Petersbury Dean considered his own injuries, finding only a couple really smarted, one arrow deep in his back – and eased out some hours ago now – and another down by his ankle that had probably clipped a bone creating a dull ache. Conversely the surviving Mor-men seemed to experience little pain, their bodies beneath the thick leather hide of a different make up to theirs, he surmised, looking them over once more. Despite their obvious difference in gestalt however, the knight turned ogre knew they were all feeling the travesties of the battle, their brushes with death filling their minds with ardent relief that the grizzled harbinger had slid them by in the melee' overlooking them in his haste to gather up as many souls as possible. It had been a fraught and terrifying ordeal – one he wouldn't want to commit to again anytime soon.

***

Rory Splengier had enjoyed the time of his life; but was thinking of his young wife, who he'd quite abruptly abandoned some days ago now – to run away with the circus.

It was, of course, no circus at all, he morosely considered, sitting somewhere amid Padworth Common.

He'd walked miles, this little copse eerily quiet once he'd stepped off the beaten tracks, even the caravans and King Arthur's reservist army having marched, walked, limped and loitered through; following on in the wake of the bloodiest battle in British history, the vanguard with the royal party probably already to the outskirts of London by now. He'd heard nothing of the abdication – was somewhat adrift of the surging tides that were converging on the capitol in order to witness the astounding celebrations that meant a truly gargantuan upheaval for the United Kingdom, only whispers and overheard conversations as crowds passed by on extremely worn paths, runners bringing news as they choroused the victory, the result presaging a complete collapse of the former royal family.

And what of his own tiny family, Rory meditated?

When he'd caught sight of that girl across the floor of the marketing suite so many moons ago, he knew she was the epitome of the go-getter he was – and, as it turned out, they were practically on the same path, both aspiring for the same goals. Who'd have thought – with all his connections and previous teachings, she would surpass him and side-step several levels in a race to the top. Who'd have thought in the two years since that day – he'd won his prize, netted the girl and one or two promotions to go along with it – then to suddenly lose interest, completely flat line – while his beloved scaled even higher echelons.

His career, his lovely partner – indeed his whole life as he knew it, seemed a million miles away now, as he sat there, as if he too had been transposed several thousand years. But it couldn't last – he told himself. How could it – these armies, cooks, jesters, soldiers, knights of the realm, these ghosts had no place here – were simply interlopers who had to return surely once the deed was done, return once again to their dusty graves.

Not ghosts however, he cogitated thoughtfully – as solid – and as deadly as a raving lunatic – only more determined and forthright than any spook.

Would Deborah have run away with him, he wondered absently, caught up in the razzmatazz, bowled over by the gleaming soldiers and knights on horseback, overwhelmed by the re-enactment soci – ?

Rory berated himself.

He'd been completely duped, a single thin thread of a vagary told him. Not *'duped'* as such, more misguided, for he knew nothing of temporal distortion, parallel time, slippages – or quantum physics gone mad. Knew nothing of the incredible power of the Sword in the Stone – and how this inexorable energy could harness space and time – perhaps even control it? How it would come to the aid finally of the land it called home, and release it from the tyrannical strangle-grip it had been dying from?

Alone, Rory watched a small mare of a pony munch happily in the sun-dappled glade of the common only a few metres from where he'd collapsed. Was it a mule of this time, he wondered abjectly, or did it belong to another, transported here along with everything else, swept up in a maelstrom that had ultimately been England's salvation?

He shook his head and stretched out further, unwilling to tramp any more, content to just sit and contemplate, nullified eventually by the traipsing, bamboozled and beguiled by the dull realisation of what was really happening – and totally at odds over the confrontation – that god awful clash of modern man against the brutal enemy of yesteryear. It was too much to comprehend, too much to take in – the terrible slaughter of so many young men – some only boys, he found as he staggered and tripped over the extremes of the Salisbury Plains, trying to avoid what had been a bloodbath in the middle of the scrubland. Somewhere in the distance, the roaring and bleating of strange wild beasts had echoed throughout the confines of the massive Dome above. He'd gazed skywards at the encroaching power grid, stunned by the unyielding energy – that force that had rammed into the brilliantly attired Horse Guards, the magnificent Blues and Royals and mounted military police like a juggernaut, reducing the regiments into the bloodiest pile of smashed bodies and animals one could not possibly want to gaze upon. But Rory had wandered and followed his feet like so many before him, not really knowing where he was going – just knowing he had to see the aftermath for himself: but now wished he'd kept to the sides and not deviated, somehow skipped the awful engagement. He zigzagged over the expanses of the scrub plains like a lost soul, finally tripping over the stiffening body of a boy scout, pausing for a brief moment to turn and gaze down at him, everything that England stood for wrapped up in his ripped and torn brown uniform; the braiding and badges signifying all that was regal and proud. He wasn't above fourteen, Rory calculated, staring down at him, the poor boy's skull smashed in. What perverse education, brainwashing or fervour had gripped that boy – what ludicrous peer pressure or gung-ho had persuaded him to race to his death with nothing but a ceremonial sword of some kind, that – in all probability had been taken down from some hall or mansion's wall, the thing as blunt as a bear's backside and about as much use as a chocolate kettle?

Rory had knelt down by him to commiserate with his passing, a stupid, selfless act that had benefited no-one.

At length he'd pushed himself to his feet and followed them as they hastily led from the killing fields through Yernham Dean, Facombe, Ashmans Worth, then crossing roads and motorways to be finally fed again by devout republicans in Old Burgclere, following then the 3051 up to NewTown, where he'd staggered to a halt in the woods of Padworth Common.

He'd not only come to a stop he considered, but to the end of his journey, not needing to progress any more – the reality of what he'd joined in – quite innocently, now leaving a sour taste in his throat, acrid and acidic, the god awful gustatory nuance of burning and charred bodies both old and young, animals and something else, something he might not have experienced even in a nightmare, one ghoulish monstrosity impaled by a rod of iron or steel catapulted from some high-powered sling-shot, he didn't wonder, backing off to trip over another, a hellish goliath of a creature that he'd only seen in fairy tales. Were these really from the days of yore or some magician's idea of fun, necromancing several human bodies into one, covering others in thick leather that smelt and looked like it had been brought from some dusty tomb.

It was all too much, he calculated. Along with those fantastic beasts he only heard but never saw, it was obvious dark forces were at play, the battle won by any means – not totally fair in his estimation, although it *was* only a battle. A battle won by one king usurping another queen, the real quest coming in running a country and hopefully turning it around, still with all the investiture, commerce and monetary infrastructure. From rumours and snippets of information he'd learnt that this King Arthur had been only a fitness instructor, a young man pure of heart no doubt, who'd stumbled upon the Sword in the Stone and, having released the awesome weapon, was impelled to follow his heart and ride on London.

Tears crept into Rory Splengier's eyes. What had he done, he chastised himself. He'd left a loving wife (without even a note to say goodbye) – had just upped and gone, disappeared on some crazy crusade and now he was miles from home in some unknown part of the Southern shires, without a hope of getting home anytime soon – unless he traipsed all the way back, perhaps following a more direct route, along the deserted motorways maybe. He was so tired, he realised, having previously walked no more than from his front door to his car – then car to office and back again at night.

What was it, he asked himself ardently, this national spirit that was engulfing the country, pulling it apart, setting land-owner against serf, factory employees against the owner, tenant against landlord, general public against nobility; swelling the worker's hearts with new hope and determination?

He searched for a handkerchief with which to dry his weeping eyes and found a grubby rag in his leggings – which were now as soiled and dirty as all the rest of the accoutrements, trying to find a clean spot. In doing so he looked down at a black leather arm bracelet that he'd found and had probably fallen from being tied to a saddle, appearing fairly new and otherwise unblemished, wondering now why on earth he'd picked it up in the first place, other than to look original or not out of place – but now that feeling of exhilaration had dwindled, crumbled, in fact, to one of despair and loneliness. He'd spent the first night sleeping on the beach at Tintagel, the next on the edge of a field, surrounded by thousands of soldiers and villagers alike, the next two under the wheels of some wagon, and now in a wooded glade that would be his last port of call. He hadn't really gone far, he realised, having replayed the trip over in his mind, yet the journey back seemed like a journey to the far side of the earth, as if this strange world he found himself in was distorting or warping his own sense of space and time. He found his watch in another pocket of his grubby leggings and put it on pointedly, stripping off his leather arm guard and tossing it aside, finding it was four in the afternoon – time perchance for a serious rest and even a nap.

The nag munched and ambled its way over to his little retreat, not noticing him at all until it got quite near, when it suddenly realised its little glade actually had a visitor.

"I'm lost like you," Rory spoke, not batting an eyelid. Odd, he reminisced, once upon a time he would be running away, frightened for his life of a horse, but now, having walked alongside so many, bumped into one staggering about the battlefield – and rubbed his forehead for a time, trying to reassure it, shared a field with many other beings – not all human or animal, he had not a care in the world, just sat, not intending to move, ready in fact for some serious shut eye, and the mule could just please itself.

The small horse ruffled itself, then, quite sure Rory was no threat, continued to munch as much of the rich grass as possible.

***

The march on London's Westminster was eerily quiet for Arthur as he passed through the Dome and into a much smaller one encapsulating part of the capitol; the Domes themselves seeming to insulate him from the clamour and noise that would rise up like a tidal wave once clear of the third dome's huge boundary. Behind and all around his armies surged, all apparently keen to be near their King when he was crowned, spilling out into Clapham and having to cross bridges at Lambeth and World's End, poring through Saint John's Wood and Westbourne like rats before a forest fire; the magical and fantastical wild beasts mingling with thousands of mounted knights of the realm, pike men, battalions of lightly-clad infantry, privateers mixing with sixth century sailors; wagon trains still herding sheep and cattle; finally meeting cheering crowds that lined the main arterial routes. Before long the *'Reserve Army'* tried to march on London's palace too, but found the roads and green spaces completely clogged, not an inch of spare ground found anywhere.

Arthur's vanguard plied their way along Cromwell Road passing the assembled crowds at Brompton Gardens, finally reaching the confluence of roads at Hyde Park Corner, all traffic suspended as mounted knights, gaily attired in the Pendragon motif clip-clopped their way toward the inevitable.

As Dan neared his destination his body seemed to fizz with exhilaration, as if all the evil and wrongdoing that had plagued the country from centuries ago would now finally come to an end, a beginning of a new epoch that would resound for the common good, restore the faith man once had for his fellow man. He would investigate dissolute traitorous immigrants to find out whatever land they felt they belonged, and enable them to get on with rebuilding those countries, instead of expecting someone else to do it; hoping around the world other countries were experiencing the same upheaval so the peoples could live within their own cultures peacefully. He'd heard rumours but that was all, apparently Merry England had been the first to be granted this exculpation.

Beside him Guinevere sat regally and stunningly beautiful, radiant and glowing in all her majesty. Her white charger held its head high as the crowds continued to line the road system, many falling over each other in order to catch a glance of the royal couple. Arthur waved so much his metalled hand made his arm ache. He swapped and twisted this way and that in order to acknowledge as many as he could, straining in his saddle. People, spilling out onto the roadways, had to be coaxed back as the vanguard of Knights of the Realm advanced. One or two well-wishers managed to skirt through the panoply of horse and rider and move dangerously close to Arthur and his Queen, but sense prevailed at the last moment as they gazed up in spellbound awe at The King, resplendent in golds and silver armour, the aquamarine, red and gold sigils of the Pendragon Clan emblazoned about his horse. The one or two zealous supporters fell back under their own volition, completely overwhelmed by such a vision, The Queen in complete comparison svelte and eminently regal in flowing white silks was the ultimate in grace and beauty.

On they trotted…on into history.

At the entrance to Green Park, situated directly behind Buckingham Palace, Merlin and his many sages, wizards and warlocks awaited their King; the small green of the expanse already full to the brim with crowds of people, a ring three or four deep of Arthur's military, pike men, lightly clad infantry and many other knights and freelance soldiers of the realm. The heavily clad vanguard meandered into the space left – a big enclosure of a tubular stage encompassing the complete royal family, dignitaries and royal officials, all mingling with a dedicated news team, a smaller complete ring of black-garbed police and armed servicemen containing the stage and people inside; the event recorded on every terrestrial channel.

Arthur scanned the environment – just as Merlin and his team had probably done earlier, eyeing the surrounding structures of Saint James' and Mayfair – the streets teeming with his supporters, nearly every roof top dangerously crowded. His direct right however and rear was screened by bushes and trees in the adjacent park of Saint James' and the palace's own gardens; Constitution Hill also crowded with mounted knights of all categories. Amidst the area of Green Park, Arthur could not see beyond too clearly for the tall standard bearers ringing the grassed space, flags and other pennants pinned to extra-long poles also obstructing a clear view – a tactic – employed by the wily wizard to encumber any snipers.

The razzmatazz and holiday spirit, buoyed by the event unfolding had everyone and everything in an excitable lather, the ebullience spilling out from the capitol in a sonic boom to infect everyone nationwide – and as The New King and Queen, with their gaily-clad entourage swarmed to fill the bottom end of Green Park, an audible hush fell upon the thousands crowding around.

***

Not a spare inch of ground could be found, Bill Nightingale worried, glancing about, still enshrouded within Arthur's royal party. He wanted to get down and try to set up a news stand of sorts nearer the former royal party, now stationed at the other end of Green Park, all looking, it had to be said, rather nervous. Unable to even get off his horse – there being not an inch of ground spare, he had to stay seated however, and try to put together his discourse on the day's events. Beside him, always inherently interested in what he was doing, Fay sat demurely. She sported a man's small gold wristwatch, donated by Mason James no less, a Rolex Oyster that he found a little too effeminate. It sparkled radiantly in the sunshine, throwing out tiny beams of light that could dazzle if too close, yet the revenant serving wench thought it the most exquisite jewellery piece she'd ever hope to see – never mind own. It was marvellous, and she had thanked him vigorously, wondering over the generosity – bowled over by the fact that by studying the small hands closely, it would even tell the time. But like many, Mason James – who was content to bring up the rear with his own entourage of financiers – was beginning to realise the folly of his ways, considering the act of giving instead of scheming, scamming, skimming and skiving his way through life – the altruism had welled up inside him, filling him with a subtle pride and sense of well-being that was hard to define, yet as uplifting as a lottery win. Instead of finding god (something of a mute point now) Mason James was all for living a much simpler life, perhaps investing everything he had – not only in his new King but perhaps his fellow man, reopen one or two engineering companies in his local area that had folded recently, place a bit more in social funding, help the local council in one or two projects. It would be nice to be a local hero for a change instead of having to suffer the same dwindling crowd of aristocrats that despised each other so much, it was a wonder they didn't wear a dagger around their waists to stab each other in the back.

***

Arthur waited patiently as Merlin coaxed his horse forward, breaking free of his crowd of mages, encouraging the royal party to join him as they walked the short distance to confront the former royal party of England. Toward the broader end that was the triangle of the Green Park space, Arthur could see the small domes' enclosure coming to an end, not far from where the Queen and all her family and officials were waiting.

At the edge of the small glistening dome, Arthur dismounted, along with his closest knights, Merlin and Bill Nightingale. They assembled into a tight group and waited for Merlin to perform a spell that would open a doorway. Beyond the sparkling curtain Arthur could see the equally small assembled crowd of the royal party, The elderly Queen heavily supported by her son and grandsons, all smartly attired in glittering uniforms, which intrigued Sir Lancelot and Galahad immensely, having never seen such gaudy displays; the ceremonial swords too were of interest.

Arthur waited patiently while Merlin performed his jiggery-pokery, taking a moment to remember a particular incantation. He waved his arms about vaguely, managing to create a rather nice circle opening, which everyone applauded but which would, in fact, be awkward to step through, especially for Arthur, it not being terribly big. Merlin dismissed the attempt and instead conjured up a rather nice arch through which several men could step together.

At once Lancelot and several others moved to be first through the portal, protecting their King by creating a virtual ring into which he could step, the immensely thick-set Green knight almost knocking Arthur off his feet as he hastened to get beyond him.

"The Shield of Light," Merlin reminded Arthur.

Arthur, regaining his balance, had to think for a moment, recalling then the enigmatic ring of bronze strapped to a side panel on his saddle. He wondered whether it was really necessary asking Merlin with a kind of small shrug, but the wily wizard insisted so he walked back to collect it while his closest knights arranged themselves to confront the dispossessed royal family, most garbed in a uniform of one kind or another, chests full of ironmongery. Intrigued and fascinated at the same time, all conferred and ruminated over the splendid arrays.

Arthur undid the shield and slid it onto his arm, the ring of metal incredibly heavy – and to a point fairly unwieldy, he mused, testing it. Merlin approached, preparing to hurl a spell at it, making Arthur flinch. "Fear not, Arthur," he intoned, "it's just a precautionary measure".

Arthur straightened, turning to hold the shield outward.

Still on horseback, Guinevere gazed on, spellbound herself over the strange aegis.

"TRI-MUF, AGAINST VIBRUM," Merlin called out, coughing slightly as he threw out the conjuration.

Immediately the shield burst into life, exploding outward at first like an erupting sun, lashing out serpent-like arms of lightening. Arthur hung on for dear life, taking hold of it with both hands, as it thrashed and jiggered on his arm, hoping the thing didn't dissolve his fingers in the process; the shield crackling loudly and spitting like a dragon disturbed. Red hot sparks and fireworks fizzled about its rim as the wild furnace of energy barked and banged its presence. Finally, after a few moments, it settled down to smoulder, the white hot centre roiling and festering with energy.

"Strewth, Merlin, do we really need this?"

Merlin hesitated. "It hasn't been activated for centuries – perhaps we can do without it. See if it settles down a bit more."

Arthur dared to peep over the rim, wondering what on earth he needed all this power for. It radiated like a miniature sun, parabolic and looking wildly unstable: The thing ultra deadly; and he had misgivings about handling it. One wrong move and he could laser away half his army.

After several more minutes he had to relax, letting go to hold the shield properly, as it simmered with violet waves of mini pyroclastic outbursts, wondering for a moment what would happen if it connected with the powerful Dome he was still to step through?

"It's an extra bit of protection," Merlin called out over the crackling and fizzing of the incredible defence.

"Hm," Arthur coughed.

"Shall we," Merlin asked, holding out a preparatory arm?

Arthur nodded, hefting the shield once again, making sure he kept it well away from the edge of The Dome as he stepped up to it, and then through – extra-carefully – from the other side, Merlin quick to follow on.

Immediately knights gave way, allowing Arthur plenty of room, the shield ruling out the chance to be protected by his colleagues on one side. He didn't know it, but any projectile coming his way from that vector would be sucked in and vaporised.

Everyone arranged themselves once again, now Arthur and Merlin had joined the party.

"That's some shield," someone mentioned from the opposing side, as if Arthur and his knights – and Merlin were not enough to tangle with.

Arthur hefted the destructive aegis with something resembling annoyance, the thing far too cumbersome – and dangerous for a meeting of this importance. At length, he turned to Merlin and asked politely if he could possibly turn it off, the crackling, hissing and spitting of fireworks just too intrusive.

Having scanned the vicinity yet again from his new vantage point, finding the erected stage did indeed hamper any firing line, Merlin at length agreed, wriggling his fingers at the bronze super power and awaiting for it to comply, the shield winking out like a light bulb. Happy it was out, Arthur slipped it from his arm, and rested it on the ground, in the entrance of The Dome behind him. He hoped the act might just show how concerned he was for a peaceful handover – and not at all worried over the possibility of a sniper targeting him.

It worried Merlin however, the wizard continually watching the nearby rooftops.

An aide for the royal party approached, detailing the arrangement for the handover, pointing out it was only fair several proclamations be ratified beforehand, making sure the immediate family would be taken care of, and assigned at least something of the lifestyle they were accustomed to. After that, the decree of abdication would be read out – and signed by both parties, then St Edward's Crown would be presented with The Orb and Sword of State to King Arthur which would ratify the act.

Arthur waited patiently as the aide read out the proclamations, Merlin listening intently with cocked ear just to make sure the family was only left with a minimal amount – enough to survive on, all off-shore accounts and gold investitures seized and given over to the state for dispersal amongst the people. Other civil monies would be similarly confiscated and used accordingly. Palaces, royal homes and other properties would also be annulled, used for better purposes. Arthur would need only one place for visiting dignitaries – the palace behind him having enough rooms for an army.

Whilst the aide droned on, Arthur happened to catch site of The unseated Queen, sitting back from the main party surrounding her, The New King finding she was just like any old lady he'd seen standing by their doorstep as he'd passed. He looked her family over finding Prince Charles and his sons all taking a leading role in protecting her. The uniforms made him smile inwardly, the array of medals on all of their chests a little unflattering, especially as none of them had got anywhere near the recent battlefield. Nor did he, he had to admit, but he did walk it afterwards which took a stout heart.

He hummed, fidgeted and passed the time with Lancelot and Galahad and others as they continued to discuss the uniforms and what they were supposed to signify, and eventually he was presented with the legislature, signing his life away at least a dozen times; then the Sceptre, Orb and Sword were handed over by several royal aides – all in one go, Arthur not knowing which to handle first.

In the end, he handed everything over to his knights. He thanked The former Queen personally for receiving him and granting him investiture of the country, implying he'd do his best to level the playing field, create thousands of new jobs and bring the greatness back into the country. He wished her well and reassured her they would always be friends, hoping she could enjoy a peaceful retirement.

As The Queen got ready to depart, Bill Nightingale – having struggled off his horse – moved in quickly for any response to the abdication.

"Dear Queen," he addressed her, calling out softly, as she was being led out of the park. "Any last words please for the public you've served for so long?"

The comment stopped her in her tracks; she paused for some considerable moments, finally turning to appraise Bill.

"We are not amused," she bleated out unhappily!

Chapter 12

Southern Chronicle

A paper for Cornwall, Devon and Somerset

Thor's Hammer Found

In a desolate part of Norway – amid the ice flows of Reipa, a young fisherman has pulled the incredible war hammer from slush ice, heaving the one tonne weapon into the air – with apparent ease, his father and other brawny sea farers unable to even shift it – together! Now the whole of Norway, Sweden, Denmark – and Iceland will have to bend the knee to young Knut who will soon be named King of all Norway and affiliated lands of Scandinavia. After a remarkable take-over of England only days ago, this is incredible news indeed, as the Northern Hemisphere braces itself for reform like we've never seen before – full story by Bill Nightingale – centre pages.

Also breaking news:
The Fabled Spear of Destiny

has apparently been discovered in a dusty archive, glowing with unbridled power and allowed to be handled by a lowly clerk as she dusted around other artefacts. Incredibly, the young woman is of Palestinian descent with Israeli parents. She already promises to halt the infighting and restore peace to the beleaguered region – full story on page 5.

The World – Ripe for Change?

Full discussion – page 17

Continuing in the same vein, take a look at the pictures of a Trident that was discovered off the coast of Brazil yesterday, the dazzling icon outshining the local sparkling beaches as a young girl hoisted it from the shores. Now the whole coastline is bracing itself for the inevitable tsunami as corruption, vice and bloodshed is routed from the country in a major overhaul. Four full pages of reports and pictures – from your No 1 newspaper – the only newspaper to bring you all the facts – as they unfold.

You may also enjoy the following other books by Christopher E. Howard

Newly released novels - summer 2022
Excalibur – *Found*
Ghost Be Mine!
River Rats II

Novels
Judgement – The Devils of D-Day – *The Return*
River Rats (1)
Thradz

Novellas
Hearts of Oak
Lost in Rem
The Hanged Monk
Those Walls – parts 1 & 2
Twelve and a Half Ghosts
Nielstroy and Chekov series:-
– Oubliette of Secrets – Soft Shell Shuffle

Short Stories
A Christmas Visitation
Harsh Illumination
The Gardener
The Internet Girls
Starlove
The Tin Legion

Short Shorts
Life is a Champagne Bubble
Last Ride out
Tremble at my name
Rebel, my friend – **poem**

Printed in Great Britain
by Amazon